Rickett, Frances
A certain slant of light.

DEC 2 '68

A CERTAIN SLANT OF LIGHT

A CERTAIN SLANT OF LIGHT

Frances Rickett

G. P. Putnam's Sons
New York

For Ned and Jean, a part of whose childhood it was, too, in a town in which all of this might have happened—and some of it did.

WITH A SPECIAL ACKNOWLEDGMENT TO HARVEY GINSBERG

There's a certain slant of light,
On winter afternoons,
That oppresses, like the weight
Of cathedral tunes.

Heavenly hurt it gives us;
We can find no scar,
But internal difference
Where the meanings are.

—EMILY DICKINSON

Chapter One

Up until the time I was ten years old, going on eleven, I thought I was a Methodist. Nobody had ever told me anything different, and my sister Kate and I always went to Sunday School at the Methodist church.

Maggie, who was the only parent Kate and I had, didn't go to the Methodist church, but she didn't go anywhere else, so I supposed she was like Genevieve McIntyre's father, who never went to church with Genevieve and her mother. He said one time he didn't need to go to church to be with God. He could go out to the woods and find Him there.

That struck me as a fine idea, and I was all set to go with him, but Kate wouldn't let me. It was just as well, since Mr. McIntyre was sitting in an easy chair in his suspenders when he said it, with the whole of the Chicago Sunday *Tribune* to go through.

Mr. McIntyre wasn't the only man in Roseville who favored taking to the woods on Sunday morning. I can remember being in a lot of group arguments with other fifth-graders about the merits of church versus the woods. But, as was the case with most such arguments, none of us knew what we were talking about. We only aped what we heard at home. And in this instance, at least, we weren't given a chance to learn, but continued finding God on Sunday mornings where the mothers of Roseville knew Him to be.

Although I was too young to appreciate it at the time, a Methodist was the best thing you could possibly be in Roseville in 1931. Not that everybody was. Quite a lot of people went to the Christian church, which was almost as good as being a Methodist and certainly the next best thing.

There was in Roseville a Free Methodist church, but it didn't have anything to do with the Methodists other than being a thorn in their side.

One time after Nathaniel came to Roseville to live with the Fletchers—Julia and Orn Fletcher were Nathaniel's aunt and uncle, and Nathaniel was my best friend—he and I were walking home from Ward's Drugstore with Julia. As we went by the Free Methodist church, he asked her what Free Methodist meant. She said she was sure she couldn't tell him—as if she didn't care whether she ever could or not—and that nobody they knew went there.

Nathaniel asked if he could go there sometime. She stared at him and said why on earth would he want to when he had a perfectly good church of his own to go to? When he said oh, just to see if it was like the Methodist church, she replied firmly that if it was like the Methodist church, it would be the Methodist church, which it most certainly was not.

My sister Kate and I weren't the only innocent frauds basking in the warm, if fleeting, sunshine of the fold. There were maybe four or five Jewish families living in Roseville at the time, and one of them, the Goodmans, let their daughter Lillian go to Sunday School at the Methodist church.

Lillian, who was better informed than we were, knew she was Jewish, but still, when she was in Chicago once and somebody asked her if she was an Orthodox Jew or a Reformed Jew, she said, "I'm a Methodist Jew."

The Methodist church was, as my Grandfather Crowley put it, "than which there is no whicher."

But that was some time later, after Kate and I—and Maggie, too—had started finding God on Sunday mornings in a place which most of the mothers of Roseville considered even more unlikely than the woods.

Maggie was not what you could call a mother of Roseville. She worked, which was unusual enough. But Maggie didn't just work. She had been elected to public office, and in Roseville in 1931 that was practically unheard of.

Maggie was a mother more by default than by choice, though Kate looked enough like her to be her daughter. She had the same fiery red hair and the same pert nose and freckled face. She had the same sparkling way about her, too, that made people turn around and look whenever she came into a room. And then look again, because she had legs like Maggie's, too.

Sam McCutcheon, who owned Ward's Drugstore and ran it almost single-handed—bustling out from behind the prescription counter to hand a bottle of pills to one customer, bustling over to the soda fountain to jiggle Coke syrup and fizz water into a glass of crushed ice for another customer, all the while carrying on a conversation with one of the people resting on the chairs in the back of his store—used to tell the story of how Maggie came in one day, and Doc Hawkins came in right behind her and went up to her and tapped her on the shoulder and said, "God damn it, Maggie, you got the best damn legs in town."

Then Sam would throw his head back and laugh and say, "Doc was right. She does."

Which meant that Kate did, too.

I didn't care about that. As far as I was concerned, legs were legs. It was Kate's front I prayed every night to have one like. I didn't have a front at all.

Maggie, who had a very fine soprano voice, had started out in life wanting to be a singer, but while she was studying at the conservatory in Cincinnati, where she lived, her father was injured in an accident at the railroad yards and died a few weeks later, so she had to quit school and go to work to help support the family.

For all the family she soon had left to support, she might as well have stayed where she was. In 1917 her brother went to France and was killed there. That so grieved her mother, who'd

11

never really recovered from her husband's death, she just gave up and died, too, leaving Maggie alone at home and no more family except her younger sister, who had married and moved to Roseville and was our mother. And when I was born in 1921 she died.

Maggie, who had come up from Cincinnati to take care of Kate and stayed on to take care of both of us, then married our father, which would have been fine, except that five years later he died, too, so Maggie ended up being stuck with us.

Not that Maggie looked at it that way. Or if there were times she did, she was too polite to say so. But other people in town—mothers themselves, most of them—were always carrying on about how wonderful Maggie was to bring us up all by herself, shaking their heads all the time they were talking. Looking in the mirror at home afterward, trying to figure out what it was the ladies had been shaking their heads at, I couldn't help wondering if I was worth all that sacrificing.

Maggie herself, when I asked her about it once, just gave me a kind of funny look, and for a couple of seconds I held my breath, thinking, from the way her hands jerked a little, she might actually be going to hug me, which was something Maggie didn't do, but she only shook her head and said not to be silly.

So I didn't ask her any more, but went back to the mirror to practice curling my upper lip off my teeth when I smiled, the way Kate's did without her thinking about it.

My lip, if I didn't think about it, layered against my teeth and looked ugly. Since I wasn't pretty like Kate to begin with—usually, after long inspection and some hesitation, I was called wholesome-looking or intelligent or lively—I thought maybe it would help some if I could improve my smile.

But I couldn't even seem to do that. Concentrating in front of the mirror, I could perform a carefully curled, beautifully thin-lipped smile time after time, but in real life, not having any advance warning, before I had time to get my mouth all set, I'd already smiled. It was discouraging.

12

In Cincinnati Maggie had worked as a bookkeeper, so when the county auditor who'd been elected in 1924 had a partial stroke at about the time our father died, Maggie applied for the job as his assistant and decided in 1928 to run for the office herself. That was where Orn Fletcher came into her life, the way he came or would come into the life of every Democrat who ever ran for office. Orn Fletcher was the Democratic County Chairman.

Orn was a big, good-looking man with a weather-tanned face and a strong, masculine build. Before the war he had worked in his father's lumberyard, but after the war he went into business for himself as a contractor. As such he had become one of the most well-to-do men in Roseville as well as one of the most powerful men politically, though he still went around dressed like a lumberman, much to his wife Julia's distress.

Orn was against married women working. He was against all the modern things women began doing in the twenties. But since Maggie had to work, and since she had demonstrated her ability to handle the duties of the office in her two years there as the auditor's assistant, he didn't oppose her candidacy. In fact, he not only gave her the backing she needed to win the primary, he helped her campaign for the fall election—to the point where a person would have thought she was the only candidate the Democrats were running on the entire ticket.

I remember one night in particular, when there was a street fair on over at North Union in the southeast part of the county. Maggie was going to go shake hands with people, asking them to vote for her, and she said Kate and I could go with her.

We had our coats on and were ready to leave the house when a car pulled into the driveway. Kate peered out the kitchen window, shielding her eyes against the light. "It's Mr. Fletcher."

Maggie sighed and said, "Now what?" but she had a smile ready for him when he came to the door.

He had an even bigger smile for her, his teeth flashing white against the tan of his face. "How about riding over to North Union with me?"

13

"Well, thanks, Orn, but I was going to take the children and go in my car."

He looked from us to her. "There are some things I want to talk to you about."

I held my breath.

"Well . . ." She hesitated, then shrugged. "I guess there's no reason why we can't go in your car."

She motioned to us, and I started breathing, only to stop all over again when he said, "Can't you leave them here?"

Maggie shook her head. "No. I told them they could go. Anyhow they can't stay home by themselves."

I was sure he'd tell Maggie to call the hired girl who cleaned for us once a week at that time to come stay with us, but he didn't. Still, I didn't relax until we were in his car and on our way, which, as Kate pointed out to me after we got there and she and I were riding on the ferris wheel, showed what a jerk I was.

"Haven't you figured out by this time, Angel," she said, getting more and more bug-eyed as we climbed toward the top, the car starting to rock now, "that Maggie doesn't want to be alone with him if she can help it?"

I shook my head at her.

"Well, she doesn't."

"Why?"

Whatever Kate was going to say got lost in her shriek as we swung over the top, the car really rocking now, and I was too intent on bracing myself against falling out to ask her.

When we got home that night Orn wanted to come in—I supposed he hadn't yet had a chance to talk to Maggie about the things he wanted to—but Maggie smiled and said she was sorry, another time maybe, but she had to get Kate and me to bed.

That was a laugh to me. Kate and I had been getting ourselves to and from bed for as long as either of us could remember, and I was all set to say so, but Kate tugged at me.

I began to get an idea of what she meant.

Orn himself must have gotten some idea from Maggie's con-

14

tinual side-stepping of him that she didn't want to be alone with him, but he was hardly the sort of man who would conclude his attentions were unwelcome. Nor would he regard her resistance as anything permanent, but merely as something that had to be expected from a woman of her character in her position, particularly under circumstances not permitting even the slightest hint of scandalous behavior on her part—expected and put up with, perhaps even cherished a little, if only to make the victory, when it was finally his, all the sweeter from the savoring.

The trouble was he'd never had his victory.

Even I, who was too young to know what he was after or whether or not he'd got it, could see how his attitude toward Maggie had changed in the three years since she'd been elected auditor. At first he was in and out of her office all the time and came to the house to see her sometimes as often as two or three times a week. But gradually his visits slackened off, and now he hardly ever came to the house at all.

Maggie's own victory in 1928 had been a smashing one. The idea of a woman running for public office gave her campaign a novelty appeal, but novelty was only half of it. The fact that Maggie had the best damn legs in town—not to mention her fiery red hair and the sparkling way she had about her—hadn't exactly worked against her. There was a Mrs. Savery out at Cedar Lake who'd been in bed for a year with complications following typhoid fever and could hardly get up to go to the bathroom, let alone go to the polls, whose husband was so determined to have her vote for Maggie he brought her an absentee ballot.

Some women whose husbands would roll their eyes and say, "Ahhh, Maggie Crowley" would pull a face and say, "Aggg, Maggie Crowley," but mostly women liked her and admired her, partly because she was a woman's woman as much as she was a man's woman, and partly because, Orn Fletcher or no Orn Fletcher, more and more women were beginning to wonder why it was their place to be in the home and only in the

15

home when there were all kinds of interesting things going on outside it and people to talk to whose chief conversational gambit wasn't "Why?"

Not that many of them could get jobs when the Depression came, even if their husbands didn't care, and no matter how much they could have used the money. People said giving a woman a job was taking it away from a man, so what jobs there were to be had in Roseville—and there weren't many—went to men. But if women couldn't do anything about wanting to be independent, they could at least think about it and admire one of their own who was.

Kate, who was fourteen in 1931 and whose idea of being independent meant being old enough to get married, thought Maggie should get married again, though she had to admit that Maggie's chances of finding another right man at her advanced age were slim. But Kate kept her eyes peeled, as the saying went, and any time a man came to the house to see Maggie whom Kate didn't know, she always managed to find out whether or not he was married—usually by asking him pointblank.

As far as I could tell, Maggie wasn't nearly so concerned about it as Kate was. Kate, when she wasn't doing her homework or practicing the piano or fussing with her hair, was always mooning—usually over somebody in a movie magazine. Maggie never mooned at all.

In the morning she was too busy preparing breakfast and getting ready to go to the courthouse. At night when she came home there was supper to attend to. After supper, while Kate and I were doing the dishes and then our homework, people would call on the telephone, or somebody would come to the house to see her about helping him get a job because he'd been laid off and his wife was expecting a baby.

Whoever it was had always been laid off for two months or three months or four months, and his wife was always expecting a baby, so I added that to my store of knowledge about where babies came from, which was one of my passionate con-

16

cerns at the time, but I was never able to make anything of it.

Or it would be a farmer wanting to know if there wasn't some way Maggie could get his tax deadline extended. The farmers' wives didn't seem to go in for having babies—I supposed because they already had a carful of children sitting with them out in the driveway—but they were always reported to be poorly or, at best, fair to middling. The farmers themselves, from what I could see of them from the kitchen, never looked too good either. Their faces were drawn, and they wouldn't sit down, but stood just inside the door, clutching at their caps and staring at the rug where it was frayed.

Or it would be somebody wanting to talk politics. They never mentioned wives or children, but smoked cigars and banged their fists on the table while they God damned this or hell's bells'd that.

Or Maggie would have the washing to do or a PTA committee meeting or something equally unromantic.

She did go out sometimes—to a party or to South Bend to see a movie and stage show—and on those occasions she always had an escort, but the only man with whom she had a continuing relationship was Harley Nichols, who owned the shoe store and who was always Maggie's partner whenever she had couples in to play cards.

Harley wasn't married, and he was around Maggie's age, but not even Kate, who could find something heart-quickening in almost every male she knew, could work up any enthusiasm for poor Harley, who was so pussy-footy and well mannered it made us want to throw up.

Sometimes Maggie would stand at the window and stare out of it, but if I asked her what she was thinking about, she'd just say oh, the weather, or oh, what we were going to have for supper, or oh, nothing.

One night in the fall of 1931, when I woke up and came downstairs for a drink of water, Maggie was sitting at the kitchen table with a bunch of bills in front of her, her chin in her hands and a faraway look on her face. When I asked her where she wished she was, she said nowhere, she was just thinking about a man she'd known once in Cincinnati.

Knowing Kate would expect it of me and be mad if I didn't, I asked Maggie if he might come to see us—which was not what Kate would have asked, but it was as close as I could bring myself—but Maggie shook her head and said he had died a long time ago, before she'd married our father.

I knew Kate would go wide-eyed over that one. Kate was almost as big on love forever lost as she was on marriage. And she did. But she recovered quickly, saying it only proved Maggie was not a one-man-in-my-life kind of person. Therefore she could be expected to find still another man to love. And since it wasn't in the law of averages for every man she loved to die on her, the next man would probably live to be as old as old Mr. Werner, for instance, by which time he and Maggie would both be too old to care if he died or not.

Kate could squeeze blood out of a turnip.

In 1931 Roseville had a population of eighteen hundred. It was not at all a one-horse town like some other small towns in the sandy flatlands of northern Indiana, where houses and stores and filling stations are strung along a state highway, with maybe four or five dirt roads crossing it, servicing a house or two on either side before petering out.

A state highway ran through Roseville north to south, but it was over on the east side of town, two blocks from Main Street, and within the city limits it was not a highway but a street, with a name to it, like all the other streets, and, except for a short distance in from the filling station at either end, curbs and sidewalks.

There were a good many streets in Roseville if you counted in all directions, quite a few of them paved or bricked or what was called improved. In fact, the total area of the town was larger than the population seemed to justify, but that was because there were also a good many vacant lots, two of them right in the heart of the business district.

Although Roseville could boast of having industry (to be

18

precise, an industry—a small garment factory), its primary reason for being was the farming which went on all around it. Farming was the reason for being of every other town in Rose County as well, but the other towns had no pretensions to being anything more than farmers' towns. Roseville did. Roseville was the county seat.

When I was ten years old, the Rose County courthouse was the grandest structure I had ever seen. An enormous gray-stoned building with red gabled roofs and a four-faced clock tower which seemed to pierce the sky, it stood in the middle of a broad, tree-shaded lawn occupying an entire block adjacent to the north end of Main Street, an occasional, now seldom-used hitching post dotting the curb of the sidewalk which surrounded it.

The heart of the business district—indeed, almost the whole of it—occupied a two-block area on Main Street between the courthouse at one end and, at the other, the Nickel Plate Railroad, which, in coming down the one hundred miles from Chicago, swung around to cut through the middle of Roseville west to east.

In spite of the two vacant lots, Roseville had two banks and more stores and offices than were average for a town its size, catering as it did not only to local residents but to farmers from all over the county who, making a trip to town to pay their taxes or take out a license or file a claim or attend a hearing in the county commissioners' office, would get a haircut or have a tooth pulled and buy groceries and patent medicines and maybe a new pair of overalls.

It's not true, of course, that in a town of eighteen hundred people everybody knows everybody else. It only seems that way, partly because, in a town like Roseville, with only one school and one library and one depot and with the business district concentrated in a two-block area, a lot of people's paths were bound to cross again and again; partly because, again in a town like Roseville, people were forever joining whatever clubs they could in order to have something to do with their spare time, so this man would play cards with that man at the Odd Fellows' Hall, and this woman would be pointed out to that woman as having read a very stimulating paper on Lesser Known Hoosier Poets at the last meeting of the literary club, and everybody would talk about the fist fight this fellow and that fellow got into at the Legion Post over whether or not the Legion should sponsor a bill denying veterans' benefits to Red sympathizers; and finally because in Roseville almost everybody spoke to almost everybody else on the street whether they knew them or not.

People in Roseville didn't just seem friendly. They were friendly. And they were hospitable, though their idea of hospitality might strike an outsider as peculiar. If a stranger driving through Roseville had a flat tire, the first man along would stop and help him change it. Or if he needed directions or had to use a phone, anybody whose door he knocked at would be happy—more than happy, eager—to oblige. But if that same stranger moved to Roseville, people would regard him in much the way a dog regards a foreign object, circling wide around it, eyeing and sniffing, as if in spite of their conviction that Roseville was the best of all possible towns, they suspected him of having some ulterior motive for coming there to live.

People in Roseville were neighborly. If they stuck their noses into other people's business, they were just as quick to stick out a helping hand. And they were practical in their neighborliness. Whenever somebody died, people swamped the family with enough casseroles and soups and pies to feed them and the gathering relatives for days—a custom that probably harked back to pioneer times, when a funeral provided the community with one of its few social occasions and the mourners, having mourned, stayed to eat.

Roseville people took as lively an interest in what went on elsewhere (in so far as they figured that elsewhere affected them) as they did in each other, but in the same way as they hung on to old customs, they hung on to old beliefs, entertaining people more readily than ideas, persuaded that being up to date meant having an indoor toilet or a Model A or an Empress Eugenie hat, seeing no need to change their way of thinking, seeing their way of thinking, indeed, as the one way of keeping safe for themselves an America which their forefathers had founded and which alien forces were trying to take over and destroy.

The opportunity to mobilize against those alien forces seldom presented itself. When it did, it had a way of turning into something more or something less—certainly something other —than had been anticipated.

Like most small towns in Indiana, Roseville was a hotbed for the Ku Klux Klan in the early nineteen twenties, determined once and for all to show those enemies to the well-being of America from within—and with the same dispatch—what our fighting men in the First World War had shown those enemies to the well-being of America from without: that America was not a country to be tampered with.

Since anyone who was not a native-born white Protestant was considered an enemy, Catholics, Negroes, Jews, and immigrants all qualified, but to the Klan in Roseville, as elsewhere in rural Indiana—indeed, throughout much of America—the most dangerous of these enemies from within was the Catholic Church.

Bad enough that this foreign church with its foreign ways and ties eschewed the simple, straightforward teachings of the Bible to indulge in a ritualistic, incense-laden mumbo jumbo. Bad enough that it condoned the loose living among Catholics that all foreigners were so notorious for (not to mention what went on among the priests and nuns, as any number of pamphlets written by those revolted enough to have quit that unnatural way of life could attest). But—and herein lay the danger—it aimed to foist that loose living and those sacrilegious rites on the whole country, because it was a known fact, so the argument went—and so a great number of people were persuaded—that the ultimate goal of this powerful foreign body with its tentacles reaching out everywhere was to take over America and install the Pope in the White House.

Unlike the people of North Manchester, Indiana, where a mob stormed the depot one day after hearing a rumor that the Pope was at that very moment on the southbound train from Chicago, only to discover when the train pulled in that the sole occupant of the single day coach was a traveling salesman who was able to prove he was not the Pope in disguise, the people of Roseville didn't look for the Pope to come there to start his takeover. Nor did they regard the Catholics who lived in Roseville as playing any vital part in the grand design—perhaps because the Catholic Church in Roseville was, even to a Fundamentalist eye, pretty small potatoes, its communicants for the most part ignoramuses or, if the communicant happened to be an otherwise acceptable friend or neighbor, an innocent who didn't know and couldn't be made to see what the Catholic Church was really up to.

Still, the Klan in Roseville was able to stir up a satisfying amount of mischief under the guise of self-appointed watchdog of the moral standards of the community, alert to the undermining of those standards by this foreign threat in its midst and by other threats which if not foreign in origin were foreign in nature to the Puritan ideal. Thus anyone, loose-living Catholic or backsliding Protestant, who violated the Klan's rigid code of chastity and clean living became a target for investigation and, hopefully, punishment.

Joe Lafferty, who was a Catholic and owned the bakery, had his bakery boycotted to the point where he was nearly driven out of business. A farmer named John Summerville, who was not a Catholic but was said to be harboring a still in his barn, had his barn burned down. (It so happened he had no still, but he did have ten Jersey cows, a team of horses, and a hunting dog, which all perished in the fire.) And any number of husbands and wives were awakened in the middle of the night to a pounding on the front door and a demand to see their marriage license.

The Rosensteins, who lived on the north edge of town, returned from a trip to Chicago one Sunday evening to find their house had been ransacked—for what, the Klan alone knew, and it didn't say—but, for the most part, the Jews in Roseville were left alone, partly because there weren't enough of them to bother with, and partly because the large room at the back of Harry Goodman's hardware store had long been the favorite gathering place uptown for men who wanted to talk politics somewhere less public than the poolroom or, after Prohibition closed down the saloon, to "have a few"—courtesy of some other, unmolested barn—and alienating Mr. Goodman would have been tantamount to cutting off one's nose to spite one's face.

In the same sense, while some Klan members and their wives boycotted Mr. Petrie's jewelry store—the Petries, like the Laffertys, being Catholics—more of them found it expedient not to. It was easy enough, after all, if tiresome, for a woman to do all her own baking, but unless the family owned a car, and not many did in those days, or a person could get a ride with someone to one of the larger towns in the surrounding counties, where else could one get a watch repaired or buy a wedding ring or a place setting of silver or china?

Outside of the financial loss suffered by Joe Lafferty, who somehow managed to hang on until the "trouble" was over, at which point all his former customers came flocking back to him with one lame excuse after another, and the blow to John Summerville's pocketbook and feelings—people said the loss of his livestock and his dog like to killed the old man—the Klan in Roseville, for all its noise, was mostly just that—noise— with a passion for robes and hoods and fiery crosses and for "klonversations" made up of such mumbo jumbo of its own— "Kigy" ("Klansman, I greet you"), "Itsub" ("In the sacred, unfailing bond"), "Sanbog!" ("Strangers are near. Be on guard!")—as to out-Catholic the Catholics, though it wasn't until the noise had died away that most people found the courage to see the Klan for what it was and say so.

There were two memorable exceptions.

The first was an incident which took place at the Methodist

church in the spring of 1924 involving the minister, a newly appointed man in his early sixties—the Reverend Mr. Shields.

Mr. Shields was in the middle of conducting services one Sunday morning when the church door was flung open to reveal five hooded Klansmen standing on the threshold bearing aloft an American flag and a Klan flag and carrying an envelope of money which they intended to deposit at the foot of the pulpit, as it was customary for local chapters of the Klan everywhere to do, visiting the various Protestant churches in town.

As the Klansmen started down the aisle, the organist signaled the choir, the choir burst into "Onward, Christian Soldiers," and the congregation, in a surge of piety and patriotism, stood up.

This, too, was customary. What happened next was not. The Reverend Mr. Shields slammed his hand down on the lectern, ordered the choir and the organ to stop, commanded the Klansmen to stay where they were, and told the congregation to sit down.

Into the stupefied silence which followed, Reverend Shields spoke, addressing himself to the five Klansmen.

"The bishop," he said, "has appointed me pastor of this church, and as such has placed the conduct of its affairs in my hands. You have not been invited here by me to take part in this service of worship, nor do I want your financial support, and if the reason for this attitude on my part is not clear to you, let me make it clear now. I don't go into the bank and tell the cashier how to conduct his business, and I don't go to the school and tell the superintendent how to run his, and nobody, not even the Ku Klux Klan, is going to come into my church and tell me how to interpret the Holy Scriptures. Now, if you will kindly remove yourselves or take off those sheets and sit down as part of the congregation, we will get on with the services."

The Klansmen stood there for a few moments, muttering among themselves. Then they turned and walked out.

By the middle of the afternoon everybody in town knew what

had happened at the Methodist church. For a week or more hardly anybody talked about anything else, the most titillating topic of speculation among the more venal members of the Klan being what would happen to the Reverend Mr. Shields.

In some places, ministers who had stood up to the Klan had been flogged and their backs branded with the KKK, but the leaders of the Klan in Roseville, somewhat sobered by the damage done to John Summerville, were not yet ready for a second try at outright violence. The Reverend Mr. Shields was neither flogged nor branded. On petition by the church board to the bishop, he was transferred.

He managed, even so, to get the last word.

On his final Sunday in Roseville he preached a sermon on brotherhood. When he had finished, he put his notes down and looked out over the congregation. "I'm an old man," he said. "In my lifetime I've seen many wrongs committed in the name of righteousness. The Ku Klux Klan isn't the first organized group to do it, and I don't suppose it will be the last. But there's one thing you can say for the Klan. I'm sure all of you are familiar with the story of the old maid who looked under her bed every night to see if there was a man there. Foolish old maid? The lawful wedded wives of Roseville might do well to take a good look under all those sheets."

The second, even more memorable, exception involved Orn Fletcher.

The incident took place in the summer of 1924 on a sultry Saturday night in August preceded by an unbroken week of temperatures in the nineties, with brassy skies by day and, at night, the intermittent flicker of heat lightning holding out the promise of relief without coming close enough to deliver it.

Until Saturday night. That night was as breathless as the ones before it, but now the western horizon was massed with black clouds, and the distant rumble of thunder preceded by a fork of lightning seemed not only to mean business, but of a kind violent enough to unwind taut tempers, soothe frazzled nerves, and satisfy the itch to spend themselves of bodies fretted almost to the point of impotence by the oppressive heat. And still the storm held off.

Afterward nobody knew for sure who suggested the idea to the seven or eight restive Klansmen rounded up to kill that Saturday night together. The consensus was that it was Orn himself, though, as some people pointed out, considering who the target was, it could have been any one of the Klansmen, particularly in view of the fact that by the time the idea was suggested, they were all well on their way to being drunk.

The target, Priscilla Rogers, was a piano teacher when I knew her in the early thirties—the best one and the best-known one in town. Kate and I both took lessons from her, as did most of our friends who studied the piano. But at the time of the Klan incident she was a newcomer to Roseville.

Barely in her twenties, she was married to (and later divorced from) the leader of a dance band which played at the South Shore Hotel and Dance Pavilion out at Cedar Lake, some six miles south of Roseville—Saturday night, of course, being a big dance night.

A blue-eyed blonde, Priscilla was as sharp-tongued as she was pretty. She was also, as more than one man who'd fallen all over himself trying to get next to her had been heard to put it, as independent as a hog on ice.

Though the stated basis of the Klan's grudge against Priscilla lay in the fact that she didn't go to church at all on Sunday but spent the morning lolling in bed with her husband, it seems more likely that the appeal of the idea lay in the unspoken suggestion that if they couldn't get her one way, they could another.

In any case, the Klansmen grabbed up their paraphernalia, piled into their cars, and drove to a rendezvous point to march in a body to her house, where they would take the defenseless Priscilla by surprise.

Once assembled, there was some grumbling about having to drape themselves in those stifling robes and hoods. One or two of the men, sober enough to doubt the wisdom of what they were undertaking, went so far as to suggest that in view of the heat and the gathering storm, they call the whole thing off.

Orn and the others hooted them down. In a sweat of anticipation—after a final fortifying round from hip-pocket flasks—they all filed off down the street, the stragglers bringing up the rear, while above them the lightning flashed ever and ever nearer and the now almost steady rumble of thunder burgeoned into an occasional doomlike crack.

Their plan, outlined as they surged forward, called for them to march into her yard, up onto her porch and into her house, there to decide—deciding it now with a wink and a leer and a laugh—what kind of punishment should be meted out to her.

Their plan began going awry the minute they turned into her yard, when the door to the house burst open, and a neither surprised nor defenseless Priscilla stepped out on the porch and leveled a shotgun at them, calling out in a clear if tremulous voice over the rumbling thunder, "I'll shoot the first one of you who comes one step closer!"

How Priscilla had learned of the Klan's intention to "get" her was never afterward made clear—she wouldn't say—but for all its pretensions to secrecy, the Klan by that time had become so brazen about running the town and so braggadocio about what it was going to do to this one and that one that everyone knew who its intended victims were and only wondered at what point the talk would turn to action.

The action in this instance ground to a halt at her command. For a few moments her hooded assailants just stood there staring at her.

Finally a man at the rear muttered, "Aw, c'mon, let's get out of here." Another man—a young man—giggled.

Perhaps it was the giggle that decided Orn. Perhaps, from the tremulous note in her voice, it was a conviction on his part that Priscilla had neither the nerve nor the proficiency to shoot a gun. Or perhaps it was simply that after waiting—and lusting—all this time, he was damned if he was going to let slide an opportunity which once lost might never present itself again.

27

He folded his arms under his robe and took a step toward her.

Though she kept her finger on the trigger, the only movement was a sudden gust of wind, the only sound a few rasps of breath.

Orn took another step forward. "What you need, young lady, is to be taught a thing or two."

Priscilla stood there eyeing him up and down as a flash of lightning illuminated house, porch, yard, and the Klansmen shrouded there together. "That may be," she said in a dry voice, "but if you don't mind, Orn, I'll take somebody who's got something to do it with."

A great peal of thunder and laughter split the night together, the thunder rumbling off, the laughter building again from chokes and gasps and hoots to a new high of hilarity.

"Why you little . . ." Orn headed for the porch.

He hadn't taken more than two or three strides before Priscilla fired.

Orn let out a howl of pain and bent almost double, clutching at his right leg.

As the men's laughter choked off into gasps of disbelief, Priscilla reloaded the shotgun and leveled it at him once again. "If you're still so anxious to show me what you've got," she said in that same dry voice, "take another step. Oh—and just to help me out," she added sweetly, "point."

Once again laughter split the night, great raucous howls of it. At that moment, as if to add the final touch of ignominy, the heavens opened up, and rain came pouring down in such torrents that before Orn could stumble back to his cohorts, dragging his injured leg and cursing it, he tripped over his now-sodden robe and fell flat on his face.

That night marked the end of Orn's participation in Klan activities. The official story given out about his lame leg—the shot splintered a bone, and he walked thereafter with a heavy, stiff-legged gait—was that he had injured it in an accident at his father's lumberyard, but it was a long time before anybody could tell that story with anything approaching a straight face. Or had the time to, they were so busy telling the true one.

And when the true story of what had gone on between Orn and Priscilla Rogers could no longer be told as a story, because there wasn't anybody left to tell it to who didn't already know it down to the last detail, the words Priscilla had used—and variations upon them—became a standard joke, a *bon mot* that could and frequently did break up many a conversation in the months and years that followed, though if the conversation took place outside the privacy of the home, the jokester first made sure neither Orn nor Julia Fletcher was within hearing—Orn because no one dared affront him, and Julia, who knew the story but not the identity of the man, because nobody wanted to hurt her feelings by taking the risk of her finding out.

That night also marked the end of any Klan activities in Roseville worth mentioning. People were tired of it all anyway —tired of the noise and the threats and the insolence and the constant living on edge. And when in March of 1925 the Grand Dragon of the Invisible Empire of the Realm of Indiana, Mr. D. C. ("I am the law") Stephenson, so far forgot his exalted office in this organization sworn to uphold the chastity of American womanhood as to sexually assault, mutilate, and cause the death of a young Indianapolis woman, it was more than most people everywhere could stomach, and his trial and conviction marked the end of Klan activities almost anywhere at all worth mentioning.

The Klan dead and done with, people in Roseville settled back into the ordinary mold of small-town life, as relieved to be able to settle back into it as they had once been happy to be stirred out of it, wondering how their mobilization on behalf of so righteous a cause could have degenerated into such demagoguery. Still, they took what comfort they could in reminding themselves that although the enemy had not been routed, the Roseville way of thinking, the only right way of thinking, prevailed in the land, and God willing—and the Congress watchful—it always would.

As for myself at the time—that is, the fall of 1931—I'd never even heard of the Ku Klux Klan. I was hardly more than aware of the fact that there was a Catholic church in Roseville.

In a way that was curious. What few relatives I had on my father's side of the family—my Grandfather Crowley, and my Uncle Donald and my Aunt Clarissa, who was my father's sister, and their children—were all Catholics, and I knew they were. But then they all lived in Chicago, and Chicago was as much of another world to me as the Catholic Church was. I suppose if I thought anything at all about it, I took it for granted that the two things somehow went together in the way that being a Methodist and living in Roseville went together, and that just as the Petries had moved to Roseville from Chicago when Mr. Petri opened his jewelry store, so all the Catholics who lived in Roseville must have moved there at some time from Chicago.

I suppose it should have occurred to me to wonder whether my father had been a Catholic like the rest of his family, but I barely remembered my father, and Maggie seldom mentioned him. The only kind of wondering about him I had any basis for was seeing other children's fathers and wondering what my own father had been like and what it would have been like for me to have a father.

I had no reason at all to wonder if Maggie was a Catholic. The only relative I knew of on her side of the family was a great-aunt in Cincinnati, and though she sent Kate and me a present every year at Christmas, we'd never met her.

It wasn't until after both Kate and I were grown, when Aunt Clarissa got to talking to us one time about one thing and another, that she filled us in on what had happened. Our mother and father, she said, had just drifted away from the Church, as much out of indifference as anything else.

With Maggie it was another story. As, one by one, the people Maggie loved were taken from her, she became bitter toward the Church, and after the man she was to marry died in the great influenza epidemic at the end of the First World War—

the man Maggie had mentioned to me that night in the kitchen —she left the Church entirely.

A few years—and two more deaths—later, when Aunt Clarissa attempted to upbraid her for it, Maggie turned to her and said, "What has God ever done for me?"

Aunt Clarissa for once had no reply.

As for the Roseville way of thinking, if anyone had asked me what that meant, I would have supposed—not without reason—it meant the Roseville way of thinking about the farmers.

Perhaps it was having to depend on them to such a large extent for their own livelihood, or perhaps it was having come, for the most part, and not too many generations back, from farm stock themselves that made the people of Roseville look down their noses at the farmers. In any case, they did.

The farmers were regarded as ignorant and unrefined—men and women who never listened to anything on the radio beyond the farm news and the weather report and who never read anything other than the Rose County *Democrat* and the Rose County *Republican* and the almanac and could therefore be expected neither to understand the importance of culture in American life nor to appreciate Indiana's contribution to that culture.

A woman who looked dowdy was said to look like a farmer's wife, which had a double sting to it, farmers' wives being seen not only as wearing ill-fitting, cheap gingham prints, but also as being fat and, because they weren't properly corseted, sloppy.

The men were considered coarse—their grammar atrocious, their humor vulgar—and, no matter how often they might wash themselves, as smelling of sweat and feed.

But then, people would say, what could you expect when you considered that a farmer's idea of getting dressed up for anything less than a funeral or a wedding was to put on a clean pair of overalls, and when his idea of what to do on Saturday night was to drive into Roseville with his wife and children and park on Main Street in the business section, so they could sit there and gawk at all the people going by.

31

The farmers were further alienated from the people of Roseville by the fact that even those farmers living in Roseville's own township did not send their children to school in Roseville (except those few who could afford the fee demanded for this privilege), but sent them to the township school just west of town. Nor did any farmers to speak of attend church in Roseville. This was partly because many of them, being of German descent, were Lutherans, and the only Lutheran church in the county was over at North Union; partly because many of them belonged to the United Brethren sect, which had two churches in the county, neither of them in Roseville; and partly because nobody encouraged them to. Certainly, with two or three notable exceptions, they did not attend the Methodist church.

The fact that the farmers used the county roads to drive their tractors from one field to another irritated motorists who had to slow to a snail's pace behind them until they could manage to get around, and they would complain that the farmers acted as if they owned the whole county, roads and all. As for the lament of people everywhere over how bad off the farmers were, the people of Roseville would retort that the farmers were no worse off than anybody else. At least they had enough to eat.

It was that kind of grumbling, so common that people no longer paid much attention to it, which made up the bulk of what was said by the young man who came to the house to see Maggie one night toward the end of September.

Kate had said she would play a game of Parchesi with me, and I was on my way upstairs to get it when the doorbell rang.

My first thought when I opened the door to him was I didn't think I knew him. My second was I didn't think I'd like him if I did.

There was still enough day left not to need to turn on the porch light, but when he angled his head down at me—neither of us had to do much angling, he was so runty—slate-colored eyes flickered at me out of a sullen face as though a beam of light had caught them. Then they slid past me into the hall. "This where Maggie Crowley lives?"

He didn't open his mouth much when he spoke, mumbling his words, and I could hardly hear him, though that wasn't entirely his fault. Kate was at the piano getting a few last licks in, and Kate's last licks being the chromatic scales, they were flourishing. And loud.

"Yes," I said.

He ran a hand over his hair—black and thick and unruly-looking in spite of the musk-sweet odor of pomade on it. "She here?"

"Yes," I said again.

Though his face remained as sullen as before, I didn't suppose he was standing there asking about Maggie for the state of his health. I opened the door wider. "Come in."

When he stepped inside I realized I did know him. At least I knew who he was. He was Chuck Sellers, who had graduated from high school a year and a half before in the class of 1930, who in his senior year, despite his runtiness, had been the captain and star player of the basketball team, the only team in the history of Roseville which had gone all the way up to the semifinals in the state tournament.

Kate came into the hall then, too, after a crashing chromatic chord, and I don't know which dumbfounded me the more, the fact that she didn't speak to him, hardly more than acknowledged his presence, or the fact that she came over to me and put an arm around me. The last time Kate had done that, at the suggestion of a photographer who was taking our picture, she broke out with the measles half an hour later, which indicated to me, fully as much as her smile in the picture, that she'd been too sick to know what she was doing.

She not only put an arm around me, she drew me to her. "Go tell Maggie somebody's here to see her, Angel."

I frowned up at her. *Somebody?*

She gave me a push, saying to Chuck, "Do you want to wait in the living room?" Then she started upstairs, calling over her shoulder to me, "I'll get the Parchesi."

I was still puzzling it out as I went to the kitchen to call out the back door to Maggie, who was in the yard visiting across the hedge with Mrs. Peterkin next door.

It wasn't that I liked Chuck Sellers any better after I realized who he was, but I hadn't expected Kate, who was an avid basketball fan, to share my opinion. To be shy with him, yes. She was only a freshman in high school. She'd only been in the seventh grade when he was a senior. Naturally she wouldn't expect him to know her. But to not even say hello to him or take any advantage at all of what must have seemed a heaven-sent opportunity to her to get next to a local hero?

I shook my head, deciding either Kate's judgment of character was improving or, what was more likely, Clark Gable had spoiled her for everybody else.

Maggie still had her apron on from getting supper. She took it off as she came up the back steps and tossed it onto a kitchen chair as she went by—Kate was the only tidy one in the family —nodding, when I told her Chuck Sellers wanted to see her, in a way that indicated she not only knew who he was, she knew what he wanted to see her about.

While Kate and I set the Parchesi out on the dining-room table, she went on into the living room and shook hands with him, pretending she didn't know, smiling and asking in a conversational way how his folks were and how he and his wife were getting along, trying to put him at ease. But Chuck Sellers was the kind who couldn't—or wouldn't—be put. After eliciting nothing but sullen grunts and monosyllables, she gave up and asked him what she could do for him.

Right away he started grumbling about the farmers, in particular one farmer who, to Chuck's way of looking at it, didn't merit even being that, since he wasn't county born and bred, but "one of them Wops over by North Union you wouldn't wipe your feet on," a man who "never would have amounted to a dime without somebody setting things up for him so he could hit it big in the onion boom," not specifying who the somebody was or what things he had set up, the particular source of Chuck's particular complaint being the fact that this man he wouldn't wipe his feet on had been his employer—until the first of August when he'd been laid off "for no good reason," his sullen face darkening as he said it, allowing as how the job wasn't nothing worth having to begin with, up before dawn every morning, his wife waiting supper every night, he didn't give a God damn about it, but he'd been laid off for near on to two months now, and his wife was going to have a baby, and he'd end up having to go on relief if he didn't find another job.

That, though he didn't come right out and say it, was what Maggie could do for him, what Maggie, judging by his attitude toward her, was supposed to be grateful to have the opportunity to do for him, his voice, and his face with it, shifting from sullen as she asked him if he'd had any experience other than being a farmhand to insolent as he retorted that he couldn't see what experience had to do with whether he could handle a job or not, just show him what needed to be done and he'd do it, he hadn't captained a basketball team up to the semifinals without proving he had plenty of what it took, though he didn't suppose he could expect a woman to see that—so insolent that Kate and I, eyeing each other across the Parchesi board, drew in our breath a couple of times in wonder that Maggie would put up with it.

There was no reason for her to put up with him at all. Finding a job for Chuck Sellers, or anybody else, for that matter, wasn't part of her job as county auditor, any more than extending a tax deadline for a farmer was within her jurisdiction. Only people didn't see it that way. Anybody who held public office was thought to have his finger on what was going on, to wield a certain amount of influence, and to be beholden to every citizen whose vote had helped elect him.

Being beholden to the citizenry had nothing to do with carrying out the duties of the office as set forth by law to the best of one's ability. That was a matter to be defended by one political party and challenged by the other—and settled by the voters— at the next election. Being beholden meant if a man had a grievance about the way his boy was being treated at school, you

35

went to see the principal, or if he had a dispute with a neighbor over a property line, you dug out the survey, or if he didn't understand how to fill out some form, you did it for him, or if he needed a job, you tried to help him find one.

Chuck Sellers, of course, wasn't old enough to have voted for Maggie. He still wouldn't be old enough to vote for her when she ran for reelection in 1932, but he told her his parents had and would—grudging her the telling of it, as if he grudged her the votes as well.

He could have saved his sullen breath. Maggie took it for granted that anyone who came to her for help had voted for her —or would say he had. Anyone known to be a dyed-in-the-wool Republican would take his problem to one of the Republican office holders. In any case, she would have tried to help him, the same as she did anybody who asked it of her—because he needed help.

"I'm not sure," she said, "Orn Fletcher can use anyone. But I think he's your best bet. Or if not Orn, his father."

Chuck grunted.

"If you'll wait here a minute . . ." Maggie came through the dining room and went on into the kitchen, where the wall telephone was.

She looked pleased when she came back. "Orn wants you to stop in to see him tomorrow morning. He didn't promise anything, but I think it's likely he has something in mind for you. Orn isn't the kind of man to waste anyone's time, his own included, just making talk."

As Chuck stood up, Kate and I gave each other a relieved look.

It was premature. Maggie put a hand out to stop him. Then she just stood there for a bit, not moving and not saying anything, frowning as if she was trying to think how best to say something she didn't want to say at all.

When she finally spoke, it was to say a bit hesitantly, "I feel I can speak plainly to you, Chuck. So I'm going to."

She paused. I frowned at Kate, but Kate only shrugged her

shoulders, meaning she didn't know what it was all about any more than I did.

"Orn doesn't have anything against a man taking a drink," Maggie went on, rather rapidly now, as if to get it out and get it over with. "Indeed he's been known to have a few too many himself at one time or another. But he will not tolerate a man drinking on the job."

Chuck didn't say anything. He nodded, his sullen face darkening again, and clenched his hand into a fist, his hands big for the rest of him, the black muck of the onion-boom earth still under his nails after all those weeks of being laid off.

"Well," Maggie said, her own face tinged with the easy pink of the fair-skinned redhead, "I'm sure everything will work out fine." She gave him an encouraging smile as she started toward the door. "Let me know, will you?"

He nodded again, following after her. When she opened the door for him and said good night, he grunted something at her and walked out.

Kate waited until she heard his car pull away. Then with a "Whew!" she went to the door and opened it wide. "What in the world," she said, wrinkling her nose, "do you suppose he uses on his hair?"

Maggie grinned at her. "I think it's called Enchantment."

We all laughed, as much out of relief at having him gone, I think, as at Maggie's jibe.

"He gives me the creeps the way he looks at you without looking at you." Kate shivered. "I hope he gets the job, if only to keep him from hanging around all the time."

I frowned at her. "Hanging around where?"

"At school. Out in front and around the playground. Haven't you noticed him?"

"No. What does he do it for?"

She shrugged. "I don't know. Maybe he's trying to recapture his past glory. But he's so—I don't know—so spooky about it."

From what I'd seen of him that evening I could believe it, but

I didn't have anything particular to say about it, so I only said, "Are we going to finish our game?"

Kate came back to the table. "I guess so."

But we didn't.

There was a light clatter up the front steps, the screen door opened, and Alice White poked her head in. "Hi."

Kate beamed at her. "Hi, yourself. What's up?"

Alice, who was one of Kate's best friends and whose father, Warren White, was a Democrat like Maggie and the cashier of the Roseville Bank and Trust Company, came in hugging a book to her. "I thought if you haven't done your algebra we could do it together."

"Good idea," Kate said. "Do you mind, Angel?"

"No, go ahead," I answered, wondering as they clattered off upstairs together to Kate's and my bedroom and shut the door how they could possibly think anybody fell for that old dodge any more, its only variant the subject they were going to "do" together.

Even Maggie grinned at me over the evening paper a little later on when the fit of giggles they were having penetrated through the door. "It's a pretty funny subject, algebra."

I grinned back at her from the dining-room table, where I was still fiddling with the Parchesi, trying to figure out who would have won if we'd played it through.

A little before eight-thirty Maggie called up the stairs to say it was time for Alice to be going home, and when Kate and Alice came clattering down again, she said it was such a nice night out, why didn't we walk her there?

Alice had ridden her bike over. Now she wheeled it along beside her as we walked from our house at the south end of Main Street to the Whites' house, which was almost uptown, just a block below the railroad and a block over from Main on Prettyman.

After we dropped Alice off, Kate asked Maggie if we couldn't go on uptown and window-shop a bit. Next to reading movie magazines and giggling with Alice and her other girl friends about boys, window-shopping was Kate's favorite pastime.

Maggie didn't seem to want to go home either, so we went window-shopping. At least they did. Mostly I just tagged after them, trying to keep from yawning and wondering what was so fascinating about looking at a lot of things you weren't going to buy.

Since it was the middle of the week, the stores were closed, but the show windows were lighted, and when the movie let out at nine o'clock, there were quite a few people on the street for a while, bunched around the theater at first, then spreading out as they climbed into cars or walked off in one direction or another, some of them stopping to window-shop, too, or to greet other people and stand with them for a few minutes, passing the time of day.

We had just finished doing the windows of the B & B Department Store when Kate noticed that all the lights were on inside the Northern State Bank across the street and asked Maggie why they were. Maggie said she supposed the board of directors was having a meeting. At that moment a door at the rear of the lobby opened, and men began coming through the lobby and out the front of the bank, walking in twos and threes.

Warren White, Alice's father, was among them. I asked Maggie what he was doing there when he belonged to the Roseville Bank and Trust Company, which was located a few doors up the street from the Northern State. Maggie said it looked as if the officers and boards of directors of both banks had been meeting together—she supposed maybe to discuss the banking situation generally.

Warren White walked off down Main Street deep in conversation with the man walking along beside him, though not too deep, I noticed, to stop and shake hands with a couple of people who were still lingering in front of the movie. I didn't suppose he could ever be too deep in a conversation to miss doing that.

I was so busy noticing Warren White that Maggie caught me

right in the middle of a yawn and said we'd better go on home, it was getting past our bedtime. Kate said all right, but just let her check first to see if her strawberry pin was still in Mr. Petrie's window.

Whenever Kate and I walked home together from the courthouse she was always tugging at me to stop so she could feast her eyes on all the rings and pins and bracelets sparkling in the window of Jim Petrie's jewelry store, and ever since she'd spotted a little red strawberry pin there some weeks before, she'd been hungering for it.

She finally worked up enough nerve one afternoon to go in and ask how much it was—and came back out pink in the face with embarrassment, because she couldn't possibly afford to buy it. It was ten dollars. Still she couldn't go by the store or be anywhere near without checking to make sure it was still there.

At that price I figured nobody else could afford to buy it either. I told her to stop worrying about it, it would be there. And it always was.

It was now.

Jim Petrie was there, too, in the store, working late at rearranging a showcase. He looked up and smiled at Kate. I think he kept the strawberry pin in the window even when he changed the rest of the display, just to reassure her. Then he waved to us.

Maggie was a friend to Jim Petrie, the same as she was to a lot of people in town and around the county, but at that time I only knew him from seeing him at his jewelry store, mostly through the window as we were seeing him now, waving back to him before we turned and started off for home.

Or times when we had relations visiting and Maggie would splurge on breakfast with bacon and eggs and sweet rolls, I'd ride my bike to the bakery early in the morning to get the rolls, and sometimes I'd see him then standing in the doorway of his store, a thin blond man, his arms folded, the same faraway look on his face I'd seen on Maggie's that night in the kitchen.

I knew a few things about him which I'd picked up the way

I picked up most of what I knew about different people—from hearing it said by someone at one time or another. I knew he was younger than Maggie—thirty-three to her thirty-seven—that he wasn't married, but lived with his mother and a maiden aunt, and that his father, who had opened the jewelry store when the family moved to Roseville, had committed suicide a few years back.

Suicides almost never happened in Roseville—as Bernice Kaiser was always saying to the other Coke ladies at Ward's Drugstore, nothing worth spending your time on ever happened in Roseville—so people tended to keep harking back to Mr. Petrie's suicide whenever anything gave them the opportunity, speculating as to why he'd done it and why the family had moved to Roseville from Chicago in the first place, though there wasn't any mystery about either one. It was common knowledge that the family had moved to Roseville because Mr. Petrie was in poor health and thought his health would improve in the country air, and he'd shot and killed himself in a fit of despondency down at the store early one morning because his health, instead of improving, had grown steadily worse.

But poor health, while cause for commiserating and even for commenting on the ability of some, such as oneself, to put up with ailments of one kind or another—enabling one to elaborate at length upon them—was disappointingly commonplace as the sole factor behind something so sensational as a suicide. Consequently, other factors were presented or presented themselves, the exact nature of them depending on what had brought the suicide up again in the first place.

The Petries were the kind of family who kept to themselves, which only made people suspect all the more they had something to hide, and the fact that Jim Petrie wasn't married only convinced them—wanting so hard as they did to be convinced —that his father's suicide had something to do with it, though just what the something was nobody had ever been able to work out to everyone else's satisfaction.

The fact that Jim Petrie wasn't married didn't interest me.

As passionate as my concern was about where babies came from, the rather vital connection between marriage and babies had somehow not yet occurred to me.

I didn't even give much thought to Maggie's getting married again, for all that Kate carried on about it, though after being at some friend's house and seeing the kind of sharing the parents had between them, I wondered if Maggie didn't sometimes feel the way I felt when Kate went off upstairs to giggle with Alice White about boys, leaving me with a half-finished game of Parchesi and nobody to finish it with.

But I supposed that, like me, Maggie didn't have any choice in the matter, not—from what I'd heard people say about how hard it was for widows with children to find another husband —while she was stuck with Kate and me. And I didn't care to consider what Maggie might do if that choice was offered to her.

I could have saved myself the worry, the same as Kate could have saved herself the matchmaking. What neither of us had any way of knowing—I doubt if Maggie herself fully understood it or would have admitted to it if she did—was that she had no intention of ever marrying again if she could help it; that underneath the stubborn independence, under the ache of loneliness, was fear; that for Maggie to give even so much as a quick little hug was not just admitting love but flaunting it before the eyes of a vengeful God.

When we got home Kate and I went to bed—by that time I wasn't even trying to keep from yawning—but Maggie said she didn't feel sleepy for some reason, she believed she'd stay up a while and read.

She often did that, so I didn't think any more of it that night than I did any other, except perhaps to wonder if it was because she still had the taste of Chuck Sellers in her mouth.

Chapter Two

At breakfast one Saturday around the middle of October, Maggie said I could go to the courthouse with her if I wanted to—I often did that, spending the day in and out of her office—but she expected to be tied up most of the morning in a hearing.

"You could sit in on the hearing, as far as that goes," she added, "but I don't know if it will interest you."

I considered. "What's it about?"

"The road around Cedar Lake."

"Oh," I said, "that."

"Well, what do you think?"

I supposed there would be a lot of speeches, but still, it might be interesting. "Okay," I said. "I'll go."

Cedar Lake was the largest lake in the county. Although some local people lived there year round, it served primarily as a summer resort for people from Chicago who owned cottages there. In the 1928 campaign Maggie had promised them that, if elected, she would try to get the county to blacktop the gravel road which went around Cedar Lake and which ran mostly between the cottages and the lake. Consequently, quite a number of them who normally voted in Chicago had that year registered and voted in Rose County.

Maggie kept her promise, which is to say she tried. She was still trying.

The county council, which met once a year to allocate the

43

money to be spent during the next fiscal year, had first to be persuaded to provide funds for it. The county commissioners, who conducted the business of the county in monthly meetings, had next to be persuaded to approve the expenditure of those funds.

The commissioners had finally approved the expenditure early in 1931, but Maggie had no sooner put the advertisement in the two Rose County papers for them, calling for bids to do the work, than farmers began streaming into her office, kicking up about as much fuss over the proposed expenditure as they did dust when they drove around the lake on summer Sunday afternoons to see what the cottage people, as they called them, were up to.

The farmers did more than kick up a fuss. They filed a protest. So the matter had dragged on. Now, after another dusty summer for the people at the lake, a field representative of the State Board of Tax Commissioners had come to Roseville to conduct a hearing on it.

Part of the farmers' driving around Cedar Lake to see what the cottage people were up to was idle curiosity. A greater part of it was resentment.

Although swamps in a few low-lying areas of Rose County had been drained to yield a rich black muck, the soil elsewhere was a sandy loam, more naturally suited to grazing cattle than growing crops. Some of the farmers kept dairy cows, some of them raised livestock, and all of them, with the help of fertilizer, grew crops of one kind or another—some rye, some wheat, a lot of alfalfa, but mostly corn.

Some of the muck farmers, such as the one Chuck Sellers had complained about, had made a fortune in the twenties growing onions—before too many of them got into the act, and the onion boom went bust—but most Rose County farmers, like farmers throughout the Midwest, had shared neither in the onion boom nor in the general boom of prosperity.

It wasn't that they didn't try. They tried very hard. They mortgaged their farms to buy more land in order to increase production. They borrowed money to pay for machinery with which to plow and cultivate and sow and harvest all that increased acreage. Still they were unable, no matter how many hours or how much land they worked, to increase their profit. They were sometimes unable, after the Crash, to make even enough money to pay their taxes or the interest on their notes and mortgages.

With people everywhere in need of food, it didn't make sense to them. And it went against their grain. They believed, as their fathers and their forefathers had believed, that hard work was the basis of success. Yet, for all their hard work, indeed, because of it, they now found themselves in danger of losing everything they owned—land, livestock, machinery, home.

The farmers who had dairy cows were better off. The Chicago market paid as high a price for milk during the Depression as it would later during the prosperous years of the Second World War. But asking a crop farmer to become a dairy farmer was asking him to change a lifetime way of doing things —and asking him to borrow still more money when he was already mortgaged to the hilt. Besides, for all the farmers knew, the dairy market could, like the onion boom, be crowded to collapse.

So they went on doing the only thing they knew how to do, unable to understand why they, who were the backbone of America, couldn't make a decent living any more, seeing with resentful eyes where the money which should be coming to them was going—into the hands of big-city Jews and foreigners.

Such a crowd of farmers showed up for the hearing it had to be shifted from the county commissioners' office, which opened off Maggie's office, to the big courtroom up on the third floor.

I supposed the farmers would come stomping in mad as hornets, but they didn't. They just poked their heads in Maggie's office long enough to find out where to go. Then they hung around in little knots in and out of the courtroom, lounging up against the wall in their overalls exchanging talk about the weather and the corn crop and aiming at the handiest spittoon.

45

The way the hearing started off, it didn't look to be any more satisfying. Any who wanted to speak their piece spoke it, while the rest of them sat back, arms folded, listening and working up another chaw. It seemed to me one speaker would have been enough. What every one of them said came down to what all of them had been saying all along—they were against the county spending the money to have the road blacktopped. But in order to agree with what had just been said, the next man had first to repeat everything the one before him had pointed out. So it took a while.

I was half asleep and wishing I hadn't come when somebody at the back of the courtroom yelled "Mr. Chairman!" so loud I nearly shot out of my seat. I turned around to see who it was, but he was already heading for the front in great, long strides, so I turned back again.

It was Mr. Wurlitzer—though it took me a minute to realize it, because I wasn't used to seeing him in overalls—here, he started out saying, shaking his fist as he said it, to show this thing up for what it was—just one more example of how the Democrats were squandering the taxpayers' money.

I sighed and settled back to listen to him, glad for what he was going to say even before he said it. In Roseville one sure way to liven up anything was to bring politics into it.

Mr. Wurlitzer pointed a finger straight at his audience. "Who," he bellowed out, "is going to benefit from having the road around Cedar Lake blacktopped?" His finger started moving. "You? Or you? Or you?"

He paused, as if waiting for somebody to answer the question, then answered it himself, which I knew all along he would do. Mr. Wurlitzer was the superintendent of the Sunday School at the Methodist church, and he was always answering his own questions. "Not a blessed one of you."

He hooked his thumbs under the straps of his overalls. On a lesser built man that might not have been impressive, but Mr. Wurlitzer wore about a size fifty-two, and he filled it all the way out. "Now," he went on in a mild voice, "I've got nothing

46

against Chicago people coming down here and buying a cottage at Cedar Lake to vacation in. I guess they've got a right to spend their money any way they want to, including showing folks around here they've got money to spend."

The farmers grunted.

John Wurlitzer had as much money as any of the cottage people, if not more. He just didn't spend it, that was all. He was, in fact, so wealthy and lived so close to the city limits, he was not considered a farmer by the people of Roseville, though he grew corn on some of his land. More important to those living closest to him or, on a summer day when the wind was right, to anybody anywhere on the east edge of town, he raised hogs.

But Mr. Wurlitzer owned real estate and was on the board of directors of the Northern State Bank, and that, along with being a Methodist and rich, was enough to put him in Roseville's upper crust, hogs and all.

Right now, however, he was being a farmer. As such he'd put his finger on the sore spot.

He unhooked a thumb to pull at an ear lobe. "Now," he said again, "I've got nothing against the cottage people wanting the road blacktopped, as far as that goes. As my father used to say to me, it's a good world to want in."

The farmers laughed.

"But can you name me one good reason the county should do it?"

Nobody could.

"Maybe the cottage people figure we owe it to them." He spread his hands. "After all, look at all they've done for us."

The farmers laughed again.

"Why, if it weren't for them, we wouldn't be enjoying the modern convenience of fast time."

More laughter.

Chicago's daylight saving time irritated the dairy farmers, who had to get up an hour earlier during the summer to milk the cows in order to get the milk to market. It irritated all the farmers in general, and a good many townspeople as well. Some of Roseville's merchants, wanting to cater to the cottage people, operated their stores on fast time, while other stores stayed on slow time, so that Roseville was in a state of confusion all summer long.

"And think of all the money they bring into the community."

"Yeah," somebody called out, "and take right back out with them, too."

The farmers hooted with laughter.

For all the catering to them, Roseville's merchants didn't get much business out of the cottage people. They brought what they needed down from Chicago with them, staying out at the lake most of the time, driving into Roseville only occasionally to get a few things at the dime store or go to the movie or cash a check at one of the two banks.

Mr. Wurlitzer made a fist again. "If the Republicans were running Rose County, I reckon they'd propose to do for the cottage people what the cottage people do for us. Nothing."

The farmers burst into applause, and the tax man conducting the hearing rapped for order.

"But the Republicans aren't running Rose County. The Democrats are. And if there's one thing the Democrats love to do, it's spend money." He started shaking his fist, really warming to his subject now. "At a time when our own people are in dire straits, with men out of work, and their wives and children going hungry—hungry, mind you—the Democrats propose to spend all this money just so the well-fed cottage people won't have to put up with a little dust!"

Again the farmers applauded, and again the chairman rapped for order.

Mr. Wurlitzer shook his head. "It kind of makes you wonder, don't it, what's really behind all this."

"Hear, hear," somebody seconded.

"It kind of makes you think maybe there's more to this than meets the eye. Considering the cottage people have gotten so used to getting things done the high-powered way they do things up in Chicago—"

"That's right," an elderly farmer squeaked out. "If they won't ante up, mow 'em down!"

The farmers burst into such shouts of laughter, the chairman had to rap again.

"I was thinking," Mr. Wurlitzer went on, "more about the high-powered way they get things done when it comes to politics. If you ask me, I'd say what's behind all this is somebody's making it worth somebody's while."

Mr. Thornapple, who was one of the three county commissioners and was sitting at a long table with the other two commissioners and Maggie, slammed his hand down on the table. "That's a lie!"

Talk broke out all over the courtroom. The chairman pounded with his gavel several times, calling for order.

Mr. Thornapple started to get up, but Maggie jumped up ahead of him. "Mr. Chairman. On a point of personal privilege."

The chairman nodded.

Mr. Wurlitzer also nodded. "I guess I've said all I had to say anyhow." He headed for a seat, pausing a moment to look over at Maggie. "Nothing personal, Maggie. You understand that."

She smiled at him. "Of course, John. How could anybody possibly think there was?"

The farmers chuckled.

"Mr. Chairman," Maggie said again. "I would like to point out two things. In the first place, if anybody runs the county, it's the county commissioners. Of the three of them, two are Republicans."

Mr. Wurlitzer, who'd no more than sat down, stood up. "She's right. They are. But the way I look at it, considering how close the commissioners work with the auditor, and considering who our auditor is these days, a man could get addled enough to forget just what he is—outside, of course, of being a man."

Even the chairman laughed at that one.

Maggie's face went almost as fiery as her hair. "Mr. Chairman," she said again.

The chairman straightened his face and rapped for order.

49

When the room settled down, Maggie said, "In the second place, although the commissioners authorized the blacktopping of the road around Cedar Lake, I'm the one—and the only one—who's responsible for proposing it. And I can tell you exactly what's behind it. I promised the cottage people if I were elected auditor I'd try to get the road blacktopped for them. And that's all that's behind it. Now if John Wurlitzer would care to examine my bank statements, he's free to do so—assuming he can bear to look at a bank account which shows expenditures as well as deposits."

The farmers howled, and Maggie smiled sweetly at Mr. Wurlitzer. "Nothing personal, John. You understand that." She sat down to a round of applause.

The chairman looked out over those assembled. "There are some questions I'd like to ask, but first, does anybody else wish to state an opinion?"

"Yes, sir. I do."

I turned around to see who had spoken, though I thought I knew from the prissiness of his voice who it was. I did. It was Lester Crabbe, whose last name fit him so perfectly I didn't realize for a long time it was his real name; I thought people just called him that.

In spite of the fact that he was always turning up everywhere, I was surprised to see him in the courtroom. It was the first indication I'd had that anyone other than farmers were there. I started to look around to see if there were any more who weren't, but Lester had started speaking, so I turned back to him.

"It seems to me," he said in his mincing way, "from the direction this hearing is taking, this entire matter is being treated as a joke. Personally, I don't see anything entertaining about it."

I sighed and thought, after things had gotten nice and livened up, now they were going to get dragged down dull again.

I was wrong. They got funnier than ever, but they got a bit ugly first.

"It seems to me," he said again, "the real issue at stake here has been entirely—and, I might add, conveniently—overlooked."

There was a small buzz of interest through the crowd—small, because from the looks on their faces, a number of those present had been subjected to Lester Crabbe's complaints before. The looks on their faces were mostly ones of weariness. Mr. Wurlitzer yawned outright.

Slipping his hand inside his jacket front, Lester brought out his wallet, from which he extracted a newspaper clipping. "I have here a recent editorial from the Chicago *Tribune* calling the attention of the local authorities to a fact which, from the behavior of those present, they obviously choose to ignore."

I looked over at Maggie. She was frowning at him, as much out of puzzlement as anything else.

"Even though this fact"—he waved the clipping—"is shaping the moral climate in which the children of this community are being raised."

I didn't know how a moral climate could be shaped. I didn't even know what a moral climate was, or why Lester Crabbe should care about the children of the community when he didn't have any children. He wasn't even married, though he was long past the age for it.

I started to yawn myself, when he added, "Including their very own children," looking straight at me.

I knew what that meant. I looked over at Maggie again. She was still frowning, an angry one now.

He waved the clipping again. "I refer to the fact that Cedar Lake is becoming nothing more than a hideout for Chicago gangsters. And far from doing everything they can to prevent this, far from cooperating with the Chicago authorities, as this editorial reminds them it is their solemn duty to do in seeing that these criminals are brought to justice, our politicians are not only bent on encouraging them to congregate here, they actually want to pave the way for them!"

The farmers burst out laughing, but Lester's humor had apparently been as unintentional as it was surprising.

He scowled. "It seems to me this matter goes far beyond playing up to these gangsters by providing them with the convenience of a blacktopped road. I suggest to you that this is part of a political conspiracy to let them come down here and take over the government of this county just as they have taken over the city of Chicago. As a citizen and a taxpayer, I protest!"

The farmers were too dumbfounded to do anything more than stare at him. Maggie wasn't. This time it was she who slammed her hand down on the table. "Political conspiracy, my foot! Lester, you make me sick. And taxpayer, indeed." She made a face. "For somebody who makes a damn good living in this town"—Lester ran an office supply and print shop for old Mr. Wheeler, who owned it and had retired—"and who drives around town in a brand-new car every year and brags about his fine collection of antiques, when the tax assessor comes around the first day of March, what do you have to show? You live in a rented house. You've sold your car the week before. Your furniture suddenly becomes nothing more than a few second-hand sticks. Taxpayer! About the only tax the county can assess you for is the poll tax, and I wonder sometimes if that isn't a mistake!"

The farmers burst into such howls of laughter, slapping their knees, you could hardly hear the gavel being pounded.

When they finally quieted down, Maggie said, "There are more than three hundred and fifty property owners out at Cedar Lake. Out of all that number, to the best of my knowledge one—and only one—is a known member of the Chicago underworld. Now how you can twist that into saying Cedar Lake is becoming nothing more than a hideout for Chicago gangsters is more than I can say."

Lester, red in the face and scowling still, snapped out, "A man doesn't have to own property to use it!"

"Are you suggesting that the cottage people rent rooms to gangsters?"

52

Even the farmers, who could believe almost anything of the cottage people, snickered at that. Lester, redder than ever and looking for all the world like Bobby Jackson at school the day before when he was trying to bluff his way through a question on some homework he hadn't read, said, "I'm saying that any number of gangsters use Dynamite Dom's place as a hideout. And," he added, blustering, "I have information to prove it."

I didn't see how anybody could believe him. I don't know that anybody did. Maggie shrugged. "Then I advise you to take your information to somebody who can act on it. I'm the auditor of the county, not the sheriff."

Lester muttered something inaudible and sat down.

"I further advise you," Maggie said, "to make sure you have something more tangible than information—your own or anybody else's—before you go shooting off your mouth again about a political conspiracy. That's something I can act on. And I'll tell you just how I'll act, too. I'll slap a suit for slander on you."

The farmers burst out laughing again.

"I can't say I've never laid eyes on Dynamite Dom, because I have, the same as you and probably most of the people in this room have. But outside of that, I know little about him except what I read in the papers. And what I read in the papers I can assure you is in no way related to the business of this hearing. As far as this hearing and my position at it are concerned, the gentleman referred to is a property owner at Cedar Lake. And that's all he is."

From the big double doorway at the back of the courtroom somebody called out, "That's right!" and clapped his hands. Only the words didn't come out "That's right." They came out "Thatsa right." And nobody applauded with him.

Probably they couldn't have, even if they'd wanted to. They were too busy gaping. So was I. Only my mouth wasn't just hanging open. My eyes were nearly bugging out of my head.

It was the gentleman referred to.

Unlike Maggie and the others, I had never seen Dynamite

Dom before in my life, but I knew from seeing his picture in the paper what he looked like. He looked like his picture—short and stocky with graying black hair and a swarthy complexion. And across his left cheek, sure enough, was the long indentation from the time he'd been grazed by a ricocheting bullet —and if he hadn't been so fast on his feet he would no longer be on them at all. I shivered.

Even if he hadn't looked like his picture, I couldn't have missed identifying him. Nobody in Roseville went around accompanied by two bodyguards.

They were just like the pictures of them, too, black-garbed and black-putteed, standing on either side of him, both of them with their arms folded and their chins jutted out, their faces so identically vacant they could have been twins.

I don't suppose they had any idea of how ridiculous they looked. I don't suppose, actually, they ever had any ideas, beyond the one they were hired to have.

At the time I didn't have any idea of how ridiculous they looked myself. My eyes were riveted on the bulge inside their jackets, or at least on what I conceived to be a bulge, and my attention was riveted on what caused that bulge.

Dynamite Dom waved a hand over the assemblage and spoke to the chairman. "This hearing. It's public, no?"

The chairman nodded. "Yes. If you'd care to take a seat."

I wondered briefly what Maggie was looking like, but I was afraid to take my eyes off the trio long enough to see.

Dynamite Dom nodded, said something to his bodyguards, then walked over and sat down with them—between them—in a vacant section of the back row of benches. He waved his hand again. "Please. Go on."

Something like a sigh settled over the courtroom as the farmers twisted back to their original positions, and the chairman rapped for order, though there was no need to.

It occurred to me to wonder how long Dynamite Dom had been standing in the doorway before he spoke. I did take my eyes off him and his bodyguards then. If I hadn't, I would have been the only one still turned around staring at them. Anyhow I had to see what Lester was looking like.

That was a disappointment. He was looking the same as ever —like a crab. Only his mouth was drawn a little tighter. I did notice, though, when the hearing finally broke up, he didn't hang around to talk to anybody, but beat it out of there. I didn't blame him. The way I looked at it, Dynamite Dom wasn't anyone to fool around with.

For that matter, the way I looked at it wasn't all that different from the way anybody looked at it. When Maggie said she knew little about Dynamite Dom, she was telling the truth. I don't suppose many people in Roseville knew more than a little about him. Or wanted to.

His name was Dominic Petrelli, but nobody ever called him that. He was always called Dynamite Dom. For all I know, he called himself that. And I never heard anybody, with the exception of Lester Crabbe at the hearing, call him a gangster. He was called, if he had to be called anything, a racketeer.

In a way this made sense. He was a racketeer. His particular racket was dry-cleaning establishments, whose proprietors paid him for protection, his favorite persuader for those who did not being a bomb.

For a routine job he sometimes used a cheap black-powder bomb, but it was his preference for the risky job and the more widely effective—and expensive—dynamite bomb which had given rise to his nickname.

But I didn't know all that then, nor was that why he was called a racketeer by those who did. To the people of Roseville a Chicago racketeer was simply an up-to-date, large-scale practitioner of the venerable art of making easy money, his precise method of making it—the Chicago *Tribune* notwithstanding —left unexplained and unexplored. As such, racketeer had a more genteel sound to it than gangster, which left no doubt whatsoever as to what methods were employed to what ends.

In the late twenties Dynamite Dom had bought some land at Cedar Lake, where he built a home—it was generally referred to as a villa—for himself and his wife and now-grown children—and, of course, his bodyguards—to vacation in. Or, as Lester put it, to hide out in.

Lester did have information to back up that charge. The Chicago *Tribune* editorial he waved at the hearing was headed CRIMINAL HIDEOUTS, and it scored Dynamite Dom and other "malefactors who have invaded the country and use hitherto respectable places for concealment."

If concealment was Dynamite Dom's aim, he was constantly defeating it. Walled in though it was, his villa was the biggest "sight" at Cedar Lake. And when he entertained guests from Chicago for the weekend, as he often did, guests who, despite Lester's dubious information to the contrary, were more celebrated than notorious, crowds of onlookers—farmers, cottage people, and townspeople alike—would line the roads and grounds nearby to be entertained in turn by the front-lawn concerts of his singer and musician friends.

But if the people of Roseville were of two minds about this member of the Chicago underworld in their midst, I was not. I was terrified of him.

At ten o'clock on those Saturday mornings when I went with Maggie to her office, I would go out to get the Chicago *Tribune* and two hot dogs, one for Maggie and one for me. I had to go down Main Street to get them, and unless I were to cross the street the courthouse fronted on in the middle of the block, which I couldn't do because Maggie made us cross streets at corners, I had to go past the southwest corner of the courthouse lawn, where the flagpole stood.

The first time I remember going by the flagpole, I looked up at it just as I was passing under it. It seemed to be leaning toward me as if it was about to fall on me. After that I tried going by it without looking up, but I never could. I suppose I thought if I didn't keep my eye on it, I wouldn't know when to jump out of the way.

If it hadn't been for the hot dog, I wouldn't have made the trip at all. The Chicago *Tribune* was always blaring forth in column after column across its front page terrors only somewhat diminished—because more distant—from the one the flagpole held for me. Those were the terrors of Chicago's kidnappings and murders and rapes, and of gangsters machine-gunning each other to death. I never wanted to go anywhere near Chicago.

So far I hadn't had to, except when my father had taken sick and died and been buried there, and Maggie had taken Kate and me up to his funeral. But I was only five years old then, too young to remember it more than vaguely, too young anyhow to have started reading the papers.

The only reason for Kate or me to go to Chicago after that would have been to visit our relatives there. So far they had always come to visit us instead (Uncle Donald and Aunt Clarissa and Mark and the twins driving down for the day on a Sunday or holiday, Grandpa sometimes coming with them, but more often coming down alone on the train and going back alone, Kate and I always wishing he wouldn't go, wanting him to stay). It was my earnest hope they would continue to.

I didn't doubt Maggie was sincere in saying that as far as her position at the hearing was concerned, Dynamite Dom was a property owner at Cedar Lake, and that was all he was. As far as my position was concerned, he was someone I was within shooting distance of.

The hearing itself, after Dynamite Dom's arrival, proceeded to wind up. The chairman, asking for and not getting any further opinions from the audience, turned to Maggie and asked her why she thought the road should be blacktopped.

Maggie said she understood the reluctance on the part of the farmers to have the county spend money for something which seemed of little benefit to them, especially now when times were hard. But the funds had already been allocated and, if allowed, the blacktopping would provide several weeks' work for a number of jobless men.

As for the road itself, she said that the cottage people, whatever money they spent or didn't spend in the community, paid

57

property taxes in Rose County. The largest part of the tax assessment was for the schools. Since the cottage people didn't send their children to school here, they didn't get any benefit from that.

"About all they do get for their tax money," she said, "are the roads. They want a good road around the lake, and I think they should have it." She spread her hands. "It's as simple and unconspiratorial as that."

The chairman considered for a few minutes. Then he said he would allow the blacktopping of the road. He banged the gavel. "This hearing is adjourned."

Dynamite Dom applauded, beaming at everyone he could. The farmers didn't beam back at him, but they didn't act particularly sore. They just got up and started heading for the door.

John Wurlitzer went over to Dynamite Dom to shake hands with him. I supposed he figured, easy made or hard, money was money, and Dynamite Dom might as well be encouraged to put some of what he had in the Northern State Bank, especially since word was going around town that Dynamite Dom was talking of retiring and settling down year round at Cedar Lake.

I sat where I was, concentrating on trying to blend myself into the bench, willing Dynamite Dom to please get up and go, hoping he wouldn't notice me before he did.

He got up, but he didn't go. His bodyguards flanking him, he walked up front and over to Maggie and pumped her hand up and down, saying what a good woman she was and what a good thing she'd done.

Maggie was polite to him, but she got flustered and pink in the face and kept looking away from him while he was talking to her, as if she were afraid the farmers would think, for all her assurances, there really was a conspiracy afoot.

The farmers didn't act as if they did. They just kept on heading for the door, talking to one another, still laughing, some of them, about Lester and the poll tax.

I held my breath against what I knew from past experience

was bound to happen. It did. Maggie sent me a come-rescue look.

I couldn't ignore it, but as I walked over to her, my feet felt as if they were already tied to cement blocks.

"This is Angel," Maggie said, drawing me to her, smiling down at me.

I tried to smile back, but nothing came of it, thin-lipped or otherwise.

Dynamite Dom beamed at me and said in his heavily accented voice, "A little one. Such a nice-a little one."

All I could think was nice-a for what?

"Angel, is it?" He nodded, beaming still. "Angelina. Such a good Italian name."

"No," Maggie said. "I'm afraid not. It's Angelica." She smiled. "Her mother came across the name in a book she was reading and took a fancy to it."

Dynamite Dom gave Maggie a bewildered look. "Her mother?"

Maggie explained about our mother and father. About Kate, too. And, under his questioning, about all her family.

Dynamite Dom shook his head over the sadness of so many untimely deaths, and though I wasn't the least bit reassured by that, I couldn't help noticing, as he went on and on about Maggie being left all alone in the world with two little ones to look after, how much, in spite of his accent, he sounded like all the think-of-all-the-sacrifices head-shaking ladies of Rose-ville.

He wound up, too, finally, patting me on the head. Then he said something in Italian to one of his bodyguards, who nodded and reached into his pocket for a package. In it was a tiny doll Dynamite Dom had bought for one of his grandchildren which he wanted me to have.

It was an exquisite little Dresden china figurine, dainty and delicate. Long after I'd given up dolls, I kept it on my dresser.

Kate could hardly stand the sight of it at first. Not because of the doll itself. Because she was so mortified when she heard about my getting it. I didn't know what Dynamite Dom had in mind when he spoke to the bodyguard. When the bodyguard reached into his pocket, I stuck my hands up.

By the time Dynamite Dom had finished with us and left, the courtroom was empty. Maggie gathered up some papers she'd brought with her, and we walked down the stairway together to the second floor.

"Did you enjoy the hearing?" she asked.

I had. In spite of Dynamite Dom. And since I'd gotten safely away from him, I could relax. I nodded. "Did you?"

She sighed. "I'm just glad the matter is finally settled."

Chapter Three

There were two drugstores in Roseville, right across the street from each other on opposite corners of Main Street where Lake Street intersected it to form the so-called center of town. (Jim Petrie's jewelry store and a filling station occupied the other corners.) But the Rexall Drugstore didn't have a soda fountain, so whenever women wanted to meet uptown, they met at Ward's.

The most habitual meeters at Ward's were the Coke ladies —Julia Fletcher, Marcella DeWitt, and Bernice Kaiser, she who was always saying nothing worth spending your time on ever happened in Roseville, looking down her nose at everything that did. At least I thought of them as the Coke ladies, because whenever I went to Ward's after school for an ice-cream cone, which was just as often as I could manage it, that was what the three of them were always there doing—having a Coke. And visiting.

Sam McCutcheon laughed when he heard me refer to them one time as that. Then he turned to a customer who was waiting for a prescription and said, "Doc Hawkins calls them the Roseville Broadcasting Company." And Sam threw back his head and laughed again.

Sam had a problem of his own in that respect. The original owner of Ward's Drugstore and its proprietor for many years was Julia Fletcher's father, Edward Ward. Then in 1927 Mrs. Ward died, and Mr. Ward sold out to Sam and went to live in Florida, so Sam took the sign Ward's down and hung up a new sign with McCutcheon's on it. But everybody kept on calling the drugstore Ward's. Sam finally got so he even answered the phone that way himself.

There was something to be said for Doc Hawkins' point of view about the Coke ladies, at least insofar as Marcella DeWitt was concerned. Marcella, whom I once heard Maggie describe as "aggressively friendly to absolutely everybody in town," owned a beauty parlor, but gossip was her life. People were always teasing her about her perpetual fiancé, Eddie Smith, joking among themselves that Marcella would never marry him for fear something might happen in Roseville while she was away on her honeymoon, and everybody, even those who were the readiest to listen to her, used to say if you wanted to get any story, no matter how outlandish, spread all over town, all you had to do was tell it to Marcella.

I didn't have anything against Marcella, but I did against Bernice Kaiser. Bernice was Barbara Kaiser's mother.

I didn't like Barbara Kaiser any better in the fifth grade than I had in the first—Barbara had explained to me back in the first grade when I tried to be friendly with her that she had to be careful who her friends were so she wouldn't pick up anything.

She didn't think I'd improved any either. I don't suppose I had. Maggie never had time in the morning to bother with nonessentials, but left it up to Kate and me to get ourselves washed and dressed for school.

But ever since the middle of September I'd been going to Ward's with Barbara to get an ice-cream cone every day after school except Tuesday, when she had to go to Mrs. Rogers for her piano lesson, because she paid for my cone. And she paid because after four years of sitting behind Bobby Jackson, who spent most of every recess picking himself up out of the dirt where he'd fallen trying to chin himself on the parallel bars, and in front of Sally Kline, who spent most of every recess spinning over the cinders around the Giant Stride, which Barbara herself would never play on because it would get her clothes dirty and ruin her shoes—and she was right, it would have— she'd managed to build up enough resistance to whatever she might pick up from me to ask me to help her with fractions.

I never could decide if the free ice-cream cone was worth going to Ward's with Barbara to get it—not because of what each of us had to put up with from the other, but because of what both of us had to put up with from her mother.

Whenever I went to Ward's with anybody other than Barbara, I didn't have to put up with Bernice. She didn't pay any attention to me at all. But she paid a lot of attention to Barbara, so when we went there together, either Bernice would make a point of looking me up and down—she didn't know about our deal but thought Barbara was being Generous to the Poor—or she'd make a point of sighing over Barbara's tendency to be a little plump—Barbara wasn't plump, she was fat, with a stolid face, and even her flaxen hair was in fat sausage curls.

Then Bernice would go on about how she couldn't understand it. Barbara was kept on a strict diet at home and never ate anything between meals other than this—if Bernice Kaiser could have seen the amount of bread and peanut butter Barbara could put away at our house, absolutely pop-eyed that Kate and I could go to the icebox or the cupboard and get something to eat whenever we wanted to, without a maid there to say we couldn't, she wouldn't have had so much trouble understanding it—but she supposed that in a couple of years when Barbara started—she never said what it was Barbara was going to start, but only raised her eyebrows and gave the other ladies a knowing look—then she'd probably slim down, and they'd be able to find clothes that fit her properly right here in Roseville without having to make special trips to South Bend or Chicago for them.

The times Bernice Kaiser was despairing over the poor being always with us, I'd just lick my cone and despair right back at her. But when she started in on Barbara, carrying on about what she was going to start doing in a couple of years to get into the right-size clothes—which Barbara supposed could only mean she was going to have to stop eating altogether—Barbara would get pink in the face and look so backed into a corner it made me squirm, even though Barbara could turn right around and pick on some kid at school the way her mother was picking on her without turning a hair.

We even talked about taking our business elsewhere, only there wasn't anywhere else to take it. There was an ice-cream and hamburger stand down by the railroad run by a kindly, cherub-faced old man named Mr. Cummings. But kindly, cherub-faced old Mr. Cummings liked to hold little girls on his lap, and even Barbara and I were old enough to have wised up as to why he wanted to. We preferred being picked on to that.

Then one Monday morning in the middle of November Nathaniel turned up in the fifth grade, come from Chicago to live with the Fletchers.

When he walked into Ward's with Barbara and me after school that day, all Bernice could say—so relieved at getting off the hook in the displaying-our-children department she was glinty-eyed—was how thin he was. "Really, Julia, so pitifully thin."

Bernice was right. Nathaniel was thin, thin to the point of being skinny. But that wasn't what most people noticed first about him.

Nathaniel had a solemn face, and he wore steel-rimmed spectacles, and his brown hair, otherwise straight, stood up in a cowlick over his forehead.

Nathaniel looked like an owl.

The first day he was at school nobody played with him. Nobody ever played with new kids or even liked them. A new kid mostly just stood around at recess watching everybody else swing or slide or spin on the Giant Stride or play cops and robbers or jump rope or whatever all we did.

If a new girl was pretty, some boy would take enough of a shine to her after a few days to sneak up and snatch her hat off so she'd chase him. Then a lot of other boys, not to be out-done, would do the same. Then the girls would start playing with her to keep her from getting so much attention.

A new boy didn't get any help from anybody. If the girls thought he was handsome, they'd just stand off and whisper and giggle and get pink in the face. Otherwise, they ignored him. The boys ignored him no matter what he looked like unless he was a better athlete than they were.

You only had to take one look at Nathaniel to figure he'd just have to wait until his newness wore off.

It wasn't because I felt sorry for Nathaniel that I went up to him after school that first day and asked him if he wanted to go to Ward's with Barbara and me. Barbara was getting better at fractions faster than I'd counted on, and while I didn't know yet whether Nathaniel would need help with anything or not—he'd hardly opened his mouth all day—I did know the Fletch-ers were rich like the Kaisers, so I figured it wouldn't hurt to get in good with him, just in case.

By the end of his second day he'd recited a couple of times. I was heading for home when he came up behind me and touched me on the shoulder, saying didn't I want to go to Ward's for an ice-cream cone. I told him I couldn't, because Tuesday was the day Barbara went to her piano lesson, explaining to him about our deal.

"I can pay," he said, digging into his pocket. He held out a fifty-cent piece on the palm of his hand.

I stared at it. I'd had a fifty-cent piece once. Old Mrs. Werner, whose husband had run Werner's Clothing Store and whose son ran it now, had called to me from her porch one day the past summer and said she'd pay me ten cents a box for all the cur-rants I could pick out of their back yard. I picked all there were, and it came to five boxes with the help of some leaves, and she gave me a fifty-cent piece. But I'd spent it a long time ago.

I shook my head finally and said there wasn't anything I could help him with, because he was smarter than I was.

Nathaniel considered a bit. Then he looked down at his feet and said, peering at me sideways, "I'm not very good at spelling."

Nathaniel was a worse liar than I was. I had a notion to ask him to spell appendicitis, which I'd missed in the last spelling bee. But I didn't. I just said okay, and we set off for Ward's.

"Are your parents rich like your uncle and aunt?" I asked him.

Nathaniel shook his head. "They used to be, but my father lost a lot of money in the Crash. And then I guess he lost the rest of it this year."

"Is that why you're here?"

"I guess so."

Nathaniel really was a terrible liar.

After we'd walked about another block, he said, "My parents are—" He stopped, so I stopped, too. "Do you tell things?" he asked.

I considered. "Not if you tell me ahead of time I shouldn't. But if you don't, then I might." I frowned at him. "And sometimes I forget anyhow."

He frowned back at me.

We walked another block or so, and then I stopped, so Nathaniel stopped, too.

"Look," I said. "We could have a club if you want to. A secret club. And we could take an oath. Would you like that?"

Nathaniel nodded.

"Okay," I said. "What shall we call it?"

He didn't know, and I didn't know, but we finally hit on A for Angel and N for Nathaniel, so we shook hands and we were the A & N Club.

"My parents are going to get a divorce."

I stared at him. "My gosh. Why?"

He shook his head. "I don't know."

"And that's why you're here?"

He nodded. "My mother said while they were doing it, it would be better if I came down here and stayed with Uncle Orn and Aunt Julia." Nathaniel's mother was Julia Fletcher's younger sister Mildred.

"For how long?"

He shook his head again. "I don't know. I guess until school is out next spring. Maybe through the summer."

"My gosh," I said again. "Does it take that long to get a divorce?"

Nathaniel shrugged his shoulders. "I guess"—he frowned at me—"maybe they couldn't decide which one of them wanted me to live with them the most after they get the divorce, and —this way they can see—I guess"—he shrugged again—"which one misses me the most."

I had to look away from him. "I guess you're probably right." Then I said, too loud, "Well, hell's bells, Nathaniel, spring isn't so far off"—it seemed years off—"and if you stay through the summer we can have a swell time swimming at the river and out at Cedar Lake."

He nodded. Then he peered at me again through his spectacles. "Doesn't your mother care if you swear?"

I shook my head. "Maggie doesn't care what we do—Kate or me—as long as we don't die."

Nathaniel got wide-eyed, making him look more like an owl than ever. "Are you about to?"

"Heck, no. It's just Maggie. She has a thing about people dying—I guess because so many she cared about have." I counted off on my fingers. "Her father and her brother and her mother and our mother, who was her sister"—I explained about Maggie marrying our father—"and then our father." I remembered Maggie's lost love in Cincinnati and counted off another finger. "And somebody else she loved once." I held my fingers out to him. "Six. That's an awful lot of people to have die on you."

He nodded.

"Anyhow," I said, "I don't swear at home or in front of Maggie."

He frowned at me. "If she was married to your father, it's

67

the same as being your mother, isn't it? So why do you call her Maggie?"

I frowned back at him. We'd always called her Maggie, both Kate and I, for as long as I could remember. "I don't know," I said, feeling about the same as Nathaniel looked. "I suppose that's what she wanted us to call her."

We were at Ward's by that time, so we went in and got our cones, and Bernice Kaiser got in a few more licks about how thin Nathaniel was. Julia said not to worry, she'd fatten him up, she just wished he would smile more. She smiled at him to give him the idea.

Nathaniel couldn't manage a smile back. He only ducked his head at her, so she sighed and asked him if he had enough money. When he said he did, she sighed again and turned back to what Marcella DeWitt had been saying about Leta Werner and her husband when we walked in.

I didn't know how anybody could keep from smiling back at Julia Fletcher. Outside of being the only one of the Coke ladies I really cared about, Julia was one of my favorite people in all of Roseville, though even now, looking back, I don't know why she was or what there was about her that made me expect so much of her.

As Orn Fletcher's wife and as the beneficiary along with her sister Mildred of the small estate their mother had left to them, Julia had more money at her disposal than her friends—except for Bernice Kaiser, who seemed to derive what little pleasure life offered her in claiming to be the richest woman in Roseville —but other than that, there didn't seem to be anything about Julia to make her different in any important way from other women of her age and social standing in the community.

Like them she was first and foremost a wife and mother— a homemaker and a housekeeper—though, in her case, as in the case of some of the rest of them, after becoming a mother she was a mother first and then a wife. She was, as most of them were, a dedicated churchwoman—she taught the young people's Sunday School class at the Methodist church and was active

68

in the Ladies Aid. And, like the others, she belonged to the PTA and to the domestic science club and to the literary club and, yet again like them, foregoing self-betterment and self-enlightenment for self-indulgence one afternoon each week, to a bridge club.

In spite of being Orn's wife, she took little, if any, interest in politics, though she was one of Maggie's staunchest admirers. I remember her saying once that as a young girl she had marched in a suffragette parade one time in Chicago, but she was quick to add she'd only done it as a lark, she didn't see how a woman could do anything so demeaning as to get herself arrested and thrown in jail for something that was bound to come sooner or later anyhow.

She was a woman of only average intelligence and—perhaps because she was Orn's wife—of stunted spirit. I doubt that her horizons extended much further beyond the confines of Roseville than my own did at the time. Yet she was an exceptionally appealing woman.

Not in her figure—she was too much on the tall and spare side—but in her face, which was beautiful in a kind of softly tinted portrait way, with haunting brown eyes and a wide and gentle smile, and her hair, truly her crowning glory, a warm chestnut brown, which she wore in a coronet braid, though most of the women in Roseville had had theirs bobbed long since. Julia was always saying she was going to get it cut in spite of Orn, but still, the coronet braid suited her height and thinness, giving her from a distance, at least, a regal look.

Perhaps it was that quality about her which made her seem special to me—someone apart and above and, conversely, because she was such a kindhearted, gracious woman, someone akin.

Or perhaps it was because a child's world is a child-centered world, and Julia Fletcher was not only devoted to her two children—and, in a peripheral way, to all children—she was completely taken up with them.

Somewhat to the amusement of her friends—and to my

never-ending fascination, brought up as Kate and I were under circumstances dictating a generous amount of do-it-yourself—Julia did not rely merely on common sense or instinct or even on other women's experiences in applying herself to the welfare of her children, or, when she was asked, as she often was, to the welfare of someone else's child or children. She sought expert advice, not only by a daily reading of the Chicago *Tribune*'s child guidance column, but by personal correspondence with the columnist.

Although she was not one to give an opinion unless it was asked of her, you had only to see the way she would look at her daughters Ellen and Mary Louise after they'd played in a piano recital or performed in a school play or brought home a good report card to realize not only how happy even their smallest accomplishment made her, but how it pleased her to have demonstrated once again the soundness of her approach to child-rearing, just as you could see from the way she smiled at Nathaniel how it distressed her to think he might not feel wanted, and how she could not understand it, really, when she was doing all that she—and the guidance columnist—could think of to instill the very opposite into him.

I understood it—more than I realized I did.

The first time Nathaniel came home with me from school, Kate said afterward, "He looks like an owl."

I was making myself a peanut-butter sandwich at the time, and the only reason I didn't throw the jar of peanut butter at her was because there was still too much peanut butter left in it, but I clattered the knife into the sink to make her jump and stamped my foot at her and yelled, "And you're a cross-eyed baboon!"

Kate was no slouch at slinging words herself, but she was so dumbfounded she only stared at me.

I was a bit dumbfounded myself. She was only saying what was true.

"Well, my gosh," I said, taking my shoe off and rubbing my foot where it stung from stamping it, "he can't help it if he has

70

to wear glasses, can he, and his hair won't lie flat? If you'd had to live in Chicago as long as Nathaniel has, your hair would be standing on end, too."

It was a wonder to me Nathaniel had managed to stay alive, living in Chicago.

"Oh, don't be such a jerk," Kate said. Then, "If he could at least smile once in a while."

It was unbelievable to me the way Kate could get to the heart of something without even knowing there was a heart of something to get to.

I tried to sigh like Julia Fletcher. "What has Nathaniel got to smile about?" But I choked on it instead, so I screwed the lid back on the peanut-butter jar and slammed it into the cupboard to distract her.

She kept on frowning at me.

"Well, my gosh," I said, turning to wipe the peanut butter off the counter so I wouldn't have to look at her, "how would you like it if Maggie decided she didn't want us any more and sent us to live with Uncle Donald and Aunt Clarissa?"

I thought she wasn't ever going to answer, but she finally did. "Maggie wouldn't do that."

I rinsed the dishcloth, wrung it out, and wiped the counter again. Uncle Donald and Aunt Clarissa were rich—Uncle Donald was an attorney in a Chicago law firm—so I knew they could afford to take us. "How do you know she wouldn't?"

Kate answered that one right away. "If Maggie didn't want us, why would she care so much if we died or not?"

My heart almost stopped. I hadn't thought of that.

"Well," I said, turning around to Kate and pressing myself against the counter to keep my legs from trembling, "that's what happened to Nathaniel. His mother and father are going to get a divorce, and they neither of them wanted Nathaniel, so they sent him down here to live with the Fletchers until they decide they want him again, which won't be for a year, at least."

"Who told you all that?"

"Nathaniel did."

Kate made a face.

"But it's true, Kate, because then I heard Sally Kline's mother tell it to Genevieve McIntyre's mother the other day, and she said she'd heard it from Marcella DeWitt, who'd had it straight from Julia Fletcher. Though Sally's mother did say," I added, "she wouldn't be surprised if Mrs. Fletcher hadn't suggested it to Nathaniel's mother, because there was a thing in the Chicago *Tribune* a few weeks ago about what a broken home does to children."

I hadn't gone back on my word to Nathaniel telling Kate about his parents. When Julia told it to Marcella she must have known it would be all over town.

Kate frowned. "How do you always hear so much of what other people say? I never hear anything."

I shrugged. "People notice you more. Anyhow, you're so busy mooning all the time, you never listen."

I didn't always listen either, unless it sounded interesting. Even when it did, I usually picked up only fragments of information, sometimes not even enough to know what or who was being talked about. Like the day, a week or so later—the last day of November anyhow—when I took Nathaniel to the courthouse after school to meet Maggie. All I knew from what I heard as we walked into her office was I'd picked a bad time in which to do it.

Maggie was standing at the high counter in the front, very sober-faced, talking across the counter to Will Short, the county treasurer. "And wouldn't that be a fine kettle of fish?"

Mr. Short, his back to us, said, "I've been trying to think if there isn't something we can do to see if it's as bad as—" but he broke off as Maggie saw us and tugged at his sleeve.

Broke off and turned around and said hello to us. Then he told Maggie he'd come back later, and he went on across the hall to his own office.

I wished, as much as Maggie must have wished, I'd picked another day to bring Nathaniel to her office, though if she was displeased at being interrupted she didn't let on. And I needn't have worried about her making Nathaniel feel welcome. Maggie had what I suppose could be called a stray-cat instinct.

But in spite of her smiles and her ready answers to his questions about what an auditor's job consisted of, I could tell she still had whatever was worrying her and Will Short on her mind. And not just then, but at home that night as well, during supper, when she only half listened to Kate and me, and after supper, when she sat down with the evening paper and only went through the motions of reading it.

What was worrying her and Will Short, she told me a long time afterward, grew out of an incident which had taken place the morning of that same day, when the assistant cashier of the Roseville Bank and Trust Company stopped by her office with some ditch bonds to present the coupons on them which had fallen due for payment.

These particular bonds, which had been issued by the county some years earlier to raise money for drainage ditches, belonged to an out-of-town client of the bank, the bank collecting the interest as each coupon came due, then forwarding that interest to the client.

Maggie always made it a practice to check the bond register before writing a warrant for the amount due. Since she was at that moment trying to get some bid notices prepared in time for the morning mail pickup, and since the assistant cashier said he had business elsewhere in the courthouse, she asked him if he would leave the bonds and coupons and come back.

The notices prepared, she checked the bonds and coupons against the register. Finding them correct, she wrote out and signed a warrant in the amount of one thousand two hundred and eighty-seven dollars. Then she took the warrant across the hall to Will Short's office for his countersignature, as required by law.

It was also his job as treasurer to designate on the face of a warrant the bank on which the funds were to be drawn. There were five banks in Rose County—one at North Union, one at Montclair, one at Jackson's Crossing, and the two in Roseville

—and the county had money on deposit in each of them in varying amounts. In this instance, since the warrant was made out to the Roseville Bank and Trust Company, Mr. Short stamped on the face of it the same institution.

A few minutes after Maggie returned to her own office, the assistant cashier strode in saying, "All ready?"

She handed him the warrant. "All signed and everything."

He stood there, she told me, for maybe half a minute eyeing the warrant. Then he looked at her. "Maggie," he said, "do me a favor?"

"Sure," she answered. "If I can."

"Will you take this back to Short and ask him to make it payable at some other bank?"

Maggie frowned at him. "Why?"

"We haven't got the funds to meet it."

Maggie stared at him, dumbfounded. "You what?"

He repeated what he'd said.

She got up and went to her account ledger and opened it. "You've got fifty-eight thousand dollars of county funds on deposit in your bank. Not to mention your other depositors. And you can't meet a warrant for one thousand two hundred and eighty-seven dollars? You're kidding me."

But even as she said it, she knew he wasn't, and he assured her he wasn't.

She stood there looking at him for a minute. "What's become of the money?"

"I don't know," he said. "You'll have to ask Warren White." Then almost in the same breath he begged her not to say anything—to anybody.

Maggie stared at him again for a bit. Then she took the warrant over to Will Short and asked him to put it on Roseville's other bank, the Northern State Bank.

Just as she had done, he asked why.

"Oh, Will," she said, "be a good scout and don't ask questions. Just do it. Please."

Maybe it was because Maggie had such a way with people

that Will Short did what she asked. More likely, from the expression she said was on his face as he rubbed out the words Roseville Bank and Trust Company and stamped in their place Northern State Bank, an expression Maggie said she would never forget for as long as she lived, he guessed what the situation was and, like herself, didn't know right then what else to do.

Since I wasn't there to see his expression, I can only imagine what it must have been—what anyone's would have been, I suppose, coming up against the realization that a sizable sum of money for which he was jointly responsible was not where it should have been, and through no fault of his. But for this particular man there was a twist to it.

I never knew Mr. Short very well. He lived over at North Union, so I only saw him at the courthouse. But I always had a soft spot in my heart for him. Just as I had to put up with wisecracks all the time about being called Angel, he had to put up with wisecracks about his last name all the years he was treasurer, and what had to have been unfunny to him for a long time now must, at that moment, have seemed a bit macabre.

That afternoon Will Short came over to Maggie's office to ask her opinion of the banking situation in Rose County. She told him she was worried to death about it.

"About all the banks?" he asked.

"No," she answered, "only about the Roseville Bank and Trust Company." But, she went on, she knew that all the banks in the county were in close association, and that in view of the nationwide bank situation they had made an agreement that if one bank experienced a run, they would all be notified and close their doors, thus tying up, among other things, all the operating funds of the county.

That was the kettle of fish she had reference to.

Although Maggie would come right out and say any number of things to Kate and me that most parents would only talk around if their children were there and might be listening—I suppose because Maggie wanted to say them to somebody, and there wasn't anybody around except Kate and me to say them to—still, there were some things she deemed unsuitable for us to hear.

The crisis at the bank being one of them, I doubt I would have found out anything about it at the time if it hadn't been for two things. The first was that Will Short came back to her office the next morning to pursue his wondering if there wasn't something he and Maggie could do to determine whether or not the bank was in fact in as grave a condition as the incident of the ditch bond coupons had indicated to them. The second was the solution they came up with.

Whenever Maggie intended to make a sizable draw on any one of the banks in the county, she made it a policy to notify the cashier in advance, so the smaller banks could get funds from the Federal Reserve Bank in time to meet the warrant when it came in. She and Will Short now decided that Maggie would call Warren White and notify him that she was going to draw ten thousand dollars against the Roseville Bank and Trust Company, her reason if he asked—though, for that matter, he had no right to ask—being that the state auditor had requested an advance, as he sometimes did, against the county's year-end settlement with the state for tax monies collected.

Maggie called him right after lunch, but he was out, so she left the message with his assistant, figuring she'd hear from White as soon as he returned, expecting it to be him each time the phone rang after that, beginning to wonder as the afternoon wore on if the assistant cashier could have been mistaken or the crisis only a momentary one now safely hurdled. When five o'clock came, with still no word, she decided it must have been one or the other, and she put on her coat and went home.

We were just finishing supper when the doorbell rang.

In our house, whoever sat next to some particular thing, like the icebox or the stove or the sink, got up to get whatever was wanted from it. Since I sat nearest to the front of the house, I went to the door.

76

When I turned on the porch light, Warren White was standing there looking so done in I blinked at him.

He wasn't a robust man to begin with, but thin, with a thin, sharp-nosed face and a prominent Adam's apple and a wan complexion—bilious-looking was the way my Grandfather Crowley once put it—and with pale, watery blue eyes which had a tendency to wander while he was talking to you, as if he had spied somebody waiting behind you and was casting about in his mind for what he would say to them. But when I opened the door I decided it must be the porch light which made him look so drawn, because he smiled and asked if Maggie was at home, and he didn't sound any different from any other time I'd ever seen him.

He stepped inside, and as I took his coat, he glanced at himself in the hall mirror. That was like him, too. He was an immaculately groomed man. With the business section of Roseville's Main Street running to farmers the way it did, you couldn't help noticing. Yet when he was standing out on the sidewalk in front of the bank shaking hands with one of them, he would dart an occasional glance at his reflection in the plate-glass window, as though to reassure himself that this was so, and he had a habit of running a finger around the inside of his shirt collar, which I always supposed was because his Adam's apple jumped around when he talked and got his collar out of whack.

He smiled a lot, but his smile was like his eyes. It came and went. Still, there was nothing unfriendly or withdrawn about him. On the contrary, he went out of his way to speak to people.

He asked me now how my piano lessons were coming, and that was like him, too. He never just said hello, how are you to anyone, but always—in spite of the wandering eyes—thought to ask some particular thing, like "I hear the wife's down with the flu. How's she getting along?" or "I understand your boy Sam had a flat tire on his way home from the sectional tourney" or "I see where you had some kinfolk over to visit Sunday before last."

It was obvious where he picked up that kind of information —from the two weekly newspapers, the Rose County *Democrat* and the Rose County *Republican*. It was also obvious from the way he preceded such remarks with "I hear" or "I see" or "I understand" that he intended his listener to realize that, thus twice pleasing him by reminding him that he or some member of his family had made the paper and that Warren White cared enough about him to read whatever it was and, having read, remember.

Considering the dozens of personals in each of the papers every week, week after week, it was a remarkable feat of memory if nothing else, though the joke a turn in the conversation would sometimes put him in mind of was not, I knew, remembered just from hearing it on the radio. Alice White told Kate and me one time her father always kept a pad and pencil by him when he listened to Amos and Andy or Eddie Cantor or Ed Wynn.

But however he managed it, it worked. People everywhere in the county felt they knew him and—even more important— that he knew them, and they talked to one another about what a well-informed man he was and, therefore, how capable. And farmers and businessmen who were Democratic precinct committeemen in their townships, upon whom he came to bestow even more of his time and attention, began asking him if he'd ever thought of running for office, wanting him to know that if he ever did, they were in a position to deliver a number of votes to him.

These same men, and others in the county who were influential in Democratic politics because of the amount of land they owned or the large number of relatives they had, also brought their business to him, the only trouble being that, after the Crash, bringing their business to the Roseville Bank and Trust Company meant, to more and more of them, borrowing money from it, so that by the fall of 1931 Warren

White's securing of the right political connections had become, for the bank, more liability than asset.

Whether Warren White was ambitious from the beginning, or whether at the beginning he only wanted people to like him, I don't know. The latter seems more likely—that, as he consoled and cajoled, asked after and commented upon, sought opinions and deferred to them, this ability to flatter the public by kowtowing to it germinated within him the idea that he was important. And when the precinct committeemen started making their offers to him, he began to see himself as belonging in public office, where he could promote the welfare of his friends and neighbors and, in an ever-widening circle, his friends' and neighbors' friends and neighbors, while at the same time reaping for himself, in ever-increasing measure from this ever-widening circle, the appreciation his attention to the welfare of the people merited, hungering not for power but acclaim, yearning, like Emily Dickinson's frog, to tell his name the livelong day to some admiring bog.

But of course I didn't know anything then about his ambition. I did know he was interested in politics. He'd been to our house a couple of times before with Orn Fletcher and some other men from the county. I supposed that was why he was here now, though I couldn't see why he'd want to get mixed up in that. He didn't smoke cigars or bang his fist, and he wasn't a God damner or even a hell's bellser. He didn't seem to me to have anything of what it took to be a politician. He was too soft-spoken to even be hearty.

As for the way he had with people, I just thought it was nice of him to take such an interest in everyone, though I wished he'd thought to ask me something other than how my piano lessons were coming. I'd been stuck for so long on "Oats, Peas, Beans, and Barley Grow," I no longer cared how they grew or if they grew.

He said not to get discouraged, his daughter Alice had had quite a struggle herself with "Oats, Peas, Beans, and Barley Grow" when she was my age.

I didn't believe him. Alice White could play the piano like nobody's business. Even Kate wasn't half as accomplished as Alice. But it made me feel so good to hear him say it that when Maggie came in from the kitchen and he went over to shake hands with her, I stood there for a minute thinking maybe his chances of getting elected to whatever he might be going to run for were better than I'd reckoned. I would have voted for him.

I went on back to the kitchen to tell Kate not to get her hopes up, it was only Mr. White come to talk politics, and he hadn't mentioned his wife, but the last time I'd seen her she looked as healthy as ever.

Kate stuck her tongue out at me and started to the kitchen door to close it, so we wouldn't have to listen—Maggie could hell's bells and bang her fist as good as any of the men if she got carried away enough—when we heard the French doors into the living room being closed.

Kate stared at me, and I stared at her. Maggie never closed the living-room doors even when somebody came to see her about finding him a job or getting his tax deadline extended. Certainly never when it was only politics.

If Mr. White hadn't come to talk politics, what had he come for? And why didn't she want us to know what it was?

Right away Kate began thinking of what I could bring out of the dining room, so I'd have an excuse to get close enough to hear what they were saying. Just to go stand at the door and listen would be cheating. Besides, I might get caught.

Even so, I couldn't hear much. Every time Warren White said anything, he talked so low it made me want to clear my throat for him. And, unfortunately, he was doing most of the talking.

Kate's idea was to have me bring her the silver out of the buffet, a few pieces at a time, for us to clean. It didn't strike me as much of an idea, but there wasn't anything except the buffet on the far side of the dining room, and since Maggie had been after us to get the silver polished before Christmas, we could always tell her, if she happened to come out while I was there, we'd thought this was as good a time as any.

"It's about the bank," I said to Kate my first trip back. "The one Mr. White works at."

Kate wrinkled her nose at me. "He doesn't just work at it. He's the cashier of it."

That didn't sound like much to me, and I said so. George Garnett had worked all the past summer as the cashier at his father's grocery and meat market, and he was only a sophomore in high school.

"Oh, don't be such a jerk," Kate said. "The cashier of a bank —here in Roseville anyhow—practically runs it. We talked about it one day in civics class."

I wanted to tell her she needn't be so superior. Could I help it if I hadn't had civics yet? But in the interest of time I didn't. "Well, he isn't doing such a hot job of running it, then, because the bank's in trouble. He said so."

Kate's eyes got wide. "What kind of trouble?"

"Don't be such a jerk yourself," I shot back at her, so glad to have the opportunity for once of saying it to Kate I could have jumped up and down. "What kind of trouble could a bank be in? They don't have any money. At least"—I reconsidered— "not enough money, anyhow. Not as much as they're supposed to have."

Kate frowned at me. "How do you know how much they're supposed to have?"

Kate could be very trying. She'd sent me in to listen. Now she wanted to argue over what I'd heard.

"I don't know," I said. "All I know is Maggie said to him she had fifty-eight thousand dollars of county money in his bank, and he said every time that something opened—the door, I suppose—he was afraid it was Mr. Somebody coming in to get a thousand dollars he had in the bank, and they couldn't give it to him if he did."

Kate's eyes got wider. "What else?"

"Nothing else."

"Then go on back."

"Okay," I said. "And you'd better get the table cleared off. If Maggie comes out, she'll think it's funny we decided to clean the silver when we haven't even done the dishes. She's not dumb, you know."

The telephone rang, and Kate flew to the table.

I answered it and then went to get Maggie, taking as much time as I could, but when she came with me to the kitchen, she only told whoever it was she'd call back in a little while. Then she went on back to the living room and shut the doors again without saying anything to Kate and me or even noticing the table.

"My gosh," Kate said, "it must be something."

"You said it, kid," I said, still basking in the glow of getting to call her a jerk when she'd really been one. I pussyfooted back into the dining room.

Kate was washing the dishes when I got back. "What's a warrant?" I asked her.

"What the town marshal arrests people with." She let go of the plate she was washing and spun around to me, wide-eyed all over again. "Is Mr. White going to be arrested?"

I frowned at her. "I don't think so. Is there some other kind of warrant?"

She thought a minute. "Search warrants. The police can't search a place without a warrant. Maybe they're going to search the bank?"

"You mean for the money they're supposed to have and don't?"

She shrugged her shoulders. "How should I know?"

"Well," I said, "it has something to do with money, but if they said anything about searching, I didn't hear it."

"Well, what did they say?"

I frowned at her again. "It's kind of complicated. Maggie said something about a warrant for ten thousand dollars that"— I frowned harder—"that she needs for the state settlement." I sighed. "Heck, I don't know, Kate. I don't even know what a state settlement is."

"Where's the dictionary?"

I jerked my head toward the living room. "In Outer Mongolia."

"Nuts."

I pointed to the table. "How about your civics book?"

She beamed at me and flew to get it. After a flurry of page turning, she ran her finger across a line, frowned at it, and said, "A warrant is the same as a check. So, a check for ten thousand dollars that she needs for—what?"

"The state settlement."

Kate frowned at the book some more, then shut it. "It doesn't say specifically, but I guess it has to do with money each county pays the state. That makes sense, doesn't it?"

I shrugged. "If you say so."

"So what did Mr. White say?"

"Something about time."

"What about it?"

"I don't know. I couldn't hear."

My next trip was my last one. I told Kate so when I got back. "I don't want to hear any more."

"Why not?"

I rubbed at the goose bumps on my arm. "My gosh, Kate, he's crying."

Her eyes bugged out so far they were almost popping. "Crying? Mr. White?"

I nodded. "He said something about the Northern State Bank and a merger—whatever that means. Only whatever it means, it must cost money, because I heard him say twenty thousand dollars. Twice. Or maybe"—I frowned at her—"maybe it's the other way around. Maybe somebody is going to give them the twenty thousand dollars twice."

"Who?"

"Beats me."

"But why would he be crying about that?"

"I don't know," I said, "except he said something about his wife and Alice and something about out of a job and pauper. What's pauper?"

"A pauper is somebody who doesn't have any money except —well, like people on relief."

"Well, and he got all choked up. My gosh, Kate, what do you suppose is going to happen?"

She shook her head. "I don't know. Maybe the bank is going to fail. Other banks have."

"Then I'm glad I don't have any money in it."

She rinsed the skillet and handed it to me. "Where would you have gotten any money to put in the bank in the first place?"

"I could have a secret fortune you don't know anything about."

"Tune in some other station," she said, and pulled the plug out of the sink.

We were on the silver when we heard the living-room doors open and Maggie and Warren White saying good night in the hall.

"Listen, Angel," Kate whispered.

"What?" I was whispering, too.

"If you breathe one word of this . . ."

"Oh, for criminently's sake, Kate," I hissed back at her, "did I ever tell anybody you sent your picture to Clark Gable?"

Maggie was so wrapped up in her thoughts after Warren White left, I had to remind her to call the person back on the telephone, and if Kate hadn't made a point of showing her the silver to admire, I don't think she would have been aware that we were polishing it.

As it was, she just said it looked very nice. Then she said she had some paper work to attend to, and she went on back into the living room.

Kate and I looked at each other and shrugged our shoulders,

figuring we'd heard all we were ever likely to hear about the trouble Warren White had got the bank into.

At that, we knew more than most people did at the time. Most people, including most of the bank's own depositors, didn't know the bank was even in trouble—a state of affairs that, considering the wildfire way word usually spread through Roseville, was nothing short of astonishing. But then, as Maggie pointed out to me that long time afterward, when she told me the full story, outside of herself and Will Short and one or two others, the only people who had found out, somewhat belatedly, what was going on in the Roseville Bank and Trust Company were its president and board of directors and the president and board of directors of the Northern State Bank, and it could hardly have been in their best interest in November of 1931 to publicize the fact that Warren White kept a loaded revolver in his cashier's cage so he could blow his brains out if worse came to worst, and that worst was precisely what worse was coming to, because in November of 1931 the Roseville Bank and Trust Company was on the verge of collapse.

Warren White could not have been unaware of the irony of his situation—that in using the bank to place himself in public office he had placed himself in jeopardy instead, despite his appeal to Maggie as family provider to family provider, for if the bank failed he would be out of more than a job. He would be out of a future—his political career dead a-borning, the esteem with which he was everywhere regarded turned to animosity or, even worse, contempt.

Nor, in trying to explain to her what had become of part of the money, at least, that was supposed to be in the bank, or available to it, and wasn't, could he have been unaware of the further irony that some of those very friends and neighbors whose welfare he had hoped to promote in public office, in whose ultimate behalf he had so witlessly exposed himself to ruin, now seemed bent, in the interests of a more immediate welfare, on becoming the final instruments of his undoing.

Not because in the two or three weeks before he came to plead with Maggie to give him time they had managed to find out, as the directors had before them, what was going on in the Roseville Bank and Trust Company. In 1931 people didn't have to know what might be going on in any bank to be nervous about money they had on deposit there.

Thus Miss Emily Pratt, for instance, who taught the first six grades in the township school just west of town, had come into the bank one morning and, red in the face and mumbling some story about a sick relation, had asked to have all her savings put into a certified check. She then took the check over to North Union and bought postal savings certificates, thinking that by using the post office at North Union the bank wouldn't know what she had done, forgetting, or not realizing, that the processed check would be returned to the bank.

Doc Hawkins, with no attempt at subterfuge at all, had simply said he was taking out every cent of his money. And take it he did—in cash.

A Mr. O'Shaughnessy from Chicago who owned a cottage at Cedar Lake had come in one day the previous summer to deposit five thousand dollars he didn't want his wife to know he had. When the Chicago bank where he had his regular account failed, he began to draw on his account at the Roseville Bank and Trust Company, and had so far withdrawn four thousand of the five—Mr. O'Shaughnessy being the man Warren White was afraid he would see coming in every time the door to the bank opened.

But the greatest irony of Warren White's predicament at the bank was how he expected to get out of it.

Maggie agreed not to present her ten-thousand-dollar warrant to the bank for payment. (Since it had only been a device to determine the condition of the bank, there would have been no point in presenting it other than to force the bank to close its doors.) She told him further that she would ask Will Short to make any warrants for current operating expenses, including salaries as well as claims filed by contractors and suppliers, payable at the other four banks in the county. But she reminded him that the county's settlement with the state, amounting to more than thirty thousand dollars, would have to be made before the end of the year, which was only four weeks away, and that she could not meet that settlement without access to the funds on deposit in the Roseville Bank and Trust Company. If the bank was in such dire straits that it could not now meet a demand for one thousand dollars, what gave him any reason to hope it could meet a demand for thirty thousand dollars in four weeks' time, assuming it managed to survive that long to meet it?

He reached into his pocket and handed her a charter showing that the Northern State Bank and Trust Company had been granted permission to do business.

In view of the national situation, he said, wiping his eyes and blowing his nose, the president and board of directors of the Northern State Bank had approached the president and board of directors of the Roseville Bank and Trust Company some time before with a proposal to merge. (Though he didn't say that it was during the discussions and examination of the assets and liabilities of both banks which followed this proposal that the true condition of the Roseville Bank and Trust Company was uncovered, Maggie assumed this was the case.)

He did say the merger would solve the difficulties of both banks, and that they were only waiting to announce it until such time as the Reconstruction Finance Corporation awarded both banks the grant of twenty thousand dollars each had applied for, adding that the RFC had a rule limiting any one bank to a maximum grant of twenty thousand, but that if two banks in a town the size of Roseville applied, each could receive the maximum. Since they were in such need of every cent they could get, they had no choice but to wait.

"But Warren," Maggie protested, frowning at him, "how can you be depending on a grant from the RFC—how can you even make application to it—when the RFC isn't in operation yet, and won't be until Congress passes the bill authorizing it? For that matter, how can you be so certain Congress will pass the bill?"

"Because a majority of both parties are for it," he answered, "and because an office has already been set up in Washington to process the applications. That's how we were able to apply, and that's how certain the bill is of passing. It's only a matter of bringing it to a vote, and the RFC will be ready to roll."

With a shake of her head Maggie handed the charter back to him. As he put it in his pocket he said, "Every time the phone rings I expect it to be the word we're waiting for—that the money is on its way. And that's all we're waiting for." He patted his pocket. "Then the Northern State Bank and Trust Company will be in business, and our troubles will be over."

"And if the word doesn't come?" Maggie asked.

"It'll come," he said. "It'll come. It's only a matter of days now. Maybe hours."

On that note of optimism on that night of December 1, 1931, he left.

The Reconstruction Finance Corporation was enacted into law on January 22, 1932.

Even without her saying anything to Kate and me at the time, it was obvious Maggie didn't share Warren White's optimism. The next morning she was still so wrapped up in her thoughts she hardly said a word all through breakfast and, when we left for school, forgot to tell us to look both ways before crossing any streets.

I supposed she would be the same that night. When she wasn't, but came in the house all sparkling-eyed and smiling, I was so relieved Warren White had managed somehow to get his twenty thousand dollars twice I almost said so, and would have if Kate hadn't kicked me.

Which was just as well, because what Maggie was sparkling-eyed about didn't have anything to do with Warren White.

88

She opened her pocketbook and took out a letter addressed to her in Grandpa Crowley's spidery handwriting. "Your grandfather," she said, beaming at Kate and me, "is coming to live with us."

Kate and I were both so thrilled we could hardly believe it was true.

Chapter Four

As superintendent of the Sunday School of the Methodist church, Mr. Wurlitzer chose the hymns that were sung each week when all the classes, from children to old people, assembled in the church for the last part of Sunday School.

One of his favorites was "Brighten the Corner Where You Are," but because the combined diction of those many diverse voices was not the sharpest, I misunderstood the pronunciation of some words, and because I had not yet been introduced to the works of Alfred Lord Tennyson, I failed to grasp the meaning of some others. As a result, I never could figure out what the Methodists, who were strictly Temperance, were doing singing a great thumping song about three drunks Sweet-Adelining under the misty light of a street-corner lamppost. At least that was what I always pictured when I sang out, "Right on the corner where you are, right on the corner where you are, someone far from harbor you may guide across the bar, right on the corner where you are."

But even though it puzzled me, it was one of my favorite hymns, too, because it always made me think of Grandpa Crowley. Until he came to live with us, Grandpa ran a speakeasy in Chicago.

Maggie told Kate and me Grandpa was retiring—he was seventy years old—but then we heard her say on the phone the gangsters had finally told him to get out or else. I looked at Kate and shivered. Knowing what the Chicago gangsters usually did to people, I thought it was considerate of them to give him a choice.

I wasn't sure they wouldn't change their minds either, so I took extra pains all the rest of that week not to step on any cracks in the sidewalk. Because of Kate's constant jeering I was beginning to think that might not really have anything to do with anything, but since I wasn't completely convinced yet and Grandpa's life was at stake, I figured it couldn't hurt any and it might help some.

When the Nickel Plate pulled in at 5:05 Sunday evening, Grandpa was on it.

I can close my eyes and see him yet, standing at the half door on the platform between two cars, his coat collar turned up against the biting wind, a black stocking cap perched on his shock of white hair, his rosy face crinkling into a smile when he spied Kate and me waving and shouting to him.

"Well, now, and let me get a look at you," he said when he'd given each of us a hug and Maggie a kiss on her cheek. He stood back to look at Kate and me, shaking his head over how we'd grown.

But it was Grandpa who was the one to see, who turned my heart over just to look at him. Towering tall he was, and straight as a flagpole, and maybe it was the way his eyes, as blue as a summer sky, were always shining, or maybe it was in the sweetness of his face, but wherever it came from, there was such an air of expectancy about him, he seemed to carry the world in the palms of his hands.

"Oh, Grandpa," I said, throwing myself into his arms again, "you're beautiful!"

He laughed and hugged me. They all laughed, and I with them, because it was true.

We'd collected his baggage—he only had two suitcases and a valise, which didn't seem like much to me, and I wondered if he'd had to get out in such a hurry he didn't have enough time to pack, but Grandpa only smiled and said what did he need with a lot of trappings—and were ready to climb into the car when another car drove into the depot.

It pulled up alongside us, and Orn Fletcher got out, come, he said, to see about a shipment of tools he was expecting from Chicago. In Roseville people always told people what they were doing and why they were doing it.

He started to go off without saying anything more, but Maggie said, "Orn, I'd like you to meet the children's grandfather," so he turned and came stomping around the back of his car toward us in that heavy, stiff-legged gait of his.

He had a red plaid windbreaker on over his Sunday suit and a peaked cap with the ear flaps pulled down against the cold. It was cold. My fingers were turning numb inside my mittens, and I hopped from one foot to the other trying to keep them from doing the same.

Although it was hard for me to imagine anyone as big and strong as Orn feeling the cold, it did seem to bother his leg. He was walking more stiff-legged than ever.

He was stiff-necked, too, but the cold didn't have anything to do with that. It was Maggie. Even Grandpa, who hadn't had Kate's and my experience at being Maggie's buffers, could tell there'd been some sort of clash between them and could sense part, at least, of what lay at the bottom of it. But then my Grandfather Crowley had a curbstone insight into people unmatched by anyone I've ever known. More to the point in this instance, he had as much of an eye for the ladies as Orn did, though my grandmother in her lifetime had done everything she could to spoil his view.

Orn was friendly enough to Grandpa when Maggie introduced them, shaking hands, exchanging the kind of remarks people made on such occasions—it looked as if there'd be a heavy frost that night, and times were bad, all right, but according to Mr. Hoover business ought to start picking up any day now, and Roseville was a fine town to live in.

I kept hopping and wishing they'd hurry up and get it over with so we could go home and get warm.

Finally they shook hands again, ready to take their leave, when a fellow came huffing and puffing out of the freight end of the depot, almost hidden behind the slatted crate he was carrying.

Both Grandpa and Orn went to give him a hand. When they helped him set the crate down on the loading platform, I saw it was Chuck Sellers.

Orn said, "Why, Chuck, you didn't have to come down here for this. I said I'd see to it."

Chuck stood there a bit panting for breath. Then he managed to get out, "I thought . . . you might . . . need some help" between pants.

Maggie had obviously been right when she told Chuck that night he came to see her she was pretty sure Orn had something in mind for him.

"Well, that was considerate of you," Orn said. "Here. Let's set it in the back of the car then."

Brushing aside Grandpa's offer to help, Orn and Chuck carried the crate to the car, though I didn't doubt Orn could have managed it without any help at all.

"How are you getting along, Chuck?" Maggie asked.

He had his back to her, bending over the crate. "Okay," he said, still panting a little.

"I'm glad to hear it."

When at last he straightened up and turned in her direction she said, "Has the baby come yet?"

Chuck favored her with one of his creepy looks—his slate-colored eyes lighting on her for a moment, then sliding past her, his face and his voice, too, I noticed, as sullen as ever. "The doc says next month."

"Well," she said, motioning to us to get in the car, by which time I was beginning to think if anybody stepped on my feet they'd break off, "I'm glad things are working out for you."

"Yeah," he answered. He climbed in beside Orn, who'd offered to give him a ride home.

They backed out and drove off in one direction while we did

the same in the other, me huddled under the lap robe in the back seat as close to Kate as she'd let me, wondering how Orn, who was such a hearty man, could put up with Chuck's sullenness—I didn't figure Chuck would dare be insolent to Orn—or find enough in common with him to like having him around.

Maggie wondered the same thing aloud to Grandpa, explaining as she turned south into Prettyman Street how Orn had taken Chuck on back in September for a bricklaying job, adding that apparently he'd thought enough of him to keep him on.

"The boy seems to be doing a bit of thinking himself," Grandpa put in.

Maggie agreed, saying if Chuck continued to show himself willing and worked hard and kept his nose clean, he wouldn't have anything to worry about, though she couldn't say much for his disposition. "But then"—she shrugged—"I don't suppose Orn hired him for the pleasure of his company."

A freight train was rumbling by on the railroad, picking up speed as the locomotive reached the outskirts of town. Maggie pulled up at the crossing. "This Orn Fletcher now," Grandpa said to her, "you ruffle him a bit, I take it."

Maggie laughed and told Grandpa all those years he'd spent in the saloon had been a waste of talent. He should have run a gypsy tearoom. "Orn and I have our ups and downs."

She laughed again. "I suppose he's still sore about last week. But it serves him right." He had come into her office, she went on, one day when she had a thousand and one things on her mind. The county commissioners were meeting, and she had a raft of contracts for building and repair work to draw up and warrants to make out to people who supplied the jail and the poor farm and the township schools and so on with food and fuel and medical services and the like. Anyhow, she was busy, and he could see she was, but he came in and sat down as if she had all the time in the world, talking on and on about one thing and another, nothing of any importance, until finally, when she had all she could do not to ask him to leave, he got down to why he was there. He wanted to know why he hadn't been awarded the contract for repairing and repainting the courthouse.

Maggie shook her head, saying he knew without coming in and wasting her time why he hadn't. The ads in both the *Democrat* and the *Republican* had stated, as they always did, that the contract would be awarded to the lowest and best bid. His was neither the lowest nor the best.

"Hell's bells," she said as the caboose thundered by, "he isn't even equipped to do the job."

"Is he not a regular contractor then?" Grandpa asked.

"Oh, indeed he is." Maggie shifted into gear and crossed the tracks. "He makes a good living at it. And gets his share of work from the county, as far as that goes. He was awarded the contract for blacktopping the road around Cedar Lake last month."

But the courthouse job, she went on to say, required, among other things, high ladders for painting the inside of the dome, and Orn didn't have them. "Nor any intention of getting any." She pulled up for a stop sign at the next intersection. "He figured on getting by with some makeshift arrangement."

But, she went on, the commissioners wouldn't allow it. They were afraid of having a lawsuit on their hands if somebody fell and broke his neck. So the contract had gone to an outfit up in Gary.

Grandpa said since the commissioners awarded the contracts, he'd think Orn would take his complaints to them. Maggie said if the Democrats were in the majority he probably would, but they weren't. "So he works on me instead."

Somebody behind us honked.

After taking another look both ways, Maggie crossed the intersection and drove on. "He knows I have influence with them, and he figures that since he endorsed me when I ran for office in '28, I ought to fix it so he gets every good contract that goes out of the auditor's office. A little thing like collusion doesn't bother Orn."

"What's collusion?" I whispered to Kate.

Kate shook her head at me, not to mean she didn't know, but

because she didn't want to miss any of what Maggie was saying. I didn't think it was all that interesting, but Mary Louise Fletcher being another one of Kate's best friends, Kate, of course, did.

"But I thought you had open primaries in Indiana," Grandpa said.

"Oh, we do," Maggie answered, "but if the county chairman favors one candidate over another, he gets the word around to the party faithful. It can make a difference. It did for me. The man I ran against in the '28 primary, Gus Hardaker, had run for one county office or another for most of the last thirty years, and he'd never once been beaten, but when he filed for the auditor's office against me, I got enough help from Orn to do it by a margin of sixty-eight votes."

"Had Orn had a falling out with the man?"

"No, I don't think so. You might say," Maggie added dryly, "that Orn had great expectations."

Grandpa laughed. "You seem to have disappointed him all the way around."

Maggie shrugged. "Orn has some rather fixed ideas about women. He has fixed ideas about a lot of things. That's his trouble." She put out her hand and turned left toward Main Street. "Orn's an odd man. There's a lot more to him than I thought when I first met him—and a lot less to him than the more gave me reason to believe."

I didn't understand that last remark of Maggie's when she made it. Even looking back on it, it seems to be nothing more than a play on words. Yet if the core of any man can be laid bare in a sentence, I think she got about as close to the core of Orn Fletcher as it's possible to get.

Not that Orn was either more or less complicated than other men, though certainly he was less sensitive, at least to the feelings of others. Nor were the contradictory elements of his personality anything more than that natural dichotomy both of personality and mores which allows any man—in this case, Orn —to be both cruel and kind, generous and mean, self-righteous and lewd. It was more that Orn had the capacity to be something other than he was and the tools with which to become it, but he not only lacked the desire, he couldn't see it as desirable.

Orn was a man of strength who believed in strength, and a man of principle who believed in principle, what failures he suffered as a human being resulting not from any conflict between the two but from the fact that there was no conflict.

He was an intelligent man and, in an era when a college degree was its equivalent, an educated man. But he was first and foremost a man of the world, in the Roseville sense of man of the world, whose education and intelligence had been so bent toward mastering that world as to make him equate knowledge with success and thinking with being shrewd.

He was that—a shrewd businessman and a shrewd politician —and, one of his principles being that the end justifies the means, a ruthless one.

Orn was one of the few people in Roseville who didn't look down his nose at the farmers either out of an honest conviction that farmers should be looked down on or because it was the fashionable thing to do. Not that Orn liked all of them or, like Warren White, went out of his way to be nice to them whether he liked them or not. Orn didn't have to go out of his way to be nice to people. People went out of their way to be nice to him. But Orn appreciated what farming meant to Roseville, and he was as baffled as the farmers were themselves—and in his heart, like them, enraged—that outside forces could have brought them to such a sorry state.

Orn was the kind of man lesser men brought their problems to, though they were sometimes sorry afterward. He was a strong believer in keeping up appearances—a man got along as best he could; if he had to pull his belt in a little, he pulled it in and kept his head up and took his family to church on Sunday—and of doing the right thing, which to Orn meant preserving the sanctity of the home, doing a day's work for a day's pay, keeping America for Americans, and voting the Democrat ticket, the Democrat ticket in Roseville being fully as conservative as the Republican one.

All of which was all very well, if small comfort to a man who'd already pulled his belt in as tight as it would go, who, if he kept his head up, had to look into the eyes of his wife, who wasn't worried about doing a day's work for a day's pay but about finding a day's pay to do a day's work for, beginning to think that, for him, doing the right thing would be to disappear.

Preserving the sanctity of the home, in Orn's view, presupposed women staying in it—not only not working, but not running around either, playing bridge and getting supper out of a tin can. And though he was the first man in Roseville to propose a Chamber of Commerce and would be the last to stand in the way of anything intended for the greater glorification and expansion of American business, still he complained that all these newfangled conveniences were going to be the ruination of women.

I can remember another time Nathaniel and I were walking home from Ward's with Julia Fletcher how her eyes, which were usually so wistful in the way only brown eyes can be, lighted up when Mr. Garnett called her into his grocery and meat market to show her the newest convenience for the homemaker—paper napkins—and how she pulled one out of the package and fingered it and said, "My land, what will they think of next?"

But if anything was going to be the ruination of Julia Fletcher, it would not be paper napkins or a Hoover vacuum cleaner or Forty Fathom Frozen Fish. It would be Orn himself, who, with his strong ideas about everything, seldom gave her a chance to think anything through on her own.

Orn was not a vicious man or a deliberately hardhearted one. Any man he respected who was down and out—and could put up with Orn's nostrums—he was a soft touch for, and for all his complaints about newfangled conveniences his wife was always one of the first in town to have them. He was just so bullheaded about having things be the way he thought they ought to be, he couldn't help being cruel sometimes. Like the way he was cruel, without meaning to be, to Nathaniel.

I can still see Nathaniel and my grandfather Crowley hunched together at our dining-room table over the Chicago *Tribune*, running their fingers down two pages of columns listing in the finest print imaginable all the winners of its "Name the Country" word-and-picture puzzle contest, Grandpa shaking his head and saying, "Jesus, Mary, and Joseph, we must be here somewhere, Nathaniel," Nathaniel peering up at Grandpa through his steel-rimmed spectacles, saying in that funny, formal way he sometimes had of speaking, "Mr. Crowley, I think I probably should have told you when you asked me to enter this contest with you that, although I am quite good at puzzles, I am not ever likely to be a winner."

Grandpa sat back in his chair, considering Nathaniel for a bit. "Is that so? And why not, may I ask?"

"Yes, certainly," said Nathaniel, not yet used to Grandpa's way of talking. "Because I am not cut out to be one."

"You don't say." Grandpa considered some more. "And where, if I may ask, did you get that idea?"

"Uncle Orn said it."

"Your Uncle Orn said you were not cut out to be a winner."

Nathaniel nodded. "He said it to Aunt Julia the day I came here."

Grandpa's rosy cheeks turned rosier. "Well, now, Nathaniel, and what makes you think your Uncle Orn knows what the good Lord cut you out to be?"

"Grandpa," I said, struck by a breathless new idea, "is that how babies are made—cut out like paper dolls?"

Grandpa waved me aside. " 'Tis only a manner of speaking, Angel. Well, Nathaniel?"

Nathaniel frowned. "Well, Aunt Julia said wasn't it nice I'd come to live with them. I mean—I don't mean live with them forever. Just until—just for a little while." He swallowed.

99

"Anyhow, Aunt Julia said wasn't it nice, because Uncle Orn had always wanted to have a boy, and now he would have one, but—well—" Nathaniel hesitated. "I guess it was the way he looked at me."

Grandpa nodded. "And how did he look at you?"

Nathaniel shrugged. "Like I wasn't what he had in mind."

Grandpa shook his head. "Well, now, Nathaniel, and I confess I'm disappointed in you."

"Oh, Grandpa," I breathed. Nathaniel looked as if he couldn't stand to have one more person disappointed in him.

"Why," he went on, "the first time Angel brought you to the house here, I thought to myself, well, now, and if here isn't a fine, bright lad!"

Nathaniel gave Grandpa a sidewise glance.

Grandpa nodded. "A little on the skinny side, maybe, but strong as an ox, more than likely, the way these skinny fellows oftentimes are."

Nathaniel was getting pink in the face.

"Why, I thought, 'tis a near miracle. Here I am, a doddering old man still struggling to make my fortune, and after all these years the good Lord has finally taken pity on me and sent this smart young lad to lend me a helping hand."

I thought I would burst.

Grandpa sighed. A great, long sigh. "And here I come to find out this smart young lad thinks his Uncle Orn's idea of a winner is the only idea there is. Why, even I know better than that."

I thought Nathaniel would burst.

Grandpa rummaged through some papers on the table and picked one up with a scramble of cut-up faces on it, holding it so Nathaniel could see it, too. "Of course, I suppose even a smart young lad is entitled to make a mistake now and then— long as he don't make the same one twice."

Nathaniel, whose passion for contests exceeded even Grandpa's, bobbed his head yes and no and yes again.

"Well, now, Nathaniel, and hadn't we better be getting at this, then?"

"Oh, yes," Nathaniel said. Then, "But Mr. Crowley—"

"Yes, lad?"

"If what you've been saying is true—"

"True as I'm sitting here."

"Then why didn't we win anything in 'Name the Country'?"

Grandpa beamed at him. "Ah, but you see, and there's the wonder of it. The good Lord cut us out to be winners, you and me, that's for certain, but in His infinite wisdom He left it up to us to find out just what it was He had in mind for us to win."

As far as I was concerned, Orn had never given me any reason not to like him. Quite the contrary. Even the night of the street fair, when he hadn't wanted Kate and me to go, he gave each of us a quarter to spend after we got there, and he sat me up on his shoulder at one of the free acts, so I could get a good look at the performers on the high wire. And whenever he drove Ellen and Mary Louise, and Nathaniel, too, after he came to live with them, to an out-of-town basketball game, Kate and I usually went along, and we always had a good time.

I can even remember feeling sorry for him once, when he came to one of Priscilla Rogers' piano recitals, at which Ellen, who was a senior in high school, and Mary Louise were both performing. Because they were relatively skilled, they were scheduled near the end of the program, and he had to sit through an interminable evening of other people's children, who played, as we always did, from memory, and who, when memory faltered, went back to the beginning and started over.

I didn't know then the story of what had gone on between him and Priscilla Rogers, which would have been enough to keep most men not only away from her house but out of her sight, but Orn, as unyielding in pride as he was in keeping up appearances and as humorless as he was proud, simply went about his business, as it were, managing where at all possible to take no notice of her, yet without seeming to make a point of it.

It wasn't always possible for him to take no notice of her. While Priscilla made no effort to seek him out, neither did she go out of her way to avoid him. Worse still, on those occasions when circumstances forced them into a confrontation on the street, she invariably gave him such a smile as would have warmed the heart of any other man—and must have smiled the more to see it only warm his face as he went stomping by, the set of his back daring the hapless onlooker, when such there was, to open his mouth.

Still, those occasions were rare, and if the hapless onlookers opened their mouths, they didn't open their mouths to him, so that Orn, his roistering days now only a rankle in his memory, was able to regard himself as a solid citizen in every way.

He was that, too. A proper if somewhat deprived husband, a devoted if only sporadically attentive father, he was a pillar of the church and the community, aware of the position he had to maintain and maintaining it—whatever straying he now did done not only discreetly but mostly out of town.

Or, as Maggie put it to Grandpa that night, "I'm sure if he thinks about it at all, he thinks of himself as a good man." She turned into Main Street a few blocks north of our house. "And in many ways he is. Good, conscientious, hard-working. And an honest man."

"A bit of collusion notwithstanding?" Grandpa asked.

"Notwithstanding. Because that's politics. And that's Indiana." She shrugged. "In Indiana all's fair in love and war and politics."

As we passed the Fletchers' I looked in the windows to try to see Nathaniel, but I didn't see him.

"Or," she added, "as Orn himself once put it to me, in politics it's what's at stake that counts, and that's all that counts."

I remembered him saying that to her. It was the night of the street fair back in 1928, after Maggie had shaken all the hands there were to shake, and Kate and I had spent all the money we had on rides and cotton candy, and we were in his car going home.

"I feel bad about Gus Hardaker," Maggie said.

Orn looked over at her. "Why should you?"

"It was all I could do to get him to shake hands with me tonight, and if I'd waited for him to introduce me to his wife, I'd still be waiting." She sighed. "I guess he's still sore at me for beating him in the primary."

Orn shrugged. "Would you rather he'd beaten you?"

"No, but—well, it must be hard after being an office holder all these years to be beaten by somebody who's brand-new to politics."

"It happens all the time."

"I suppose so."

"You get into politics, you got to learn not to let hurt feelings bother you—your own or anybody else's. It's what's at stake that counts. And that's all that counts."

"I suppose so," she said again.

"Besides, he'll get over it."

Maggie shook her head. "I don't think so. Not Gus."

Maggie slowed now to a stop to let somebody from the Laramores' back out of their drive. "Politics is a dirty game in this town. You scratch my back, I'll scratch yours."

She shifted into gear and started on again. "And the times when you can do a person a favor without cheating the taxpayers, you only make a lot of other people sore at you." She shook her head. "I'm sick and tired of the whole business."

I perked up. "Aren't you going to run again next fall, Maggie?"

She sighed. "Yes, I'm going to run again. I don't know what else I can do here to make a living."

I huddled back under the robe, supposing the ladies would have another sacrifice now to add to their list.

"Well," Grandpa said, "and won't you be needing Orn Fletcher's endorsement again?"

103

"Oh, Orn'll endorse me, all right. He pretty near has to, since I'll be running for reelection."

"Still," Grandpa said, "I think we might all hope and pray he doesn't lose out on too many more contracts."

Maggie laughed. "It isn't losing the contract for repairing and repainting the courthouse Orn's so sore about. It's what I said to him."

We turned into the drive and were home.

Maggie started laughing again, so hard I thought I must have missed something. I looked at Kate, but she only shrugged her shoulders.

Maggie gave a long sigh and wiped her eyes. "I'll tell you about it later," she said to Grandpa, her voice still shaking from the laughter in her.

While Kate helped Maggie get supper, I helped Grandpa unpack and hang up his clothes.

"What's this, Grandpa?" I held out a strange-looking contraption that had been packed in with his socks.

"That, Angel, my love, is a clock."

I stared at it. "It is?"

Grandpa took it from me. " 'Tis a special kind of clock I was working on a few years back." He turned it over in his hands. "I about had the answer to it, too, but then I got interested in a canning process." He frowned. "Or maybe it was the gasoline engine." He shook his head. "There've been so many of them over the years, I don't rightly remember which came where. But it doesn't matter."

He put the clock in a bureau drawer. "I don't know why I bothered to bring it with me. Oh, sometime I might get back to it, but—" He rummaged through the valise and held up a brown paper bag. "This, Angel, this is what's going to make our fortune."

"What is it?" I stood on tiptoe.

He opened it to show me what he had inside.

I frowned up at him. "But, Grandpa, it's only some dried-up ears of corn."

"That it is."

"Well, you can get corn anywhere. All the farmers around here grow it."

"Ah, yes, but not these particular ones they don't."

I took another look at them. "I don't think they'd want to. They're kind of scrubby looking, don't you think?"

He nodded. "That I do. But 'tis not what they look like, Angel, that counts. 'Tis the secrets they hold inside."

"Secrets?"

He twinkled his eyes at me. "Secrets. Of corn that will shoot up straighter and taller and greener in the spring than any corn you've ever seen before. Corn that will stand up to the hot summer sun and to wind and drought and to the ravages of insects and disease." His blue eyes were shining. "Corn that will harvest big, full, golden yellow ears and yield sixty or seventy, maybe a hundred or more bushels to the acre."

The world Grandpa held in his hands was rimmed with magic. Without even shutting my eyes I could see whole fields of corn shimmering in the sun, and I wanted it to be spring the next day, so we could run out and start them growing. But still . . .

I pointed to the spindly, shriveled ear he held, unable to keep the disbelief out of my voice. "From that, Grandpa?"

He nodded. "From this, Angel. And the others here."

"But how?"

He beamed at me. "Through a new process called hybridization."

I shook my head at him. I didn't know any more than I had before.

He tried to explain it to me. Did I understand, he asked, that all plants had to be pollinated in order to bear fruit?

I didn't know if I did or not, but I nodded my head.

Well, he said, that was the key to understanding this new process.

He went on to say that the corn farmers now grew was pollinated every summer the way many other plants were—by the wind. It carried pollen from the tassel of one stalk and dropped it on the ear-producing silk of some other stalk. When the corn grew and ripened, it might be good or so-so or poor. It all depended on chance.

But now, he said, suppose a farmer grew some corn that had better qualities than the rest of his crop, and he wanted to preserve and develop those better qualities. How could he do it?

I didn't know.

Well, he said, the farmer might preserve them for a while, at least, by saving enough of that corn to use as seed for all his fields the next year. If all went well, and he harvested a good crop, then he could do the same the next year.

But that was only preserving what he had, and only for as long as the whims of nature would allow. What about developing those better qualities into something really fine? Something really fine that would last. How could he do that?

I shook my head.

That, Grandpa said, was where hybridization came in.

First you started with what was called inbreeding—breeding the corn to itself in order to fix those better qualities permanently. You did that by what was called controlled pollination or selfing.

You planted the seeds of the good corn, and when the stalks grew high in the summer, you tied brown paper bags over all the tassels to keep the pollen in the tassel from being carried away by the wind. And you tied brown paper bags over all the young ears to keep the silk from being pollinated by that same wind. Then, when the bag over the tassel had collected the pollen, you exchanged it with the one over the silk, so the corn would be self-pollinated. And you snapped off the tassel, so no more pollen could be produced.

He held out the spindly, shriveled ear. "And at harvest time you get an ear of corn like this."

I hadn't understood too plainly the process he'd explained to me, but I could see plain enough what it had produced.

"Now," he said, before I could object, "you take another ear of corn from a different strain that's been inbred the same way." He pulled another spindly, shriveled ear out of the bag. "This time you plant the seeds from each of your two ears of corn in alternating rows. Now this year when your plant grows high, you snap the tassels off the stalks in one row. On the next row you leave the tassels on. Now, the ears of corn produced on the rows which have been pollinated by the tassels on the other rows are called a single-cross hybrid. Do you see?"

"I guess so."

He twinkled his eyes at me. "That hybrid, Angel, my love, will be a union of all the good qualities which each of these two parents, poor-looking as they are, have within them. If the cross is right, that hybrid will grow into a hardier, richer, more abundant corn than any ever produced before."

I guessed he knew what he was talking about. I guessed if anybody could grow the finest corn ever produced from those poor, scrubby ears, Grandpa could do it. As far as I was concerned, Grandpa could do anything. But what interested me most was his use of the word parents.

I hadn't ever thought of plants as parents, or as babies either. I wanted to ask him if there was a connection there somewhere with people. But with all that talk about tassels and silks and brown paper bags, it didn't seem likely. Anyhow I didn't get a chance to.

Grandpa dropped the ears of corn back into the bag and stood there holding it almost as if he were caressing it, his eyes shining again. "Ah, child, 'tis a lifetime I've waited for this. When I think of all the years I've spent tinkering over one thing and another, while all the time this"—he patted the brown paper bag—"this was what the good Lord had in mind for me."

Seventy years seemed an eternity to me. Looking back over his life, even Grandpa must have thought the Lord had taken rather an undue amount of time getting around to pointing out to him what it was He had in mind for him, though Grandpa not being one to question the ways of the Lord, he more likely thought the defect lay in his ability to see just where it was the Lord meant him to look.

He'd started out looking in the right direction. When he immigrated to America as a young man in 1881, farming was his life's dream. He was only going to tend bar, which he'd learned in Ireland as a boy, until he could save up enough money to buy a farm.

But then he'd married my grandmother, and the two children—my father and my Aunt Clarissa—had come along. What with the family needing first one thing and then another, it was hard to get enough money together to do it.

Nor had his idea of buying a farm set well with my grandmother, who was, as Grandpa put it, "a remarkable woman, God rest her soul, but she had not the true Irishman's love for the land."

I didn't remember my Grandmother Crowley, but I knew she had no love either for any of the other ideas Grandpa was always turning to in his spare time to make his fortune with. She thought he should devote every waking minute to his proper business of running the saloon.

I remembered Maggie saying once that Grandma had kept an electric prod in Grandpa's behind from the day she married him until the day she died, which of course I thought she meant literally until Kate said not to be such a jerk.

Grandpa gave the bag another pat and tucked it away in a drawer of the bureau. "Ah, well, 'twas a long apprenticeship, that's all, and not without its blessings. If you'll hand me that sweater, Angel, there's a spot for it here."

We had almost finished putting things away when I came across a small book with a pebbly black cover and gold-topped pages, bright satin streamers sticking out of the bottom of it. "What's this, Grandpa?"

He turned from hanging up a suit in the closet. "Why, that's my missal."

I frowned at him. "What's a missal?"

"Why, to follow the mass with, to be sure."

I kept on frowning. "What's a mass?"

"Why, child—" It was Grandpa's turn to frown. "Surely you know—" He sighed. "No, I suppose you don't."

Kate called up the stairs for us to come to supper.

"We'll talk about it later," Grandpa said.

After supper, while Kate and I did the dishes, Maggie and Grandpa sat on at the kitchen table so Grandpa could have his pipe. Maggie asked him if he wouldn't rather smoke it in the living room, where he'd be more comfortable, but he said Grandma had never liked the living room smelled up, and he'd gotten so in the habit of having his pipe in the kitchen, he'd gone on doing it even after she died and he was living on alone there over the saloon.

I couldn't imagine why my grandmother had been so particular about Grandpa's pipe, but I was glad she had been, so Kate and I wouldn't have to miss any part of his first evening with us.

Kate asked Grandpa if he would go to a basketball game with her sometime. He said he'd be proud to go anywhere with someone as pretty as Kate, and she blushed.

I asked him if he'd help me with a scrapbook on food I had to make for health class. He said he didn't like to say so, but he was probably the best scrapbook-maker ever to come out of Cook County. "Alive," he added, winking at me.

Maggie said she hoped he would find enough to interest him in Roseville, which struck me as peculiar. I figured if he hadn't thought he would, he wouldn't have come to live with us.

Grandpa said he didn't like to horn in on other people's lives, but—well, it was mighty fine to be here, which struck me as even more peculiar. But then I supposed it was just one of those times when people were so excited about something happening the way they wanted it to, they couldn't find the proper words for it.

It never occurred to me that Grandpa had come to live with us because he had nowhere else to go.

I supposed he could have gone anywhere he wanted to—to

109

Florida, like Julia Fletcher's father—or he could have stayed on in his apartment over the saloon, the way old Mr. and Mrs. Werner had stayed on in their house in Roseville after their son took over the clothing store. Or he could have chosen to live with Uncle Donald and Aunt Clarissa and Mark and the twins.

Indeed, the one thing I feared when Grandpa first came to live with us was that he would change his mind and decide he'd rather go live with them because they had more to offer him than we did.

The truth would have been incomprehensible to me, the truth being that Grandpa didn't have the money to go to Florida or even to stay on in his apartment, and Aunt Clarissa had made it plain to him without putting it into so many words that although she was prepared to do her Christian duty by him, she didn't want him.

Aunt Clarissa, who was seldom without an opinion, had a way of making her opinion plain on any matter without putting it into so many words—whenever she came to visit us, she had her nose wrinkled so much of the time, she gave me the feeling I smelled. And though she regarded herself as a charitable woman, devoting time and energy to the volunteer service of a number of worthy organizations, she would have been dismayed to hear that charity had anything to do with love.

In Aunt Clarissa's opinion, Grandpa's failing lay not so much in the fact that he'd never amounted to anything as in his blithe disregard for the fact that he never would. It was that kind of old-man foolishness she didn't want to have to contend with day in and day out, wasn't able to contend with, Aunt Clarissa being the kind of person who, if somebody offered to let her look at the world through rose-colored glasses, would have said, "Mercy sakes, what for?"

After Kate and I finished the dishes, we all went into the living room, where Grandpa told Maggie and Kate about his corn. Maggie thought to ask him something I hadn't—how he'd come by the spindly ears he had. I thought he'd bred them himself somehow—maybe out behind the saloon—but he hadn't. One of his regular customers had been a young agricul-turalist who had spoken to Grandpa about the experiments he was doing in hybridization. After he saw how interested Grandpa was, he'd given him some of his inbreds, so Grandpa could experiment, too.

At nine o'clock we turned on the radio for Eddie Cantor's program. When it was over Kate and I went to bed.

While I was waiting to go to sleep, I lay there listening to the sound of Maggie's and Grandpa's voices floating up from the living room, thinking how nice it would be, now that Grandpa was here, to have somebody to come home to after school.

Maggie started laughing again, the way she had earlier in the driveway, the laughter pealing through her voice and shaking it, fading away to bubble up again a little later, with Grandpa's deeper laughter joining in. I supposed she was telling him what she'd said to Orn Fletcher to make him sore at her.

I wondered, trying to piece together the few words and phrases I could make out—something about a clan and not equipped to do the job and no business bidding for it in the first place and fractious and couldn't resist saying—how it could have made him so sore when Maggie thought it was so funny, but I was too sleepy to care or even be much interested. I turned over on my stomach, pushed my head under the pillow, and went to sleep.

It wasn't until the next day that I remembered Grandpa hadn't talked to me later about the little black book. When I asked him about it, he only said again we'd talk about it later.

Later turned out to be the next Sunday, by which time I'd for-gotten all about it.

Sunday morning Maggie asked Kate and me if we'd mind not going to Sunday School that day, which naturally we didn't. She said she and Grandpa were going somewhere together. When they came back home we'd talk about it.

When they came back home a little over an hour later, they told us they'd been to church and that pretty soon we'd start going there with them, but Maggie thought we ought to get some idea about it first.

She told us we weren't Methodists at all, but when Kate was small, she'd wanted to know why she couldn't go to Sunday School at the Methodist church with her friends. Since she wasn't going anywhere else, Maggie had let first her and then me.

But all this time we, and Maggie, too, should have been going to the church we belonged to. She and Grandpa had talked about it many times before, and they'd talked about it again this past week, and now we were going to.

When I asked her what church it was, she said the Catholic church.

As soon as I got Kate alone I said, "What's a Catholic?"

"You know," Kate said. "Like Frank Zurini and Jerry Schultz. And like Grandpa and Aunt Clarissa and Uncle Donald and Mark and the twins."

"Well, yes," I said. "But what is a Catholic?"

Kate thought a bit. "Somebody who has holy pictures around everywhere and wears a thing around his neck and can't eat any meat on Friday."

"Oh," I said.

"And," she added, "they go to church at eight o'clock one Sunday and ten o'clock the next."

I frowned at her. "Why?"

She shrugged. "Beats me."

Chapter Five

How the Roseville Bank and Trust Company managed to keep going from one day to the next after Warren White came to the house that first night of December to tell Maggie what the situation was I doubt that even Warren White or any of the others who worked at the bank could have said afterward—or cared to think back on—but I suspect that when the shade was pulled up at the door each morning at nine o'clock, tellers, assistant cashier, cashier all prayed that the day's deposits would outweigh—or at least equal—the day's withdrawals, and not just in the aggregate, and when at three o'clock the shade was pulled down once again, they sank back on their stools like so many survivors of a mirthless game of musical chairs.

And as each day came and went its precarious way, so endless by the clock, so fleeting by the calendar, Warren White must have been—was, according to Maggie's telling of it—nearly driven out of his mind with worry trying to think of some other way out of the jam he was in if word didn't come from the RFC, still clinging to the hope that the next ring of the telephone would bring that word, because he couldn't think of any other way out.

Nor was Warren White the only one who worried. Along about the middle of December the board of directors of both banks—each board included the president and four other men

—began meeting almost every night, working together to try in their turn to come up with some way of shoring up the Roseville Bank and Trust Company enough to keep it from going under and dragging them and their good names down with it.

As the end of the year—and her settlement with the state—drew nearer and nearer, Maggie had the bank on her mind almost as much as Warren White and the directors did, wishing there was something she could do to relieve the situation, as unable as the rest of them to come up with anything.

As for me, in the excitement of Grandpa coming to live with us, I forgot all about Warren White's predicament at the bank and didn't think of it again until the Saturday before Christmas when Grandpa and Nathaniel and I went Christmas shopping and ran into him.

I could tell then he had money on his mind. For that matter, so did I.

Before she left for the courthouse that morning Maggie gave me a dollar to spend. As Grandpa and I set off for town after lunch, picking up Nathaniel on the way, I practically came unglued over the absolute certainty I was going to have money left over after I bought all the presents on my list.

We stopped at Ward's first for Grandpa's pipe tobacco—I'd asked Sam McCutcheon after school Friday to please have it already in a sack so Grandpa wouldn't know what I was getting him—and that cost a dime.

When we went into Woolworth's across the street, I was so goggle-eyed over all the things I'd like to have myself and so busy trying to steer Grandpa and Nathaniel past the right counters, watching them out of the corner of my eye, it was hard to concentrate on getting something for Kate.

From all the hints she'd been dropping, I knew Kate wanted a lipstick—after we'd had a laugh or two about me getting her the strawberry pin in Jim Petrie's window.

The lipstick was only ten cents, so I was all set to buy it. Then over at the games counter I noticed a game of tiddly winks.

Ordinarily I couldn't have afforded it, because it cost twenty-nine cents, but this one had a cracked cup, so it was marked down to seventeen.

I went back and forth from one counter to the other, persuading myself that if I bought Kate the lipstick, Maggie probably wouldn't let her wear it. If, on the other hand, I bought her the tiddly winks, I could play with it. On that happy note I splurged an extra seven cents.

In the exchange at school I'd drawn Barbara Kaiser's name, and I could hardly wait to get back at her for what she'd given me the year before—a handkerchief, of all things. It wasn't even one she'd bought, but an ugly orange- and purple-flowered one their maid had given to her mother.

The trouble was I couldn't find one for her anywhere near as awful as I wanted. Then I got to thinking she'd treated me at Ward's two different times after I'd stopped helping her with fractions, so I ended up buying her ten cents' worth of orange slices and only ate two of them before I got them wrapped.

That left Nathaniel and Maggie. Actually, it only left Maggie. Nathaniel's present wasn't going to cost anything. All I had to do was mail thirty-five bread wrappers to Chicago for a free jigsaw puzzle, and as soon as I collected three more wrappers from old Mrs. Werner and young Mrs. Werner and Marcella DeWitt, who were saving them for me, I'd have enough.

So there was Maggie, and I still had sixty-three cents.

Grandpa suggested I might find something at the B & B. Nathaniel frowned at his list through his spectacles and said he had to go there, too, to buy presents for his mother and father and his Uncle Orn and Aunt Julia. That made me more relieved than ever that Maggie hadn't sent Kate and me to live with Uncle Donald and Aunt Clarissa. Then I'd have had to buy them presents, too.

But Nathaniel could afford it. He had an unbelievable four dollars and fifty-four cents he'd saved up from his allowance and from different times when his Aunt Julia would look at him as if she wished there was something she could give him that he didn't have. Then she'd sigh and reach into her pocketbook and give him a nickel or a dime or even a quarter.

Maggie would look at Kate and me that way sometimes, only Maggie didn't have Julia Fletcher's wistful brown eyes. Maggie's eyes were hazel, and when she was laughing or happy or excited, yellow flecks danced in them. Other times, times when she would look at Kate and me that way, or sometimes when I'd come upon her unaware, it was as though a shadow had come over them, the way it hides the sun.

But Maggie wasn't rich like Julia Fletcher, so she'd only say drink our milk or button up warm or be careful crossing streets. Anyhow I didn't suppose anybody paid anybody not to die— not when they were as healthy as Kate and I were.

When we left Woolworth's Grandpa had a wide, flat paper sack in his arms. I was sure he'd bought me the paper dolls I wanted, but when we went into the B & B, and he stopped to look at a sweater for Kate, I sidled up to him, pretending to look at it, too, and peeked into the sack. It was only Christmas wrappings.

After I looked around a little, I found what I thought was a perfect present for Maggie—a beach ball, left over from the summer and reduced from seventy-nine cents to forty-nine. But Grandpa said with all the campaigning she'd have to do next year, she probably wouldn't have time to play on the beach. How about that nice pair of woolly black gloves?

I didn't think woolly black gloves were very exciting, but I supposed Grandpa knew best, and they were only thirty-nine cents, so I bought them.

Then while Nathaniel and Grandpa finished their shopping, I sat on a bench by the door and started thinking of all the things I could buy with the twenty-four cents I had left over.

Until Tommy Bassett came and sat down beside me.

I didn't know what he was even doing in the B & B, unless he'd come in off the street to get warm. The Bassetts were the poorest family in Roseville, with a raft of runny-nosed little children starting with Tommy, who was only seven or eight.

He didn't say anything. He just sat and stared at me and the packages I was holding, until the twenty-four cents I had in my mitten began sweating off on my hand.

I didn't see how he could possibly know I had it. I hadn't taken it out and counted it again after he came and sat down.

I wished if he had to sit, he'd go sit somewhere else.

But he didn't, and when I tried staring back at him, I only got clammier, so I finally went over and stood behind a rack of men's coats, and the fourth time I looked out he was gone.

When Nathaniel and Grandpa were finished—Grandpa had all his packages in a string bag by that time, so I couldn't tell what anything was—Grandpa said he'd treat us to an ice-cream cone at Ward's before we went up to the courthouse to see if Maggie was ready to go home yet.

I thought that was the best idea anybody had had all afternoon—until we walked in, and I saw who was sitting at the soda fountain eating a caramel sundae. It was Miss McCray, who'd been the third-grade teacher in Roseville for so many years she'd taught half the people in town.

It wasn't that I didn't like Miss McCray. I didn't like her or not like her. I tried to steer clear of her.

I was so dumbfounded to see her at Ward's—Miss McCray didn't strike me as the kind of person who'd do something so frivolous as to eat a caramel sundae—that when she said, "Good afternoon, Angelica," instead of good-afternooning her back the way Nathaniel had, I started babbling about how we'd been Christmas shopping, and I'd bought all my presents, and I still had money left.

But then I probably would have babbled at her anyhow, dumbfounded or not. Miss McCray affected me that way.

She even had to remind me to introduce her to Grandpa.

I hoped he'd keep her occupied until Nathaniel and I finished our cones, but just when I'd decided to practice one smile between each lick in the mirror behind the fountain and had my mouth all set to curl, I had to unset it, because she turned to me and said she was pleased I'd been such a thrifty shopper, and she hoped I'd save the money I had left.

I knew she was going to say that.

I don't suppose the field trips of most third grades include a visit to a bank to see how it operates, but Miss McCray, who had a sign over her blackboard, "Waste Not, Want Not," was positively obsessed with the virtue of saving money, and the trip climaxed a year of frequent exhortations to develop the habit of saving, a person was never too young to start—exhortations which, to our class, at least, assembling before her in the pre-Crash September of 1929, looking, for the most part, as grubby then as we did in the Depression year of 1931, must have seemed to her to be her Christian duty, the fostering of this virtue being sadly lacking in the home.

Miss McCray was a living example of the frugality she preached. A small, tidy woman, her white hair drawn up in a knot, she wore dark brown dresses which she made herself, all of them apparently cut from the same bolt of silk, all with ruching at the high-necked collar to hide the scrawniness of her neck, and each of them, because of a pleat here or a flounce there or a brooch for that one and beads for this one, managing to look different from all the others.

She lived alone on the north edge of town in a house which had belonged to her parents, and she drove, at a maximum speed of ten miles an hour, an ancient Model T Ford, which looked, in spite of the gleam of its hood, as if it wanted to retire but didn't dare.

It was almost impossible to imagine, let alone have, a traffic jam in Roseville in the early thirties, but I can remember seeing Miss McCray's Model T come quavering down Main Street toward the school, with one or two, maybe even three cars inching along behind, she sitting bolt upright, hands firmly on the wheel, stopping at the corner of Pearl Street to look left and right, even though Pearl Street was the stop street. Then, satisfied that no collision threatened from either side, she would start up again, begin to slow down almost immediately, put her hand out, pull over to the opposite curb, and—in the spring or fall—reach over to pick up and enjoy a sniff of the damp-wrapped garden flowers for her desk, while the exasperated motorists behind her muttered or cursed or simply sighed with relief as they kicked into second and shot off down the street.

It did no good to honk at her to try to hurry her along. If anybody did, she was likely to stop and get out and go back and ask the honker was he in some kind of distress, asking it with such grace and sincerity it was impossible to tell whether she really meant it or was taking this means to upbraid him for rudeness.

Whatever her motive, it was like Warren White's wooing of people—it worked. So well, indeed, that a husband trapped behind a farmer dawdling along the highway on a Sunday afternoon was likely, after several minutes had passed, to get an irritated "For land's sake, Fred, give him the horn. It isn't Miss McCray."

Miss McCray had the reputation among adults of being the best-loved teacher in Roseville. They said it of her then, they would say it of her when she retired (if she ever did) and again when she died, and she would go down that way in the history of the town. But what they meant was she was the most respected teacher. They were too uncomfortable in their minds about her to love her—too uncomfortable still, after all the years that had passed since they themselves had had her back in the third grade.

Not because she had inflicted violence upon them or held them up to ridicule. For all her sternness, Miss McCray wasn't mean. She was a good person in the truest sense of the word, with an abiding faith in the goodness of God and the goodness of America and the goodness of a way of life which had made Roseville what it was. Even her exhortations were not scoldings, but little maxims delivered in the spirit of "Let us then be up and doing."

Nor was there anything formidable in her appearance. Besides being small, she was as thin as a reed, with a brittleness about her, as if any man with an ounce of strength in him could pick her up and snap her in two.

It was a small thing, really, that made people shy away from her, even after they were old enough to not have to care. It was a way she had of looking at you—into you—that made you wish she could find whatever it was she was looking for, without, as time went by, much hope that she ever would.

It was not surprising that Miss McCray was firmly convinced in 1931, and said so to other teachers in the hallway, that the people in Roseville who were hardest hit by the Depression were hardest hit because they'd squandered money which they should have saved.

I didn't doubt she was right. I didn't doubt she was right when she also said that if Harvey Jones—or Charles Fitz or William Osgood—really wanted to work, he could find some kind of a job somewhere. I only felt a kind of fellowship with Harvey Jones and Charlie Fitz and Will Osgood and all the squandering hardest hit.

Especially Charlie Fitz and Will Osgood. I supposed Miss McCray had said to each of them when they came into the third grade the same kind of thing she'd said to me.

"A nickname," she said, her thin face pink in the earnestness of its welcome, her snapping brown eyes already searching into me, "is a familiar kind of name we give to someone who is a good friend or a schoolmate or a member of the family, and it says to that someone that we like him or her, which is why a nickname is nice to have. But, by the same token, a nickname doesn't ask very much of us, does it?"

I shook my head, not because I had any idea of what she was talking about, but because she seemed to expect it.

"Now in the third grade," she went on, "I intend to ask a great deal of my pupils. Not more than they can give. But perhaps"—she smiled—"more than they may think they can."

I nodded. I knew what she was talking about there from Kate, who'd had her four years earlier. Miss McCray wasn't against learning being fun, but she wasn't against it being work either.

"In the same way," she continued, "that we speak of Mr. Garnett as having a business because he owns a grocery and meat market, or of Mr. Kaiser as having a business because he practices law, so it is the business of boys and girls to learn, to make their minds stretch and grow even as they themselves are growing."

I was beginning to wish I didn't have a nickname.

"And because I expect every one of my boys and girls to take their learning seriously, to give me the best that's in them, the very best of which they are capable, then they should expect me to take them just as seriously, don't you think?"

I nodded again. I was willing to agree to anything if only she'd get through what she had to say.

"That is why I believe in calling boys and girls by their proper names."

I wanted to *whew,* but I didn't. Anyhow she wasn't through.

She smiled at me again. "Angelica is a name you should want people to call you. Do you know what the name Angelica means?"

I shook my head.

"It's from the Greek. It means lovely."

I knew then what she meant about a nickname not asking much of us. Miss McCray was the only person in Roseville who ever called me Angelica. Everybody else called me Angel.

As for the twenty-four cents I had left over from my Christmas shopping, I had no intention of saving it. I certainly wasn't about to put it in the bank—any bank. I was tempted to tell Miss McCray if she was as smart as I figured she was, she'd go to the Roseville Bank and Trust Company, where I knew she did her banking, and get her money out while the getting was still good. But even if I'd dared tell her, which I didn't, I doubted she'd believe me.

I doubt now she would have done it—or tried to do it—even had she known the shape the Roseville Bank and Trust Company was in. Nor would she have approved of what Doc Hawkins and Miss Emily Pratt and some others like them had done. For all that Miss McCray's understanding of job opportunities during the Depression was flawed by a naïve faith that can in an industrial society was still the sole determining factor of his position in that society, her belief in banks as an instrument of the common good was grounded in a common-sense understanding that banks operated—could only operate—on a basis of mutual trust, which meant that no bank, no matter how sound, could withstand a run.

What I did tell Miss McCray was I'd try to save my money. I figured I wasn't telling her a lie. I'd tried before without any luck at all, so I knew it couldn't possibly hurt to try again.

But I didn't look at her when I said it.

On our way to the courthouse Grandpa said what a fine, upright person she was. He'd like to get to know her better. I hoped if he did, he'd do it on his own.

We had just climbed the staircase to the second floor when Warren White came around the corner from Maggie's office, nearly bumping into us. He looked so terrible I thought he must be sick, until I remembered his predicament.

Still, he smiled at us and said hello, so I introduced Grandpa to him.

He told Grandpa he'd heard he was interested in hybrid corn. They'd have to get together sometime to talk about it. He'd grown up on a farm. He was sorry he didn't have time to talk now, but he had to get on back to the bank.

After we went into Maggie's office Grandpa said to her Mr. White must be having trouble with his liver, he was so bilious-looking. Maggie said it wasn't his liver. Then she asked Nathaniel and me if we'd like to go on into the commissioners' office. There were pencils and paper in there.

I figured she wanted to tell Grandpa about the bank, but I also figured I wasn't missing anything. From the look on Warren White's face, it was obvious he still hadn't gotten his twenty thousand dollars twice, or even once.

Anyhow I had more important things to tell Nathaniel. I'd

intended waiting until the next meeting of the A & N Club, because it would give us something to talk about. But our next meeting wouldn't be until after Christmas. I thought by that time I could surely think of something else.

After Nathaniel had shown me all the presents he'd bought —I was hoping he wouldn't show me what was in the biggest package, but it was only a mixing bowl for his Aunt Julia— and I'd shown him all of mine, I said, "Guess what."

"What?"

I took a breath. "I just found out I'm not a Methodist."

He frowned at me. "You're not?"

"No."

"Then what are you?"

"Something a whole lot different."

His eyes lit up. "A Free Methodist?"

"Hell's bells, Nathaniel, no. It's more different than that."

He thought a minute.

"Give up?"

He nodded.

"A Catholic."

His eyes widened. "You are?"

I drew a stick man on the tablet in front of me and waited for him to ask me what a Catholic was. I hadn't figured out what I would tell him. I thought I'd wait and see what came out. But he didn't ask me.

I looked up at him. "Don't you want to know what a Catholic is?"

He frowned at me. "Isn't it just somebody who goes to some other church?"

I sighed. "Yes." And wondered why I'd sighed. "But it's more than just that. A Catholic has to go to church. I mean, it's not like Mr. McIntyre, who can stay home if he wants to and read the Chicago *Tribune*. You have to go to church every single Sunday. If you don't, it's a sin. And every holyday."

"What's a holyday?"

"I don't know. Like Easter."

"Well, Easter's on Sunday anyhow."

"Well," I said, "there are some holydays that aren't." I frowned. "Like Christmas. Christmas is on different days."

He shrugged. "We always go to church on Christmas."

"I guess you're right," I said, and made a mental note to get Grandpa to explain it to me again.

"What's it like inside?" he wanted to know.

I told him I didn't know yet, because I hadn't been. "We're going the first time Christmas Eve. And guess what."

"What?"

"It's at midnight."

Nathaniel's eyes widened again. "Boy, that is different."

I told him church was only at midnight on Christmas Eve— I supposed to make it special. Usually it was at eight o'clock one Sunday and ten o'clock the next.

Nathaniel thought that was pretty different, too, but I explained it was because Roseville and Montclair shared the same minister, who wasn't called a minister but a priest. "And you know what else?"

"What?"

"Church isn't called church."

"It isn't?"

"Well, I mean you don't call the services church. It's called a mass."

"A mass? Why?"

I shrugged. "Beats me."

I tried to think what else I knew about it. "If you were a Catholic, Nathaniel, you could be a server, because you're a boy. Girls can't be servers. Only boys."

He frowned at me. "What's a server?"

I frowned back at him. "I don't know. But I suppose everybody is in the room kneeling—Catholics kneel a lot—and probably the server goes around with a platter of fruit and serves it to them. Don't you suppose?"

He shrugged. "I suppose."

"I'll try to get an orange for you when I go Christmas Eve," I said.

"Okay," he said. "Or if you can't get that, an apple."

When Christmas Eve came I was glad I'd said it to Nathaniel and not Kate, because I was being a jerk again. The servers didn't serve fruit or anything else. They served the priest.

Nothing turned out the way I'd imagined it, and I imagined so much I almost threw up and didn't get to go at all. But Maggie made me lie down after supper, and I finally went to sleep. Then when she woke me I didn't want to get up—until I remembered where we were going.

Kate, of course, hadn't gone to bed at all. She was so excited about getting to stay up past midnight she was glassy-eyed.

On the way to church Grandpa told us he and Maggie had a surprise for us. I couldn't think what it could be, but when we got there, everything was such a surprise, I supposed that was all he meant. It was enough.

Just seeing the inside of the church was almost enough. The Catholic church in Roseville may have been small potatoes, but to my uninitiated eye, it had it all over the Methodist church in looks alone.

It was smaller. I could see that. And it was a different shape. The Methodist church was square, with row after row of benches curving to form a great wide semicircle. The Catholic church was a narrow rectangle, with one center aisle and an aisle along the wall at either side of the pews, which faced straight front, seating maybe one-fourth as many people.

But it wasn't size and shape. It was color and content.

Except for wine-colored carpeting on the floor and short green velvet draperies on brass rings bordering the pulpit, everything in the Methodist church was brown—brown benches with brown hymnbooks in brown hymnbook holders, a brown pipe organ centered against the back wall of the brown wood-paneled pulpit, with more brown benches in the choir section to the right of the organ.

The walls and ceiling weren't brown, of course. They were white, but there wasn't anything to look at there except cracks in the plaster, and unless the crack was a big one, it was too far away to make anything interesting out of it.

There wasn't even much to look at in the pulpit—only the lectern, also brown, and Mr. Wurlitzer, sometimes in brown himself, presiding over it, talking, for the most part, about things I didn't understand or making announcements about things which didn't concern me, which was why, for lack of anything else to do, I was always trying to find something to look at.

In the Catholic church I didn't have to try. There was so much to look at, in so many different colors, I hardly knew where to start.

Around the walls were fourteen pastel paintings which Grandpa told me represented The Way of the Cross, showing me how to look at them in sequence. On the ceiling was a painting of a fierce-faced God the Father looking as if He had just created the wind and was having second thoughts about it, His white hair streaming, His dark blue robe billowing, while rosy-cheeked cherubs hung on for dear life all around. (There were cracks in the plaster here, too, in the vacant places—more and closer if not bigger—but I saved them to fall back on after I got used to everything else, assuming I ever did.)

The organ and choir were upstairs at the back of the church, out of sight unless you turned around, which I kept doing, because for some reason I couldn't figure out that was where Maggie had gone to sit, until Grandpa whispered to me it wasn't polite to turn your back on God.

I turned around to him, wide-eyed. "Where is God?" I whispered back. In the Methodist church, according to what our Sunday School teacher had told us, God wasn't any special place. He was just there, an unseen Presence.

Grandpa pointed to a little door in the middle of the altar—which was something the Methodist church didn't even have.

I stared first at the door and then at Grandpa. "You mean He's behind there?"

Grandpa nodded.

I wanted to ask him how He could possibly fit into such a small space, but Kate was frowning at me, so I let it go.

Above the altar there was a statue of Jesus hanging on the Cross. At each side of the altar there were statues, one of the Virgin Mary and one of St. Joseph. (There was a statue at the back of the church, too, of St. Francis of Assisi, which somebody from Chicago had found in Europe and given to the church, that I'd had a glimpse of on the way in. I couldn't see it at all now, even by turning around, but I didn't mind. Kate had told me one of his feet had been kissed by so many people for so many hundreds of years, it was partially worn away, and that didn't appeal to me a whole lot.)

Best of all in my opinion was the altar itself, all white-spired and trimmed in gold, with red poinsettia plants and white candles everywhere.

I hadn't finished feasting my eyes on that when a boy in a red robe with a white blouse over it came in through a doorway at the side and lighted all the candles, using a long taper, bobbing down on one knee each time he crossed in front of the altar.

He'd hardly more than gone out when the organ struck up, and he came back in again with three other boys dressed the way he was, followed by the priest in long gold and white robes. As the priest came in, the congregation stood up, and the mass began.

For all the explaining Maggie and Grandpa had done in the preceding two weeks to prepare Kate and me for the Catholic church, I had only a vague idea of what was going on.

Except for the announcements and the sermon, which came about halfway through the mass, the priest had his back to us most of the time, kneeling in front of the altar or climbing the steps up to it to hover over one thing or another with his hands raised, mumbling words I couldn't make out and wouldn't have understood anyhow since it was all in Latin. The few times he did turn toward us for a moment or two, he didn't look at us but at some point off in space, raising his hands again and singing—if you could call it that—some Latin phrase to the choir, who responded with a phrase of their own, generally the same one each time.

From start to finish he was hardly still a minute, and the congregation was just as active—standing, kneeling, sitting, kneeling, up and down, up and down.

It was all so breathtaking I hardly had time to think.

I wasn't worried any more about the next meeting of the A & N Club. I was going to have plenty to tell Nathaniel. Including the surprise Grandpa had mentioned.

About two-thirds of the way through the mass, after we'd already done so much kneeling my knees ached, we had to kneel some more while bells rang and the priest held things up in the air. Then nearly everybody in the church, including Grandpa, got up and went to Communion.

Before he went, he poked Kate and me and said to pay special attention. The surprise was coming.

It nearly bowled us over.

The organ started playing an accompaniment that sounded familiar to me. The next thing I knew, Maggie was singing Gounod's "Ave Maria."

We'd heard her sing it at home, and other songs, too, which she'd learned when she was studying at the conservatory, but I'd never heard her sing in public before. Whether it was polite or not, I had to turn around and look. And then look to see if other people were liking it. But those who weren't standing in the Communion line were kneeling with their heads bowed and their hands covering their faces, so I couldn't tell. Then Kate tugged at me, so I bowed my head, too, and covered my face with my hands and found out why they did it—so they could yawn without anybody knowing.

In a night which had been full of surprises, another surprise was yet to come. After the mass was over, we went out by the side aisle near us. I was moseying along in the slow-moving crowd, looking at the stained-glass windows as I went by them, reading the names of the donors engraved on each of them, when I came to one which read "Mr. and Mrs. Dominic Petrelli."

I was past the window before it hit me who Mr. Dominic Petrelli was. Dynamite Dom.

I couldn't imagine him giving a stained-glass window to a church. I couldn't imagine him in church. But then I supposed if he was a Catholic, he had to go to church whether he wanted to or not, no matter what he did the other six days of the week, and that considering what he did the other six days of the week, his stained-glass window was probably also bulletproof.

Outside, on the way to the car, people came up to Maggie to tell her what a beautiful voice she had, and the yellow flecks danced in her eyes. I was so perked up by the frosty air, I thought when we got home I'd ask if we could sing some Christmas carols, but when we came into the house, the warmth made my eyelids so heavy I had all I could do to keep them open long enough to see to get to bed.

I was too sleepy even to wonder any more if it would snow before morning or if there'd be any presents under the tree.

It snowed.

It was snowing when I woke up and crawled out of bed. Kate was still sound asleep. I had to poke her to wake her up.

I thought she was going to bite me, but I quickly said, "Merry Christmas."

She groaned and rolled over on her other side. I poked her again.

She sighed. "I'm coming."

I started on ahead, but when I reached the turn in the stairway, I couldn't go on, so I sat down to wait for her.

When I was still young enough to believe in Santa Claus, the only thing I ever worried about was being good, and so far as I could see, nobody paid much attention even to that. But after I found out that there wasn't any Santa Claus, that it was mostly Maggie who was buying the presents, then I had to start worrying about whether she could afford to or not.

She always gave me a dime on Saturday afternoons to go to the movies, and it was easy enough to get a penny for a Dum-Dum sucker and even sometimes a nickel for an ice-cream cone at Ward's when I didn't have the deal with Barbara Kaiser or when Nathaniel was off with Bobby Jackson trying to learn how to chin himself—I did think Nathaniel could have picked a better teacher, but beggars can't be choosers, and Nathaniel had an aggie Bobby Jackson wanted—but Christmas was more than a dime for the movies or a nickel for an ice-cream cone. It was more, even, than something special for your birthday.

I didn't know what a Depression was or why we were having it or why people like the Kaisers and the Fletchers didn't seem to be affected by it when almost everybody else was. But I knew that, like almost everybody else in Roseville, we were poor.

Not poor like people at the poor farm, who were too old to work and whose families, if they had any, couldn't take care of them. And not poor like the Bassetts, who were perennially down and out, good times or bad, and lived off county relief.

Not poor, even, like Loretta Gudeman's parents, who, George Garnett told Kate, would send Loretta to his father's store with a note saying what they wanted, because they hadn't paid their bill and didn't have the nerve to come themselves.

But we were poor, and even though Maggie had always managed Christmas before, I didn't know if she could again. Or if maybe she wasn't so tired of making sacrifices, she'd feel she couldn't make another one even if it killed us.

The thing was, I felt, not to get excited and go charging down to the living room and, if there weren't any presents there, end up making a fool of myself for everyone to see. That was what I couldn't bear the thought of.

So I waited on the stair to let Kate go first. That way I could mosey around the turn, peeking ahead to see if there was anything to get excited about. If there wasn't, then I could pretend I didn't care, I hadn't been expecting anything anyhow.

Kate, when she finally came, said what was I sitting there like a jerk for? Why didn't I go on down? But she didn't say it with any heat. Kate probably felt the same way I did, but since she was four years older, she had to act as if she wasn't afraid of anything.

It turned out there wasn't anything to be afraid about. I got enough of a look rounding the turn to make me quiver down the last half of the stairs. When I got to the living room I just stood there staring. Then I turned around and went flying back up the stairs and banged on Grandpa's door and Maggie's door and shouted, "Hurry up! It's Christmas!"

Kate was very nice about the tiddly winks, even playing me once. I thought I might let her beat me that first time, since it was her game, but I could have saved myself the thought. She beat me anyhow.

Maggie said she'd been wanting a pair of black woolly gloves all fall, and Grandpa said how did I know he was running low on tobacco?

But it was Kate who gave Grandpa the best present—better even than the bathrobe Maggie gave him, which he put right on and walked up and down in so we could all admire it.

None of us could figure out ahead of time what Kate's present was. It was in an enormous box, but so lightweight I thought it must be a lampshade. Maggie guessed eight cones of cotton candy. Grandpa said two hundred egg shells. Kate blushed and giggled and told him to open it.

It was brown paper bags for covering the silks and tassels of his corn. Dozens and dozens of them. She must have gone to everybody's house in town collecting them. Grandpa couldn't get over it. His eyes were so shiny when he looked at Kate I was afraid he was going to cry.

He didn't, but he blinked several times and gave her a big hug before he reached under the tree to pull out a present for somebody else.

It was for me. I could tell what it was before I opened it. The paper dolls I wanted. Only they were from Kate, not Grandpa.

Nathaniel's present was an autograph book. Maggie gave me two new *Nancy Drews*, a giant pencil box, and a navy blue suspender skirt with a white blouse. There was a fountain pen on a neck ribbon from Uncle Donald and Aunt Clarissa—for somebody who found it so hard to show any affection, Aunt Clarissa had a positive genius for choosing presents that were not only in impeccable taste but something you really wanted—and a pair of pajamas from Great Aunt Helen in Cincinnati.

But nothing from Grandpa.

I supposed he must have forgotten, though he had given Kate a white Angora sweater and Maggie a carving knife with a curly handle. So I didn't see how he could have. But I looked, and I didn't see any more presents.

Then, when Maggie said we'd better get dressed for breakfast, and what on earth was I doing crawling around behind the Christmas tree, Grandpa slapped his thigh and said, "The saints preserve us, Angel, and didn't I leave your present upstairs!"

He went right off to get it, and I crawled back out and pulled some icicles off my hair and waited for him.

When I heard him come thump-thump-thumping down the stairs, I couldn't imagine what it could be. When he came through the doorway I almost fell over.

It was a sled. A sled bigger than I was.

"Oh, Grandpa," I breathed. He beamed at me, and Maggie beamed at me, and Kate beamed at me.

It was truly a Christmas.

But what made it a memorable one was not, after all, the sled bigger than I was.

The day after Christmas, which was a Saturday, two things happened. The first was that Orn Fletcher went to Chicago for several days on business. The second was that Maggie came up with an idea of how to save the bank.

Maggie was in her office at the courthouse when the idea came to her. Excited about it, and wondering why on earth it hadn't occurred to her before, she put on her coat and went over to the bank. There she took Warren White aside and said to him, "Warren, if I could get you as much as twenty thousand dollars for deposit, would that help?"

He stared at her open-mouthed. "Help? My God, Maggie, it would save us. But where can you get that kind of money?"

"I'm not sure I can get it," she said, "but I think I can." Then she told him it would mean driving down to Indianapolis, which she would do the first thing Monday morning. As soon as she found out anything she'd call him.

On Monday morning she drove to Indianapolis, but the man she was looking for—the state auditor—was out of his office and didn't return until four o'clock. It was almost five before she called Warren White and asked him if he could get the directors of both banks together at the Roseville Bank and Trust Company at eight o'clock that night. She'd be there with a proposition for them. He said he would and asked her if she had gotten the money. She told him it would depend on the directors. She'd explain when she saw them.

She pulled up in front of the bank a few minutes before eight, but the ten directors were already assembled inside waiting for her, sitting at the table in the counting room, looking, she said, in spite of some desultory remarks she heard exchanged as she approached the room and in the moment before they realized she had come into it, as if each of them was wrapped in a private despair—Karl Kaiser holding the lawyer's briefcase he was never without propped against the edge of the table, running his thumbs up and down the sides of it, John Wurlitzer patting his pockets with the halfhearted air of a man who has already forgotten, and no longer cares, what it was he was looking for, Mr. Thornapple, the county commissioner, staring at the sheaf of papers in front of him, Harry Goodman staring at nothing at all—as if all of them had been hoping against hope for so long now, they no longer had any hope left to summon forth, the only exception a pale but sweaty-browed Warren White hovering over Orn Fletcher's father, a director of the Northern State Bank, assuring him that "Maggie must have something, she wouldn't have me drag you down here for nothing," Mr. Fletcher not looking up but only brushing a hand at him the way you would a fly.

When they realized Maggie was there, they all stood up, and Warren White came over to take her coat and pull out a chair for her, saying he hoped the long drive hadn't been too tiring. At least, as she said afterward, she thought that was what he said. She was so stricken by the sight of the men before her she didn't really hear him, but found herself saying to them, although she was ahead of schedule, "I'm sorry to be so late."

It wasn't until she told them what her idea had been and what she had done about it and what the directors must now do on their part to secure the money she was prepared to offer them, which was not the twenty thousand she had hoped for but forty thousand, that despondency changed to astonishment, astonishment to hope, hope to uncertainty, and uncertainty— when she offered to make still another trip for them, not to Indianapolis this time but to a bank in Chicago where certain bonds and other securities were deposited in her name as county auditor—to determination, and with determination came the final breakthrough from the cocoon of despair into the meeting place of ideas.

And, in the exchange of those ideas, the stunning, almost belated, realization that the bank was going to be—had been— saved.

That they would never forget what Maggie had done for them was avowed by each of them, each in his way, the most touching perhaps, certainly the most demonstrative, being the avowal of Warren White, who all but got down on his knees to her.

And Maggie, wrapped now in a cocoon herself, the cocoon of their gratitude, went home and went to bed.

Since Orn Fletcher was in Chicago, he didn't know what had taken place in Roseville until he returned the following Thursday afternoon. Since I happened to be where I was when he returned, Maggie didn't have to explain to me, when she told me her story years afterward, what her idea of how to save the bank had been. I heard all about it for myself.

Chapter Six

Kate was always saying I was going to get in trouble for listening to things I shouldn't, even though a lot of times, when she was more curious about something than I was, she egged me on to do it.

But intending to listen was different from not being able to help listening. That was what I kept telling myself all the way home afterward, wishing every step of the way we lived farther from the Fletchers' than the two blocks we did.

Telling myself, too, it wasn't my fault Nathaniel and I had had to hold our A & N Club meeting where we did.

Since nobody outside of the two of us was supposed to be aware of the existence of the A & N Club, let alone that we were having a meeting, we normally met at our house, where in winter we could use the attic and in summer what had once been a hayloft in the old barnlike shed at the back of our property. The Fletchers had neither attic nor shed. Nathaniel did have a room of his own, but the Fletchers' hired girl, Elmira, was always grumbling at us for messing around, as she put it, after she'd just finished cleaning in there, which, according to her, she always just had.

But the Thursday following Christmas we had no choice. Elmira had the afternoon off, Mary Louise was at our house with Kate and Alice White and Sarah Frances Wunderley, Ellen had a date, and Julia, who was going to Bernice Kaiser's to play bridge, asked Nathaniel if he and I could play there so he could answer the phone and take care of anything else that might come up.

She was just leaving when I arrived, stopping in the entryway to pull on her gloves and to say she'd be home around four-thirty or five. If we got hungry there were cookies on the kitchen table and apples in the Frigidaire—the Fletchers didn't have an icebox like ours with a pan under it, which, if we forgot to empty it, overflowed and ran all over the floor, but a new Frigidaire with a great cylindrical motor on top.

We decided to eat first. Then Nathaniel had to show me all his Christmas presents, and then it took a while for us to decide where we could meet that would be secluded enough and still within answering distance of the telephone.

We finally hit on behind the davenport, which had been moved cattycorner across two walls at the front of the living room to make room for the Christmas tree. When we got all settled back there, it was as shadowy and secret as we could have wished.

We conducted our meetings the way the PTA committee did when it met at our house, except we didn't bother to keep any minutes of the last meeting, our reasoning being that everything we said was secret, and we didn't need to remember it anyhow. So Nathaniel started out by asking if there was any old business, and I said no, which he knew I was going to say, because we never had any old business, but I made him ask it anyhow.

That left new business.

Sometimes we didn't even have much of that, but this time we had the Christmas Eve mass, which took a long time. Then when I'd told him everything about it I could think of and answered all the questions I could, he asked to have the floor.

Making me shake hands first, he pulled an *Open Road for Boys* out of his pocket and showed me an ad from Charles Atlas saying how even the weakest man could be made strong if he'd send for Charles Atlas' special strength-building equipment.

Nathaniel had. He'd had the box of equipment—an elastic cord with jump-rope handles and a coil spring to be squeezed in your hand—for over a month. I didn't know how he'd been able to keep from telling me about it before, but then Nathaniel was a better secret-keeper than I was.

Taking the cord out, he demonstrated it, asking me to look and see if his arm muscles were any bigger yet. I couldn't see that they looked any different than they ever had, but we were in a cramped space, making it hard for him to stretch the elastic very far. Anyhow I didn't want to hurt his feelings, so I said I thought they were.

We must have spent an even longer time over Charles Atlas than we had on the Catholic church. When I looked out the window it was getting dark.

I told Nathaniel I had to go home, but just then Julia came in the front door and, after a few seconds, into the living room to turn on the tree lights and some lamps.

We were only waiting for her to finish and go on out to the kitchen so we could come out. In my experience, as well as everybody else's, parents never understood what you were doing or why you were doing it where you were, and when you tried to explain, it only made matters worse.

She finally finished and went out. We stood up and were about to push out the end of the davenport enough so we could wriggle past it when we heard a stomp-stomp-stomping on the front porch, the front door burst open and slammed shut, and we hardly had time to bob back down again before Orn Fletcher yelled, "Julia!" and came storming into the living room without even stopping to take off his galoshes.

My heart was beating so loud I was sure he could hear it. And then she came in and said he was getting snow all over the rug.

He said he didn't give a good God damn about the rug, but at her insistence he took his galoshes off. Then he threw his overcoat onto the davenport.

She said, "What on earth's the matter with you? When did you get back?"

"Nothing's the matter with me," he growled at her, "and when do you think I got back, for Christ's sake? Just now."

"Orn, I wish you wouldn't swear. This isn't a poolroom."

"That God damned woman," he said, not paying any attention, "thinking she could pull a trick like that and get away with it. Well, she's not going to get away with it." He snorted. "I made up my mind a month ago to get her out of there, and by God if she hasn't given me the way to do it!"

"What are you talking about? What woman?"

He banged his fist on a table, and I jumped. "That God damned woman in the auditor's office."

I frowned and thought he couldn't mean Maggie. But what other woman was there? I sighed. Maggie's secretary.

"Maggie?" she asked, right in the middle of my sigh.

"Who do you think?" he snapped.

I guessed I had thought wrong.

There was a pause. I supposed she must be frowning at him. I knew I would have. "Well, my land, surely you can't be angry at her because of what she did for the bank."

"Which bank?"

"The Roseville Bank and Trust Company."

"What do you mean, what she did for it?"

"Well," she said, "I thought that's what you were talking about—the bank."

"No, I wasn't talking about the bank. I don't know anything about the bank. I told you I just got back. What about the bank?"

"Why, Maggie saved it from going under."

He roared at her so ferociously I reeled backward. "She what?"

"She saved the bank from going under."

"Who said so?"

"Your father. He called this morning to speak to you, and I told him you were still in Chicago. Then he told me about Maggie. Did you know the bank was in trouble?"

"Yes, I knew it."

"Well, you didn't say anything."

"It's not the kind of thing you spread around."

"Well, no, I suppose not. Still, I think you might have said—after all, all the money Mama left me when she died is in there. And all of Mildred's money, too. Did you talk to Mildred?"

"Did I what?"

"Did you talk to Mildred?"

Beside me Nathaniel twitched. Mildred was his mother.

"What in hell does Mildred have to do with—"

"I just wanted to know if you talked to her."

He sighed. "Yes, I talked to her. For all the good it'll do."

She sighed, too. "There, you see? I knew I was doing the right thing in persuading Mildred to let me handle her money for her, and Dr. Terrapin agreed with me, and—"

"Who in hell is Dr. Terrapin?"

"Well, really, Orn. You know perfectly well who he is. My land, I've talked about him enough. He's the child-guidance columnist in the *Tribune*."

"What does handling Mildred's money have to do with child guidance?"

"Well, I write to him sometimes about related things. He's always so helpful. Anyhow, he agreed with me it was probably best for me to handle Mildred's money, so she wouldn't be able to go right through it, but he did point out that I'd be responsible for it. You knew that, too, so I don't see how you couldn't have said something to me about the bank."

"If you'll remember," he said, sounding testy, "I told you not to put the money there in the first place. I told you to put it in the Northern State."

"Well, I know, but—well, after all, Warren's an old friend, and I thought—"

"You thought. You don't have anything to think with. It's because of your friend Warren the bank got into trouble."

"Orn, how can you say that?"

"Because it's true, that's how I can say it. Warren White has

140

about as much judgment as a beagle pup. How in hell he ever got where he is is beyond me."

"People like him."

He started roaring again. "You're God damn right, people like him. Why shouldn't they? Anybody sticks his ass out to him, he'll kiss it."

"Orn!"

"All right," he said, disgusted.

I stole a look at Nathaniel. Nathaniel was trembling all over now. But then, so was I.

"You want to know what I think of Warren White, that's what I think of him." He stomped over to the mantel, and the floor trembled, too. "How'd she do it?"

"Who?"

"Who do you think? Who've we been talking about?"

"Maggie?"

He sighed. "Yes, Maggie."

"Oh. Well, your father said the Roseville Bank and Trust Company and the Northern State Bank were planning to mer—"

He cut her off. "I know that."

"And they were only waiting for each of them to get a grant from the RF—"

He cut her off again. "I know that, too."

"Well, Maggie knew the Roseville Bank and Trust Company was in trouble, because she tried to write a warrant against it, and Warren told her they couldn't meet it, and then he told her how bad off the bank—"

"For Christ's sake, get to the point."

For a minute she didn't say anything. Then she said she was trying to, if he'd only let her. She said Maggie was concerned about the bank and was concerned, too, about her year-end settlement with the state, and she'd been racking her brain trying to think if there was anything she could do to keep the bank from going under.

The floor was trembling almost continually now as Orn paced

back and forth across the room—*thump-thud, thump-thud, thump-thud.*

"And then while she was in her office the day after Christmas it came to her." Julia snapped her fingers. "Just like that."

He stopped pacing.

She gave a little laugh. "Really, it's quite simple when you stop to think about it. Not that I don't think it was clever of her. I do." She laughed the little laugh again. "But when I think of your father telling me how the directors of both banks had been meeting almost day and night trying to come up with something. Even Christmas Day. Well," she said, as if she'd just realized something, "no wonder he had to get right up from the dinner table. I couldn't think at the time what he could be rushing off to on Christmas."

I thought Orn was going to explode. "Will you get to the point?"

"Oh. Well, I just thought that—well, anyhow, Maggie drove down to Indianapolis Monday to talk to the state auditor, and when she got back, she went straight to the bank, where Warren had all the directors waiting for her, and she told them if they could get twenty thousand dollars together in approved securities—Liberty Loan bonds and U.S. Stock and Land Bank bonds and gravel road bonds and the like—they could have forty thousand dollars in cash to deposit in the bank. Well, they didn't have any securities at all and didn't know where they could get any, so she offered to go to some bank up in Chicago where she keeps all the securities which the county holds in —in what did your father say? Oh, yes, in escrow—and she'd take out twenty thousand in bonds and give it to them if they would each sign a personal bond until such time as they could replace the one for the other. And then they all got to thinking about where else they could get the twenty thousand, and they ended up borrowing it the next day from a correspondent bank in Indianapolis long enough to get the forty thousand dollars in cash she had for them." Julia sighed. "And that was that."

Except it wasn't. Orn banged his fist so hard down on a table

I would have thought he'd fracture his hand. And he roared at her again. "Forty thousand dollars cash from where?"

"Orn, I wish you'd stop banging on that table before you break it."

He sounded as if he was strangling. "From where?"

"Why, I told you, didn't I?"

"No, you did not."

"Oh. Well, I started to, and then you got me off the track. That's what I meant about it being such a simple idea, really."

"Julia," he said, as though he could hardly keep from hitting her, "where did the money come from?"

"I'm trying to tell you. From the state."

"From the state?" He seemed dumbfounded.

"Yes. Maggie told the state auditor—it turns out he's a friend of hers, by the way, so I suppose that helped—anyhow, she told him the banks in Roseville were having a hard go of it, what with the Depression and so much panic around, and she asked him if he could deposit some state funds in one of our banks, the same as she distributes county funds to each of the five banks in the county. And he said if the bank would put up security, he would. And he did. And that's all there was to it."

"I'll be God damned."

She laughed that same little laugh again. "You see what I mean about it being such a simple idea?"

If he saw, he didn't say so. He just made another strangling noise.

"I guess," she said, "the directors of both banks were nearly bowled over by it. And Warren—why, your father told me he was ready to kill himself, he was so desperate to save the bank—"

"As well as his own neck."

"I suppose so. Anyhow, he was beside himself, he was so grateful to Maggie for thinking of it."

"Why couldn't the lily-livered son of a bitch think of it himself?"

"I'm sure I don't know. And I wish you'd stop using those vulgar expressions. I don't see any need for them. The point is, he didn't. And neither did any of the others. She did."

"She would."

"Really, Orn, I'm surprised at you. What have you got against Maggie all of a sudden? My land, you'd think she was trying to ruin the bank instead of save it. Your father," she went on, an edge to her voice, "thought it was a fine thing for her to do."

"He would. He's always been soft on her."

"It seems to me," she said, as if she were walking on eggshells, "you used to be soft on her yourself."

"That's hogwash!"

"Orn, there's no need to shout. Do you want the whole neighborhood to hear you? I don't know where Nathaniel is—" Her skirts rustled toward us, and I clutched at Nathaniel. "He and Angel Crowley were playing here this afternoon." Her skirts rustled over to the doorway, and my heart started beating again. "I suppose she's gone home now, and he's up in his room. But do keep your voice down."

He snorted as she rustled back to him. "Soft on her. There was a time when I felt sorry for her—after that husband of hers, who, God knows, never amounted to anything, died and left her with those two kids on her hands and a house mortgaged to the hilt and God knows how many unpaid bills. Now, do you want to call that being soft on her?"

"I wouldn't blame you if you were. Maggie's a very attractive woman. And—well—appealing."

"Appealing, hell. She's as bullheaded as an ox. And as for feeling sorry for her, I got over that a long time ago. She hasn't given me anything but a hard time ever since I put her in that God damned office."

"I thought," she said, and I didn't know how she could keep her voice so mild, "it was the voters who put her in."

It was awfully quiet for a bit. Then he stomped over to the mantel again and said there wasn't any sense in trying to talk politics with her, because she didn't know anything about it. She said she supposed she didn't, and from all the shouting

144

and swearing and cigar-smoking that went with it, she was just as glad. She didn't see how Maggie, for all her get up and go, could stand to be mixed up in it.

"Well, she's not going to be mixed up in it much longer, I can guarantee you that."

"What do you mean?"

"Just what I said. When election time rolls around next year, Maggie Crowley is going to find herself out."

"What makes you think you can get her out?"

"Wait and see."

"And why do you want to anyhow?"

He kicked at a log in the fireplace, and it thumped. "On the way into town just now, I stopped off at the office to leave some equipment I picked up in Chicago. Chuck Sellers was there waiting for me."

"Chuck Sellers?"

"The boy who's been working for me the last three months."

"Oh. Him. Well?"

"He had something to tell me. Something he thought I'd be interested to know."

It was quiet again. Then she said, "Well, really, Orn, talk about me. Go on."

He kicked at the log again, harder.

"Orn, for the love of heaven, you're getting ashes all over the hearth. Elmira just cleaned in here this morning. Can't you leave anything alone?"

"Why didn't you tell me about Maggie?"

"Tell you about Maggie?" she said, puzzled. "I just did."

"I'm not talking about the God damned bank."

"If you don't stop swearing, you're not going to be talking to me about the bank or anything else. I'm not one of your cronies down at the poolroom."

"No, and I'm not one of your drugstore biddies."

"I'm sure," she said, "I don't know what you mean by that."

"Considering all the time you waste down there, and all the drivel you bring home with you, I find it damn peculiar you didn't say anything to me about Maggie. If you ask me, you're the one who's soft on her."

"If I had anything to say, I'd have said it. My land, I don't know what's got into you. What did Chuck Sellers tell you that's so terrible, for heaven's sake?"

When Orn finally spoke, every word he said had a little space after it. "Maggie Crowley is a God damned Catholic."

I frowned. I supposed she was frowning at him, too, but when she answered him, she didn't say anything like I expected her to. She said, "Maggie?" in a horrified tone. "I don't believe it."

"Well, she is."

"Because Chuck Sellers said so?"

"Because she's going to church there."

"Since when?"

"The last two or three Sundays."

She let out her breath. "Oh, for heaven's sake. You and your Chuck Sellers. She probably went there once or twice to see what it was like—though why anybody would want to, I can't imagine. But I suppose one of those Polacks who voted for her asked her to, and I suppose she felt she had to. Really, Orn. To make a great big something out of nothing."

"Have you ever known of a drop-in visitor at the Methodist church to sing in the choir?"

"What's that got to do with anything?"

"Have you?"

"No."

"Well, all right. She sang in the choir there Christmas Eve at their midnight hoopla. She even sang a solo."

It was quiet again.

"Well," she said, sounding a little uncertain. "Maybe they asked her to. Maggie has a very fine soprano voice. Everybody knows that."

"Then why hasn't she ever sung at the Methodist church?"

"Because she never comes to the Methodist church."

And again it was quiet.

146

"Well, but," she went on, "a lot of people don't come to church who ought to. And Maggie's girls come to the Methodist Church to Sunday School. Why, they have for years. What would they be doing in our Sunday School if they were Catholics?"

"What's the Goodman kid doing there?"

She sighed. A long sigh. "It just isn't possible."

I wished I was home. I wished I was anywhere but where I was.

Her skirts started rustling again.

"Where are you going?"

"To call Marcella. I haven't seen her since the weekend. First she was sick for three days, and then today I was at Bernice's playing bridge."

He snorted.

"Well, really, Orn, I'm not going to sit home all the time. If you don't like it, you'll just have to not like it. If you'd learn to play bridge, you'd stop calling it a waste of time. It can be very stimulating."

He snorted again, and she rustled out. I hoped he'd go after her, so I could get out of there. But he didn't. He just paced around, and then she was back.

"Well?"

She sighed again. "Yes. It's true. I don't know why Marcella couldn't have called and told me." She sighed another time. "I just can't believe it. I've always admired Maggie so much, and she's had such a struggle raising those two children all by herself. When they weren't even really hers to begin with. And now to have a thing like this happen. It just doesn't seem fair. Orn . . ."

"What?"

"Couldn't you talk to her?"

"Are you out of your mind?"

"Well, she surely can't be very much of a Catholic if she's gotten along all these years without going there to church."

"If she's a Catholic, she's a Catholic."

147

"Well, yes, I suppose you're right."

"And what do you think her chances would have been of getting elected to the auditor's office if people had known she was?"

"Well, yes, I suppose that's right, too."

"God damned connivers, every last one of them. No wonder she was so anxious to get into that office. And now coming up with an answer for the bank. I suppose she figured she'd end up running the whole damn town. Well, we'll do a job on her."

Whether or not she frowned at him, her voice did. "You act as if you're pleased about it."

"You bet your sweet life I'm pleased about it." He didn't sound pleased. He sounded bullish.

"Well, I don't see why."

"I wouldn't expect you to. You don't understand these things."

"I'm sure I don't know what 'things' you're talking about," she said in the same tone of voice I used with Kate when she lorded something over me, "but I understand perfectly well what it means to have two children to feed and clothe and house —and now her father-in-law, too. If you take Maggie's job away from her, how will she make a living?"

"That's her worry."

Julia got even angrier. "Orn, I'm ashamed of you. All right, so Maggie's a Catholic. I don't like that any better than you do, but, after all, she can't help being what she is. She certainly wouldn't have chosen to be one if she'd had any say in the matter. And there are worse things. She could be a drunkard or a —a thief. And she certainly isn't either of those."

"I wouldn't put it past her."

"Orn!" This time she banged a table. Or rapped on it, anyhow, with her ring hand. And she told him she wouldn't listen to him talk that way.

He grumbled something about there wasn't any point in any more talk of any kind. He'd made up his mind to get Maggie out, and that was that.

She said just because he'd made up his mind didn't mean he'd be able to do it.

He said who did she think ran the Democrat party in Rose County?

She said he might run the Democrat party, but he didn't run the Republican party, too, and there were more Republicans than there were Democrats. As far as that went, he'd have a hard time getting other influential Democrats to go along with him. His own father, for one. And Warren White for another. After what Maggie had done for Warren White, he'd certainly campaign for her, and considering how well liked he was around the county, his backing would carry a lot of weight.

"Warren White," he said, "won't be campaigning for her."

"How can you say that?"

"He has political ambitions of his own."

"Well? I don't see that that—"

"He can't get anywhere with his ambitions without me."

The room was quiet again.

"And you intend to . . . ?" She didn't finish.

"Exactly."

"Orn, that's despicable."

"Maybe it is," he said, as if he didn't care whether it was or not. "It also happens to be politics."

"Well," she said after a minute, "politics or no politics, I can't believe Warren would turn his back on Maggie now, whether you like it or not. He may not be as ambitious as you think he is."

"You don't know your friend Warren very well."

"I suppose you do."

"Why do you think he fawns all over everybody the way he does? Because he gives a good God damn about them? He's thinking of the time when he'll need their votes. And why do you think he's been toadying up to me the last few months? He wants to run for the state senate next year."

"Well, he surely doesn't need you to run for that. After all, we do have open primaries, don't we?"

149

He snorted and said couldn't she get any understanding at all of politics through her head? Open primaries didn't mean a thing. Whoever had the party backing won. In any case, it took money to run for public office, and Warren White didn't have that kind of money.

She said she didn't see how it could cost very much to run for the state senate, and he snorted again and said did she think he'd waste his time on Warren White if it was only a state senate seat at stake? Warren White had a bigger political future in mind than that.

She said she couldn't understand why he'd want to waste his time on Warren White, whatever he had in mind, considering how he felt about him.

He said he didn't have to like the son of a bitch to recognize his political potential. Anyhow, his spinelessness could be turned into an asset. Unlike Maggie, Warren White wasn't likely to forget which side his bread was buttered on. Or who was doing the buttering.

"Well, I don't care," she said after a bit. "I can't believe Warren could be so mean and contemptible he'd turn against Maggie, even if it means giving up his political future. If it wasn't for Maggie, he might not have any future at all."

He grunted.

"And you're forgetting," she said in a more spirited way than I had ever heard her talk, "how well liked Maggie is herself. And everybody I've ever heard say anything about it thinks she's a good auditor, too. So you can scheme all you want to about doing a job on her, but so far as I can see, you don't have much of anything to do it with."

He roared at her as if she'd bitten him.

I thought I must have missed something. I thought she must have missed whatever it was, too, because she didn't say anything about the profanity he used. She didn't say anything at all for a long time.

"Well," she said finally, as if she wanted to laugh but was too close to crying to be able to do it, "I've often wondered, and now I know. You weren't even at the lumberyard that night, were you, Orn? It was you Priscilla Rogers shot."

While I was still trying to figure that out, and before he had a chance to say anything back, the front door opened, and Mary Louise came in, calling out, "Hi, Daddy. When'd you get back?"

"Just now," he said.

Julia went to greet her, and Mary Louise said, "Mother, what's the matter?"

"Nothing. I just got something in my eye is all."

"Oh. Where's Nathaniel?"

"Upstairs in his room reading, I imagine. Why?"

"Kate said to send Angel home."

I started trembling again.

"Why, she's already gone home. Or at least I thought she had. They certainly are being awfully quiet if they're here."

I wondered that they couldn't hear us shake.

"Look there in the coat closet," Julia said, and I clamped a hand over my mouth. "Oh, never mind. She must be upstairs in his room with him. Go on up, will you, dear, and tell her, while I get supper started. I don't know what's keeping El-mira."

"Her new boyfriend, probably," Mary Louise said as she started upstairs.

Julia rustled on out toward the kitchen. I held my breath to see if Orn would go or stay.

He went. Into the downstairs bathroom and shut the door. I figured he needed to, after all they'd been through. I did myself.

Not that I wasted any time thinking about that. Quick as a flash Nathaniel and I got up—my legs aching so, I could hardly stand—and pushed the end of the davenport out and wriggled past it. I grabbed Nathaniel's hand and flew on tiptoe to the coat closet, where I grabbed my coat and galoshes and his coat.

He frowned at me, and started to grab his galoshes, but I tugged no at him. Then we tiptoed to the front door and opened it as quietly as we could.

We made it to the porch all right. I threw my coat on, then jammed my feet into my galoshes and started buckling them. "Put your coat on," I hissed at Nathaniel. "You don't want them to guess you were in the living room, do you? You've got to look like you just came in from outside. Come on."

We hurried down the walk to the sidewalk, and my heart nearly stopped all over again. The Fletchers' hired girl, Elmira, was standing under a street light on the corner across the street with her boyfriend.

I clutched Nathaniel's arm and frowned over at her. Then I relaxed. They were necking. When people were necking, I'd learned, they didn't pay any attention to anything else.

"But what'll I say?" Nathaniel asked.

"Hell's bells, Nathaniel, don't you ever do anything you're not supposed to and have something figured out to cover it? Say you've been uptown for something. To the library. For a book."

"I don't have a book with me."

"Well, say you couldn't find the one you wanted. Here. Stand in the snow a bit."

"Why?"

"Then your Aunt Julia probably won't even ask you where you've been. She'll be too busy noticing you've been out without your galoshes. You know how mothers are about that. Pinch your cheeks, Nathaniel."

He pinched.

I sighed. "Well, I've got to go." I didn't wish now I was at home. I wished I didn't have to go home at all.

"Angel . . ."

"What?"

He frowned down at the snow a bit. Then he peered at me in that sidewise way of his. "I don't think—well, they probably didn't really mean any of what they said."

I hoped his Aunt Julia wouldn't ask him where he'd been.

"It's okay," I said.

"Well," he said. He stuck his hand out, and I shook it.

I'd just started off when a car whooshed up to the curb, and Ellen Fletcher got out and waved to the boy driving it. "See you."

He raced the engine and roared off.

"Nathaniel," she said, "what are you doing standing out here in the cold? And what are you doing without your galoshes on?"

As they went into the house, I set out for home thinking what a dandy mother Ellen was going to make.

Chapter Seven

On the way home I told myself that since the trick with Nathaniel's galoshes was working so well, and I was a better liar than he was, I ought to be able to work a few tricks of my own.

The thing was to act nonchalant.

Assuming it meant what I thought it did.

I practiced acting nonchalant past the Bedfords' and the Taylors' and the McIntyres'.

Hi, Maggie. I know you're wondering what kept me so long at Nathaniel's. Well, I just couldn't get away, that's all.

"Heck," I said, and scuffed at the snow.

I went past two vacant lots.

Hi, Maggie. Remember what happened to you that day at the courthouse? Well, the same thing happened to me. I was all set to come home at least a half hour ago, and Mr. Fletcher could see I was, but he came in and sat down as if I had all the time in the world, talking on and on about one thing and another, nothing of any importance, until finally, when I had all I could do not to ask him to leave—

I wondered if maybe I could just sweep in the door and give them all a thin-lipped smile, and they'd be so astounded, they wouldn't think to ask me anything.

Only my lip cracked when I tried to curl it.

And then it hit me that even if they didn't ask me anything, how could I not tell Maggie Mr. Fletcher was going to try to get her out of the auditor's office? I didn't know what she could do about it, but I was sure she could do something.

The thing was, she had to know.

Maggie, I heard the most peculiar thing while I was standing in the hallway at the Fletchers' putting my galoshes on. I can't think why Mr. Fletcher would have said it, because he could see me standing right there. In fact, he was buckling my galoshes for me. And he looked up at Mrs. Fletcher and said, excuse my language, but we've got to get that God damned woman out of the auditor's office.

I wondered if maybe I could write her an anonymous letter.

I went past the Peterkins'.

Well, I don't know why you're all staring at me like I was late or something. It's only four-thirty, isn't it?

I was home.

I could see Grandpa through the window sitting at the kitchen table, laughing about something. I wished I had something to laugh about.

I figured maybe they were all out there, and maybe I could sneak in the front door and get my coat and galoshes off and pretend to be asleep on the davenport, but I hadn't any more than opened the door when Maggie called out from the kitchen, "Is that you, Angel?"

So there went my last hope.

"Yes," I called back. I went to the coat closet to put my things away, still trying to think of something.

"Well, come on," she called again.

So I went out to the kitchen. I hadn't been able to think of anything that was any good anyhow.

Maggie was making gravy. "Are your hands clean?"

Kate was carrying a bowl of mashed potatoes to the table. "Pour the milk, will you?"

Grandpa was working on a crossword puzzle. "Angel, who is that idolatrous Egyptian sun god in two letters I never can remember?"

I just stood there and stared at them, my teeth still chattering from the cold.

At least I thought it was the cold, until Grandpa jumped up from the table, almost knocking the potatoes out of Kate's hands, and came running over to me and knelt down and said, "Angel —love, love. What is it?"

Maggie turned from the stove and started toward me, and Kate, too, and then I blew the whole thing as I fell against Grandpa and blubbered at him, "Oh, Grandpa, he said Catholics are God damned, and he said my father never amounted to anything!"

Although Maggie was more concerned about what I had overheard than how I'd managed to overhear it—she said she'd been trapped that way herself once, only she was fifteen, and it wasn't behind a davenport, it was behind a screen, when her brother was telling some girl he couldn't live without her, and Maggie started shaking so hard with laughter she knocked the screen down, and he nearly skinned her alive—she was less concerned about what effect, if any, it might have on her than she was about the effect it might have on me. And Kate.

"Orn Fletcher," she said, "is a bigot."

I frowned at her through blurry eyes. "What's a bigot?"

She considered a bit. "Someone who's so opinionated, especially about the church he goes to, he can't stand for other people to have some other opinion or go to some other church. So he says a lot of things about them, and about their church, that aren't true."

"Because he wants to hurt their feelings?"

"No. He doesn't think about their feelings."

I hiccupped. "Then why?"

"Because he wants to discredit their opinion and their church."

I frowned at her again. "But if the things he says aren't true, how can he? I mean, why would anybody believe him?"

"Well, that's just it," Maggie said. "Hardly anybody does."

I think she might have let it go at that, but Kate spoke up. "What about when people here were burning crosses?"

Maggie looked at Kate for a bit. "I thought you were too young to remember that."

"No," Kate said. "I remember it. A little anyhow."

Maggie sighed. "Well, there was a time, some years back, when the Ku Klux Klan filled people's heads with a lot of malicious nonsense about the Catholic Church and got everyone so worked up—" She broke off to ask us if we knew what the Ku Klux Klan was.

I said I didn't, and Kate said she didn't really, so Maggie told us what it was and some of the things it had done, including, in a general way, the incident involving Priscilla Rogers, finishing up by saying that the Klan was long dead and done with and most people in Roseville were ashamed they'd ever had anything to do with it.

"There are a few people around here," she went on to say, "who are still so prejudiced against Catholics, they'll say— and believe—almost anything about them. Like Orn Fletcher. And Julia, too, I suppose," she added, shaking her head, "though I can't help feeling sorry for Julia, she's such a nice person in every other respect. Anyhow, the thing to do is just not let what they say bother you, because they're ignorant people. If they weren't, they wouldn't talk the way they do. Here, Angel." She took a handkerchief out of her apron pocket and handed it to me, and I blew my nose.

"Indeed," Grandpa said, nodding to me, "Mr. Fletcher has provided you with a way to show God you love Him."

"He has?" I frowned at him over the handkerchief. "How?"

"Well, now, and why did God send His only begotten Son, our blessed Lord and Saviour, Jesus Christ, to suffer and die on the Cross for us?"

I frowned at him some more. "Because God loves us?"

Grandpa beamed. "That's right. And when we are called upon to suffer the Orn Fletchers of this world, how do we do it?"

That one I couldn't frown my way through. "I don't know," I said.

"We do it for Christ's sake, to show God how much we, in our turn, love Him."

"We do?"

He nodded at me again.

"But, Grandpa—"

"Yes, love?"

I shook my head. "Nothing." I wanted to ask him why suffering for Christ's sake was all right when getting back just now for Christ's sake wasn't, but I was afraid of being a jerk. I was having enough trouble trying to figure out how God the Father and God the Son and God the Holy Ghost could be one Person and three people all at the same time and in different places.

Grandpa went on to say that the Catholic Church was the one, true faith, and poor, miserable sinners though we were, we were fortunate indeed to have been born into it by the grace of God.

Which was something else I wanted to ask him—why Kate and I had been going to Sunday School at the Methodist church all our lives and Maggie hadn't been going anywhere at all, when the one, true faith was right over there on East Washington Street.

I'd tried asking Kate, but she only shrugged her shoulders and said she didn't know. Then I'd worked up enough nerve to ask Maggie.

Maggie said it was a long story, so I sat down to listen, but she just went and stared out of the window for a while and then said hadn't I better practice my piano lesson. Which meant it was something sticky, and there was no use asking.

So I let it go.

As for my father, Maggie said he'd been a fine man and—well, after all, he'd been Grandpa's own son, and didn't Kate and I think Grandpa was someone special?

She also said a man didn't have to be rich to amount to something. As for the house being mortgaged, almost everybody who owned a house these days had a mortgage on it.

I wanted to ask her more about him while we were on the subject, since we seldom ever were, but I didn't know what Kate might do.

The year before, when Maggie had dug an old winter coat of Kate's out of the cedar chest for me to start wearing, Kate had taken one look at it and burst into tears.

When Maggie asked her what on earth was the matter, she said that was the coat Maggie had bought for her to wear to our father's funeral in Chicago, and she'd been so thrilled at owning a brand-new coat it was all she could think of when she was walking down the aisle of the church. How could she have been so callous? And she started crying again.

In the interest of one of us in an evening being enough, I let that go, too.

For her own part, if Maggie was surprised to hear that Orn Fletcher had made up his mind to get her out of office, she didn't let on. She just said it would take more than Orn Fletcher to do it. Then she grinned at me. "If they can't lick Mr. Gilligan—"

I grinned back at her and clapped my hands. "—they can't lick me!"

Who Mr. Gilligan was or had been, or who "they" were, or why they couldn't lick him, I didn't know. It was just a refrain Maggie had taught us that we used at different times. Times like that one.

In view of what I'd been through, Maggie may have said it to reassure me, but I don't think so. I think at that moment she was fired up by the idea of Orn trying to take her on. Maggie liked a challenge.

And, like Julia Fletcher, she felt she had more going for her than Orn realized. She knew how well liked she was around the county, and since she would have the record of her first four years to run on, she'd have an advantage over any candidate he might put up against her.

But there were other advantages, too, which she could expect to accrue to her from her years as auditor, the advantages of having been beholden—the jobs she'd found, the tax deadlines she'd managed to get extended, the other favors she'd done wherever she could, like getting up in the middle of the night to drive a sick woman to the hospital over in the next county, or arranging for a needy family to get county relief— the kind of favors the people she'd helped, and their relatives and friends, weren't likely to forget when it came time to vote.

Nor were the bank directors likely to forget her after what she had done for them, and they were all influential men, whether Democrats or Republicans.

As for Warren White, she had more than Julia Fletcher's conviction that he couldn't be so mean and contemptible as to turn against her. He had stopped up to see her that very day and had sworn to her, as God was his witness, he'd campaign the whole county for her reelection.

All in all, Maggie saw little reason to worry. And since she wasn't worried, neither was I.

I suppose you could say that in a way, Maggie's situation right then was like that of the new Northern State Bank and Trust Company—everything seemed just fine.

Both of the weekly papers, the *Democrat* and the *Republican,* had come out that afternoon with banner headlines and front-page stories about the merger—the forty thousand dollars Maggie had secured from the state to keep the Roseville Bank and Trust Company from going under having enabled the two banks to proceed with it at once, without waiting for the RFC.

There was no mention in either account, of course, of the crisis at the Roseville Bank and Trust Company or of the roles Warren White and Maggie had played in it. To have made a public revelation even then of the old bank's near failure would have been, in those shaky times, to invite a run on its successor—of which, curiously enough, Warren White had been appointed cashier, though not, as would be seen later, without certain restrictions placed upon the office.

Instead, the merger was described as a move on the part of the boards of directors of both the Roseville Bank and Trust Company and the Northern State Bank toward strengthening their financial position—and thus the financial position of all of their depositors—and the wisdom of this move was confirmed by pointing out—at some length and in laudatory prose—the fine rating accorded the new Northern State Bank and Trust Company.

In all the describing and extolling, there was something else the papers didn't mention.

One Friday near the end of January, I had gone to Ward's with Nathaniel after school and then gone home and was playing double solitaire with Grandpa when I realized I'd left my catechism in my desk, and I needed it for Sunday. So, as late as it was, I had to go back to school to get it.

Just as the Catholics didn't call church church, so, I had learned, they didn't call Sunday School Sunday School. They called it Catechism, and instead of being held before, it was held afterward.

Nobody ever said it would be a sin if you didn't go to Catechism. Sin didn't come into it. You just went. But in spite of the fact—and to my relief—it was in English, it was so different from anything I'd ever encountered, it was worth it.

At the Methodist church, Sunday School was in two parts.

During the first part, the different classes met in separate rooms and did whatever it was their class was doing. The primary classes sang "Jesus Wants Me for a Sunbeam" and talked about how God made flowers to bloom and rain to fall and children to be good little boys and girls, which took better with the girls than it did with the boys.

In our class that year the teacher had been reading Bible stories to us. Since the boys were always sticking pins in the girls or untying our sashes and we were frowning at them or jabbing our elbows into them, we sometimes missed the moral of the story—I thought, for instance, that Lot's wife was turned into salt for not looking where she was going—in which case

161

the teacher would point the moral out, and that would be our Thought for the day.

During the second part of Sunday School, all the classes would go down—or up, as the case might be—into the church to sing hymns and listen to Mr. Wurlitzer make his talks and read his announcements and, if it was Christmas or Easter or Children's Sunday or some other special occasion, have a program of poems and piano pieces and the like.

Catechism wasn't anything like that.

There was only one class, made up of children from the first grade to high school. And we met right in the church, down in the front pews, our teacher the priest himself, Father Kolchek.

There were no hymns, no announcements, no poems, no piano pieces, no blooming flowers or falling rain or Jesus wanting anybody for a sunbeam. There weren't even any Bible stories.

We got right down to business.

"In the name of the Father, and of the Son, and of the Holy Ghost, Amen," Father Kolchek would say, and we with him, all of us crossing ourselves.

He would glance at his catechism. "From the first lesson," he would say, pointing to some first-grader. "Who made the world?"

"God made the world," the first-grader would answer.

"Who is God?" He'd point to another first-grader.

"God is—is—is—the Creator of Heaven and earth, and of all things."

"Very good," he might say. Then he would point to somebody else. "What is man?"

"Man is a creature composed of body and soul, and made to the image and likeness of God."

He would nod to the same kid and ask, "Is this likeness in the body or in the soul?"

The kid would nod back at him—right in the spirit of the thing—and answer, "This likeness is chiefly in the soul."

So you'd quick sneak a look at the next question—Q. How

is the soul like to God? *A.* The soul is like to God because it is a spirit that will never die, and has understanding and free will—and then he'd fool you by saying, "From the second lesson. What is God?" and point at you.

Your mind would race ahead to the second lesson—what is God, what is God, what is God—and you'd take a breath and blurt out, "God is a spirit infinitely perfect." It didn't do to say God is perfect, or God is infinite, or God is a spirit, or God is anything but exactly what the answer in the catechism said He was.

Even a question which sounded as if it would take a simple yes or no, didn't.

"Had God a beginning?"

"God had no beginning; He always was and He always will be."

"Does God see us?"

"God sees us and watches over us."

"Does God know all things?"

"God knows all things, even our most secret thoughts, words, and actions."

The Catholics didn't waste questions any more than they wasted time.

And if you wanted to squirm at God knowing your most secret thoughts, the place to do it was at home while you were studying your catechism. Otherwise, you might find yourself staring at Father Kolchek, while everybody else stared at you, waiting for you to answer some question he'd obviously just asked you. "I'm sorry, Father. I didn't hear you."

"Is there but one God?"

An easy one. "Yes; there is but one God."

To the boy next to you. "Why can there be but one God?"

"There can be but one God because—because—because—"

You put your hand up over your mouth and coughed and then whispered, "God, being supreme and infinite—"

"—because God, being supreme and infinite, can't—"

Father Kolchek: "Cannot."

"—cannot have an equal."

Whew.

To Kate: "How many persons are there in God?"

"In God there are three Divine Persons, really distinct, and equal in all things—the Father, the Son, and the Holy Ghost." Good old Kate.

To Kate again: "Can we fully understand how the three Divine Persons are one and the same God?"

"We cannot fully understand how the three Divine Persons are one and the same God—"

You said it, kid, I thought. And then thought, oh, dear, the Lord knows what I'm thinking.

"—because this is a mystery."

You had to be on your toes all the time. If it wasn't Father Kolchek, it was God Himself.

Father Kolchek flipped some pages and pointed to a big boy in the back row. "From the eleventh lesson. Why did Christ found the Church?"

"Christ founded the Church to teach, govern, sanctify, and save all men."

"Are all bound to belong to the Church?"

"All are bound to belong to the Church."

"And—?"

Not as easy as it had sounded. A flurry of pages turning.

He had to admit he didn't know. Criminy!

Another boy did. "All are bound to belong to the Church, and he who knows the Church to be the true Church and remains out of it cannot be saved."

It was enough to make you sigh. Somebody had come up with the right answer, and we were all of us going to be saved —assuming we did all the things we had to, which, for Kate and me right now, along with six first-graders, meant learning enough catechism to be ready to make our First Holy Communion in April.

As I trudged back to school to pick up my catechism, I thought how lucky Kate and I were that God—or Grandpa,

164

anyhow, through the grace of God—had snatched us out of the hands of Mr. Wurlitzer and away from the Gates of Hell.

I only wished the Catholics, who weren't Temperance at all, would sing "Right on the Corner Where You Are" once in a while. I did miss that.

The school building was still open, and there were lights on in some of the rooms where I supposed the janitor was sweeping up, but the downstairs hall was deserted, and so were all the rooms I went by. Or I thought they were.

I'd gotten my catechism and started back out, when I came up to the third-grade room. There was Miss McCray still in there sitting at her desk. And the blackboard not cleaned off, which struck me as odd, because as soon as the last bell rang, she always collared some poor kid who wasn't fast enough on his feet.

I tiptoed by, hoping she wouldn't see me and stick me with the job. I had to get home and study my catechism, didn't I?

But after I'd made it by, I stopped and wondered if something could be the matter with her. She had the sharpest eyes and ears of anybody in the entire school. Even if she hadn't seen or heard me this time, she must have heard me when I'd gone by before, not knowing there was anything to be quiet about.

Hell's bells, I thought. And then thought I shouldn't have thought it. Only it was too late by then.

Being a Catholic was no breeze.

I sighed and went back almost to her door. Then, after arguing with myself for a little bit, I went the rest of the way.

She still didn't seem to know I was there.

"Miss McCray—" I said.

She didn't stir.

I wondered if I'd only thought I'd said her name out loud. I took a couple of steps into the room. "Miss McCray—"

She turned her head then to look at me, but not in her usual way of at you and into you, right through to your very soul. She didn't seem to even see me.

"It's Angelica," I said. I didn't know whether I felt more scared or more like a jerk.

She nodded. "Yes, Angelica."

Miss McCray was a thin person anyhow. Now, with the spirit gone out of her voice and the snap gone out of her eyes, she looked little and frail and old.

"Do you want—I had to come back to school for my—for something, and I was just going by, and I—" I was babbling again. I swallowed. "Do you want me to clean your blackboard and erasers?"

She reacted as if she didn't know what I was talking about —like, what blackboard? But then she turned and looked, and sure enough, there was a blackboard there needing to be cleaned.

She turned back to me. "That would be kind of you."

I was glad to have it to do. Anything was better than standing there seeing her look like that.

After erasing the blackboard, I went to the cloakroom and got the pail and filled it with water in the girls' restroom. Then I got the cloth to wash the blackboard with and started in.

From time to time I stole a look at her over my shoulder, but she'd just be sitting there, the same as she had before.

There was a letter open on her desk, but I couldn't make out who it was from or what it said, only that it was typewritten. I wondered if maybe somebody she cared about had died. It seemed to me it would have to be somebody she cared about an awful lot to act like this. Maybe a sister or a brother. I figured she was too old to have some man to love.

I thought I probably ought to say something to her, like, it certainly is cold out, isn't it, or, how did your day at school go, or something, to take her mind off what was bothering her, but I couldn't bring myself to say things like that to her even when there wasn't anything bothering her, so I just kept on washing the blackboard and wringing out the cloth. And thinking how still it was.

166

I wished she'd say something to me, ask me a question, even, so I'd know she was all right. But she didn't say a word.

When she finally did, it startled me so, I jumped.

"All my life," she said. "All my life."

I didn't know what to say to that. All your life what? What all your life? It wasn't exactly a remark you could respond to. And she didn't seem to be saying it to me anyhow. I wasn't even sure she knew she'd said it out loud. So I went on washing and wringing, wondering what she could have been doing all her life she'd just found out she shouldn't have.

Sinning?

I wiped my hands against the sides of my skirt and went over to my coat and took a handkerchief out of the pocket and wiped my nose—in case she asked me what I was doing. Then I picked up my catechism and turned to the lesson on sin. The last question was the one I was looking for.

Q. Which are the chief sources of sin?

A. The chief sources of sin are seven: Pride, Covetousness, Lust, Anger, Gluttony, Envy, and Sloth; and they are commonly called capital sins.

I wasn't sure what all of them were, but none of them sounded like anything Miss McCray would have anything to do with.

I went back to the blackboard. What, then?

She'd been teaching all her life, or most of it. But I didn't think that could be something she'd feel this bad about, or she would have quit when she'd had our class.

I didn't know enough about her to know what else she could have been doing all her life, other than things everybody did, like eating and sleeping and listening to the radio and wishing they were rich instead of poor—except that since she was so obsessed about saving money, she likely wasn't as poor as everybody else.

I'd finished the blackboard, so I dried my hands against my skirt again and put my coat on and gathered up the erasers and

took them outside to beat them against the side of the building—and got to thinking about the time two years before when
Miss McCray had taken our class on the field trip to the Roseville Bank and Trust Company.

She had introduced Warren White to us, saying he'd been
one of her third-grade pupils a long time ago when she'd first
started teaching.

One of her best pupils, she added, who always knew his lessons. And then he'd grown up and started working for the bank,
and now, along with Mr. Elliott, who was the cashier of the
Northern State Bank, he had the safekeeping of all the money
of the business community and of people like herself and our
fathers and mothers, and wasn't it a fine thing to know their
money was in such trustworthy hands.

I remembered looking at his hands and thinking they looked
like anybody else's hands, except they were cleaner.

She said she hoped our little trip to the bank would add to
our understanding of what she meant when she said America
was the best country to live in in the whole world, because it was
a free country.

Did we remember last week talking about how people in
America were free to worship God as they chose? And how our
parents were free to elect the men they wanted to govern them?
And how we had free public schools so we could learn to read
and write and spell?

Then she rapped on Mr. White's desk and told Bobby Jackson to keep his hands off that inkwell—nobody was to touch
anything—and straighten up and pay attention. His father
paid good tax money to send him to school, and he wasn't to
waste it.

I couldn't figure out how school could be free if it cost
Bobby Jackson's father money, but it was awfully stuffy in the
bank with our coats on and everybody jammed together, and
I'd been watching Genevieve McIntrye's nose running, so I
supposed I'd missed something.

Well, she went on, another thing America had was free enterprise, which meant that Mr. Werner could own a clothing store, and Mr. Blakely of the B & B could own one, too, and they could compete with each other for our mothers' trade. It was the same with all kinds of stores, big and little, all over America. And banks were the backbone of this great free enterprise system, because banks loaned the money needed to start a store. And where did banks get the money they loaned?

My nose was running, too, by that time.

Banks, she said, got their money from people like our parents and herself, who worked hard and saved something out of what they earned. And when they put that money in the bank, it was called investing it, because banks paid you for the privilege of using your money to lend to somebody else.

I wished somebody would lend me a handkerchief.

So when you saved money—and she hoped we would all develop the habit of saving, a person was never too young to start—you were not only helping to keep America a free country, you were also building up security for your old age.

What it all seemed to boil down to when she finally got through, by which time I'd had to use my coat sleeve, was we should put our trust in banks, which appealed to me a lot more than putting money in them did.

Which made me think now of what Julia Fletcher had said to the other Coke ladies that afternoon just as Nathaniel and I were coming into Ward's after school, which had struck me as queer. She jiggled an envelope at them and said, "Well, it looks like I'll get half of Mama's money back from the Roseville Bank and Trust Company anyhow. Maybe more."

When I got home, I asked Grandpa what she meant. His explanation, in simplified form, was the something else the papers hadn't mentioned.

When the Roseville Bank and Trust Company and the Northern State Bank merged, they had, of course, under the terms of the merger, to pool their assets, both good and—in bank terminology—slow. But in order for the new Northern State Bank and Trust Company to stay in business, and to operate on any kind of sound footing, those slow assets (such as foreclosed mortgages) had to be liquidated.

To permit the liquidation of those slow assets, a majority of the depositors—also now pooled—had to sign a waiver settling for a return of whatever amount on the dollar the court-appointed conservator was able to collect, the money collected—when, as, and if it was—to be distributed to the depositors.

From the majority point of view, a return to all depositors of fifty cents or seventy-five cents or more on the dollar was better than risking a total loss or, as in the case of many banks which failed during the Depression, receiving such a meager return on the bank's liquidated assets as to make it not much better than nothing, and the majority point of view prevailed.

But the intellectual soundness of a majority point of view does little to assuage the feelings—or mitigate the shock—of the individuals composing that majority, especially after experiencing, as each of them must have, such blessed relief—and warm security—upon reading in glowing terms in the *Democrat* or the *Republican* or both that the merger had strengthened the financial position of the depositors and that the rating accorded the new bank was a fine one.

Or, as Grandpa put it to me that afternoon, it must be a hard, hard thing to lose even a part of your money, especially if you were old, and it was your life's savings.

I always tried to keep my head turned whenever I was beating erasers, so the chalk dust wouldn't blow in my face, but it always did, and it did now. I finished up with a sneeze and went back inside.

And then it hit me.

Miss McCray must have received a letter, too, telling her she wasn't going to get back all of the money she'd been putting in the Roseville Bank and Trust Company all her life.

I stood stock still for a minute.

And after she'd trusted them so, and let them use her money to help Mr. Werner and Mr. Blakely start their stores so she'd have something for her old age.

Criminy.

I was glad I wasn't Mr. White. If he was as smart as she claimed he was, he'd stick his trustworthy old hands in his pockets when he saw her coming, so maybe she wouldn't think to say anything to him.

Even so, I didn't know how he could ever look her in the face again. I had a hard enough time of it myself, and I'd never done anything more than say I'd do something she wanted and then not do it, like saying I'd try to save the twenty-four cents at Christmas, which I'd spent so long ago I couldn't remember now what I'd spent it on. Candy, probably.

I wondered if that had been a sin. Maybe I should mark it down for my first confession. "Bless me, father, for I have sinned. This is my first confession, and I am accused of the following sins: I told Miss McCray—"

On the other hand, my first confession wasn't until April, and there was a thing at the end that went, "For all these sins and those I have forgotten and those of my past life . . ." It could be part of my past life.

I bet Mr. White wished the bank was part of his past life, and that Miss McCray was, too.

When I went in with the erasers, she had one hand up at the side of her face, which gave me a queasy feeling. I hoped it was only the light bothering her eyes.

I distributed the erasers along the blackboard and then leaned down to pick up the pail of water to dump it out. As I did so, she blew her nose.

My skin crawled.

I wanted to be away from there so fast I slopped some water out of the pail carrying it out. I didn't want to go back either, but I had to—as far as the cloakroom, anyhow, to put the pail away. So I did. Then I just stood there like a jerk, listening to her blow her nose some more and wondering what I ought to do.

I wished Grandpa was there.

I wished I hadn't forgotten my catechism in the first place.

171

My gosh, I thought, does it have to matter all that much to her?

I tried to think what Kate would do if she were me, but since she wasn't me, that didn't help.

I supposed I could go in there and tell her I was sorry she'd lost so much money, but if she was anything like me, that would only make her cry more.

I wished she didn't have to cry. Crying wasn't so bad when kids did it. Kids were always doing it. But grown people shouldn't.

Maybe the thing was to pretend she wasn't. Just go in there and say, well, Miss McCray, I'm all finished, and if you are, too, why don't you go on home?

That was the thing to do. It would let her know I knew she felt bad, without being sticky about it.

I marched over to the doorway and opened my mouth so I'd be all set when she looked at me. Only she didn't. She had the letter clenched in her hands, with her head down on them.

I stood there for a minute, but she didn't look up. I tried to say something anyhow, but even after I swallowed a couple of times, I couldn't get anything to come out. So I finally just turned and left. I figured there wasn't anything I could have said to her anyhow that would bring her money back. And that was what she wanted, not me babbling away about me being finished and go on home. She'd go home when she felt like it.

When I came out of the building a gust of wind hit me. I shivered and stuck my hands in my pockets. As for the money, I supposed she'd manage somehow.

That was what other people were always having to do when they lost their jobs or had another baby or needed a new coat and couldn't buy one. They managed somehow.

I hunched up my shoulders against the wind and headed down Main Street. I supposed it was all part of having a Depression.

Chapter Eight

In spite of his active participation in the Klan, I've often thought that if Maggie had been willing to play along with Orn, giving him the contracts he wanted, he would have been willing to overlook the fact that she turned out to be a Catholic, choosing to regard it as Julia and most other people in Roseville regarded it when they first heard about it—as a misfortune, a peculiarity, a flaw in the character of an otherwise admirable woman.

Perhaps he might have been willing to overlook it even so if she hadn't poked fun at him, reminding him not only of the humiliation he had suffered at the hands of Priscilla Rogers, but of her own rebuff of him, indicating, however unwittingly, by laughing at him that she shared Priscilla's view of him.

Priscilla had made a fool of him and got away with it. That Orn had no intention of letting Maggie do the same he himself made clear when he told Julia that afternoon in my hearing he'd made up his mind a month before to get Maggie out, and by God if she hadn't given him the way to do it.

In view of the chronology of the two things—and his choice of words—it seems unlikely that Orn was motivated even then by pure bigotry, but, though it showed him to be more craven than I would have believed possible for a man of Orn's strength and rectitude, that he intended to use bigotry as the means to achieve the end he had in mind.

Julia's remark during that same conversation that there were worse things than being a Catholic, that Maggie could be a drunkard or a thief, and she certainly wasn't either of those, plus his own retort, made in the heat of anger, "I wouldn't put it past her," may have given him the idea of how to use it.

That and his approach to the problem of what to do about Warren White.

Just when the confrontation between Orn and Warren White took place I don't know, other than it had to have been some time before the second day of March.

Exactly what was said between them I don't know either, but based on what took place afterward as well as on what had taken place before and considering the character and personality of the two men, I would imagine that the conversation between them—once the amenities had been dispensed with— went something like this:

"Well, Orn," (trying to sound hearty and as equal speaking to equal, but without success) "you said you had something you wanted to see me about?"

"Yes. Sit down, Warren." (Spoken with a brusqueness which does nothing to dispel his visitor's constraint.) "I had a talk with Joe Spencer a few days ago." Joe Spencer was the Democratic County Chairman of Jefferson County, an adjacent county which along with Rose County made up the local state senate district. "He gave me the go-ahead on your bid for the senate seat."

"Well, that's fine." (Visibly relieved, he settles back in his chair.)

"So it looks like you're in business."

"Yes, I'd say it does." (A faint blush suffuses the pallor of his skin as he permits himself the satisfaction of contemplating his nearly blighted, miraculously restored, and now at last about-to-flower political career.)

"There's just one thing."

"Yes?" (Some formality, he supposes. A statement to prepare, a committeeman to reassure, a hand to shake, or— Of course. He should have realized at once. The signatures for the primary. He would have to get twenty-five signatures to file for the primary.)

"A matter I need your help on."

(Not a formality, then. Something Orn needed his help on.) "Of course, Orn. Of course. Anything." (His face now pink with pleasure as he realizes how he has misjudged the man.) "Anything at all."

"I want Maggie Crowley out of the auditor's office."

(His mouth falls open, his jaw goes slack.) "You—you—what?"

"I want Maggie Crowley out."

"But—but—but—"

"And I expect you to help me do it."

"You—but how can I? I gave Maggie my word I'd campaign for her. I owe it to her. I—" (He swallows.) "Why do you want her out?"

"Because she's a God damned Catholic, for one thing."

"Well, yes, I know, and I agree with you that it's unfortunate, most unfortunate, but I think we might—under the circumstances—"

"And because she's too God damned independent, for another."

"Well, yes, I—"

"She seems to have forgotten who's running things around here."

(A silence. Rather a long silence.) "Yes, I—I see."

"Well?"

"But Orn, I—what I mean to say is I understand your position, of course, and I—under ordinary circumstances I'd be the first to—I mean, I want you to know I appreciate what it means to have your support, but—but surely, after what she did for me—making it possible for me—surely you can't expect me to—" (He swallows again.)

(With a shrug.) "I understand Lippincott's been talking of retiring in '36."

Charles S. Lippincott was the senior United States Senator (Rep.) from Indiana.

"Yes, I—I heard something to that effect." (Running a finger around the inside of his shirt collar.)

"Even if he doesn't, I think a good, strong candidate on the Democrat ticket can beat him. Somebody the people can get behind. Lippincott's a cold fish."

"Yes, I—yes, he's always struck me that way."

"Of course, it'll take a lot of hard campaigning to do it— with enough money to give our candidate the exposure he needs. And it ought to be a man with legislative experience to back him up. The convention's more likely to go for a man with experience."

"Yes, I—yes. I see that."

(Another shrug.) "Ed Rensler spoke to me the other day about entering the race for the state senate." Ed Rensler owned the Home Hotel on Main Street alongside the Nickel Plate Railroad. "He might not make a bad candidate. Everybody likes Ed."

(Another silence, also rather long.) "I—in other words, it's Maggie or it's me."

"That about says it."

"But I—" (running a finger around the inside of his shirt collar again) "—I don't see how I—I mean, even if I did this thing for you, what's to keep it from backfiring onto me? You have to think about that. I mean, if I talk against Maggie, what's to prevent her from telling everybody what she did for me at the bank?"

"I'd say that's up to you."

"Up to me? But how?"

"By seeing to it she can't bring up the subject of the bank."

(Another silence, longer than either of the others, his face drained now of even its normal pallor, looking a pasty white.) "But I don't see how—I don't see any way—"

"Think it over. You'll see a way."

Thinking it over myself—and thinking back on it—I won-

176

der if the confrontation between Orn and Warren White might not have taken place about two weeks before the second day of March.

I say that because one Saturday morning in the middle of February, when I was spending the day at Maggie's office, she had to go to the bank to make a deposit, and I went with her.

I thought Warren White looked awfully drawn—as much when his smile was coming as going—but then I'd gotten so used to seeing him look that way over the past few months when he thought the bank was going to fail—and I supposed he'd had to face a lot of people since the merger, Miss McCray among them, about playing fast and loose with their hard-earned money—I didn't think too much about it.

In spite of his drawn face he bowed and scraped all over the place to Maggie and, after she'd made her deposit, handed her a piece of paper, saying, "You've got a little note here, Maggie, that's a few days past due. I made a new one out for you to sign."

Maggie looked at the note. "I don't need it for sixty days, Warren. I can meet it next payday." She crossed out the word sixty and wrote in thirty. Then she signed it and gave it back to him. She pulled her change purse out of her pocket. "How much do I owe you?"

He smiled and raised his hand in a deprecatory way. "Just forget the interest."

Maggie opened her purse and took out a couple of dollars. "How can you run a bank if you don't charge interest?"

He smiled again, a rather bleak smile. "I was thinking it's just a little something I can do for you."

Maggie handed him the money. "The only thing I want you to do for me, Warren, is to keep your promise about campaigning for me."

Even as he nodded he looked away from her to a man just coming in the door. Then he turned back and repeated what he had said to her before, his voice shaking a little. "As God is my witness, Maggie."

He handed her some change, and we left, the man who had just come in stepping up now to take our place, Warren White greeting him—wondering, I supposed, if he still had to go on pretending to be interested in the man's wife's flu or his boy Sam's flat tire or the visiting kinfolk now that he no longer had any reason to, because I assumed from what he'd just said to Maggie that, faced with Orn Fletcher's take it or leave it, Warren White had, however disheartened by this death blow to his political ambitions, left it.

The fact that Maggie had had to borrow money from the bank—even so petty a sum that she could pay all of it back out of her next monthly paycheck—may have triggered Warren White's thinking of a way to keep her from bringing up the subject of the bank, but certain elements of the story about Maggie as it was first told, and most of the elements of the story about her as it finally came to be told, suggest that Warren White, in trying to square his conscience, to rationalize his need to view—and portray—Maggie as scoundrel rather than friend, fell back on an incident which had taken place between Maggie and himself early in 1931, for which he had held a slight grudge against her ever since.

The incident involved those securities Maggie had offered to draw upon at the time of the bank crisis, supplying the necessary twenty thousand dollars in bonds to the directors of the two Roseville banks in return for their personal bonds until such time as the directors could replace them.

The securities were the property of the five banks in Rose County, held in escrow by the county because the law required all depositories of county funds as well as state funds to put up collateral in the amount of half the initial deposit.

At the time of Maggie's election to office in 1928, the securities, in the amount of eighty-seven thousand dollars, were stored in the vault of the Roseville Bank and Trust Company, but a couple of years later a man from Chicago who owned a cottage at Cedar Lake and who was a friend of Maggie's suggested to her that in view of the rash of robberies then plaguing small-town banks, she would be better off storing the securities —for which she was personally liable—in one of the large banks in Chicago.

Maggie agreed with him. In any case, though this was some months before the crisis at the Roseville Bank and Trust Company, Maggie was aware—as anybody who read the papers was aware—that robberies weren't the only thing plaguing small-town banks, and she was not so convinced of Warren White's honesty as to be sure he wouldn't make use of some of those bonds which were negotiable if he had to. So she removed the securities from the Roseville Bank and Trust Company and deposited them in her name in Chicago's Continental Illinois Bank.

Stung by what he considered Maggie's lack of trust in him, in spite of her protestation to him that her sole motive in removing the securities was for their better protection, and perhaps reflecting now that had the securities remained in his possession he could have made temporary use of them to shore up the Roseville Bank and Trust Company, in which case he would not have needed Maggie to save it, Warren White was able to conclude, in a comforting if somewhat remarkable turn of thought, that it was Maggie's fault the bank had been brought to the verge of collapse.

His next turn of thought, now that he had established in his mind what amounted to criminal intent on Maggie's part, was to decide he would say she had taken county funds for her own use.

This posed a problem. Such a charge could lead, undoubtedly would lead, to a filing of charges and an investigation by the grand jury, and—most unthinkable of all—to a naming of names.

Actually a dual problem.

How to solve it?

By saying, first of all, that Maggie's embezzlement of funds had been revealed to him in confidence, he himself was revealing it in confidence, certain it would go no further, and by saying—

What?

That the money had been replaced before the embezzlement could be discovered.

Good. But how had the money been replaced?

Somebody—some friend—had given it to her out of his own pocket.

His?

Yes. More logical that it be a man. Not many women had that kind of money to give, and it would be too easy for the two or three or four who were known to have it to deny doing it.

What man, then? With what motive, what undeniable motive, sufficient to want to get Maggie out of a jam?

The sparkling, fiery-headed, best-God-damn-legs-in-town ahhh, Maggie Crowley?

He could, he thought, leave that open.

Only one problem remained: how to get the story spread around town without having to do the distasteful—and risky—job himself.

Warren White must at that point have allowed himself if not a smile—surely he couldn't have *smiled*—a small sigh of relief.

Marcella DeWitt.

All he had to do was tell it to Marcella—tell her in pious tones and with much shaking of head what an unfortunate thing it was that Maggie, whom he had always thought to be honest to a fault, had so betrayed the people's trust in her that etc. etc.

Marcella would take it from there.

And tell it to Marcella he did on the second day of March. Only Marcella did more than take it from there. Marcella gave his anonymous man a name.

Not because she was vicious. Marcella wasn't a vicious person, nor was she so contemptible that she would make a story up out of whole cloth the way Warren White was doing. She was just so empty-headed she believed anything anybody told her, and she was always so thrilled to have something to gossip about—because otherwise nobody paid any attention to what she said—she was always trying to put two and two together.

In this instance she didn't have to try. She already had the other two, had gotten it the day before in her beauty parlor from what Marcella would have considered practically the horse's mouth. She had gotten it from Kate.

Chapter Nine

It was because of Kate's eyes that Maggie agreed to let her get a permanent.

One Sunday evening early in February we were all at home about ready to eat supper. Nathaniel was there, too. He and I had been out sledding all afternoon, and when we came in, Maggie asked him to stay, because we were going to have our Sunday-night favorite—waffles.

Nathaniel and Grandpa were sitting at one end of the dining-room table working on the Chicago *Tribune*'s "Name the Country" contest. Although Grandpa was more convinced than ever as spring approached that he was going to make his fortune in hybrid corn—and more impatient than ever for spring to get here—he wasn't one to let some other opportunity for making it slip by meanwhile. The way he looked at it, for all he knew, the Lord intended him to be a winner more than once.

I was sitting at the other end of the table studying my catechism, Maggie was in the kitchen making the waffles, and Kate was in the living room with her nose stuck in a movie magazine, as usual.

Grandpa smacked his hand down on the table. "Germany!"

Nathaniel frowned at him. "Do you think so?"

Maggie called in from the kitchen. "Chocolate, pineapple, or plain?"

"I was thinking," Nathaniel said, "it was Argentina."

"Pineapple," Kate called.

"Argentina? Well, now, and how, if I may ask, do you make that out of it?"

"Chocolate," I said. "Nathaniel, do you know how the Holy Ghost came down upon the Apostles?"

"Dad?"

"Hm? Oh, anything, Maggie. Whatever the children want. Of course, I suppose the man could be a gent."

"Chocolate," I said again. "Nathaniel?"

"I don't know. How did He?"

"We had chocolate last Sunday! Pineapple, please, Maggie!"

I read from my catechism. " 'The Holy Ghost came down upon the Apostles in the form of tongues of fire.' How about that for making you sit up and take notice?"

"I'd sit up and take notice," Nathaniel said, "if He came upon me as a ghost."

"Here's a picture of Tom Mix."

"I don't think He's that kind of ghost," I said, getting up to go see. "Can I have it?"

"You don't think it could be Germany, then?"

"When I'm finished."

Maggie came in from the kitchen. "What did you decide, Nathaniel?"

"Argentina."

"She means about the waffles, goofy," I said, "not the country."

"Oh." He looked confused. We tended to confuse Nathaniel. "Heck, I don't care. Pineapple, I guess."

"Nathaniel, how could you?" I turned to Maggie to make another pitch for chocolate, but Maggie was looking at Kate.

"Kate," she said, "why are you frowning so?"

"She probably just lost Clark Gable to some movie star," I said.

Kate looked up. "I didn't know I was."

"I wonder," Maggie said, "if you need glasses."

When Kate got her glasses, she cried. I couldn't see what

183

there was to cry about. They weren't ugly steel-rimmed things like Nathaniel's. They didn't have any rims at all. And she didn't have to wear them all the time, only when she was studying or reading or practicing the piano. But the way she carried on, you'd have thought they were false teeth. I did think that would be something to cry about.

Kate said nobody would ever look at her again. I told her I would, but she said not to be such a jerk, she didn't mean me.

I knew who she meant. I couldn't see what there was there to cry about either. She wasn't allowed to date any of them yet. Not until she was fifteen.

Anyhow, from the way the phone kept ringing after she started wearing glasses, if the boys weren't looking at her any more, they were still talking to her.

But Kate, who was as smart as a bloodhound sniffing out a trail, had got on to a good thing, and she knew it. Ever since school had started in the fall, she'd been begging Maggie to let her get a permanent. Maggie had kept saying no. What did she need with a permanent when her hair had a natural wave to it? It would be a waste of hard-earned money.

Now Kate said, with tears welling out of her eyes, if she could have a permanent like all the other girls did, instead of her dumb old windblown bob, which was so grade-school none of them would be caught dead with one like it any more, then people wouldn't think about her wearing glasses. They'd be too busy looking at her hair.

Kate was right about people looking at her hair after she had her permanent. They couldn't have missed it if they'd tried.

It was one big red frizz.

Not that Kate cared. She thought it was grand and went preening about the house like a peacock.

Grandpa said, well, now, and it was different, wasn't it?

Maggie said if Marcella would pay attention to what she was doing, instead of talking so much, she wouldn't have let Kate stay under the machine so long.

Marcella did talk a lot.

184

I wasn't Kate's first choice to go with her the Tuesday afternoon she got her permanent. She wouldn't have chosen me at all if she could have found anybody else. But her appointment was for four-thirty—school let out at a quarter to four, but Marcella never had any appointments between then and four-thirty, because that was her time to gossip with the other Coke ladies at Ward's—and she wouldn't be through until six or six-thirty, and all her friends either had to go to the dentist or take a piano lesson or be home before that. I was all she had.

Marcella had her beauty parlor in her house, which was located one block east of Ward's. When we got there she wasn't back yet, but the door wasn't locked, so we went on in. In Roseville people never locked their doors, or if they did lock the front door, they put the key in the mailbox or under the doormat or on the ledge over the door, so you wouldn't have to traipse all the way around to the back to get in.

We'd been there only a few minutes, just long enough for Kate to paw through all the movie magazines and latch onto one she hadn't seen yet, when Marcella came flapping in.

Marcella was a gawky woman—tall and thin and angular—who never just came in anywhere. That afternoon, what with her scarf trailing after her and her coat down off her shoulders and an enormous pocketbook clutched in her arms, she gave you the feeling she was barely making it all in one piece.

The cold had heightened the color in her cheeks, which were always pink because she rouged them, but it was her mouth, rouged or not, which drew your eyes, because it so dominated her round moon face.

Marcella had what we called horse teeth, which showed a lot because she talked a lot and smiled a lot and even listened with her mouth open, and she had blond hair which she wore in a little-girl Dutch bob—I suppose she was so busy setting everybody else's hair she didn't have time to bother with her own.

She gave us one of her big, toothy smiles, dumped her pocketbook onto a chair, and jerked out of her coat.

"Well, lambs," she said—Marcella called all children lambs, and she insisted we call her Marcella, because she said Miss DeWitt made her feel like she'd just parked a broomstick—"I would have been here sooner, but I ran into Elsie Watkins, and she had to tell me about all the trouble she's been having with her boy Fred. Kate, lamb, you sit right over here—bring the magazine with you, that's all right. Angel, lamb—look in that jar over there"—she jerked her head toward the doorway—"there are some more bread wrappers for you—you sit anywhere you want to."

She slapped an apron onto Kate, spun the chair around so Kate's neck was up against a metal trough, turned on the tap, pulled Kate's head back, and hosed down her hair.

I'd never watched Marcella work on anybody before, and I began to see why she always seemed at such a loss over what to do with her hands when she was at Ward's or talking to somebody on the street and could only resort to jabbing her finger in the air or waving her arms about.

While she was shampooing Kate's head, she told us all about Mrs. Watkins' troubles with her boy Fred—as long as a story wasn't something children wouldn't understand, Marcella didn't mind telling it to them, especially if there wasn't anybody else around to tell it to—and from the way her fingers rubbed and dug and scratched and wrung, you could tell Mrs. Watkins would like to take her boy Fred and snatch him bald.

The climax of Mrs. Watkins' troubles was that Fred had taken his father's car without permission and wrapped it around a telephone pole, at exactly which point Marcella flipped Kate's head upright and spun a towel around it. I breathed a sigh of relief Mrs. Watkins' boy Fred hadn't broken his neck.

After Marcella combed Kate's hair, she picked up a pair of scissors. Kate's eyes, already big from sharing all of Mrs. Watkins' troubles, got bigger. "Oh, Marcella," she wailed, "you aren't going to cut my hair, are you?"

In the three weeks since Maggie had agreed to let her get the permanent, Kate had been brushing her hair for hours on end, trying to make it grow as long as possible.

"No, lamb, just trim it a bit to make it even all around. You don't want any scraggly ends hanging down to spoil the look of your permanent, do you?"

I wondered afterward why trimming it or not trimming it mattered. After Kate got her permanent, no ends of any kind hung down anywhere. It all stuck straight out. But Kate agreed she didn't want anything to spoil the look of her permanent, so Marcella snipped away while Kate kept an anxious eye on her, hoping, I knew, Marcella didn't have anybody else's troubles in mind right then.

While Kate sat under the drier, Marcella let me use her push-broom to sweep up all the hair she'd trimmed off everybody that day. She herself jerked around setting things out for the permanent and answering the phone and smiling toothy smiles at Kate, who was looking pink and sweaty.

The last thing Marcella did before lifting the drier up and deciding Kate was dry was to wheel over the permanent machine, which looked like a skinny-legged octopus on a pole.

"Well, lamb," Marcella said when she had Kate back on the work chair again, and Kate was now eyeing the octopus the way she'd eyed the scissors, "how are Maggie and Harley Nichols getting along these days?"

Kate wrinkled her nose. "Oh, all right, I guess."

I wrinkled my nose, too, but not over Harley Nichols. I did more than wrinkle my nose. I coughed. Marcella was putting some kind of lotion and a paper on a section of Kate's hair.

Marcella smiled her toothy smile at me. "It's ammonia, lamb. Pretty soon you get so used to it you don't even notice it." She wound the paper-wrapped hair around a metal curler, stuck a hairpin in it, and attacked another section.

Kate blinked her eyes, and I coughed again and wondered what Marcella meant by pretty soon.

"I thought maybe they might get married."

Kate's eyebrows shot up. "Maggie and Harley Nichols? Oh,

Marcella. Maggie doesn't feel that way about Harley. They just both like to play cards, that's all. Anyhow, Maggie couldn't marry Harley now, even if she wanted to, which she never did, because he isn't a Catholic."

I was the one who'd found it in my catechism and shown it to Kate.

Q. Does the Church forbid the marriage of Catholics with persons who have a different religion or no religion at all?

A. The Church does forbid the marriage of Catholics with persons who have a different religion or no religion at all.

That killed off every prospect Kate had been able to line up so far. But Kate recovered quickly, as always, saying it opened up a whole new field of prospects, and the very next Sunday she began eyeing every man who came to mass by himself.

Her first choice turned out to be married, after all. He'd only come by himself a couple of Sundays while his wife was having a baby, which, according to the latest theory on where babies came from, as expounded to me by Barbara Kaiser, meant she was up in Chicago picking it out at Sears & Roebuck.

Since you could get everything else at Sears & Roebuck, I supposed Barbara was right, only I couldn't understand why, then, a woman said she had a baby. Why didn't she say she got one?

Barbara's answer for that was nobody talked the way people did in the Bible any more, which didn't satisfy me, but it shut me up. Otherwise I'd have had to admit to her I didn't know what she meant.

As far as the man was concerned, Kate just shrugged and said she didn't think he would have appealed to Maggie anyhow.

I decided if you could get to heaven on virtues, Kate would make it on fortitude alone.

Marcella attacked another section. "Well, we'll just have to find somebody for her who is a Catholic, then, won't we?" She beamed at Kate. Marcella wasn't one to waste her time on something that nothing was likely to come of. "It would be a pity if somebody as attractive as Maggie didn't get married again. I'm sure she must want to." Marcella wound the paper-wrapped hair tight around a curler and jabbed a hairpin into it.

Kate winced. "Oh, Maggie'll get married again. I know she will." Marcella had done more than jab at Kate's scalp. She had jabbed at her soul. "She's had lots of opportunities. She's just choosy, that's all."

It was news to me, both the opportunities and Maggie being choosy. I wondered where Kate was getting her information.

"But she'll probably get married again probably soon. In fact, I wouldn't be surprised, actually, if she got married any time now."

Kate coughed, but it wasn't at the ammonia, which I was coughing at, and I knew now where she was getting her information. She was making it up.

Marcella's eyebrows shot up this time. "Really?"

"Well," Kate amended, wincing again as Marcella jabbed again, "I didn't mean today or tomorrow, actually. Or even next week. But—well—I mean, Maggie's awfully popular and goes out a lot, and men call her and come see her all the time."

I rolled my eyes. I would have thought Marcella would, too, but she only beamed and said, "Well, isn't that interesting."

After Marcella had every inch of Kate's hair lotioned and wrapped and wound and pinned, she clamped a padded octopus leg to each curler, then switched on the machine. Kate looked as if she expected to be electrocuted, but that was partly because the curlers had been wound so tight her eyebrows were pulled up almost into her hair. I stood back a way to inspect her. What she looked like, I decided, was Medusa.

"It's so heavy," she told Marcella. "And so hot."

"I know, lamb." Marcella moved a blower machine over and turned it on. "But think how snazzy you'll look when you're all done."

Kate had been cooking for about fifteen minutes when Marcella turned from straightening up her work counter to jab a finger at her. "Say, wasn't that Jim Petrie I saw Maggie and the rest of you with on Sunday?"

Kate started to nod and winced instead. "Yes. He brought us home from church. Maggie couldn't get the car started."

Marcella sighed. "I wonder why he's never married."

"I don't know," Kate said. "I suppose he couldn't find just the person he was looking for."

I frowned at Kate. She knew perfectly well why Jim Petrie had never married. At least she knew Maggie's theory of why he hadn't.

On the way home from church one Sunday after Maggie had introduced Grandpa to Jim Petrie and his mother and maiden aunt, she'd told Grandpa a little about the Petries, including the fact that when they had moved to Roseville from Chicago, Jim, who was an only child, had been somewhere in Illinois studying for the priesthood. Three or four years after that he had left the seminary and come to work in the jewelry store with his father.

Nobody knew why he had left the seminary, she said, and if they depended on the family for finding out, they never would. Maggie had supposed he'd simply found he didn't have a vocation. But then from something he'd let drop once, she had the impression it must have been a personal problem of some kind —something to do with his mother or perhaps his father's health.

In any case, after his father's suicide, he'd taken over the store, and there he still was, and there he was likely to stay, though he had never married, perhaps thinking he might still go back to his studies for the priesthood. And perhaps, she added, he might. Older men than he had done it. Certainly he was devoted to the Church, ushering every Sunday and serving Father Kolchek at the six o'clock mass on weekday mornings in place of the schoolboys.

Marcella jerked the blower around to a different angle. "He certainly is handsome."

"Oh, very," Kate said.

"I should think he'd make a splendid opportunity for someone."

I'd never seen Medusa smirking in any of her pictures, but I got an idea now of what it would be like. "I wouldn't be surprised."

Kate might not be, but I was. I stared at her, dumbfounded. Marcella beamed. "Well. Think of that."

I wanted to ask Marcella, think of what? But the phone rang, and she went charging over to it.

She'd hardly more than answered it when she squealed, "Sophie Miller? You don't mean it!"

Whoever was on the other end apparently did. After a minute or so, Marcella looked over at us and then said, "Hold on. Angel, lamb, will you hang this phone up when I pick up the one in the kitchen?"

As soon as I did, I flew over to Kate to ask her why she'd said what she had.

Kate tried to raise her eyebrows, but they were already stretched as high as they would go—not permanently, I hoped. She blinked her eyes, and even that wasn't easy. "What do you mean, what I said?"

"That Mr. Petrie is an opportunity for Maggie."

Kate reared her head back, and the octopus legs danced. "I didn't say—ouch! I didn't say any such thing!"

"You did so."

"I did not! All I said was I wouldn't be surprised if he made an opportunity for someone."

"Well, you made it sound like the someone was Maggie."

"I can't help what it sounded like. That's not what I said."

"Anyhow, how could you say he's an opportunity for anyone? You were there in the car with the rest of us when Maggie told Grandpa about Mr. Petrie and the priesthood."

"Well, he can change his mind, can't he?"

I started to say something more, but I sniffed instead. "What's burning?"

I thought Kate's eyes would jump out of her head. "Get Marcella!"

Marcella took it very calmly. After she had Kate unhooked and unpinned and unwound and unwrapped, she went snip, snip at a couple of frazzled spots and smiled her toothy smile and said not to mind, it wouldn't show. Before Kate could get more than a fleeting glimpse of herself in the mirror, Marcella spun her around to the trough again, poured some new kind of lotion on her hair, then gave her another shampoo.

We never did hear what Sophie Miller's troubles were. This time Marcella just hummed a happy little tune while her fingers danced and squeezed.

Kate's hair, when Marcella combed it, hung in crimps. Kate frowned and asked if the permanent hadn't taken right, but Marcella said not to worry, that was how they always looked wet. Just wait till it was set and dried.

While she was twisting a crimp into a pin curl, Marcella said, "Wouldn't it be nice, after getting your hair fixed so pretty, if you had some special occasion to go to?"

"Oh, I do," Kate answered.

Marcella beamed. "Really?"

"Angel and I are going to make our First Communion next month."

"Oh. Well—yes, that will be special, I guess." Marcella twisted another crimp. "I was thinking more of a special occasion for Maggie." She beamed again. "You know. Like a wedding."

"Oh. Well . . ." Kate squirmed a bit. "Well," she said finally, "you never can tell. I suppose, actually, our First Communion might be a kind of special occasion for Maggie, too. I mean—well, probably Mr. Beebe will be here for it. And Mr. Owen, too, I wouldn't be surprised."

"Mr. Beebe?" Marcella asked. "And Mr. Owen? Now who are they?"

I was wondering that myself.

"Oh," Kate said, smirking again, "they're two of Maggie's

friends I was telling you about. They're very devoted to her. And to us, too, of course. Naturally."

"Naturally," Marcella agreed.

While Kate sat under the drier again, I waited for the phone to ring, so I could ask her who Mr. Beebe and Mr. Owen were, but it didn't ring.

Marcella didn't ask any more about them either when she combed Kate out, so I didn't find out until we were walking home. If you could call it walking. We practically ran all the way, Kate was so anxious to get home to show Maggie and Grandpa how she looked. I would have thought she'd want to run the other way, even faster.

I might have guessed who Mr. Beebe and Mr. Owen were. She'd made them up, too.

"Why?" I asked.

"Because you were so afraid Marcella would think I meant Mr. Petrie wanted to marry Maggie. So I decided to throw in a couple of other names, just in case. After all, you don't want Marcella to think Maggie doesn't have anybody, do you?"

"Why not?"

"Oh, you're impossible," she said.

I supposed I was.

The next evening—a shivery, raw evening already starting to get dark—I'd just had my piano lesson and was on my way to the courthouse to go home with Maggie, when a boy with a pack of newspapers raced past me, almost knocking my music book out of my arms.

When I crossed the street over to Ward's, he was standing there on the corner yelling, "Extra! Extra!

I stared at him, open-mouthed. We'd never had anything like that in Roseville.

"Extra!" he yelled again. "Extra! Lindbergh baby kidnapped!"

I shivered and hunched up my shoulders.

"Extra!" he yelled again. "Read all about it!"

I started walking backward toward the courthouse, staring

at him, and had gone past the now-vacant Northern State Bank, the post office, Joe Lafferty's bakery, Mr. Goodman's hardware store, and the vacant lot next to the hardware store when I backed into somebody.

It was Marcella. She was standing on the sidewalk in front of the Roseville Bank and Trust Company—or, rather, now that the two banks had merged and elected to locate there, the Northern State Bank and Trust Company—with Warren White.

"Oh, excuse me," I said. "I wasn't looking."

"That's all right, lamb." Marcella smiled, but hardly long enough to show her teeth. Then she smiled the same way at him.

I thought if he asked me how my piano lessons were coming, I could tell him I'd finally made it past "Oats, Peas, Beans, and Barley Grow," but he didn't ask. He didn't say anything at all. Or even look at me. He looked off over my head and ran a finger around the inside of his shirt collar.

I could tell it was a wrong time, but I didn't know why. Just before I bumped into Marcella, I'd heard him say the word money, but I supposed he talked about money most of the time.

"Did you know the Lindberghs' baby was kidnapped?" I asked. I pointed. "There's a boy down by Ward's with newspapers about it."

"Yes, we knew," Marcella said, jerking her head up and down.

She didn't say any more, and he still didn't say anything, and I'd said all I could think of. I guessed they wished I would leave anyhow, so I shivered and started on, walking frontward this time.

As I was crossing the street in front of the courthouse, I could still hear the boy yelling. When I reached the other side I turned back to look at him once more.

Warren White was talking to Marcella again. She was listening to him with her mouth hanging open, the way she al-

194

ways did. Then she said something to him, jabbing at the air in front of her.

I couldn't hear what they were saying, but I supposed he must have told her something he wanted everybody in town to hear about, which would be why he'd tell it to Marcella.

I started on my way again, keeping a wary eye on the flagpole as I trembled past it, the flagpole leaning at me the way it always did, thinking Marcella could probably even beat an extra. And she didn't charge you anything.

It took about a week for the story Warren White had told Marcella—and Marcella's contribution to it—to get back to Maggie. A friend of Maggie's called her up one night while we were eating supper and told her what was being said. Not that Maggie let on anything to us. She just listened, frowning. After she hung up, she didn't come back to the table but stood on by the telephone.

"Is something the matter?" Grandpa asked.

She turned toward us, giving a little shake of her head, which could have meant she was angry, but I could tell from the stillness on her face and the shadowed look in her eyes that she was too stricken to be angry. Without saying anything she picked up her coat from the back of the chair she'd tossed it on when she came home and went out the back door and got in the car and drove away.

Grandpa frowned out through the window after her. "Maybe she received word someone is sick."

Kate, who'd been looking out the window, too, shook her head. "She's running away."

Grandpa turned from the window to stare at her. "Running away?"

"Yes," she said. "She's done it before." Kate shrugged. "When things get her down, I guess. But don't worry about it, Grandpa. She'll come back in a while. She always does, even the times when she says she's never coming back."

Grandpa looked from Kate to me. I nodded. Kate was right.

But I couldn't have said it the blithe way she did. In spite of the fact that Maggie always did come back, I never could be sure she would until she did.

That night she was gone for over an hour. When she came back the shadow was still there in her eyes.

All she said in front of Kate and me was that some people had made up a lie about her to use against her in the election campaign, and she'd been trying to think what was the best way of combatting it—if there was any way.

I looked at her for a minute. "Maggie—"

"Yes?"

I was afraid to say it, afraid it wouldn't work, as much afraid of destroying the magic of it if it didn't work as wanting to remind her that it always did. "If they can't lick Mr. Gilligan—"

She nodded. "—they can't lick me!"

I gave such a big sigh of relief she even smiled a little.

Chapter Ten

Any lingering hope I had that Orn Fletcher might waver in his determination to get Maggie out was dispelled the same week Maggie received the phone call. She told us one night when she came home that Dale Helford, who ran the grain elevator and was a long-time crony of Orn's, had filed for the primary as a candidate for the auditor's office.

Maggie's determination to win soon got a boost, however, from an unexpected quarter. Somebody else filed for the auditor's office, too.

The somebody else was a man from Jackson's Crossing named German Dunkelberger, and the boost lay in the fact that he was a lifelong Democrat, an active supporter of the party, and a big man in his part of the county.

Orn, Maggie reported to us, was fit to be tied, but there wasn't anything he could do about it. Anybody who wanted to could run in the primary as long as he made application to the clerk of the court and rounded up twenty-five voters to sign a petition in his behalf.

The filing period for all candidates of both parties was from February 22 to March 24. The two surprises yet to come came on the last day, though one of them didn't come as a surprise to anyone but me.

Warren White had gone to Indianapolis and filed for the state senate.

Grandpa's reaction, when Maggie told him, was, " 'Tis no more than I expected."

It was a whole lot more than I expected, but I supposed Warren White must have decided he'd go ahead and run for office
without Orn's backing, the same as Maggie was doing, and see
if he couldn't win anyhow. At least, I supposed that until I saw
the knowing look on Kate's face.

As soon as I could get Kate alone I asked her what she knew
that I didn't. She didn't want to tell me, but I reminded her she
still owed me fifteen cents for the movie magazine I'd let her
buy out of the quarter old Mrs. Werner had paid me for sweeping snow off her front walk, and if she told me I wouldn't
press for payment. So she told me what was behind the phone
call to Maggie—that people were saying Maggie had embezzled county funds and that a man had covered up for her.

After she explained embezzled to me I frowned at her. "You
mean Mr. White is the man?"

She shook her head. "No."

"Then who is?"

"I don't know. I tried to find out, but I couldn't."

I frowned at her again. "Well, how does Mr. White come into
it?"

"He's the one who started the story."

I gasped. "Mr. White?"

She nodded.

"Oh, Kate," I said, "I can't believe it."

"Well, it's true."

"How do you know?"

"I heard Maggie say so."

(Maggie's friend, as I would learn eventually, had not only
told Maggie what people were saying, but had managed to pry
out of Marcella—by promising not to tell another soul, and by
offering some other confidence in exchange—her source of information. As shocking as the news was to her, it hadn't taken
Maggie long to figure out how the story had been "revealed"
to Warren White. And why. Even Kate, with her limited
knowledge at the time, was able to figure out that much, as she
demonstrated to me.)

"But how could he?" I said.

"You shouldn't have to ask me that. You heard what Mr. Fletcher said that day about Mr. White wanting a political career and needing Mr. Fletcher's influence and money behind him to have it."

"Well, I know, but Mrs. Fletcher said—"

"Mrs. Fletcher was wrong."

"My gosh," I said. "But Kate, how could he even so? I mean, if he had to turn against Maggie, couldn't he just be against her without making up a terrible story like that?"

Kate shrugged. "I suppose if he just said he was against her, Maggie could tell everybody how she'd saved his bank for him and what kind of gratitude was that?"

I frowned at her. "Well, why doesn't she tell them anyhow?"

Kate had Maggie's shadowed look in her eyes. "Who'd believe her now?"

"My gosh," I said again, beginning to see what Maggie had meant when she said politics was such a dirty game in Roseville. "But Kate," I said again, "I was with Maggie just a few weeks ago when Mr. White swore to her he would campaign for her. How could he say that and be saying the other?"

"I don't know. I suppose he doesn't have nerve enough to tell Maggie straight out."

"Is Maggie going to face him down with it?"

"I don't know."

"Well, I would."

Kate shrugged again. "Maybe she figures it wouldn't do any good. I suppose he'd only deny it."

I nodded. "I suppose so."

Kate had mowed down every objection I could think of, but I still had a hope left. "What makes Mr. White think people will believe a crazy story like that?"

"Some people," Kate said, "will believe anything. I suppose it all depends on how many believe it. And how many believe Maggie when she tells them it isn't true. I guess we'll just have to wait and see."

The other filing didn't surprise anybody but Maggie, because the name didn't mean anything to the rest of us, and Maggie was as much puzzled as surprised. A man named Pete Bolen—a young man, Maggie said, who taught commercial subjects in the high school over at Montclair—had filed for the auditor's office on the Republican ticket.

Pete Bolen, she added, handing us the surprise, was Gus Hardaker's nephew.

"It's possible," she said, "it's just a coincidence. But I wonder."

"Wonder what?" I asked.

"If Orn Fletcher had anything to do with it."

I stared at her for a moment. Then I remembered Maggie telling Orn that night coming home from the street fair how Gus Hardaker still carried a grudge against her for defeating him in the 1928 primary, and how she didn't think he'd ever get over it.

"But why," Kate asked, "would Mr. Fletcher have anything to do with a Republican?"

"If Orn wants me out of office bad enough and thinks he might not be able to swing it in the primary now because of German Dunkelberger, he might have approached Gus and got him to persuade his nephew to run, offering to make a deal with the Republicans to help put Pete in office."

Grandpa frowned. "In return for their help in putting one of the other Democratic candidates on the ticket in?"

Maggie nodded. "That, or the promise of a lot of good contracts for Orn out of the auditor's office. Maybe both."

"And what," Grandpa wanted to know, "would Gus Hardaker get out of it?"

Maggie shrugged. "You know the old saying—revenge is sweet."

"Well," Grandpa said after a bit, "Pete Bolen has to win the primary first, does he not? And he has—how many—three others up against him."

Maggie nodded again.

"And, as you said," he added, "it might be nothing more than coincidence."

"And"—Maggie shrugged—"if I don't win my own primary, it won't make any difference whether it is or not. So I guess we'll just have to wait and see."

I didn't know how I could stand all that waiting and seeing. Primary Day wasn't until Tuesday, May 3. But I had so many other things to do and think about, the days and weeks went by the way they always had—like lightning.

Mostly they were things at school, like finishing up my food scrapbook for health class and being so relieved at finally finding a picture of butter, the hardest picture of all to find, in a Land O'Lakes magazine ad. And being chosen as one of Martha Washington's children for a play whose performers, except for the other child, were all high-school students, so I was nearly bowled over by the thrill of it.

Or they were things at home, like watching, along with Grandpa, for the first signs of spring, yelling at him to come over to the front window—then making him walk on tiptoe— to see a robin on the lawn. And making final preparations, along with Kate, for First Communion, thinking how much I knew about God I hadn't known before, even though I didn't halfway understand it.

But there were also three outside things that happened during those six weeks before Primary Day—three apparently unrelated things that happened to me, to Maggie, and to Kate, in that order. I thought some about them, too, but they were each so odd, I hardly knew what to make of them.

The first thing, the one that happened to me, was precipitated partly by Julia Fletcher and partly by Nathaniel's mother coming to visit him.

The visit by Nathaniel's mother was pretty odd in itself.

Nathaniel's mother Mildred had the same tall, spare build that Julia Fletcher had, but outside of that there wasn't much family resemblance between them. Mildred was a blonde—or had been anyway—with green eyes and a thinner, more sharply featured face. She was pretty, prettier in a magazine way than Julia, but she didn't have Julia's appeal, and though she was three years younger, she looked older, with shadows under her eyes and the hard look about her skin of a woman who bleaches her hair when it begins to darken but can't do anything about making her complexion stay the complexion of a blonde.

She wore her hair bobbed and marcelled the way Bernice Kaiser did, but unlike Bernice, who always looked as if she'd just come from Marcella DeWitt's beauty parlor, Nathaniel's mother, every time I saw her, looked as if that was where she needed to go.

But what struck me most about her when Nathaniel invited me over to meet her that Saturday evening, and what made her seem most different to me from Julia, was her manner. Even when she was with the other Coke ladies at Ward's Drugstore, Julia was quiet—almost to the point of being vapid. She moved with the same quietness. Mildred didn't have much to say to Nathaniel and me either—the Fletchers had all gone off to South Bend for the day to let Nathaniel have his mother to himself, so there were just the three of us—and she seemed to have trouble finding even that much, but she was hardly still a minute. If she wasn't smoking, in quick little puffs, she was pushing at her hair or straightening her collar or checking the seams of her stockings. Or she'd get up and move about, finding a piece of bric-a-brac on the mantelpiece to adjust or a drapery to poke at. Or she'd go out of the living room altogether, usually in the middle of a dying conversation, leaving Nathaniel and me sitting there unable to find anything to say either.

When she came back a couple of minutes later she'd smile at us, her eyes a bit brightened, as if she were greeting us for the first time. Then she'd sit down and start a new conversation, sitting quietly for maybe a couple of minutes, and then it would start all over again—the smoking and the tapping and the pushing and the straightening and the checking and the adjusting and the poking until by the end of the evening I was a nervous wreck just watching her.

Nathaniel had asked me to come for supper, so I supposed his mother's trips out of the living room were trips to the kitchen to see how the supper was coming along. Only I couldn't smell anything cooking.

Just when I had about decided we were never going to eat, the front doorbell rang, and there at the door was a man from Mr. Cumming's ice-cream and hamburger stand with our supper in three paper bags.

I thought it was a smashing idea. We never did anything like that at our house. Nathaniel thought it was a smashing idea, too. As we helped his mother set the food out on the dining-room table, he was positively beaming. But not because he'd never done anything like that before. Because he had. It was obvious even without his mother saying after we sat down to eat, "Like old times, huh, Nathaniel?"

Nathaniel had his mouth so full of hamburger and French fries he couldn't do anything more than duck his head at her as he reached out for his chocolate malted to wash the mouthful down.

Looking at him eat as I'd never seen him eat before, his face pink with pleasure, I couldn't help wondering what Julia Fletcher and the guidance columnist would make of it. Even Nathaniel's mother looked for a time as if she was enjoying herself, though she didn't do any more than pick at her food.

But the oddest part of the evening, odder even than the way Nathaniel's mother said good night to me before Nathaniel walked me home—as if she wasn't sure I was the same person who'd come there earlier—was what she said to Nathaniel during the evening about his father.

She didn't say much. And she didn't say it all in a piece, but fidgeted around it the way she fidgeted around her person, which may have been why it made such an impression on me.

203

That and the fact that I couldn't figure out why, when she'd been alone with Nathaniel the whole day, she'd wait until after I arrived to talk to him about something so personal.

She asked Nathaniel first if his father wrote to him, and what did he have to say. Then before Nathaniel had more than a chance to say yes, he'd had a letter a few days before, she was up adjusting a photograph of Mrs. Ward on the mantelpiece, saying she never had cared for that picture of her mother, she didn't know why Julia had picked it to display. When she sat down again, she just looked at us for a while. Then she smiled at Nathaniel and said, "You haven't told me what you're studying in school."

Another time she said she supposed Nathaniel knew his father was moving to New York City, adding, "as if he couldn't get far enough away."

The only thing Nathaniel could find to say to that was yes, he knew.

It didn't matter. She was already up when she made that remark, and she was on her way out of the living room almost as soon as he finished answering her.

While we were eating supper she told Nathaniel his father was going to get married again as soon as the divorce was final. A little later on she said the woman his father was going to marry had once been a friend of hers, which showed you what kind of friends some friends turned out to be. Still later she said the woman had two children of her own, and she'd find out soon enough what kind of a father Nathaniel's father was when he couldn't take the time to visit his own son and probably didn't even so much as write a letter to him.

I expected Nathaniel to remind his mother about the letter he'd just received, thinking either she hadn't listened or she'd forgotten, but he didn't. We all just sat there for a bit, and then his mother got up and went out to the kitchen again, and I looked at the clock and said I had to go home.

It was obvious even to me that Nathaniel's mother felt bitter toward his father and wanted Nathaniel to be on her side.

What I couldn't understand was why she felt she had to try so hard to win Nathaniel over when he could hardly take his eyes off her as it was. Or why, if she was all that crazy about him, she'd sent him to live with the Fletchers in the first place, making Nathaniel feel she didn't want him around any more than his father did. Or why she didn't say anything at all during the evening about how she was looking forward to his coming home again. Or even when he would be—unless, of course, she'd said it earlier, before I came.

The only thing I heard her say even remotely connected with Nathaniel's coming home seemed to be a reverse of it, when she said she hoped Nathaniel liked his Uncle Orn and he should go see him at his office once in a while so he could get to know him better.

Whether Nathaniel liked Orn or not I don't know. I don't suppose Nathaniel himself could have said at the time. Orn was his uncle, and uncles were people you were supposed to like. Even his mother's saying what she did was only a manner of speaking—putting into words what was taken for granted.

Maybe what his mother was trying to say was she hoped Nathaniel could get his uncle to like him. It would have been more to the point. Not that Nathaniel needed his mother to tell him to try. He was always trying. And never getting very far.

My own feeling about Orn at that point was an ambivalent one. When I heard him say the harsh things he did the day Nathaniel and I were trapped behind the davenport I didn't ever want to see him again, even after deciding he'd only said them out of spite. But then the very next afternoon Mary Louise Fletcher called to say her father had said he would take all of us ice skating out at Cedar Lake, and I didn't want to miss out on it, so I went.

I didn't see how Orn could want to take Kate and me. I supposed at the very least he'd be as stiff-necked to us as he had been to Maggie that time at the depot. But he wasn't. He was the same as ever—hearty, and making sure all of us had our mittens, building a fire in a bucket on some bricks in case we needed to warm our hands even so, taking us for hot dogs and milkshakes afterward.

If he was hard on anybody it was Nathaniel—because Nathaniel couldn't skate as well or last as long in the cold as Orn wanted him to. Nathaniel could skate better and last longer than I could, but Orn didn't expect as much from a girl and said so.

I supposed, thinking about it on the way home, it was politics that made Orn feel the way he did about Maggie, and since Kate and I weren't mixed up in politics we didn't come into his feelings.

In any case, as far as Kate and I were concerned, things went on the way they always had. Kate and Mary Louise were as friendly as ever, and if Nathaniel wasn't at our house with me, I was generally somewhere with him.

Nathaniel and I had talked off and on about going to see Orn at his office, not because either of us figured it would help Nathaniel get to know Orn any better, but because his Aunt Julia was always encouraging him to go there, too. When she mentioned it again at Ward's the Monday after Nathaniel's mother had visited him, we decided we might as well go on over.

Orn's office was located at his father's lumberyard, beside the railroad tracks a few blocks west of the depot. When we got there he had somebody in his office with him, so we went across the way to old Mr. Fletcher's office, but he wasn't there, so we started wandering around looking for something to do.

We came across a long two-by-four and wedged it, narrow side up, between two stacks of lumber. Then we practiced walking back and forth across it without losing our balance until eventually we got tired of doing it.

The air was turning sharper as the sky, already overcast, began getting dark, so to keep warm, we started chasing in and out of and around all the stacks of lumber, hiding from one another and jumping out to yell "Boo!"

I had stopped alongside a stack to catch my breath and

thought I heard Nathaniel pussy-footing along the other side. I crept toward the end. When I heard him come around the corner I jumped out at him, yelling "Boo!"

Only it wasn't Nathaniel.

It was Chuck Sellers.

He didn't say anything. He just stood there staring at me in that creepy way of his, his eyes sliding away from me, coming back to me, sliding away again, coming back again, his chest heaving with each breath he took, as if he'd been running.

I figured if he didn't have anything to say to me, I didn't have anything to say to him, and I started to go on past him. He put his arm out against the stack of lumber, blocking my way.

When I turned to go back the way I'd come, he put his other arm out the same way, trapping me.

Still he didn't say anything, but only looked at me.

I frowned at him and grabbed hold of one of his arms to pull it loose. I couldn't budge it.

I turned to face him. "Let go!" I said, hitting his arm with my fist. "Let me go!"

He didn't move.

I twisted around and pulled at his other arm, but I couldn't budge that one either. When I tried to duck out underneath it, he shoved his leg forward so I couldn't.

I backed up against the stack of lumber, staring up at him. As he started to close in on me I frowned at him again. Then I let out a yell for Nathaniel.

Nathaniel came tearing around the end of the stack, and Chuck looked at him and backed away, letting his arms drop to his sides, muttering something about us chasing around there messing things up.

I couldn't see any sense to what he was saying at all. In the first place, we hadn't messed anything up, and in the second place, it wasn't his lumberyard anyhow. I was all set to say so, but Nathaniel shook his head at me. He took my hand, and we headed for Orn's office.

Orn and the man who had been inside with him were just coming out of it. They stopped in the doorway to finish their leave-taking, and Nathaniel and I went on in and sat down by the stove to get the numbness out of our hands and feet.

After a couple of minutes the man left, and Orn came back in and sat down at his desk, asking what he could do for us, trying to sound friendly but looking as if he hoped whatever it was it wouldn't take much time.

Nathaniel said we hadn't come for anything. I said we'd just come over to visit him. Orn said he supposed his wife had put us up to it, she was a great one for visiting.

That seemed to put an end to the conversation. I figured we ought to go, so I started to, but Nathaniel tugged at me. "Uncle Orn—"

Orn looked at him. "Well?"

Nathaniel's cheeks were already pink from the cold, but they turned pinker. "I don't think Chuck Sellers is a very good person for you to have working for you."

Orn frowned at him. "What in the name of tarnation put that idea in your head?"

Looking down at his feet, hesitant and stumbling over the words he used, Nathaniel told Orn what Chuck had done.

Orn barely had enough patience to hear him out. When he had, he shook his head at us, saying Chuck was just trying to beat us at our own game.

Nathaniel blinked. "I don't think so. I think," he said, his cheeks pinker than ever, "he was—he had some other idea."

"Such as what?"

Nathaniel struggled again, but this time nothing at all came out. He shook his head, looking embarrassed.

"You read too many books," Orn said. He stood up. "The both of you had better get on home. It'll be dark soon."

Nathaniel didn't say anything on the way home, but when we reached the Fletchers' house and I started to say I'd see him tomorrow, he put his hand on my arm. "Listen, Angel."

"What?"

He frowned at me. "I don't care what Uncle Orn says. You keep away from Chuck Sellers. Okay?"

"Sure, Nathaniel," I answered, thinking he didn't have to say even that much. I wasn't too clear about what Chuck Sellers had on his mind, but I had no intention, if I could help it, of ever getting near enough to him again to find out.

The other two outside things, the ones that happened to Maggie and to Kate, took place at the time Kate and I made our First Communion the last Sunday in April—the one to Maggie the night before we made it, the one to Kate the night after.

Saturday night Maggie was supposed to take Kate and me uptown to buy white shoes to go with our white communion dresses and veils which Aunt Clarissa had sent to us from Marshall Field's in Chicago.

Primary Day was now only a little over a week away, and Maggie had been out in the county all day campaigning. When she came home she looked so tired I was sure she was going to say Kate and I would have to manage somehow without white shoes. I was scared to even bring it up.

Kate wasn't. Even though Kate had more to lose than I did —she didn't just want white shoes, she wanted them with high heels—she asked Maggie right off. To my relief, Maggie said we'd go right after supper, which Kate, with an eye on the high heels, had been scurrying around the kitchen most of the afternoon cooking.

Once inside Harley Nichols' shoestore, it took me only a few minutes to get mine. There was only one choice in children's shoes to wear for good—T-straps.

It took Kate forever. Maggie asked Harley to see some pumps with low heels. Then while she went over to shake hands with somebody and ask them to vote for her in the primary, Kate quickly told him to bring some out with really high heels. She ended up with five or six boxes stacked at her chair.

I said to Grandpa why didn't he and I go over to Ward's for an ice-cream cone.

Grandpa reared back, giving me his A-1 super-duper beetle-browed frown. "What? After that magnificent supper Kate concocted for us? How could you?"

I giggled. "It's easy."

He sighed, and I giggled again. I knew what was coming next.

He patted his pockets. "Sure, and I think I left all me money at home."

"Try that one." I poked at his chest.

"Well, the saints preserve us, if the child doesn't have X-ray eyes." He pulled out a little ancient black leather purse and peered into it. "And how much now is an ice-cream cone?"

"Oh, Grandpa." I giggled some more. "A nickel."

"A nickel? Well, and I believe we can just about make it." He nodded. "If we share one between us."

As Grandpa and I came out of Ward's, Maggie and Kate came out of Harley's store. We all headed for the car.

"How high?" I said to Kate as we came up. Maggie had stopped to shake hands with somebody on the street.

Kate hugged the box to her and beamed.

Maggie came along in a couple of minutes, and we were standing there while she tried to think if she needed any groceries from Garnett's, when an old man, in clothes like a tramp's and with white stubble all over his face, came weaving up to us and tapped Maggie on the shoulder.

Maggie smiled and shook hands with him, which wasn't as easy as it sounds. "Hello, Sam."

He poked a finger at her coat collar. "Listen, Maggie."

"I'm listening, Sam."

He had to think a bit. "I'm your friend. Right?"

"Right," she said.

He leaned back to get a better look at her, and Grandpa put out a hand to steady him.

"Is something troubling you, Sam?" Maggie asked.

His mouth worked, but nothing came out.

She dug in her pocket for her change purse. "You want a cup of coffee?"

He shook his head. "I'm your friend. Right?"

"Yes, Sam. You're my friend."

He poked at her again. "Listen to me, Maggie."

"I'm listening."

His eyes were watering, and he wiped at them with his coat sleeve.

"What is it, Sam?"

His mouth worked again, and he jerked a hand over his shoulder. "Whole damn dirty lot, that's who."

"Who, Sam? What are you talking about?"

He nodded at her, then turned and started back the way he had come. "Whole damn dirty lot."

She called after him. "You want a ride home?"

He weaved off down the street without answering.

Maggie stood staring after him for a minute. Then we climbed into the car and headed home. "Whew," Kate said, "what a smell."

Maggie shook her head. "Poor old soul."

"I wonder what that was all about," Grandpa said.

"I suppose they threw him out of the poolroom. I don't know." She shrugged. "Maybe he had a run-in there with Otto Karshman. Harley Nichols told me Karshman was in his store spouting off to him earlier this evening."

"Who is Otto Karshman?" Grandpa asked.

"A farmer over in South Township, near Montclair. One of Orn Fletcher's stripe. Harley was so distraught about it and about me 'doing this thing,' as he put it, so close to election time, he almost forgot to charge me for the shoes."

Grandpa turned to her, frowning. "Is there cause for him to be distraught?"

Maggie shrugged again. "For somebody like Harley, yes. Harley's a great one for never doing anything for fear somebody somewhere might take offense." She smiled at Grandpa. "He once worked himself up almost to the point of asking me to marry him, but I guess he was afraid his other girlfriends might be so put out they'd take their shoe trade somewhere else." She shook her head. "If I were married to Harley Nichols I'd lose what sense I've got."

Kate beamed at me.

"You don't think, then," Grandpa said, "there's any reason for you to be concerned?"

"No. Oh, there'll be a few others like Orn and Otto Karshman, but I can't believe it'll amount to anything much. If anything's going to hurt me, it's this story going around town, and I'm doing everything I can to put the kibosh on that."

"I don't know how the man could do it," Grandpa said.

"I don't know either," she answered. "But there you are. Not that I don't intend to have it out with him one of these days, because I do."

I wanted to ask her when, but I didn't. I was afraid she'd decide Kate and I had already heard more than we should and not say any more.

She didn't say any more right then anyhow.

When we passed the Laramores' Kate said, "There's a car at our house."

"So there is," Maggie said. "I wonder who it can be."

"Mr. Beebe, probably," I said, "come for our First Communion. Or Mr. Owen. Or probably both of them. I wouldn't be surprised, actually, if they came together."

"Who on earth," Maggie wanted to know, "are Mr. Beebe and Mr. Owen?"

"Oh, they're friends of Kate's," I said, as she raised her shoebox at me. "They're very devoted to her."

"Don't pay any attention to her," Kate said. "She's looney." She sat up on the edge of her seat. "It's Uncle Donald's car!"

And so it was.

They were all there in the living room—Uncle Donald and Aunt Clarissa and the twins, Jeanne and Joanne—all except Mark, who was away at college. When we came in, the twins yelled, "Surprise!" and everybody hugged everybody, and you could hardly hear what anybody was saying, because everybody was talking at the same time.

Maggie said why didn't they let us know they were coming, we could have had supper for them. Uncle Donald said he'd been tied up in court all day and didn't know until the last minute if he could get away in time. Aunt Clarissa wanted to know if the dresses fit all right. We said they were perfect. Kate brought her shoes out to show the twins, who were seniors in high school and wore high heels all the time, and I went and got the rosary Grandpa had given me to show them, while Maggie put the kettle on for coffee. Uncle Donald asked Grandpa how he liked it here in Roseville, and Aunt Clarissa wrinkled her nose.

Kate put her shoes on to practice walking, teetering and tottering so we all laughed at her. She went pink in the face. Then, with a giggle, she weaved over to Maggie and poked her in the collarbone and said, "Listen, Maggie, I'm your friend!"

We all howled, even though Uncle Donald and Aunt Clarissa and the twins didn't know what they were laughing at until we explained it to them.

Aunt Clarissa wrinkled her nose again. "Disgusting old drunk."

The words were hardly out of her mouth when a sound like a gunshot went off in the kitchen.

I jumped, and Kate nearly sprained an ankle.

Aunt Clarissa said, "Mercy sakes. What was that?" But she didn't look scared, only offended.

We all stared at each other. *Bang!* it went again. *Bang!*

Grandpa slapped his thigh. "The saints preserve us, Angel. 'Tis our root beer."

He and I tore out to the kitchen, the others at our heels. It was. Three bottles of the batch we'd made the week before were splattered on the ceiling and trickling down the walls.

"Mercy sakes," Aunt Clarissa said from the doorway, Kate standing behind her, peering over her shoulder. Kate had had to stop and take her shoes off, so she was stuck where she was. When Aunt Clarissa stood in a doorway, she filled it. "Mercy sakes," she said again, "get the rest of it outside somewhere before it goes off, too."

Grandpa and Uncle Donald and the twins and I grabbed the rest of the bottles and hustled them out the door, holding them at arm's length.

"Why in the world," Aunt Clarissa said when we trooped back in, "would anybody want to make root beer when you can go to the store and buy it? Really, Papa."

I didn't mind what she said—she was always complaining about something—but I minded the way Grandpa looked at her. I went over and stood by him. "It's cheaper," I said. "All those bottles only cost fifteen cents. Anyhow, it's fun, isn't it, Grandpa?"

He touched his hand to my cheek. "That it is, love."

Maggie had brought the mop out, but Grandpa took it out of her hands, telling her to go sit down in the living room with Uncle Donald and Aunt Clarissa, she'd had a hard enough day as it was. He'd get the kitchen cleaned up in a jiffy while one of us made the coffee.

Kate wanted Joanne to help her set her hair, so they went upstairs while Jeanne made the coffee, and I helped Grandpa clean up.

Grandpa had just finished mopping the floor and I was wringing out the dishcloth from wiping the last bit of root beer off the wall, when Aunt Clarissa came into the kitchen for a glass of water to take two aspirins with.

After she'd dug them out of her pocketbook, she dug around some more and took out some folding money. She gave it to Grandpa, saying she'd meant to send it to him, but what with her bridge club and doing volunteer work for the hospital and a committee meeting for civic improvement and one thing and another, it had slipped her mind.

Grandpa thanked her and felt around in his pockets for his little black leather purse.

I supposed it was money she'd borrowed from him and was paying back, but then she said, "Will that be enough to get along on for a while?"

He said it would be and thanked her again. She snapped her pocketbook shut and went on back to the living room.

Grandpa turned to me as he put the mop away. "Coming, love?"

"In a minute, Grandpa. You go on."

I stood at the sink pressing the dishcloth against it, thinking how Grandpa always made such a joke about not being able to afford an ice-cream cone at Ward's.

It hadn't ever occurred to me Grandpa didn't have any money of his own. I supposed after working all his life he had money saved up in the bank, the way Miss McCray said people did.

I wondered if maybe the bank with his money in it had gone under, and he'd lost not just part of his life's savings, but all of it.

I shook my head. It didn't seem likely. Wouldn't he have said something about his bank going under when the Roseville Bank and Trust Company almost had?

I frowned. Could people work all their lives and not have any money saved up at the end of it?

That didn't seem likely either. But then, Maggie had been working for a long time, and she didn't have any money saved up. She always said she didn't have any left over to save. Maybe Grandpa hadn't had any left over either.

I frowned again. What had Mrs. Fletcher said that time Nathaniel and I were trapped behind the davenport? About she understood what it meant for Maggie to have two children to feed and clothe and house, "and now her father-in-law, too," making it sound as if Grandpa didn't have anywhere else to go, when of course he did. Even if he didn't have enough money to go to Florida like Mr. Ward or to stay on by himself in his apartment over the saloon, he could have gone to live with Uncle Donald and Aunt Clarissa.

I bunched the dishcloth up and smoothed it out again, stretching the sides of it to try to make it hang even all around.

Only, how could he plant his corn at Aunt Clarissa's? She'd wrinkle her nose and say she wouldn't have that mess in her back yard. And if she was cleaning out his bureau drawers and came across the clock that didn't look like a clock, she'd say it was a piece of junk and throw it out. And she'd fuss about him smelling up the living room, the same as Grandma had. And nag at him the way she nagged at Uncle Donald.

Except it was Uncle Donald's house as much as it was Aunt Clarissa's. If he didn't like her nagging at him, he could tell her to stop. But what could Grandpa do?

I shook my head. No wonder Grandpa had promised me he wouldn't leave us and go live with them. He didn't want to any more than I did.

It was bad enough having Aunt Clarissa come visit and scold him for doing something she didn't approve of, like making root beer that exploded.

I scowled at the dishcloth. What gave her the right to do even that? Just because he'd maybe scolded her a time or two when she was a child. He was still her father, wasn't he?

I shook my head again. Grandpa probably figured that since he didn't have any money saved up in the bank after working all his life but had to go to her for money to get along on, he had to let her scold him.

I supposed he did, but it made my stomach hurt to see her do it.

Maggie called in to me it was time to take my bath, so I went along upstairs. Both twins were up there now with Kate, laughing and having a high old time while Kate teetered and tottered around some more.

I didn't have to practice walking, but I opened the shoebox and ran my finger along the shiny white leather, wondering how I could wait until morning. But then I supposed it was wrong to be thinking about wearing new shoes and a new dress when I should be thinking about receiving the Lord. I put the shoebox away and printed DON'T DRINK WATER on a piece of paper and stuck it in the bathroom mirror.

Which was being smart for once instead of being a jerk, because that was the first thing I headed for when I crawled out of bed the next morning over whichever one of the twins I had in there with me.

Maggie worried about me throwing up. I told her it had been so long since I'd eaten, I didn't have anything to throw up. The only thing that worried me was I might have committed some sin since going to confession Saturday afternoon.

According to my catechism, however, the only sins that really counted were mortal sins, and for a sin to be mortal, it had to have, among other things, sufficient reflection. Since I'd spent nearly all my time after coming out of the confessional reflecting first on whether I'd get new white shoes and then, after getting them, on having them, I guessed I was still in a state of grace.

The First Communion class occupied the two front pews, four on one side of the aisle and four on the other. I was scared we'd miss our cue—I still hadn't figured out how people knew when it was time to get up and go to Communion, especially when you were supposed to keep your head bowed all through the part preceding it—and what with trying to peer out the side of my veil, and wishing I'd gone to the bathroom again before we left home, being more and more sure as time dragged on that any minute now Father Kolchek would turn and say, "*Ite, missa est*—Go, the mass is ended," I almost threw up anyhow.

But pretty soon Jim Petrie came and tapped the aisle kids on their shoulders. We all stood up and filed out, met our partners from the other side, and started up toward the altar.

Kate and I, being the tallest as well as the oldest, were the last two. She did very well. She only tottered once and had to grab my arm, which she'd told me to have ready, just in case.

As we walked up the steps, Maggie sang, "O Lord, I am not worthy that Thou shouldst come to me, but speak the words of comfort, my spirit healed shall be." As we knelt and Father

Kolchek put the curious, sweet-crumbling wafer in our mouths, she sang, "And humbly I'll receive Thee, the Bridegroom of my soul, no more by sin to grieve Thee, or fly Thy sweet control."

We walked back to our pews and filed in to kneel and pray while other people went to Communion. A few minutes later Father Kolchek did turn and say, *"Ite, missa est*—Go, the mass is ended," the choir responding with *"Deo gratias*—Thanks be to God," which always struck me as hardly even polite, but then I hadn't written it, somebody else had, and thankful it was ended or not, it was, and we went.

I would have thought Kate would be as starved as I was when we got home, but she only picked at her breakfast and hardly ate anything for dinner either.

I knew why, though I didn't see why. Maggie had backed down from saying Kate couldn't have a date until she was fifteen—which was only a couple of weeks away anyhow—and had said she could go to the movie that night with Bill Kaiser.

Kate pretended she wasn't the least bit excited, but by the time Uncle Donald and Aunt Clarissa and the twins went back to Chicago in the late afternoon, she was so beside herself she could hardly sit still.

The minute they were out of the house, she flew around the living room picking up the Sunday papers and emptying ashtrays from Uncle Donald's cigars, opening windows to air out the smoke. Then she dusted and ran the carpet sweeper and straightened cushions, saying if anybody used the living room to please not make a mess.

When I asked her if it would be all right if Grandpa and I put a jigsaw puzzle together in the middle of the living-room rug, she nearly had a fit. So we spread it out on the dining-room table, which was where we were going to put it all along.

Grandpa said I shouldn't have teased her, she was nervous enough as it was. And she was. When she sat down to put on her nail polish, her hands shook so, it went on crooked on her right hand, and she had to do it over.

She said she didn't want any supper, she wasn't hungry. Maggie told her if she didn't eat, she couldn't go. So she picked around again, and as soon as Maggie let her excuse herself, she flew upstairs to take a bath.

She'd just had a bath the night before, which I thought should have been enough to last her for a few days anyhow, but I supposed after being in such a sweat all day she was probably afraid of having b. o. According to all the magazines, if you had b. o. you couldn't expect to have any friends, let alone dates.

Bill wasn't supposed to come after her until a quarter to seven, but she was all dressed and ready to go by twenty after six. Grandpa and I were back at the dining-room table working at the jigsaw puzzle again, and he said why didn't she help us, it would make the time pass more quickly. She said no, thanks, she'd read a movie magazine.

She went into the living room and sat down with one, but she didn't read it. She didn't even put her glasses on. She just thumbed the pages and looked at the clock and straightened her skirt and looked at the door and fussed with her purse and stood up and sat down and looked at the clock again and straightened her skirt again, and on and on, until I was as much of a nervous wreck as I had been watching Nathaniel's mother.

When the clock chimed three quarters, I breathed a sigh of relief and waited for the doorbell to ring. It didn't.

When more minutes went by, and it still didn't ring, I began to watch the clock, too.

Kate got up and pretended to be looking at some sheet music on the piano. Then, when she thought nobody was looking, she peeked out the window to see if he was coming. Since she didn't say anything, I didn't know if she'd seen him or not, but when five more minutes went by and he still hadn't come, I guessed she hadn't.

When the clock struck seven, with no sign of him yet, Kate said, with a little tremor in her voice, "If he doesn't hurry up, we'll miss the coming attractions."

"You can see them the second time around," I said.

"That's true." She sighed. "I hate people to be late."

Maggie, who was at the desk in the living room working on a campaign speech—having assured Kate she wouldn't make a mess—looked up and said she agreed with her, but not to fret. Boys didn't tend to be as punctual as girls.

By seven-fifteen Maggie was watching the clock.

Kate said maybe he was sick or something, but she'd have thought he could at least call. Or have somebody call.

"Why don't you call him?" I said. It made sense to me, but she said she wouldn't call him if her life depended on it.

Grandpa said, "Maybe you misunderstood him. Maybe he said a quarter after seven, not a quarter to."

"But it's past that now," Kate wailed. "Anyhow I know he didn't. He said six forty-five. Besides, the newsreel goes on at ten after." She went to peer out the window again, not caring now if anybody saw her do it. "I don't understand it," she said when she'd looked and looked, apparently with no sign of him.

I didn't understand it myself. All the past summer whenever we'd go swimming at the river or out at Cedar Lake, if Bill Kaiser was there, he'd come and hang around Kate the whole afternoon, showing off his diving to her. And he'd been calling her and asking her for dates for months now. Even her frizzy permanent hadn't seemed to make any difference to him. I figured if he stuck through that, he'd stick through anything.

For the next several minutes Kate alternated between being angry with him for not calling to say he'd be late and being worried he'd been hit by a car or stricken with pneumonia and couldn't call, but when the clock showed a quarter to eight, by which time he was a whole hour overdue, she said she wouldn't go out with him now if he did come, no matter what had kept him, and if he called she wouldn't speak to him.

When the phone finally did ring, she flew to answer it, but it was only somebody for Maggie.

When it rang again a little after eight, Kate got very airy, saying it could ring its head off for all she cared. When I came back out of the kitchen from answering it, she was sitting on the edge of her chair. "It's for Maggie again," I said. Kate drooped.

She must have decided about then he wasn't going to show up at all. She came over and sat with Grandpa and me to help us with the jigsaw puzzle and didn't look at the clock any more and only out toward the kitchen every now and then.

She hardly said a word the rest of the evening. Nobody else did either. I supposed Maggie and Grandpa were like me. They couldn't think of anything to say.

When we went upstairs to bed she had such a shiny-eyed look about her, I was afraid she'd cry, but if she did, I didn't hear her.

Walking home from school with me the next afternoon, she said Bill had had to go to South Bend with his family for the day and didn't have a chance to call and let her know. By the time they came back, it was almost ten o'clock and too late to call.

I would have thought she'd be hopping mad with him, but she just shrugged her shoulders and said she didn't know why she'd ever wasted her time on him. She hadn't liked him all that well to begin with.

By the time she'd repeated it to Grandpa and again to Maggie, she sounded almost convincing.

I thought he'd call her on the phone to try to make up with her, but he didn't. I supposed he didn't have the nerve.

By the next weekend Kate apparently didn't care if he did anyhow. She had a date for the movie Saturday night with George Garnett.

I didn't see how I could go through it all again this soon, let alone Kate. But Saturday night didn't turn out anything like Sunday. George not only showed up, he showed up early, before Kate was even ready.

He didn't look too happy about the whole thing. In fact, he looked so miserable sitting on the davenport with his cap in his hands and his black shoes so shiny he must have spit on them till he was dry, I thought maybe Kate had engineered him into taking her.

As usual, I thought wrong. When Kate came teetering into the living room he jumped up as if he'd been shot at, and when she said, "Hi, I'm ready," he looked at her as if she personally had deflected the bullet.

The next Tuesday was Primary Day.

I was torn between being afraid Maggie would lose because of Warren White's lie about her and the two men on the ticket against her and being sure she couldn't possibly lose, no matter what had been said or how many opponents she had, simply because she was Maggie.

She told us she wouldn't be home for supper. She wanted to stay uptown until the returns were in. But she also said she wouldn't be late.

After supper I practiced for my piano lesson the next day, Grandpa listened to the radio, Kate did some homework, and we all watched for her headlights to turn into the driveway, which they finally did.

The minute she stepped into the house I knew. I clapped my hands. "If they can't lick Mr. Gilligan—"

She beamed at us. "—they can't lick me!"

The party faithful Orn had rounded up, she said, had had a hard time deciding whom to be faithful to and had split their votes down the middle between Dale Helford and German Dunkelberger. Maggie had not only won, she'd won hands down.

There was only one discordant note to the evening. Pete Bolen had won, too.

Chapter Eleven

Grandpa planted his corn the Saturday after Primary Day. He'd decided, he told Nathaniel and me while the three of us were sitting on the back steps cooling off with a lemonade after hoeing the plot a final time, to plant two rows of seeds from one strain of corn and inbreed that, plant another two rows of seeds from the other strain and inbreed that, and plant three rows of seeds alternating the two strains and crossbreed them. "I think," he said, "that should cover all the possibilities."

"How do you know," Nathaniel asked, "when you've inbred as many times as you have to?"

Grandpa took a handkerchief out of his pocket and wiped the sweat off his forehead. "That I don't know. 'Tis a new idea, this crossbreeding of corn."

"Didn't your agriculturalist friend know?" I asked.

Grandpa shook his head. "Not for certain. He was of the opinion that perhaps the two strains had each been inbred enough already. But he said 'twas only an opinion. He'd thought the same last year and then decided he'd been wrong." Grandpa reached for his bag of corn. "We'll just have to plant it and see what the good Lord makes of it." He took an ear out and broke it in half. "Have you the piepans, Angel?"

"They're right here." I gave one to him and one to Nathaniel and kept one for myself.

"Maybe you could talk to some of the farmers around here," Nathaniel said. "They ought to know something."

Grandpa gave us each a half ear to shell. "Indeed they should, but I'm afraid they don't put much stock in the idea of cross-breeding. 'Tis a pity, but"—he sighed—"a fact."

"Have you talked to some of them already?" I asked.

He took another ear out of the bag and started shelling it. "I have that."

Nathaniel took a drink of his lemonade. "The kernels don't come off as easy as you think."

I sucked at my thumb where I'd scraped it against the point of one. "You said it. Grandpa—"

"Yes, love?"

"How will we keep them separate from each other? The corn, I mean."

"I have a record book. We'll mark down in it which row is which. With letters or numbers. Or we could name them if you like."

"Oh, let's!" I clapped my hands. "I've got just the names!"

"What?" Nathaniel asked.

I could hardly wait to tell Kate. "Mr. Owen and Mr. Beebe. And"—I'd had an even greater idea—"we can call the cross-breed Mr. Owen Beebe. How about that?"

"Not bad," Nathaniel said. He knew all about Kate's friends.

Grandpa said it was fine with him, and we marked it down in his book.

After we'd shelled enough corn, we started planting. "If hybrid corn is going to be so much better than ordinary corn," Nathaniel said to Grandpa, "why don't the farmers think what you're doing is a good idea?"

Grandpa looked over from his row. "You know of the Apostle Doubting Thomas?"

Nathaniel nodded.

"They're his relatives."

"Oh, Grandpa," I said.

After we finished, we sat down on the steps again to admire our work and have another lemonade.

"I wish I was going to be here next November to see how it comes out," Nathaniel said.

"I wish you were, too," I answered, wondering if his mother had said something to him, after all, about his coming home. "Isn't there any chance of it?"

"I don't think so. I'll probably go back to Chicago probably as soon as school is out."

In spite of the fact that he didn't sound too convincing, I stared at him in dismay. "But that's next week!"

He nodded. "I know."

"But Nathaniel, the corn won't even be up out of the ground yet."

"I know," he said again.

"Well, you can't leave before that. And right after that it will be summer. I know you don't want to stay here forever, but you have to stay here for that. Summer's the best time of all. Couldn't you ask your mother to let you stay on at least until school starts in the fall?"

As it turned out, he didn't have to ask. His mother wrote him a letter saying she hoped he wouldn't mind staying on in Roseville through the summer. She missed him terribly, but he'd be much better off in the country. The city was no place to be in hot weather.

So Nathaniel stayed.

His mother was right about the weather. It turned hot early in June and stayed that way, with hardly any let-up, all summer long.

His mother was also right, as far as I was concerned, about Nathaniel being better off in Roseville. In fact, I couldn't imagine anybody who had any say in the matter wanting to be anywhere else, though I would have been hard put at the time to decide whether it was the familiar things we did or the discoveries it held which made that particular summer one of the best times.

The first big event of the season was the Fourth of July celebration out at Cedar Lake. Sponsored by the Cedar Lake Community Club, it always started with speeches and a picnic in the afternoon and ended with a fireworks display at night. That year it had the extra added attractions of speedboat races and a bathing-beauty contest. It also marked my second encounter with Dynamite Dom.

It wasn't easy to avoid him. He was all over the place, shooting off the gun—naturally—to start each race, presenting the silver trophies—he'd bought them—to the winners, helping the girls get lined up for the beauty contest, and introducing himself with a handshake and an effusive welcome to so many people you'd have thought he was running for office.

I kept my distance, jumping every time the gun went off, but after the boat races were finished, he spied Maggie and came over—his two bodyguards, who were having a busy time of it, trailing after him—to pump her hand and exclaim over her as if she were some long-lost relative, asking how the little ones were and how her campaign was going, exclaiming all over again when Maggie introduced him to Kate at how much Kate looked like Maggie.

I tried standing behind Grandpa, but it was no use. He saw me, and I had to come out and shake hands with him and be patted on the head and exclaimed over like Maggie and Kate.

He was wearing dark blue trousers and a flashy sport shirt and an even flashier diamond ring, and the summer sun had turned his complexion swarthier than ever, giving the long indentation across his left cheek a terrifying lividness, but I couldn't help noticing as the afternoon wore on that nobody else seemed to be afraid of him.

People didn't exactly warm up to him, as he so obviously wanted them to do, but then neither would they have warmed up to Fritz Kreisler or John Barrymore or Andrew Mellon if one of them had descended into their midst.

Even Grandpa, who had had personal, if limited, dealings with the Chicago underworld, didn't seem to be afraid of Dynamite Dom, but then, as Grandpa remarked to Maggie that night on the way home, Dynamite Dom appeared to be an altogether different person at Cedar Lake than, from all the accounts of him in the newspapers, he was in Chicago.

Maggie agreed, saying he struck her as a very kindhearted and generous man, so much so, indeed, she sometimes found it hard to remember there was another side to him.

Sitting in the back seat of the car clutching the unbelievable dollar bill Dynamite Dom had given me—he'd given Kate one, too—I was finding it a bit hard at the moment myself.

The biggest discovery of Kate's life that summer—boys—could hardly be called a discovery, since she'd known all along they were there. She just hadn't been old enough before to take advantage of the situation. She did now.

As soon as the weather turned hot we started going swimming every afternoon, usually in Platt River at the north end of town, where the water was so swift and cold it took us only about an hour to turn blue, and our teeth chattered all the way home.

Kate's didn't, but then for the amount of time she spent in the water she might as well have stayed home and taken a bath, which she did anyhow the minute we got back. She took so many baths I thought she was revolting.

At the river she mostly sat on the bank with her girlfriends, all of them talking away as if they hadn't seen each other for a year instead of a day, not to mention all the phone calls in between. And every time the boys splashed water on them they shrieked and carried on as if they were wearing their Sunday best instead of bathing suits.

Bill Kaiser, I noticed, was showing off his dives this summer to Sarah Frances Wunderley. Not that Kate cared.

Jerry Schultz, who was a classmate of Kate's, was always on the lookout for her at the river, and whenever he could get his dad's car, he drove us out to Cedar Lake to swim—and then after we were there had to fight off a lot of Chicago boys for her attention. And George Garnett, who worked during the daytime for his dad, showed up every Saturday night, looking as miserable and shiny-shoed as ever, to take Kate to the movies.

I couldn't understand why she couldn't be ready when George arrived, so he wouldn't have to sit in the living room sweating out conversations with Grandpa and Maggie, George's conversations leaning mostly to questions and answers—them asking and him answering—but Kate just looked superior and said you weren't supposed to be ready when a boy came for you. You were supposed to make him wait. That way he appreciated you more.

It didn't make sense to me, but since boys were appreciating her left and right, I figured she must know what she was talking about.

Except for the matters of Jim Petrie and Alice White, Kate was in seventh heaven all summer long.

The matter of Jim Petrie came up at a band concert.

Band concerts were held every Wednesday night during the summer in the center of town on a bandwagon pulled out into the intersection of Main and Lake streets. All the stores stayed open through the concert (stayed open, indeed, until the concert was long over and the last prospective customer had vanished from the streets), and the sidewalks were jammed with people, farmers and townspeople alike, with cars parked bumper to bumper along both sides of Main Street and along all the cross streets throughout the business section and beyond it.

One night after we'd just gotten there, Kate and I were standing in front of Werner's Clothing Store so she could admire the dresses in the window, when Jerry Schultz spied us from across the street and hotfooted it over to hang around through the concert with Kate.

Jerry said he'd buy me a bag of popcorn if I'd make myself scarce. For a bag of popcorn I would have disappeared into thin air if I could.

After he bought it for me I ducked around to the side of Jim Petrie's jewelry store and, since it wasn't very secluded even there in the shadow of the wall, ate the popcorn as fast as I could before anybody could come along and want some of it.

I made it and was just wiping my hands on the crumpled sack, preparing to go look for Grandpa, when I heard Maggie's voice and looked over to see her come out of the jewelry store, pausing in the doorway to talk to Jim Petrie. She saw me at about the same time, so I went over and stood with her while they finished their conversation.

We were just on the point of leaving when Kate came pushing through the crowd on the sidewalk, her eyes wide and brimming with tears.

I didn't know what in the world could have happened to her, and just as she said, "Oh, Maggie," the band struck up "The Stars and Stripes Forever," and I couldn't hear myself think, let alone what Kate was saying.

Maggie and Jim Petrie exchanged looks, and then he motioned us to come inside, shutting the door after us.

Tears started running down Kate's face as she blubbered out that she and Jerry had been moseying along the street when they happened to see Maggie inside the jewelry store. At that moment some woman a few steps away turned to the man she was with and said, "I'd think Jim Petrie would be the last person Maggie Crowley would want to be seen with in public."

I stared at Kate, taking about as long as she had to come up with Jim Petrie as the man who was supposed to have covered up for Maggie—and, as she sobbed out, "It's all my fault!" hardly able to look at Maggie, totally unable to look at him, to figure out how he happened to be the one chosen for the honor.

I wished I hadn't eaten the popcorn so fast. I wished I hadn't eaten it at all.

Maggie didn't understand, of course, how it could be Kate's fault, and I didn't see how, with Jim Petrie standing right there, Kate could explain it to her, but she did, more or less—the less being to leave out as much of what she had told Marcella as she honorably could.

Maggie could hardly have lived with Kate as long as she had without being aware of Kate's romantic schemes and dreams for her. She said Kate should have known better than to suggest anything, however remote, to Marcella, but as for it being all Kate's fault, it was no such thing. One of these days somebody was going to take Marcella and knock her teeth down her throat.

Marcella's teeth being the size and fullness they were, I thought that presented a marvelous picture. I was so taken with it, indeed, I almost missed Maggie's next remark, which was directed to Jim Petrie rather than Kate—a remark to the effect that she was sorry for any embarrassment he'd suffered, but she believed that as far as he was concerned, at least, the worst was over. They'd found other fish to fry now.

I supposed she meant Marcella and Warren White and whoever else "they" were had found some other person to tell a story about, but looking back on it now, I realize that the "other fish to fry" was the second version of the story about Maggie.

Just how or when it started Maggie was never able to tell me. She didn't know. More important than the how or when of it was the why, and that was easy enough for us to figure out. Orn was as well aware as Maggie of her popularity throughout the county and of her good record as auditor. Although he had, in fact, made a deal with the Republicans which could be counted on to deliver a certain number of votes from the hard-core faithful of both parties, in order to be sure of getting Maggie out he had to do something which would damage both her popularity and her record with the voters at large.

Warren White's original story, while a step in the right direction, was only that. Once Orn had been given the raw material from which the story had been made, he must have found it hard to conceal his contempt for Warren White, if, in fact, he bothered to conceal it. For in the raw material lay the makings of a far better story, a story which gave Orn the link he needed to the Ku Klux Klan—a story to stir up those passions which, contrary to Maggie's belief, had not died with the Klan but, for the most part, were lying dormant.

The story now being spread around was that Maggie had removed the eighty-seven thousand dollars in securities from the Roseville Bank and Trust Company and deposited them under her own name in a Chicago bank not to protect them from theft by others but to facilitate her own theft of them, and that she had done this not at the suggestion of a friend from Chicago but in connivance with "that Chicago crowd," with whom she had entered into a conspiracy with intent to defraud the people of Rose County.

Jim Petrie probably knew what "other fish" Maggie was referring to that night in the jewelry store. That may have been what Maggie went in to talk to him about. As for the story about the two of them, he told her the whole business was so patently ridiculous he didn't see how anybody with a grain of sense could believe it, and from the margin of her victory in the primary, obviously very few did.

When Kate, still hardly able to look at him, apologized to him for what she'd said to Marcella, he patted her on the shoulder and told her not to feel bad. After standing there a bit looking down at her, he walked over to the window and, taking out her beloved strawberry pin, put it in her hand, saying he wanted her to have it.

I was about ready to cry myself at the look Kate gave him then. But she shook her head and handed the pin back to him, saying she couldn't take it. And she didn't.

She didn't even want to hear the band concert. When we went back outside she shook her head at Jerry Schultz, who'd been hanging around waiting for her to rejoin him. Then she went and climbed into the car and sat there by herself the rest of the evening.

The matter of Alice White was no more than might have been expected.

The first time I noticed anything wrong between Kate and Alice was one night toward the end of the school year when Alice came over, the way she had so many times before, to "do" some subject with Kate, only to have Kate say she'd already done all her homework and she'd promised me she'd help me with mine.

It was news to me, Kate's promise, but I was too dumbfounded by her turndown of Alice to say so. I was even more dumbfounded when I realized, looking from the one to the other of them, Kate not smiling, keeping her eyes averted, Alice clutching her book to her, trying not to let her own smile fade even for a moment, that Kate knew I didn't have any homework that night to be helped with.

I thought it was only some squabble they'd had which they'd patch up sooner or later. Alice had, after all, been one of Kate's best friends, along with Mary Louise Fletcher and Sarah Frances Wunderley, ever since they'd entered the first grade together. Alice seemed to think it was only temporary, too. When we started going swimming she sat with Kate's group on the riverbank—though never next to Kate, I noticed—and she knocked herself out early in the summer trying to do things for Kate and ask her places and fix up double dates.

Kate was civil to her, and that was about all.

When I finally asked Kate about it, she said she knew it wasn't Alice's fault what her father had done to Maggie, "but the way she tries to act like nothing happened, and things ought to be the same as they always were, when she knows as well as I do what he said—well, I just can't stomach her."

After a while Alice stopped trying.

As for Warren White himself, he was to all appearances—and with a surely by now perplexed God still as his witness—going to campaign for Maggie in the fall election. At least so he kept telling Maggie whenever she ran into him, and so he maintained to Grandpa when he came over after work one day to look at Grandpa's corn. Grandpa, like Kate with Alice, was civil to him, and that was about all.

I didn't know what to make of him, but I thought maybe he'd had a change of heart after all those people had laughed in his face about the lie he'd told, probably upbraiding him while they were at it for being so ungrateful to Maggie after all she'd done for him. And I supposed Maggie must have had it out with him, too.

She hadn't. She said she was going to wait and see what developed when the campaign got under way after Labor Day. So there wasn't anything for me to do but wait and see, too.

The summer was dry. Although Grandpa's corn passed the first test, being knee-high by the Fourth of July, Nathaniel worried that it wouldn't be able to pass any more.

Early in August we tied the brown paper bags Kate had given Grandpa over all of Mr. Owen's and Mr. Beebe's tassels and silks. In the crossbreeding section, Grandpa snapped the tassels off the middle row as soon as they appeared, so its silks could be pollinated from the tassels on the row at either side, thus producing Mr. Owen Beebe.

He seemed to thrive, but as August wore on with hardly any rain, both Mr. Owen and Mr. Beebe turned so wan and shriveled, I didn't think they'd survive at all, and even Mr. Owen Beebe began to droop.

Nathaniel said why didn't we sprinkle the hose on them, but Grandpa said the whole point of inbreeding and crossbreeding corn was to produce a hybrid which would stand up to drought and other ravages. If it couldn't, what would be the use of it? So if it was going to die, let it.

Not that he let on to Mr. Owen or Mr. Beebe or their offspring that he felt that way about them. He was out walking up and down the rows of his plot every morning sometimes before the sun was hardly up, and again in the evening when the sun was going down—just to see, he always said, how they were doing. But from the way he acted, it was more as if he was trying to breathe encouragement at them.

Aunt Clarissa wrote saying they might come down one weekend, and my stomach hurt from thinking of what she'd have to say about all that field corn growing right there in the back yard and all tied up in brown paper bags, for mercy sakes. Didn't he have anything better to do than make a spectacle of himself? Really, Papa.

But they didn't come.

When other people kidded Grandpa, wanting to know if he

was afraid the crows would get at his corn or was he expecting an early frost—mopping the sweat off their brows as they said it—he just smiled and said he hated to throw anything away, even a brown paper bag, and that seemed a handy place to keep them.

The Saturday before the Labor Day weekend, Grandpa decided the bags over the tassels in the inbreeding rows had collected as much pollen as they were likely to. As soon as Nathaniel and I removed the protective bag from over the silk of each stalk, he covered the silk again with the bag from the stalk's tassel. Then he snapped the tassel off.

There wasn't any more we could do now, he said, but wait and see.

So there I was, waiting and seeing again, not wanting the summer to be gone, but anxious for the days and weeks to hurry by, so Maggie's election and Grandpa's harvest would both be over.

It was along about that time that all thoughts of either one were driven from my mind, for a few days at least, by what was to me the most thrilling discovery of the entire summer.

Sally Kline called me up one morning, all excited, to come over and play paper dolls with her. I didn't think paper dolls were all that exciting any more, but I didn't have an excuse ready and I couldn't think of one on the spur of the moment. So I went.

She met me at the door absolutely pop-eyed. As soon as we were upstairs in her room she shut the door, saying she'd only said play paper dolls on the phone in case her mother could hear her or somebody was listening on their line. She had the most fantastic thing to show me and *shh!*, to walk on tiptoe and not make a sound.

She opened her bedroom door and we tiptoed down the hall to the door to the attic, went in, shut it behind us, and crept up the stairs.

It was like a furnace up there.

Motioning me over to a corner where there was a bookcase

with a lot of old magazines and some books piled in it, she pulled a book out and showed it to me. It was a textbook her mother had used when she'd studied to be a nurse.

I said, "What the heck—"

"Look," she said, cutting me off. She opened the book to somewhere in the middle.

I stared at it, dumbfounded.

"And look here," she said, turning the page.

I stared again.

"And here." She turned another page.

"My gosh," I said, still staring.

There were six pictures in all.

"My gosh," I said again, when we'd looked at all of them at least three times, "how'd you find it?"

"I just happened to," she said. "Mother gave me some boxes of stuff to bring up here to the attic to store, and I was poking around, and I found this."

I crossed my fingers. "Have you told anybody else?"

She shook her head. "I just found it this morning."

It was all I could do to keep from clapping my hands. Wait till Barbara Kaiser heard this!

I thought at first I'd wait until we went swimming that afternoon, but I was so afraid she'd be out at Cedar Lake and we'd be at the river, or the other way around, that as soon as I left Sally's, I rode my bike over to the Kaisers' and asked the maid to tell Barbara to come out.

The minute I told her I knew where babies came from, and it wasn't Sears & Roebuck, like she'd palmed off on me, this was the real McCoy, her eyes flew wide. "Where?"

I poked her in the stomach. "There."

"There?" she said, her voice shooting high. "I don't believe it."

"Well, I don't care if you don't," I said. "It's true."

"How do you know?"

I was tempted not to tell her, she was so hoity-toity. Barbara hated not being the one who was doing the telling, which was why I'd raced right over there. She still hadn't forgiven me for telling her back in the third grade there wasn't any Santa Claus.

"You're making it up," she said when I didn't answer right away.

"No, I'm not." I told her about the pictures. "Go see for yourself if you don't believe me."

She couldn't get over it.

"Well," she said at last, "if that's where they come from, how do they get there?"

I sighed. I knew she'd ask me that.

"Well?" she demanded.

I'd only been able to think of one thing. I didn't suppose it was right, but I knew she'd never admit she didn't know what it meant. And it sounded good.

I beamed at her. "Cross pollination."

Chapter Twelve

Labor Day marked the traditional starting point of the campaign for the fall election, but no self-respecting candidate for public office ever let the calendar stand in his way when it came to politicking. Before the summer was over, campaign posters were appearing on telephone poles all over the county, and any gathering, no matter how slight, served as a vehicle for the inevitable handshake and the smiling request for "your vote for me in November."

Whenever Maggie had occasion—or could manufacture one —to drive out into the county, she made it a point to stop at as many farm homes on the way there and back as she could. She did so for two reasons. The farm vote was much heavier than the town vote, and the farmers, more than the townspeople, appreciated a personal visit from the candidates, perhaps because in addition to the sense of importance it gave them to be thus individually sought out, it provided them with company, and the day-to-day routine of their lives affording them little in the way of socializing, company was always welcome.

Nathaniel and I sometimes went with Maggie on these drives. I don't know why we wanted to since she didn't take us inside with her, and we spent most of our time sweating it out in the car wishing she'd hurry up and get finished talking to them so we could get a move on. But we went—I suppose mainly because of the drive itself.

Maggie seldom said anything to us one way or the other about how she was doing, but we got so we could predict, or thought we could, anyhow, whether people were going to vote for her or not.

No matter how the visit had gone, either the farmer or his wife or both of them—sometimes children, too—would accompany her out of the house at least as far as onto the porch, where there would be handshakes and a "nice to see you" all around, but it seemed to us the ones who were going to vote for her put more enthusiasm into it.

It also seemed to us she garnered more enthusiasm at the beginning of the summer than at the end of it, but by the end of summer the weather had been hot for so long, people were always saying it was an effort just to get through the day, and they tried not to exert themselves any more than they could help because it only made them feel the heat more.

Even Maggie was beginning to look a bit wilted.

After one particularly unenthusiastic morning (according to our barometer: three calls, no votes) we stopped at a farmhouse just off the state highway a few miles south of town.

Maggie told us it would be her last call for this trip, so after she went inside we started debating whether to choose orange pop or grape pop when she treated us at the Standard station on the way in.

She was gone an even longer time than usual, but just when we'd decided we couldn't stand it another minute without expiring, out she came accompanied by a tall, thin, elderly farmer.

He walked all the way down to the car with her. After she got in and was stepping on the starter, he leaned down to the open window. "The wife and I are going to vote for you, Maggie. You can depend on it. The son and his wife, too."

Nathaniel and I beamed at one another.

Maggie said, "Thanks, John," and smiled at him, but it was such a fleeting smile and she looked so discouraged after it was gone, I thought she mustn't have believed what he said. I turned to look back at him as we headed down the drive.

He was standing where we'd left him, looking after us. "What's his name, Maggie?" I asked.

"John Summerville."

I frowned, trying to think why the name was familiar to me. Then I remembered. John Summerville was the man Maggie had told Kate and me about who'd had his barn burned down in the heyday of the Ku Klux Klan.

Since the Republicans were in the majority in Rose County, Maggie needed a substantial number of their votes to ensure a margin of victory, especially so this year in order to counteract the loss of those Democratic votes which Orn's deal would cost her. She called on Republicans, therefore, as well as Democrats.

One day, coming back to town from the east, we passed John Wurlitzer out feeding his hogs. As Maggie slowed down, which meant she was going to stop, Nathaniel and I looked at each other in dismay, the smell of the hogs and the slop almost more than either of us could bear. But when she turned into his yard and parked, we were in an upwind position, so it wasn't so bad after all.

Maggie went over to speak to him where he stood, taking care, I noticed, to stay upwind herself.

Even so, the sun was broiling hot, and they were right out there in it, Mr. Wurlitzer mopping his balding head with a red bandanna, another one tied around his neck to catch the sweat that trickled down before he could get to it.

They talked for about as long as she and John Summerville had, and, like Mr. Summerville, Mr. Wurlitzer walked back to the car with her, saying as they came into our hearing, "A story like that's always hard to stop once it gets started. It's hard enough just to keep it from getting any worse. But I'll do what I can."

He opened the door for her. "I've never voted for a Democrat in my life. I must say it kind of goes against my principles." He grinned at her. "But then I guess it would have gone against my principles even more to lose my reputation as a smart man with a dollar."

Mr. Wurlitzer leaned into the back window toward me. "Your granddad still nursing that popcorn of his along?"

"It isn't popcorn," I said, knowing he knew it wasn't.

"Oh? I thought that's what he was keeping all those brown paper bags so handy for." He grinned again and, as Maggie drove out of the yard, waved to Nathaniel and me waving back to him.

Not all of Maggie's calls were at farm homes. She drove out to Cedar Lake a few times to call on people there.

Now that the road around Cedar Lake had been blacktopped, Maggie didn't expect many of the cottage people to drive all the way down from Chicago on Election Day just to vote for her, but some of them said they would anyhow, and some others of them who had been forced to sell their homes in Chicago because they'd lost their jobs and were too old to compete for another one, lived at the lake all year round now like the few local people there.

Nathaniel and I didn't miss any of the trips to Cedar Lake. Even Kate and Mary Louise Fletcher went along on those. Maggie would drop all of us off at the public beach so we could go swimming, picking us up again when she was ready to go back to town.

Except one Sunday afternoon in August, when Kate and I were the only ones along, and Maggie asked us if we'd mind staying with her. When she asked that, I knew where we were going before she told us.

I didn't suppose Maggie was afraid of Dynamite Dom. Nor did I have the impression she thought he might be entertaining the kind of idea about her Orn Fletcher once had. I supposed it was more like that day at the hearing in the courtroom, though how the presence of Kate and myself could prevent people from thinking she was in some sort of conspiracy with Dynamite Dom was more than I could figure out.

I was wrong, as usual. As Maggie eventually explained to me, she wasn't concerned that day about any talk of a conspiracy between herself and Dynamite Dom. She saw no connection between Lester Crabbe's outrageous charge that blacktopping the road around Cedar Lake was part of a political conspiracy to let the Chicago gangsters come down and take over Rose County and the equally outrageous but more likely-to-be-listened-to charge that she had entered into a conspiracy with "that Chicago crowd" to defraud the people of Rose County of the eighty-seven thousand dollars in securities. The Ku Klux Klanners for whose benefit the latter charge was being circulated were not interpreting "that Chicago crowd" as gangsters, nor were they meant to. "That Chicago crowd" meant Catholics and other foreigners who were all too eager to use any means they could to get in power in this country, including buying their way in with stolen money.

What Maggie was concerned about was the original Jim Petrie version of the story about her. Contrary to her expectation, it had not been supplanted by the second version, but was still being circulated—at least, in some quarters. In some other quarters it was being circulated right along with the second one. What it came down to, I suppose, was who listened to whom—and which version who was prepared to tell.

In view of the fact that the second version was potentially far more damaging, and realizing as she must have even then how any story passing through so many willing hands could become more and more distorted, Maggie's concern that day seems almost funny now. Yet I suppose it would have been uppermost in the mind of any woman. Maggie could, after all, point out that the securities were still in the bank where she'd put them, and she was under bond to see they remained there in safekeeping, but as far as Jim Petrie was concerned, she had only her word against someone else's that he had not given her any money nor—the obvious assumption—was anything going on between them to have made it worth his while.

If people thought that about her and Jim Petrie, they could think it about her and Dynamite Dom. Therefore she wasn't taking any chances.

She told Kate and me on the way out to the lake that Dynamite Dom—who almost never spoke on the telephone himself, but let his flunkies do it for him—had called her that morning and asked her to come out at three o'clock. She didn't know what he wanted. He hadn't said, and she hadn't asked. She supposed maybe he wanted to make a campaign contribution.

He did. A somewhat unique, if characteristic, one.

Dynamite Dom's walled-in villa was built on a point of land between the road and the lake, directly across from the South Shore Hotel and Dance Pavilion. When we pulled up by his gate, I noticed a lot of cars parked around, but I supposed they belonged to people at the hotel.

A guard opened the gate for us, tipping his cap to Maggie and addressing her as "Miss Maggie." I'd expected him, so I wasn't surprised, but by the time we reached the door of the villa, so many other guards had popped up out of the bushes at us as we passed by them, I was about ready to come apart.

Each of them tipped his cap to her, too, and said, "Miss Maggie," but that didn't make up in my mind for scaring me half to death. When Dynamite Dom himself opened the door, I had so far forgotten my almost friendly feeling toward him after he gave me the dollar bill that, for all his beaming "Hello, hello. Come in, come in," I had all I could do to bring myself to go inside.

I didn't know what horror awaited me there, and as we followed him down a dimly lit corridor toward the living room, the fact that I couldn't see too well didn't help.

When we reached the living room, which had windows on three sides, making it nearly as bright as the outdoors, I blinked my eyes and gasped outright. The room was filled with people.

Maggie was as astonished as I was, though since she wasn't expecting to be mowed down at any moment, she didn't gasp. She said, "Well, for goodness' sake."

I took another look.

Dynamite Dom had invited—ordered, more likely—every Italian in Rose County to come to his villa that afternoon.

There were more Italians in Rose County than might be

expected in a rural area dominated by people of German and Scandinavian stock, and there was a reason for it.

Shortly after the turn of the century, some Chicago promoters decided that the sand hills near North Union contained qualities which would produce excellent glassware, most particularly the then-popular cut glass. In a burst of enthusiasm they purchased more than a hundred acres of land, divided it into lots, and proceeded to bring prospective customers down from Chicago by the trainload Sunday after Sunday so they might feast their eyes—and their imaginations—on the bright future in store for them. Lots were sold, homes were built, and a large number of families, many of them Italian, moved in, only to have the bubble of excitement burst when experts declared the sand unsuitable for making any kind of glass except Indian beads.

Some families had gone back to Chicago. Others stayed, making what living they could as hired hands for farmers or as farmers themselves or as storekeepers or mechanics in North Union.

His captive audience assembled and Maggie there to greet them, Dynamite Dom made his campaign contribution. He told them he wanted all of them to vote for her. In keeping with his Cedar Lake personality, he didn't add "or else." But Republicans though most of them were, as, indeed, he was himself, I counted on some more split tickets come November.

After the assembly broke up and everybody left, Dynamite Dom insisted on our staying to meet his wife and have some refreshments.

Mrs. Petrelli was as quiet as Dynamite Dom was voluble—a small, slender woman with black hair drawn into a bun at the nape of her neck, dressed, in spite of the summer heat, all in black.

We went outside onto a terrace where she had laid a table for us. As we were sitting down, Dynamite Dom asked her something in Italian.

She shook her head at him, saying, *"No, caro, mi dispiace. Posso prenderli?"*

"No, no," he said. "You stay. I get." He beckoned me to come along.

Maggie nodded to me, so I turned to go with him. I thought he meant for Kate to come, too, but apparently he didn't. When I shot her a look meaning come along anyhow, she only grinned at me.

I followed him back down the corridor again, our footsteps echoing in the silence, into a room off one side of it. Once again I drew in my breath, but only out of astonishment this time.

Except for being smaller, the room was like the back room at Joe Lafferty's bakery, a great brick oven with an iron door built into one wall, in front of it a metal worktable with all kinds of cloth-covered pans and trays on it, against another wall cupboards and a sink and a small stove.

Dynamite Dom beamed at me. "You like?"

I nodded.

"It's my bakery. You know I'm a baker?"

I shook my head.

"In the old country that's what I do."

I wanted to ask him why he'd changed his occupation, but even if I'd had the nerve, I didn't have the voice.

"Americans"—he shook his head—"they make"—he stopped, frowning, gesturing—"lousy bread." He laughed at the slang word which sounded so strange coming from him. "I make very fine bread. And for you I bake something special this morning. Come. See." He pulled the cloth off a pan.

It was filled with tiny chocolate frosted cakes in the shape of mounds. *"I dolci,"* he said. "Sweets. For you, Angela." He gestured. "Take."

I took one and bit into it. The bottom part inside the chocolate frosting was like sponge cake, the top a very sweet jam with a nutty, figlike flavor. It was unlike anything I had ever tasted.

He gave me an anxious look. "You like?"

244

I nodded and put the rest of it in my mouth. I liked it very much indeed.

He beamed. "That's good." He filled a plate with them. "When I come to live here all the time, maybe in the spring, you come visit me, and I show you how to make *i dolci*, yes? You like that?"

I didn't know if I did or not, but I nodded anyhow.

"And bread. We make good bread, not—not—" He gestured helplessly.

"Lousy," I said, and jumped at the sound of my own voice.

He nodded, beaming. "Lousy. Not lousy bread. Come now. We go back."

At that moment the door burst open, and a white-faced guard came tearing through. This time I really gasped. He was carrying a Tommy gun pointed straight at me.

He was also spewing out something in Italian, but Dynamite Dom stopped him cold with one word, *"Idiota!"* stepping up to him and pushing the gun aside, gesturing back at me.

The guard looked at me as if I didn't exist and nodded. Then he turned back to Dynamite Dom and spoke to him in rapid-fire Italian, pointing with his free hand in the direction of the road, waving his arm in a circle over his head.

I couldn't understand a word of what he was saying, but I gathered we were being surrounded. I wondered which way I should run, then wondered why I bothered wondering that when I was so rooted to the floor I couldn't even lift my feet.

Dynamite Dom asked a couple of questions, also in Italian, shaking his head at the answers. Then he said something to the guard, and the guard nodded and left.

Dynamite Dom turned back to me, beaming again. "Come."

I still couldn't move. I just stood there quivering.

His beam changed to a look of distress. Muttering *"idiota"* again, he came over to me and took my hand. "It's nothing, little Angela. Nothing to be afraid about." He jerked a thumb over his shoulder toward the door. "He thinks he saw someone ride by. He's a very excitable fellow, that one. He's always seeing someone ride by. He makes even me afraid sometimes. I think I get rid of him."

I swallowed, and he frowned at me. "You know. How you say it?"

I knew how, but I couldn't help him out this time.

He beamed. "Fire him. Discharge him. Yes?"

"Oh," I managed then, "yes."

But what little progress I had made toward warming up to him was wiped out once again. He knew it. He said and did everything he could the rest of the time we were there trying to get me to like him. He even showed me pictures of his three grandchildren, saying the next time they came down for a visit I must come play with them. But it wasn't much use.

As we were leaving he told Maggie about the plans he'd made for the Labor Day weekend as chairman of the Cedar Lake Community Club's entertainment committee.

Every year the club sponsored a farewell carry-in picnic supper and dance, open to anyone who wanted to come. Not on Labor Day itself. That was the day the summer people packed up and drove back to Chicago. On the Saturday night preceding it.

The affair was to be held this year at the South Shore Hotel across the road. Determined to make it the biggest and best one yet, and no more of a one to let the calendar stand in his way than the candidates who were running for office, Dynamite Dom was personally contributing a fireworks display—not only, he assured us, bigger and better than the one the club had staged on the Fourth of July, but the most spectacular fireworks display anybody around here had ever seen. After the fireworks, of course, there'd be the dance in the hotel's pavilion.

Kate was starry-eyed just listening to him tell about it. The minute we got into the car she asked Maggie if we were going to go. Maggie said she supposed we would. And we did.

So did nearly everybody else around, including, of all people, Lester Crabbe, who couldn't find anything to crab about for once other than the mosquitoes. It seemed to me, in fact, that half of Roseville was there, not to mention a great crowd of people from the lake. After supper there were even some farmers parked along the road, come to see the fireworks.

A lot of candidates were there, of course, and, of course, shaking hands all around soliciting votes.

Other than Dynamite Dom, who was all over the place again welcoming people and making sure everybody was having a good time, Warren White was the busiest man there, moving from one picnic table to another to clasp somebody's hand, his eyes already darting ahead to the next somebody, unable, with so many voters to get around to, to give each one more than a smiling "Hello, how are you?"

Except when he came over to our table. Then you would have thought, except for the wandering eyes, he had all the time in the world and nothing he'd rather do more with it than talk to Maggie.

He was full of promises, as usual, but as Grandpa remarked when he finally went on his way, he noticed Warren White didn't suggest Maggie accompany him on the rest of his rounds so he could start fulfilling the promise.

Maggie just shrugged and repeated her intention to have it out with him one of these days. All she was waiting for was the right moment.

The right moment, as it turned out, was about four hours away.

The most interesting candidate there to me was Pete Bolen, whom Maggie pointed out to us. A little later he came over to our table, very earnest in the face if a bit limp in the handshake, saying he didn't suppose he could count on any votes from this table, ha-ha, but he hoped, however the election turned out, there'd be no hard feelings. Looking at him and listening to him, I didn't see how he could possibly beat Maggie, and my hopes rose.

The Fletchers were there, of course. Julia came over to tell Maggie she'd be happy to help her with mailings or in any

247

other way she could, to just let her know. At one point I saw her talking to Warren White, and I wondered what she had thought of the lie he'd started circulating about Maggie and if maybe she was having it out with him herself, but they were too far away for me to hear what they were saying.

Orn Fletcher didn't come over. Nor did he have any contact with Pete Bolen that I was aware of, but I did see him talking to Gus Hardaker a couple of times during the evening and to Warren White every now and then.

Priscilla Rogers came over and sat down with us for a few minutes, saying to Maggie in her dry way, "Welcome to the club."

I had to get Kate to explain it to me. As usual, she didn't want to, but also as usual she was in to me for money. I was glad Miss McCray's exhortations had had even less effect on Kate than on me or I wouldn't have been able to find out what little I did about what was going on.

As it was, Kate's explanation left something to be desired, since she was as unaware as I was at the time of the second version of the story about Maggie.

She asked me if I remembered Maggie telling us how the Klan had trumped up a charge of immoral behavior against Mrs. Rogers that summer back in the middle of the twenties. When I nodded she said, "Well, that's what she meant."

I frowned at her. "But it was Mr. White and Marcella who did it to Maggie."

Kate shrugged. "It amounts to the same thing."

I supposed, after thinking about it for a minute, it did. "But there isn't any Klan any more, is there?"

"Maggie said there wasn't."

"Well, then?"

She shrugged again. "I don't know."

I didn't know either, so I had to let it go at that. In any case, it was getting dark by then, and Kate went off to meet her friends to watch the fireworks with, so I hunted up Grandpa and Nathaniel.

The fireworks lived up to Dynamite Dom's promise—skyrocket after skyrocket bursting into showery umbrellas high over the lake, the grand finale a breathtaking American flag in red, white, and blue lights.

A lot of people went home after that, but just as many or more stayed for the dance. We stayed, mostly because Maggie was politicking, but also because Kate would have had a fit if we hadn't.

As we were coming back from the lakeshore, crossing the road to the hotel, Nathaniel poked me and pointed to somebody up ahead of us. It was Chuck Sellers.

He turned to look in our direction, and I ducked behind Grandpa, staying there until Nathaniel nodded to me that it was okay to come out. When I did, I couldn't see Chuck anywhere at all.

After we got up to the pavilion Nathaniel and I both looked around, but we didn't see him there either. We decided he'd gone home with the others.

Grandpa went off to the verandah of the hotel to play pinochle with a group of men. Nathaniel and I hung around the side of the pavilion for a while watching Kate and Mary Louise and Ellen dancing with their various boyfriends. When we grew tired of that, we went outside to swing in the big two-seater over in the side yard of the hotel.

Dynamite Dom was standing in the doorway talking to Maggie and some other people when we went out. He waved to us and sent one of his bodyguards over to start us off with a push.

After we'd swung for a while we decided we were thirsty. Nathaniel said he'd go get us some pop, and I said I'd sit in the swing and wait for him, but he was gone so long I got tired of sitting there. I hopped off and wandered around the yard, looking up through the trees at the sky, trying to find the only two constellations I could recognize—the Big Dipper and the Little Dipper.

I wandered farther away than I intended to. It wasn't until I heard a rustling and a snap and peered around me that I realized I was well beyond the area of light cast through the windows of the hotel.

I was hotfooting it back when somebody popped out from behind a bush and grabbed me. As much as it scared me, I thought it was one of Dynamite Dom's guards, and I was all set to yell at him he was on the wrong side of the road when I realized he didn't have a cap on. I looked into his face.

It was Chuck Sellers.

I started to yell for Nathaniel—or anybody—but he clamped a hand over my mouth and pulled me tight against him. My mouth was already open when he did it, so I bit him, and he reacted enough to give me room to shout. But my shout only came out as a squawk before he clamped his hand over my mouth again.

I was pushing and pulling and twisting and kicking at him, the breath half choked out of me, but he was so much stronger than I was I wasn't accomplishing anything. When he started dragging me back behind the bush with him, I pushed and pulled and twisted and kicked with all the strength I had in me, but I still couldn't accomplish anything.

His breath reeked of liquor, and his eyes were more creepy than ever. I thought my own eyes were going to bug right out of my head if somebody didn't come quick.

Somebody did.

An arm shot out from somewhere, and I heard a crack as a fist landed on Chuck Sellers' jaw, sending him sprawling to the ground. I turned and looked straight into the barrel of a gun, and from the gun at Dynamite Dom holding it.

At that particular moment I wouldn't have thought I could be any more scared than staring into Chuck Sellers' face or into the barrel of a gun could make me, but the look on Dynamite Dom's face as he stood over Chuck Sellers was enough to drain what little breath there was left in me out.

The look on his face, and the sound of his voice. "Get up," he said, kicking a foot against Chuck.

Chuck staggered up, his eyes going from face to gun and back to face.

"Pig," Dynamite Dom spat at him. *"Bastardo."* He waved the gun. "Move."

By this time the two bodyguards were there. One of them poked his gun into the middle of Chuck's back.

Dynamite Dom tossed his own gun to the other bodyguard. "Take him to the house." As they moved off, he knelt down beside me. "Angela, little one, you all right?"

I was, in spite of the fact that I was shaking all over and couldn't make myself stop.

He picked me up, called one of the bodyguards back and told him to get Maggie, then carried me across the road and into his villa, patting me on the back and murmuring things to me in Italian.

He'd no more than sat me down on the davenport in the living room and started explaining to his wife when Maggie came flying in, with Nathaniel and Orn Fletcher and Warren White right behind her. Nathaniel had come back with the two bottles of pop just in time to see Dynamite Dom send Chuck Sellers sprawling. He'd gone tearing off to get Orn, who was with Warren White, so they had both come running back with him.

"It's all right. It's all right," Dynamite Dom said to Maggie, who was white-faced and wide-eyed. He nodded to a guard. When Chuck was brought in, Dynamite Dom told Maggie and the others what had happened.

They all went white in the face then, but Orn did more than that. In three great stiff-legged strides he crossed the distance between himself and Chuck and struck him across the face with the back of his hand. For the second time Chuck went sprawling.

Nathaniel shrank back onto the davenport beside me as Chuck lay on the floor staring up at Orn.

"You dirty, rotten son of a bitch," Orn said to Chuck.

But it was Maggie who carried the day. "Take a good look at him, Orn," she said to him. "It's yourself you're looking at."

Orn turned to stare at her.

"The county born-and-bred one hundred percent white Protestant American."

He started to speak, but Maggie put her hand up. "Oh, no, you wouldn't assault a child. Is that what you wanted to say? Or give any other man the license to do it. To any child. No matter who the man is or who the child is. But then children aren't your particular bent, are they?"

Orn's face went whiter than before.

"In politics it's what's at stake that counts, is it? And that's all that counts?" She pointed to me. "That's what counts, Orn. And that's all that counts."

Orn looked over at me as if he was going to throw up, but he didn't.

All he said to Maggie, and that in a dead voice, was, "Do you want to prefer charges against him?"

"You're damn right I want to prefer charges against him."

Orn went to the telephone and called the sheriff.

Chuck heaved himself up to a sitting position, and one of the guards brought his gun up, but Chuck wasn't going anywhere. He didn't even look at the guard or at anybody else, but sat staring down at the floor, one hand shielding his face against the light from a nearby floor lamp.

Maggie turned to Warren White. "And don't think you don't have a share in this. You, with your fawning as-God-is-my-witness gratitude to me for saving your worthless neck, while all the time you're going up and down the alleys routing out the Kluxers to spread your lies about me." She eyed him with contempt. "All for the soul-satisfying achievement of adding Honorable to your name."

He raised a protesting hand. "Why, Maggie," he bleated.

She made a face. "Don't Maggie me. It was a different story when it was your child who was in jeopardy, wasn't it? Your child who might have to go hungry because her father would be a pauper. Now see what you've done to my child with your filthy, rotten bigotry. You make me sick."

Orn had come back, and she turned to him again. "You both make me sick."

Orn nodded as if he agreed with her. He turned to Dynamite Dom, saying if it was all right with him, he'd wait outside until the sheriff came.

Warren White went with him, but when Nathaniel and Maggie and I came out a few minutes later, Orn was standing by himself outside the gate, down a way from it.

It wasn't until Maggie had collected Grandpa and Kate and we were in the car going home that I realized I hadn't said one word to Dynamite Dom for rescuing me from Chuck Sellers.

I thought of asking Maggie to take me back so I could thank him, so I could tell him, too, that I did want him to show me how to make the little *i dolci* cakes when he moved to Cedar Lake the next spring for good. But I didn't suppose she'd want to go back after all we'd been through, so I decided to let it wait until the next time I saw him.

I never saw him again. One afternoon in the middle of October he was machine-gunned to death as he was walking up the steps of his home in Chicago.

Chapter Thirteen

Nathaniel came over on Labor Day to say good-bye. His mother had come down the day before, and he supposed she'd take him back to Chicago with her that night.

"What do you mean, suppose?" I asked him.

We were sitting on the back steps. Nathaniel frowned out at Grandpa's corn, which stood stiff and dry and forlorn-looking. "Well, she hasn't said anything yet, but—" He frowned down at his shoes. "That's what she came here for, wouldn't you think?"

I would have thought so, but I didn't know. "I guess so."

"I'm all packed."

A wind stirred up from somewhere, rattling the corn. I shivered. It had turned cool in the night, and it felt more like fall than summer. "I think," I said, "I would have waited till I knew for sure."

He frowned out at the corn again. "She has to take the train at six o'clock. I didn't want her to go without me because I wasn't ready."

"You'd think, since she's been here since yesterday, she would have said something before now."

"I guess she just took it for granted I'd know."

I tugged at my ankle socks, which had slipped down at the heel into my shoes. "I guess so."

Nathaniel stood up. "Well, I guess I'd better go."

I stood up, too. "I wish you didn't have to. I mean, I know

you'd like to go home, but I wish your mother would move to Roseville. Then you could be home here."

Nathaniel nodded. "I'll speak to her about it."

"If you don't go," I said, "I'll see you at school tomorrow."

"Yeah," he said. "Well—good-bye."

He stuck out his hand, and I shook it. "Good-bye, Nathaniel."

When I walked into the sixth-grade room the next day, Nathaniel was there.

"What did she say this time?" I asked him.

"She has to get adjusted."

I frowned. "What to?"

He shrugged. "Beats me."

Nathaniel didn't come home with me so much that fall. He was always saying he had somewhere else to go, though sometimes after he said it and I'd started on down the street, he'd call to me and run and catch up and come home with me after all.

One time after we'd been to Ward's, when he said he couldn't come home with me, I asked him why. He said, "I'm not supposed to be with you so much."

"Why?"

He frowned down at the sidewalk. "Uncle Orn said so."

"But why?"

Nathaniel frowned some more and got pink in the face. "Because you're a—because you're a girl."

"Hell's bells, Nathaniel," I said, "I've been a girl all along."

"I thought you said it's a sin to swear."

"Well, it is. I forgot."

"Will you have to confess it?"

I nodded.

I didn't tell Nathaniel I was glad I'd forgotten, but I was. It would give me something to say the next Saturday besides quarreling with Kate and thinking up ways to get out of helping her clean the house, which was about all I was ever able to come up with.

I thought it must sound monotonous to Father Kolchek,

though he'd never said so. At least, not so far as I knew. In the confessional he sat behind a screen with a handkerchief up to his face, so I didn't always catch everything he said. And since it didn't seem to me to be the kind of place where you said, "What did you say?" or "Would you mind speaking up?" I just made out the best I could.

I didn't know whether Orn wanted Nathaniel to stay away from me because of what Maggie had said to him the Saturday night of the Labor Day weekend or because he was afraid Nathaniel would turn into a sissy if he was with me so much. At any rate, Nathaniel started spending more time with Bobby Jackson and Orville Watkins.

He asked me a couple of times if I wanted to go along, but all they ever did was chin themselves or toss a football around or work with the Charles Atlas equipment or go out to the woods and get their hands stained picking black walnuts. I couldn't see anything interesting in that.

I wondered if that was the sort of thing Kate had to do when she went out with a boy and they didn't go to a movie or a dance, but I was afraid if I asked her she'd say I was a jerk. I decided to wait and find out when the time came. If it ever did. I wasn't any nearer to getting a front than I had been the year before.

Nathaniel did come over the first Saturday in November, when Grandpa harvested his corn. I was glad we had it to do. Election Day was the next Tuesday, and I was beginning to get nervous.

A lot of things had been happening. And not happening.

One thing that didn't happen, to nobody's surprise, was Warren White's campaigning for Maggie. Grandpa went to the Legion Hall one night to hear him speak. When he came home he said to Maggie, "If you can call 'vote the Democrat ticket in November' campaigning for you, then he campaigned for you."

Maggie made a face.

"Maggie—" I said.

"What?"

"Did Mr. White campaign for you last time?"

She shook her head. "He'd hardly more than started taking an interest in politics in 1928."

"Well," I said, "if you didn't need him then to win, you can win without him this time, too, can't you?"

She smiled at me. "I guess I'll have to."

"And you've still got the bank directors, haven't you?"

"Most of them."

It was a surprise to me to hear she didn't have all of them. I waited for her to go on, but she didn't, so while Kate and I were getting into bed I asked her who it was Maggie didn't have.

"Mr. Kaiser, I suppose," Kate said.

"Why?"

She shrugged. "Because we're Catholics."

I waited for her to go on, too, but she didn't. "Because we're Catholics and what else?"

"Nothing else."

I stared at her. "You mean just because we're Catholics?"

"That's what I said, didn't I?"

"Well, yes, but—"

"It's like Maggie told you that time about Mr. Fletcher. About being a bigot."

"You mean Mr. Kaiser is one, too?"

She nodded. "And Mrs. Kaiser along with him."

"But why?"

Kate shrugged. "How should I know? They just are, that's all. Why do you think Bill Kaiser didn't show up that night for the date I had with him?"

"I don't know. Why didn't he?"

"Because his mother and father wouldn't let him."

I stared at her some more. "Wouldn't let him?"

"That's right."

"But what does Bill Kaiser dating you have to do with politics?"

It was Kate's turn to stare at me. "Politics? It doesn't have anything to do with politics. Why should it?"

"I don't know. I thought—"

"Well, think again. They just didn't want him to go out with me, that's all."

"But why didn't they?"

"How many times do I have to tell you? Because we're Catholics."

"But Kate—you mean Mr. and Mrs. Kaiser wouldn't let Bill even take you to a movie—after he'd already asked you to go—just because we're Catholics?"

"That's right," she said again.

"And no other reason?"

"None whatever."

I shook my head at her. "Well, if that isn't the dumbest thing I ever heard."

"Yes," she said, "isn't it?" She snapped off the table light between our beds.

Another thing that didn't happen was Chuck Sellers didn't go to jail, other than for the one night after he was arrested by the sheriff. The next day he was out on bail to await trial, though not through any effort by Orn in his behalf.

A few nights before the trial was scheduled to take place at the end of October, the prosecuting attorney came out to the house to talk to Maggie. He told her that since Dynamite Dom was the only witness to the attack, and he was dead, the chances of a conviction were slim. If I took the stand to testify as to what had happened, I would have to undergo cross examination by a defense attorney whose business it would be to try to tear my testimony down. Did she want to put me through such an ordeal, with all the attendant publicity, possibly for nothing?

Maggie, who I suspect was beginning to think she'd already put both Kate and me through more than she had bargained for, talked it over with Grandpa, and they decided the prosecuting attorney was right. So the case was dismissed, and Chuck

258

Sellers went free. He also, having been fired by Orn, went on relief.

What was happening with Orn himself I didn't know. I hadn't understood too clearly what Maggie had meant when she accused him of being the same as Chuck Sellers, but I knew he understood it. I supposed he was so ashamed, not just for that, but for whatever else he and Warren White had brought on Maggie because of his bigotry, he must be doing whatever he could in the time that was left to make up for it.

As for the campaign itself, the biggest happening there—at least, the one people talked about most—was something I didn't understand too clearly, either.

One day after school as Nathaniel and I were coming into Ward's Drugstore I heard Marcella DeWitt say ". . . and the real reason he committed suicide—" Then she saw us and broke off.

It didn't mean anything to me at the time. I just figured something new had come up, the way it did from time to time, to set people off again about Mr. Petrie's suicide, speculating in the same old way as to why he'd done it and why the family had moved to Roseville from Chicago in the first place.

It didn't make any sense at all to me when I saw the ad Jim Petrie put in both the *Democrat* and the *Republican* the first week in October, the week before Dynamite Dom was killed.

Headed "To Whom It May Concern," his ad stated that while he was proud to be considered a friend by the county auditor, he had never on any occasion given or lent her any money whatsoever, nor had she ever asked him for any money, nor had she any cause to do so; that furthermore she had never discussed with him those securities which the county held in escrow other than to inform him of the scurrilous lie being circulated about her custodianship of those securities; that furthermore his name was James Edward Petrie, his father's name had been Arthur Allen Petrie, his paternal grandfather's name had been James Allen Petrie, and that at no time in the history of his family had the name been anything other than Petrie; that

259

no member of his family, either now deceased or now living, had ever had any connection whatsoever, by blood, marriage, business association, or otherwise with Mr. Dominic (Dynamite Dom) Petrelli, that the death by his own hand of Arthur Allen Petrie, his father, had been the result of despondency over long deteriorating health and nothing else; finally, that he was hereby serving notice that any individual heard making any statements contrary to the facts as herein stated would be sued for slander by the undersigned James Edward Petrie.

People were goggle-eyed over that for days, and when the news came that Dynamite Dom had been machine-gunned to death by a Chicago hoodlum, they talked about it even more—after first looking over their shoulders.

I tried to get Maggie to explain what the ad meant other than the part I already knew about, but she just said it had to do with some loose talk that had been going around. It was too complicated for me to understand. She was having a hard enough time trying to keep up with it herself.

Kate was there with me when I asked, but she only shrugged her shoulders when I looked at her, meaning she didn't have anything to tell me, so I knew there wasn't any point in asking her.

Maggie went up to Chicago for Dynamite Dom's funeral, and people talked about that, too, though she wasn't the only one to go, and since John Wurlitzer and his wife were among the mourners, and he was such a pillar of the Methodist church, it was hard to make anything much out of Maggie's going.

The morning of the funeral I thought of Dynamite Dom's wife—that small, quiet woman dressed all in black—and I thought of him and the day in his bakery when he beamed at me and said, "Americans make lousy bread. I make very fine bread. And for you I bake something special this morning. Come. See."

I wished, through my tears, he'd stayed a baker.

Julia Fletcher, true to her word, came to Maggie's office one Saturday afternoon to help get out a mailing. She also gave

Maggie a campaign contribution of ten dollars. But she must have been sore beset, what with not wanting to believe any of the things she'd heard about Maggie and being firmly of the opinion, as I'd heard her say to Bernice Kaiser and Marcella at Ward's, that where there's smoke there's fire. Julia being the kind of person she was, however, feeling that Catholicism was a misfortune Maggie had been stuck with through no choosing of her own, she no doubt also felt that whatever trouble Maggie might have gotten herself into was somehow the result of circumstances beyond her control.

There was one matter in which Julia displayed no ambivalence. I never had gone to the Fletchers' as often as Nathaniel had come to our house and I seldom went there any more at all, but I was there one day during the first week of school. As I was leaving, Julia and Orn were having something out behind the closed doors of the living room. What it was I didn't know until I heard her say, "I don't ever want to hear his name mentioned in this house again."

"How was I to know the son of a bitch was what he is?" Orn said. "As far as that goes, it was Maggie who sent him to me about a job."

"And that's the thanks she gets."

There was a moment's silence. Then Julia said, "Really, Orn, I wonder sometimes how you can live with yourself."

Over the years I've wondered it sometimes myself. I've never doubted that Orn was in fact as stricken with shame that Saturday night as I supposed him to be, but contrary to my other supposition, he was not doing whatever he could in the time that was left to make up for what he'd brought on Maggie, but continued, along with Warren White, to go "up and down the alleys routing out the Kluxers" against her.

But then I had no way of understanding at the time the full measure of what stirred within Orn Fletcher, that although he chose to use bigotry as a means to an end, it was neither the end he desired—to get revenge on Maggie while replacing her with a more cooperative auditor—nor his belief that the end justi-

261

fied the means which made his choice so easy. He was as much of a bigot himself as Maggie had claimed him to be—a man so narrow in concept, so strong in conviction, and so blind to reality that after maiming himself while trying to destroy a phantom he was able, like some self-renewing organism, to face the phantom whole again.

In spite of her detractors, Maggie didn't lack for support. Any number of people came up to her on the street to shake hands with her and pledge their votes, including old Mr. Fletcher, who told her he still hadn't forgotten what she'd done for the bank, and he never would—at the same time expressing his regret that, in view of the continuing deterioration of the banking situation generally, the board of directors could not risk having the bank made a campaign issue by offering a public statement to that effect.

Nor did Maggie lack in appeal. As Mr. Savery out at Cedar Lake loved to point out to her whenever we stopped at his filling station for gas, she still had the same things going for her she'd had the first time around, to which Mrs. Savery, now recovered from her typhoid fever complications and no longer in need of an absentee ballot, good-naturedly agreed.

There seemed to be general agreement on that point. Whenever Maggie went anywhere to make a speech, she always attracted a good crowd. Even those hand-shakers who didn't go so far as to pledge their votes at least wished her well.

In public Maggie acted confident, the way all the candidates had to, though it gave me the shivers to watch them, knowing they knew as well as I did only half of them could win.

At home she acted confident most of the time. Even after one of the discouraging days she didn't stay discouraged long, because, as Grandpa pointed out to her one night, she had something else going for her in this campaign. Pete Bolen wasn't very bright and showed it.

She also had the record of her first four years to run on, though I heard her say one time that whenever she was able to stop denying things long enough to bring it up, if the audience was a farm crowd some heckler was sure to ask her about the blacktopping of the road around Cedar Lake.

As the campaign neared its end, it was hard to tell from looking at her just how she felt, she looked so tired. Every candidate I saw looked tired. They had reason to. After working all day they were out every night appearing at some function or making a speech or going from house to house soliciting votes.

Maggie couldn't even be around the Saturday morning we harvested Grandpa's corn. She had to get up early and drive over to Jackson's Crossing to canvass the town before attending a noonday rally there.

We offered to wait until she returned, but she said she expected to be out all afternoon as well and for us to go ahead. We could show her our harvest that evening.

From the looks of Mr. Owen and Mr. Beebe I didn't think we'd have anything much to show her there. We didn't. The ears turned out as puny and shriveled-looking as I'd expected. A couple of the shucks didn't have any ears in them at all.

Grandpa wasn't discouraged. He said that proved the two strains had now been inbred as much as they needed to be.

As soon as we had those ears marked and stored away, we all crossed our fingers at each other and went back to the plot to harvest Mr. Owen Beebe. Nathaniel and I did one-potato, two-potato, and he won, so he picked the first ear.

When he brought it over I said, "It looks bigger anyhow."

After Grandpa shucked it, we all stared at it. It was not only bigger, it was beautiful. Grandpa turned it over and over in his hands, beaming at it. "Well, now," he said, "and I think we're on the right track."

I yelled to Kate to come out and see, then frowned at him. "On the right track? Isn't this it?"

He said to be patient until we'd picked the rest of it.

When we had it all picked and shucked, we went inside and laid the ears out on the kitchen table. Kate, who'd come running out without her coat on and had to go shivering back in, looked them over and said she thought they were beautiful, too, except didn't Grandpa think those three over there weren't quite as nice-looking as the others?

Grandpa nodded and said he'd send an ear from each of the rows to his young agriculturalist friend to look at, but he was pretty sure we'd done the right thing in inbreeding the two strains one more time. Our crossbreeds next year ought to really be something.

"Next year?" I sighed. "That's such a long time away, Grandpa."

"So many things will happen," he said, " 'twill be here before you know it."

"I suppose so," I said.

At school Tuesday afternoon we held a mock election, and Maggie won by a landslide. I felt good, but I kept reminding myself that Pete Bolen didn't have anybody in the sixth grade in Roseville.

When school let out, I sat on at my desk for a while, pretending I had to finish reading my geography, so everybody would go on ahead of me. When I figured they'd left the school ground, I came out of the building. I knew that what I was going to do was silly. I would have laughed at them the same as they would have laughed at me. But I had to do it anyhow. I walked all the way home without stepping on any cracks in the sidewalk.

Maggie had told us she'd get something to eat uptown, and if she wasn't home by bedtime not to wait up for her—the returns would probably be a long time coming in.

Grandpa said it was a good year for Democrats everywhere. People were sick and tired of waiting for President Hoover to do something besides tell them prosperity was just around the corner. Since the local Republicans had to say they were for President Hoover whether they were or not, they'd probably get beaten right along with him.

I thought Maggie might call sometime during the evening. Even Kate wouldn't talk to anybody on the phone for more than a couple of minutes, so the line wouldn't be busy when she tried. But she didn't call. Grandpa said she probably had too many things on her mind to think of it.

I went to the front window every now and then to look for her headlights, but I didn't really expect to see them.

Kate and I stayed up until after ten o'clock, and then Grandpa said we'd better go on to bed, we had to get up for school in the morning. He'd stay up awhile. If any word came, he'd let us know.

I asked Kate when we were getting undressed if she thought Maggie would win. Kate said of course she would. She'd won in 1928, hadn't she? And that was a Republican year. Besides, look how well she'd done in the primary.

I lay in bed thinking about what Kate had said, and I felt good again. But it was like Christmas morning. I was afraid to get excited until I'd rounded the turn and made sure there was something to get excited about.

I didn't think I'd be able to go to sleep, but I did. I woke up once when I heard somebody on the stairs. "Maggie?" I called out. But it was only Grandpa coming to bed.

The next time I woke up, it was so still I knew it had to be late, yet it wasn't pitch black in the room. I sat up in bed and looked out the window. The sky was turning gray.

I crawled out of bed thinking Maggie must be home by now, and I could round the turn.

I tiptoed out of Kate's and my bedroom and down the hall to hers. She was in bed.

I supposed she was asleep, and maybe I shouldn't wake her, but I went in and over to her bed to make sure.

She stirred then, so I whispered, "Maggie?"

"Yes," she said.

I took a breath. "Did you win?"

She shook her head. "No."

I stood there thinking I had rounded the turn, and there wasn't anything to see. I couldn't believe it.

But it was true.

"Oh, Maggie," I said, wanting her to reach out and hug me.

265

She just said, "Go on back to bed, honey. I'll tell you about it in the morning."

"All right," I said. But I didn't go back to bed. I got dressed without waking Kate and went downstairs and had a bowl of cereal and a glass of milk. Then, since the sun was up and I didn't know what else to do, I put my coat on and walked to school.

The playground was empty. I went over and sat in one of the swings, staring at first one thing and then another, not knowing what I saw.

A long time later somebody rounded the corner of the building and came across the playground toward me. It was Nathaniel.

"Hello," he said.

"She didn't win," I said, "and if you say anything sympathetic to me, I'll start crying."

He dug in his pocket and held out a handkerchief. "You already are."

He suggested we take a walk until it was time for school to start, so I blew my nose and we set off. He didn't say anything, and I didn't say anything. We just walked.

I was all right when we got back to school. The bell was ringing, with all the grades lining up to go inside, and nobody said anything at all to me, even the ones who turned around to look.

At morning recess I stood against the wall at the side of the school building and watched Sally Kline and some others spin on the Giant Stride. And tried to think why Maggie had lost.

I supposed she knew, and if I'd stayed home until she got up, she could have told me.

I wondered if maybe it hadn't been a Democrat year after all, but I knew that couldn't be so. I'd heard our teacher congratulate the fifth-grade teacher on Mr. Roosevelt winning.

I supposed Orn Fletcher had had a lot to do with it, in spite of Maggie saying it would take more than Orn Fletcher to get her out of office. I supposed the story Warren White and Marcella had made up between them about her and Jim Petrie had been at least part of the more, in spite of my not understanding, along with Jim Petrie, how anybody could have believed it.

From what little Maggie had said, I supposed the things I hadn't understood about his ad—the securities and the business about his name not being changed from Petrelli and his father's suicide being due to ill health and only that—had figured in it somehow. But I didn't know how.

Any more than I knew how all the men who liked Maggie so and all the ladies who admired her so for making all those sacrifices to bring up Kate and me could have voted against her.

But I had to stop thinking about the ladies and their sacrifices before I started crying again and made a fool of myself in front of everybody. If Maggie didn't know of anything else she could do in Roseville to make a living, then it wouldn't matter whether she wanted to go on making sacrifices or not. She wouldn't have anything to make them with.

And what, I wondered, would become of Kate and me and Grandpa, and Maggie, even?

I supposed we'd have to go on relief, like the Bassetts. And Grandpa would have to go live at the poor farm, because where else could he go? Aunt Clarissa didn't want him.

I took Nathaniel's handkerchief out of my pocket and blew my nose and thought it didn't do to think of things like that.

I screwed up my face and thought, Who made the world? God made the world. Who is God? God is the creator of heaven and earth and of all things. Why did God make you? God made me to know Him, to love Him, and to serve Him in this world, and to be happy with Him for ever in the next. Of which must we take more care, our soul or our body? We must take more care of our soul than of our body.

I blew my nose again and thought what a jerk I'd been not to think of my catechism in the first place, when it had the answers to everything that really mattered. The thing was to take care of our souls and stop worrying about living off county relief or sending Grandpa to the poor farm. We didn't have to do either one. We'd manage somehow, the same as Miss Mc-

Cray was doing, the way other people did when they had another baby or lost their jobs or needed a new coat and couldn't buy one. That's what you did when you were having a Depression. You managed somehow.

I shifted position against the wall and wished my catechism had the answer to why Maggie had lost.

It was shifting position that made me notice Barbara Kaiser. She was standing a little way over whispering something to Inez Blakely. I couldn't hear what, but out of the corner of my eye I saw her keep looking at me, so I knew it was about me.

I was surprised. Whatever differences Barbara and I had had over the years, we'd always had them out between us. She'd never stooped to this before.

I turned and looked straight at her to make her stop. She did, but it was only because she'd finished what she had to say. Genevieve McIntyre came along just then, and Barbara started in all over again.

I ran over to her and grabbed her arm before she had a chance to back away, twisting it around behind her back. "If you have something to say about me, say it to me."

She struggled to get her arm out, but even though she was bigger than I was, she was all fat, so I had her.

"Ouch!" she said. "Stop! You're hurting!"

"Then say it."

"I won't! And you can't make me!"

"Can't I?" I twisted her arm harder.

"Ow!" she yelled. "All right! But let go first."

"Talk first."

She glared at me, her round face pink.

"Talk," I said.

"All right," she snapped. "You think you're so much. Well, you're not. And everybody knows it now."

I stared at her, so dumbfounded I almost let go of her. "What's that supposed to mean?"

"You know as well as I do."

"I don't either."

"Well, if you don't, you should. It's why Maggie didn't win the election."

I frowned at her. "Why didn't she win it?"

"Because the Klu Klux Klan saw to it she didn't."

I let go of her then. "It's Ku, not Klu. And there isn't any Ku Klux Klan any more. Maggie said so."

"Well, I don't care what she said." She stood there rubbing her arm. "If there isn't one any more, how could they make her lose the election?"

She had me there.

I frowned at her again. "Why did they?"

"Why did they what?"

Barbara could be as exasperating as Kate. More so. Kate, at least, wasn't dumb. "Make her lose the election."

Barbara got a superior look on her face. "You ought to know that without having to ask me. You're one of them yourself, just like all the other Catholics."

"One what?"

"Con—conspiriator."

"What's a conspiriator?"

She rubbed her arm.

I shook my head at her. "You don't even know what you're talking about."

"I do, too," she answered. "It's the Catholic Church. Daddy says it's a big foreign conspir—conspir—"

"Conspiracy," Inez said.

Barbara nodded. "—conspiracy to take over America from the Protestants and put the pop in the White House."

"Pop?" I frowned at her, thinking of the sign old Mr. Cummings had had in the window of his ice cream and hamburger stand all the past summer: *We Don't Know Where Your Mom Is, But We've Got Your Pop On Ice.* "What do you mean, pop?" She wasn't making sense.

Genevieve spoke up. "She means Pope."

I looked at Genevieve, but she wouldn't look back at me. Neither would Inez.

"Well, anyhow," Barbara said, "that's what they're trying to do."

"You're crazy," I said.

For all the good that did. She said she wasn't, and I said she was, and we might have gone on that way forever, but the bell rang, so we had to go in.

I made it through the rest of the day one way and another. I would have made it through without any more tears if Miss McCray hadn't come up to me just as we were going outside for afternoon recess and said to me in that earnest way of hers, "I'm so very sorry, Angelica."

I nodded and turned away, my eyes swimming again.

During recess I sat on the steps playing jacks. Or playing at them. I couldn't concentrate on them. Barbara's words kept going through my mind.

You think you're so much. Well, you're not.

I frowned down at the jacks. Did I think I was so much?

I didn't know. I supposed I did. I supposed I must have. Why else would she say it?

I frowned at the jacks some more. Why would she say it anyhow?

You think you're so much. Well, you're not.

I rolled the little red rubber ball around in my hands, telling myself, let her think what she wants to about me. She's never liked me much anyhow.

I shook my head. It wasn't what Barbara thought about me that bothered me. It was her saying it to me. That was what I kept coming back to, what I couldn't understand.

Saying it to me and to anybody else who would listen to her. Making them not look back at me when I looked at them.

You think you're so much. Well, you're not. And everybody knows it now.

I swept up the jacks and squeezed them in my hand until the points bit into the flesh of my palm.

I didn't know what gave her the right to say it.

When school let out that afternoon, I went up to the court-house to see Maggie. I didn't know if she'd be there. I thought maybe she hadn't wanted to face anybody either and had stayed home in bed, the way I wished I had. But she was there.

She was alone in her office when I came in, not doing anything, just sitting at her desk with her chin in her hands, staring out the window across from her.

She looked tired. More than tired. She looked—the only thing I could think of I didn't like to think of, because it was what she was—defeated.

I wanted to say to her, "If they can't lick Mr. Gilligan—" but the words stuck in my throat, the way Barbara Kaiser's words were stuck in my craw.

They had licked Mr. Gilligan. There wasn't any magic in him any more.

I swallowed a couple of times and ended up saying what I always said when I came to her office. "Hi, Maggie."

She looked away from the window at me. "Hi, Angel." It was what she always said, too.

I wished it was still the day before, with a different turn to round. But it wasn't.

I went through the gate at the counter and back to her desk and sat down in the chair beside the desk, looking at the scuffs on my shoes. "Barbara Kaiser said you didn't win the election because the Ku Klux Klan saw to it you didn't."

As I looked up at her she nodded.

"I thought there wasn't a Klan any more."

"I thought so, too."

"Barbara said the Catholic Church is a conspiracy to take over America and put the Pope in the White House."

"That's nonsense."

"That's what I told her. Or the same as." I frowned at Maggie. "Do people really think that?"

She sighed. "Back in the twenties, in the heyday of the Klan, I heard a lot of people around here say it. I thought that kind of thinking was over and done with, like the Klan itself. But apparently some people still feel that way." She shrugged. "More people, I guess, than I realized."

"Why do they?"

"Because they're ignorant." She frowned at me. "What made Barbara say those things to you?"

I wanted to tell her I wished I knew, that the main reason I'd come to see her was to have her ask me that, so I could tell her what else Barbara had said. She would know what had made Barbara say it, and she could explain to me what gave her the right.

But sitting there looking at her, I didn't have the heart to somehow. "Oh," I said, "you know Barbara. She likes to be the one who does the explaining. She heard her father say why you didn't win, so she said it, too. I guess if her father is a bigot like Mr. Fletcher, he would be one of the people you said still felt that way."

Maggie nodded. "Yes, he is. Though it's hard for me to believe it of him."

"Why?"

"I should think he'd be smart enough to know better."

I wished I'd been smart enough to say that to Barbara.

The election returns, by precinct, were lying on Maggie's desk. I pointed to them. "Was it the farmers mostly?"

She shrugged. "Only because there are more of them." She sighed. "It was pretty nearly everybody."

I stared at her. "Even the people in Roseville?"

She nodded. Then she said, "Why do you ask that?"

I frowned at the scuffs on my shoes, trying to grasp enough of a thought to put it into words, but I couldn't. "I don't know."

It was a long time before I was able to work it out, before time and distance gave me enough perspective to understand what I couldn't come up with that day—that the people of Roseville were just as bigoted as the farmers whose ignorance they despised.

Not all of them. From the way the phone was to ring at home

that night and over the next few days and from the number of people who would go out of their way to speak to her on the street, Maggie still had many friends—people who had voted for her and were appalled at the skulduggery which had been indulged in to defeat her.

Ironically, some of the people who had voted against her still considered her a friend—now that she was no longer a threat.

"Mr. Petrie's ad," I said. "Was that because of the conspiracy talk?"

"All kinds of talk," she answered, shaking her head. "It's amazing the lengths some people will go to believe what they want to believe."

I wanted to ask her exactly what they had believed, but I didn't. I didn't want to talk about the election any more at all.

We didn't talk about it any more. Maggie got up from her desk and said, "Well, now that it's over, maybe people will find somebody else to gossip about and give me a rest. Come on. Let's go home."

All the way home I tried to work up enough nerve to ask her the one thing I still wanted to. We were turning into the driveway before I did. "Maggie," I said.

"Yes?"

"What will we do?"

She turned the engine off and sat there for a minute staring out the windshield. "I don't know," she said at last. "But we'll manage somehow."

It was what I had hoped she would say.

Chapter Fourteen

Maggie started looking for a job as soon as she was rested, but she didn't have anything to tell us until shortly before Christmas, and that wasn't to say she had a job but a reprieve. Her term of office was up the first of January, but Pete Bolen was having such a hard time learning the duties of the office, the county commissioners were paying her to stay on another month to teach him.

I hadn't expected Maggie to find anything right away. By definition, managing somehow wasn't easy, especially in Roseville.

It wasn't until her month of reprieve was almost up that she came home one night all smiles to say she'd found a job.

One of the people she'd written to after the election was her friend the state auditor, who had been reelected and who had promised to use whatever influence he had in her behalf. She'd been expecting him to write or call. Instead, he had been in Roseville that day on a routine visit to check the state's account with the Northern State Bank and Trust Company and had stopped up to see her to tell her the good news in person. She was to start the first of February as a relief administrator for the state welfare department.

After we'd all beamed at each other I said, "Where's their office here?"

"They don't have one," Kate put in. "But they'll open one. Is that it, Maggie?"

Maggie looked at us for a minute, her smile fading. "No. That's the only bad part of it. I won't be working here."

I stared at her. "Not here? Not in Roseville?"

"No."

"Not even some place you can drive to from here?"

She shook her head. "Not back and forth, no. I'll be working down in the southern part of the state. In Terre Haute."

Kate's eyes lit up. "You mean we're going to move?"

Maggie shook her head again, and the light in Kate's eyes died out. "No. Not right away anyhow. Not until I can work things out."

I didn't know why Kate should get so excited at the thought of moving away from Roseville. Or look so disappointed when she found out we weren't going to. I didn't want to move away from Roseville. Not right away or any time. But Roseville without Maggie in it? I thought I understood then the reason for Kate's disappointment. "You mean," I said, "we can't go with you?"

She nodded.

She put it more specifically to Uncle Donald and Aunt Clarissa when they drove down from Chicago the following Sunday to spend the day with us.

Maggie had no sooner told them what her new job was and where she'd be working than Aunt Clarissa, in her customary broadside way, turned to Uncle Donald and said, "I expect Papa had better come live with us now. Maggie has enough on her hands to worry about."

My stomach hardly had more than a chance to twinge before Maggie said she couldn't possibly get along without Grandpa. She needed him.

Grandpa beamed at her and said that was right. She wouldn't be able to take any of us with her, so he had to stay in Roseville to look after Kate and me.

I was afraid Aunt Clarissa would offer to take Kate and me along with Grandpa, but she only said, "Well, for mercy sakes, can't you sell this house and buy one down there or rent one?"

Maggie said, "When you have a five-thousand-dollar mortgage on a house that's only worth four, who do you think is going to buy it?"

Uncle Donald said, "I've told you all along you ought to be paying something on the principal."

"Saying is easier than doing," Maggie said.

"Well," Aunt Clarissa said, "you can't go on living like that indefinitely. You'll have to get rid of this house sometime."

That was when Grandpa came up with the solution I'd been searching for ever since Maggie had told us she was leaving. He said if things worked out the way he expected them to, we wouldn't have to get rid of the house, and Maggie could come back to Roseville to live.

Aunt Clarissa wanted to know what things, looking at him as if she expected him to say he was going to rob a bank.

Grandpa said his corn experimenting. He was sure this next summer would bring him the results he was looking for, and then all our worries would be over.

I beamed at him, and Aunt Clarissa wrinkled her nose.

When the first of February came, Maggie left.

I could hardly bear to see her go. I was afraid she'd never come back, even though she said she'd come up the first weekend she could. For the first time in my life I wished I had a younger sister, so she could say what I was thinking, and I could tell her not to be such a jerk.

The house wasn't the same after Maggie left, but then by that time not much else was the same either.

Although I hadn't been able to forget what Barbara Kaiser had said to me the day after the election, I finally told myself she was just talking through her hat. Until a couple of other things happened.

One Saturday afternoon in December I went to the movies, the same as I always did on Saturday afternoon. When I got there Loretta Gudeman was sitting in my seat. She knew it was my seat. It always had been, the way other kids' seats had always been their seats. But she wouldn't get up and move. So I finally went and sat somewhere else.

I didn't know what to make of it. The only thing Loretta had ever had against me that I knew of was the fact that I'd been chosen queen of the May Day parade when we were in the fourth grade. Loretta, who was far and away the prettiest girl in our class, couldn't have been any more dumbfounded about it at the time than I was, until I found out why I'd been chosen. I was supposed to set an example, all right, but it didn't have anything to do with looks. It didn't even have anything to do with grades or character or personality. I got to be queen because I'd had my diphtheria shots.

It seemed to me if anybody was still carrying a grudge about that, it ought to be me, not Loretta. It also seemed to me she'd been a mighty long time getting around to doing something about it. But if it wasn't that, I didn't know what else it could be. If anybody had told me right then it had something to do with her mother and father, I wouldn't have believed it. I didn't even know her mother and father.

The other incident took place on the playground at school. One morning during recess I was standing near the parallel bars waiting my turn to jump rope when I heard Kenneth Parker say to Bobby Jackson, "Is it true Angel Crowley's a Catholic?"

It wasn't his asking. It was the way he asked—as if I'd turned into a leper.

I didn't say anything to Maggie about either incident, though she was still at home at the time, partly because I didn't know what there was to say, and partly because I was beginning to suspect Barbara hadn't been talking through her hat at all. I'd been talking through mine—which left even less to say, and no point in saying it.

Although Maggie put a good face on, I could tell as much from what she didn't talk about as from what she did that it hurt her to think Kate and I might be suffering from the big-

277

otry Orn Fletcher and Warren White had stirred up around her. Just as, when I stopped going to the movies on Saturday afternoon, I could tell from her not asking me why, she was relieved not to have to give me the ten cents she could no longer afford.

It took me a while to figure out for myself what was happening, just as it took a while for the bigotry of the parents to filter down to their children—and for the children to realize what Barbara Kaiser had seen at once, that just as their parents had toppled Maggie, they could topple me.

Not that I understood it. I didn't understand it at all. I kept thinking if they'd liked me all right before, why didn't they like me all right now? I was the same person I had been.

I did talk to Kate about that, pointing out to her that Mike Reilly had been in our class all along, and he'd been a Catholic all along, and nobody was giving him sidewise looks or whispering about him.

Kate said she supposed it was because our friends had always taken it for granted we were the same as they were, and they didn't like finding out we weren't.

I frowned at her. "But aren't we the same?"

She shook her head. "Not exactly."

I started to ask her why, but she said, "Don't ask me, because I don't know."

Kate was having her own problems.

A few weeks after Kate and Alice White called it quits, Sarah Frances Wunderley started dating Bill Kaiser, and she and Kate stopped speaking to each other. Sarah Frances wasn't dating him any longer, and I didn't see why she and Kate couldn't be friends again. They tried, but it didn't work.

That left Mary Louise Fletcher.

Unlike Alice, Mary Louise admitted to Kate that she knew her father had worked against Maggie, but she reminded Kate that her mother had helped Maggie and voted for her and was terribly upset over Maggie losing. So that part was all right. But then she would make the most outrageous remarks.

278

One time when she was at our house, and Kate said she had a date with George Garnett for the movie Saturday night, Mary Louise said, "I wonder why he keeps on dating you."

Kate frowned at her. "Why shouldn't he?"

"Well, after all, he can't marry you—unless he became a Catholic. And you certainly can't expect him to do that."

"For heaven's sake," Kate said, "who's talking about marrying him?"

I asked Kate afterward why she didn't light into Mary Louise for being so insulting, but Kate shrugged and said Mary Louise didn't mean to be. She was so used to hearing people talk that way about Catholics she just didn't think.

But it was Julia Fletcher herself, considering her indignation over Chuck Sellers and her distress at knowing that Orn himself had once attempted something only somewhat less base, who was the most astonishing.

One time that winter when Kate had bronchitis, I went to Ward's after school to get the prescription filled which the doctor had given Grandpa. Julia was there at the soda fountain. So was Marcella DeWitt—her teeth as firmly fixed in place as ever.

Both of them smiled and said hello and asked how Maggie was. When I told them about Kate, they asked how she was, too. But then while I was waiting at the prescription counter, Julia sighed and said in a low voice she worried so about Maggie's girls now that Maggie wasn't here to look after them. Kate particularly was at an age when she might run wild. She seemed as nice and polite as ever, but you couldn't tell what she might do, now that she was a Catholic. There was so much loose living among Catholics. Why, they actually condoned it.

At that moment Bernice Kaiser burst into Ward's shrieking, "Julia, what's this I hear?" almost before she was in the door. "Let me see! Let me see!"

Julia took her hat off.

I gasped. She'd had her hair bobbed.

"Well, it's about time," Bernice said. "Turn around."

Julia said, "Oh, Bernice," looking flustered. She turned her head first to one side, then the other.

Bernice nodded. "It looks marvelous."

I thought it looked chopped. But then, I hadn't thought much of Kate's permanent, either, and all of her friends had raved about it the way Bernice was raving now.

Bernice settled herself on a stool. "How'd you manage to talk Orn into it?"

. "She didn't," Marcella said. "She let me talk her into it."

"Well, well." Bernice looked at Julia. "The Emancipation Proclamation?"

Julia went pink in the face and took a sip of her Coke. "Orn," she said at last, "can't have everything his way."

"I've been telling you that for years." Bernice called out to Sam McCutcheon where was he, she wanted a Coke. He called back he'd be right there, his girl must have stepped out for a few minutes.

Julia laughed, a nervous little laugh. "You won't believe this, but I dread going home."

"Pooh," Marcella said. "What can he say? It's done, isn't it?"

Julia sighed. "Yes, it's done. But he's not going to like it."

"You said yourself," Bernice reminded her, "Orn can't have everything his way." She shrugged. "Let him learn to live with it."

"I suppose so," Julia said. She sighed again.

Sam McCutcheon bustled out with the prescription and flipped open his account book. "Charge it, I suppose?" He frowned at me.

My hands went clammy inside my mittens. "If it's all right." I wished I hadn't told Grandpa I knew it would be.

He entered it in his book. "Next time Maggie gets up from Terre Haute, tell her to stop in and see me, will you?"

"Yes," I said. I took the prescription and left, hoping Julia Fletcher was too concerned about her bob to hear what he'd said, though I didn't see how she could blame our being poor on our being Catholics. We were still the same as other people in that way, at least.

I wished, now that she'd changed her hair style, she could change some of her ideas, but I supposed Orn would like that even less.

I suppose, Orn being the kind of man he was, the fact that she could work up enough courage to bob her hair was something. She may even have thought it was enough.

The thing Kate hated most about that winter was pork liver. We had it for supper almost every night. Grandpa said it was good for us, and Kate sighed and said she supposed it was, but why did so many things that were good for you have to taste so awful? So Grandpa would frown over a recipe book and then go to Garnett's and buy some beef to make a stew or pot roast, and we'd have that for a couple of days. But we always ended up going back to pork liver. It was the cheapest meat you could buy—probably, I decided, because of the way it tasted.

Even the tramps who came to our kitchen door couldn't work up much enthusiasm for it.

I didn't mind the pork liver. What I minded was Maggie not being there. Since she'd never been there to come home to after school, I didn't miss her then. But I missed her the rest of the time—in the mornings and at night and on Sunday. Most of all I missed the Saturdays we used to have together at the courthouse.

A girl named Opal Rittenhouse, who lived in Montclair and whose father was in his third term as the county recorder, kept calling me up on Saturday morning to come spend the day at the courthouse with her. Opal and I had played there together a lot whenever she came over with her father, holding mock trials in the courtroom and sliding down the banister when the janitor wasn't looking. But I never went. I didn't want to. Nathaniel and I had a set route we always took when we went bike riding, and we even changed that so we wouldn't go past the courthouse. I didn't want anything to do with the courthouse at all.

Maggie only came home about once a month. It wasn't just the long time it took to drive to Roseville from Terre Haute. It was the gas and oil it took to make the trip. And the wear on the tires.

We were always so glad to see her when she did come, Kate and I hardly stopped talking from morning until night. Except the time she came home around the end of March, when there was a letter waiting for her from the bank.

She went out the first thing Saturday morning. She wasn't gone long. When she came back Kate and I were still doing the breakfast dishes.

I saw her come in the driveway, and the minute she opened the kitchen door I started jabbering to her about the map I was making for geography class, but then I took a look at her and quit. She looked almost the same as she had that day at the courthouse after losing the election.

I supposed whatever it was she wouldn't say anything about it in front of Kate and me, but when she went into the living room to talk to Grandpa, she didn't close the French doors, so of course we listened.

She told Grandpa the bank had a new rule. From now on you couldn't just pay the interest on a mortgage. You have to pay part of the principal, too. So, as much as she hated doing it, she'd gone in to talk to Warren White. Well, he'd greeted her like she was the bank's chief depositor, bowing and scraping all over the place.

Kate and I stared at each other.

Maggie laughed—if you could call it that. "And never once looked me in the eye."

"I don't wonder," Grandpa said.

Maggie said she told him she understood the logic of the new rule, and the need for banks to have it, but if he could only give her a little time. He surely could understand she was having a hard go of it right now just making ends meet.

Oh, indeed he understood. If it were his decision to make, he'd give her as much time as she wanted. Unfortunately, the new board of directors had laid down very rigid requirements for him to follow in the matter of loans and mortgages. The bank did, of course, take extenuating circumstances into consideration, but those circumstances had to be a prolonged illness or the loss of work. She wasn't sick, and she had a job, so, sorry as he was, he was afraid he couldn't help her, though of course he'd give anything to be able to.

"Even," Grandpa said, "his seat in the state senate, no doubt."

"No doubt," Maggie said.

After a minute Grandpa said, " 'Tis a curious thing how all of the man's shortcomings end up on your doorstep."

Maggie agreed that it was.

Grandpa asked her what she was going to do about the mortgage.

"Try to meet the payments," she said.

Grandpa said it might be a sin to wish your life away, but he wished May would hurry up and get here, so he could plant his corn. Then, God willing, we'd show Warren White and his extenuating-circumstances bank a thing or two.

I beamed at Kate.

Kate smiled back at me, but after she pulled the plug and wiped the sink out, she stood on where she was for a while staring out the window to the field across the road at the end of Main Street, and past the field into whatever lay beyond it.

May finally did come.

The Saturday we planted the corn was more than a big day for Grandpa. It was a big day all around. Maggie was home, and it was Kate's sixteenth birthday.

For my birthday in April Kate had sent away for a free copy —in a plain brown wrapper—of *Marjorie May's Twelfth Birthday*, so I got back at her. For her birthday I gave her a kiss.

She didn't care. She hardly cared that Maggie was home. All she could think about was her date that night with George Garnett. Not for a movie. For his junior prom.

Aunt Clarissa had sent her a yellow organdy formal one of the twins had worn, and Kate was as nervous as a cat George would get her the wrong color corsage. I figured if he did, he must be deaf and dumb both. The last time he'd taken her to a movie she'd worn a yellow sweater, and when they set off down the street, you could hear her all the way back at the house going on about how yellow was her favorite color, everything she bought from now on was going to be yellow, didn't he think gardenias, for instance, would look beautiful with yellow?

I didn't know why she didn't come straight out and tell him.

Nathaniel came over early Saturday morning, and we planted nine rows of corn, alternating the Mr. Owen and Mr. Beebe from the previous year's inbreeding.

In the afternoon while Kate did her nails and washed her hair, Nathaniel and Grandpa and Maggie and I went for a ride out in the country. As we drove past a farmer out planting his field, Grandpa said wait till the farmers around here got a look at Mr. Owen Beebe this fall, sure and they'd all be clamoring for the seed.

Nathaniel frowned. "You won't have enough seed for even one farmer, will you, Mr. Crowley?"

Grandpa shook his head. "No. But they'll be wanting it, all the same. 'Tis that that counts."

"How, Grandpa?" I asked.

"Well, now, in order for any product to be a success, there has to be a demand for it, does there not?"

"I guess so," I said.

"Indeed there does," he replied.

"But if you can't supply the demand," Nathaniel said.

Grandpa beamed at him from the front seat. "When the gentlemen from the bank see the demand, they'll make possible the supplying of it."

"How?" I asked.

"Why," he answered, "by providing the money with which to obtain land to produce our Mr. Owen Beebe on a large-enough scale."

Nathaniel frowned again. "But you won't have enough seed even for that, will you?"

"In time we will," Grandpa said. "In time." He reminded Nathaniel that our last year's crop of final inbreeds had produced a lot more seed than we'd used to plant our nine rows this morning. So we had that. Then, too, we still had seed left over from the original ears his young agriculturalist friend had given him, not to mention the agriculturalist's own supply. It would take time, that was all, to repeat the final inbreeding on a larger scale and then to produce again, on that larger scale, the same Mr. Owen Beebe we were going to harvest this fall. "Time," he said again, "and money."

I shivered. It was like Christmas morning and Maggie's election all over again. What if our new Mr. Owen Beebe didn't turn out the way Grandpa expected him to? I could hardly bear to ask.

As it turned out, I didn't have to. Maggie did.

Grandpa beamed at her and said he was sure he would. He had great faith in Mr. Owen Beebe.

Maggie said she hoped Grandpa's faith was justified.

Maggie wasn't a nose-wrinkler like Aunt Clarissa. I remembered her telling Kate and me one time it did her heart good to see how much pleasure Grandpa got out of all the different things he'd worked on all his life trying to make his fortune, adding, in one of her rare comments about him, that our father had had dreams, too, but, unlike Grandpa, they never gave him any pleasure. They only made him restless and unhappy.

Maggie just didn't have any faith in dreams, that was all.

I did and I didn't. But I figured if Mr. Owen Beebe turned out anything like the day we planted him did, he'd be a smashing success.

We had fried chicken for supper, followed by cake and ice cream. George showed up early, looking shinier than ever and not the least bit miserable. George had become so used to us by that time he even asked a question of his own now and then.

When Kate swirled in in her yellow organdy, circling around for us, we all let our breath out over how pretty she looked. Kate no longer had a permanent—and couldn't understand now why she'd ever wanted one—but wore her hair down to her shoulders in a long silken bob that swirled when she did.

"Here," George said, handing her a florist's box as if to say he didn't know how he happened to have this thing along, would she mind dropping it in the wastebasket for him.

She opened it and took out a corsage of gardenias. "Oh, George," she exclaimed, as if he was the cleverest thing imaginable, "aren't you wonderful! How'd you ever guess?"

George looked pleased as punch.

For all that I didn't understand the workings of Kate's mind, I sighed and thought maybe I ought to pray for that as well as for her front.

The only thing to mar the perfection of that day was the call a man from the bank made on Maggie while Grandpa and Nathaniel and I were out planting the corn, and since I didn't know—and wasn't told—he was calling to serve notice of foreclosure on the house, it didn't mar the day for me.

Under the law a property owner was given one year in which to prevent foreclosure after the notice was served—prevent it by paying the mortgage, the interest, and the court and attorney costs.

Under certain circumstances there was another way to prevent it. If the value of the property was greater than the amount of the mortgage, and if the property owner paid a portion of the mortgage—and could demonstrate his or her ability to continue such payments—the bank would generally agree not to foreclose.

In the case of farm properties, some banks reached a point during the Depression where they had so many foreclosed farms on their hands they couldn't dispose of, they began allowing the farmer to stay on his property if he would agree to keep farming it and pay the taxes, which the bank, to avoid forfeiting the property, would otherwise have had to pay.

Whether or not the same kind of arrangement was ever made with homeowners, I don't know. It wasn't made with Maggie. She had the year the law provided her to come up with the five thousand dollars plus, or with enough of it to enable her to persuade the bank not to foreclose.

If Maggie and I were not looking for quite the same thing in that spring of 1933, we were at least looking in the same direction—the one miracles come from.

The summer was hot and dry again, even more so than the summer before. Grandpa didn't mind. He was out walking up and down the corn plot every morning before breakfast and every evening after supper, and at night he'd sit at the kitchen table figuring things on paper or reading books on farming or writing to his agriculturalist friend.

Early in August we snapped the tassels off the four inside alternating rows which were to be cross pollinated, thus producing Mr. Owen Beebe. From then on whenever Kate asked me or I asked her where Grandpa was, the answer, without either of us thinking, was, "He's out back with the corn," because he nearly always was.

Maggie came home for the Labor Day weekend, and after mass on Sunday morning we drove out to see how John Wurlitzer's cornfield was doing, his being the nearest field to town.

It wasn't doing well at all. In fact, it looked terrible.

Grandpa had all he could do to keep from rubbing his hands together, he was so excited. Our tasseled rows looked even worse than Mr. Wurlitzer's, but Mr. Owen Beebe, so far, at least, was standing straight and tall, and his ears were growing big.

I hated to see Maggie go back to Terre Haute without us on Labor Day worse than any other time. For all the differences there were between him and us, I was beginning to understand how Nathaniel felt.

Nathaniel's mother came down for Labor Day, too, but this

time Nathaniel didn't pack. And when I went into the seventh-grade room the next morning, I didn't ask him why he was there.

Grandpa said not to fret. It would be harvesttime before we knew it. Then things would begin to happen.

The Saturday morning in November we harvested the corn, Nathaniel arrived before we'd finished breakfast. This time we didn't bother with one-potato, two-potato. Nathaniel and I both went into the plot and picked an ear while Grandpa crossed himself and said a Hail Mary.

Both ears were big, and they were heavy. When we had them shucked, we just stood there and stared at them, waiting for Grandpa to say something.

"Jesus, Mary, and Joseph!" he said.

I yelled for Kate.

When we had all the ears picked and shucked and laid out on the kitchen table, all we could do was walk around the table and look at them and try to believe our eyes.

They were absolutely perfect.

Kate was all for Grandpa going to the phone right then to call Warren White, but Grandpa said no, he needed time to compose himself and think over what he wanted to say.

I said, "But Grandpa, you've been thinking all summer what you're going to say."

Grandpa touched his hand to my cheek. "I know, love. But—well—" He shook his head. "I have to sit down."

He sat down and blew his nose and wiped at his eyes where the cold had stung water out of them. Then he asked Nathaniel and me if we'd mind riding our bikes out to Mr. Wurlitzer's to ask him for a couple of ears of his corn. He wanted them to take with him when he went to the bank, so the gentlemen could compare them with Mr. Owen Beebe, in case they needed convincing.

Nathaniel said, "Heck, no," and we set off.

"Gosh," Nathaniel said, "it's really something, isn't it?"

288

"It really is," I said.

Mr. Wurlitzer was very jovial. "Well," he said, "I suppose your granddad's been fooling around with that ratty-looking stuff of his for so long he's forgotten what a good ear of corn looks like."

I started to say it wasn't that at all, but Nathaniel tugged at me, saying to Mr. Wurlitzer, "I guess he has, all right."

On the way home Nathaniel said, "Let him think it. When Mr. White calls him to come see, he'll really be bowled over."

Grandpa decided he'd go to the bank the first thing Monday morning, which meant Kate and I wouldn't know until after school, because we didn't come home for lunch. Grandpa said we already knew the important thing. The bank was just a detail.

Monday morning when we came down for breakfast, Grandpa was in his Sunday suit, his white hair brushed until it glistened, his shoes as shiny as George Garnett's. On the table he had two brown paper bags, one with Mr. Wurlitzer's corn in it, the other with Mr. Owen Beebe.

I gave him an extra hug when we left. Kate said, "I'll say a prayer."

Grandpa beamed at us and said maybe that night we might be extravagant and call Maggie on the long-distance telephone.

Kate said she'd settle for being extravagant by having something besides pork liver for supper.

"That, too," Grandpa said.

When we got past the Peterkins', by the first vacant lot, I turned and waved to him the way I always did. He waved back from the kitchen window, still beaming.

That afternoon after school Nathaniel and I wanted to run all the way home, but Kate said she couldn't in high heels. It was all she could do to keep up with us as it was.

When we reached the house, we couldn't see any lights on, which struck us as peculiar, because it was starting to get dark.

"Do you suppose he might still be at the bank?" Kate asked.

"My gosh," Nathaniel said, "that really would be something."

When we got to the kitchen door, I hung back. "You go first," I said to Kate.

"Silly," she said, and went on in.

There weren't any lights on anywhere.

We trooped through the kitchen and on into the dining room. "I bet he isn't here," Kate said.

But when we got to the living room he was there, sitting in his favorite easy chair.

Kate stopped so abruptly, Nathaniel and I bumped into her. "Grandpa?" she said. She reached out to a lamp and pulled the cord.

He only nodded.

"Grandpa, are you all right?" I asked.

He nodded again and looked up at us. "Yes, I'm all right." The light was gone out of his eyes.

"Oh, Grandpa," I said. It was all I could do not to throw myself at him. "What happened?"

Grandpa sighed. "It didn't turn out just the way I thought it would."

Nathaniel frowned. "You mean they didn't like Mr. Owen Beebe?"

"Oh, and they liked him very much," Grandpa said with a glimmer of his old self. "One of them, indeed, admitted it was the finest corn he'd ever seen in Rose County."

I breathed a sigh of relief.

But what could it be then?

Nathaniel asked.

Grandpa shook his head as if he still couldn't believe it. "The one thing I didn't even question."

Kate frowned. "What, Grandpa?"

He spread his hands. "That the farmers wouldn't want it."

Nathaniel and Kate and I stared at each other.

"Not want it?" Kate's voice shot up.

He shook his head again.

"But why wouldn't they?"

"I suppose," he said after a bit, "John Wurlitzer put it as well as anybody. He wanted to know why he should pay eight or nine dollars a bushel for seed corn, when he had plenty of his own that didn't cost a cent."

"But his corn's nowhere near as good as Mr. Owen Beebe," I said. "Is it, Grandpa?"

"No," he said, "it isn't." But, he went on, times were hard, and it would take more than a sampling of Mr. Owen Beebe to prove to Mr. Wurlitzer and all the other farmers that their eight or nine dollars a bushel wouldn't be a needless expense but an investment that would pay off in top-quality corn with maybe double the yield to the acre.

And, he said, the gentlemen at the bank weren't interested in supplying the money it would take to produce enough Mr. Owen Beebe to give the farmers that proof. To tell us the truth of the matter, in spite of their admiration for Mr. Owen Beebe, the gentlemen at the bank weren't any more convinced of his great possibilities than the farmers were themselves. And considering how little profit, if any, was being realized from corn in today's market, he could see their point of view, shortsighted though it was.

Kate said Grandpa should try some other bank. Mr. White would say no to anything that had to do with us.

Nathaniel said maybe Grandpa's agriculturalist friend would know where to get some money.

I said maybe we didn't need any money. Maybe Mr. Wurlitzer or somebody would let us use one of their fields the next year.

It didn't do any good. Grandpa said he'd been sitting there all day thinking of first one thing and then another, until he'd finally had to face what he should have faced long before—his corn experimenting had been only another dream.

All his life he'd lived on dreams, sustained and comforted by them and—he shook his head—beguiled by them into believing that one day one of them would come true and make his fortune. And now when he most needed help for us, what use had his corn experimenting been? He shook his head again. Like all his other dreams, no use at all.

It wasn't that he didn't have faith in the future of hybrid corn. He did. If he had come to it as a young man, perhaps . . .

He sighed. He'd come to it too late in life. He needed more than money to carry on with the experiment. He needed time.

"But, Grandpa," I said, "we have lots of time."

He shook his head. The Lord, he said, had been good to us in sending Mr. Owen Beebe, but, as magnificent as he was, he was only a start. Anybody who wanted to make a business of raising hybrid seed corn would have to work with many different strains and with double crosses as well as single crosses.

Nor would they all come as easily as Mr. Owen Beebe.

Even there he hadn't done the hard work. His young friend had. With his scientific know-how and his practical experience, he had known which corn to select each year to inbreed further.

Grandpa shook his head again. It would take more time than he had any call to hope for to learn what needed to be learned and do what needed to be done. John Wurlitzer was right when he said what made an old saloonkeeper from Chicago think he knew anything about raising corn?

I gasped. We all did.

Grandpa had been staring off into nowhere. Now he looked at us, bewildered, wanting to know why we'd gasped.

When we told him, he said he was sorry, he hadn't meant to repeat that, it had just slipped out, he supposed because it had been on his mind so much that day. But we mustn't be distressed. John Wurlitzer hadn't said it to his face.

"He had no right to say it at all," Kate said.

Grandpa shook his head, saying he might as well recognize the truth when he heard it, even accidentally. And in truth that was indeed what he was—an old saloonkeeper from Chicago. "Probably," he said to me with a trace of a smile, "the oldest saloonkeeper ever to come out of Chicago alive."

I ran to him and hugged him. "Oh, Grandpa, I love you so!"

Grandpa asked Nathaniel if he'd like to have an ear of Mr. Owen Beebe for a keepsake. Nathaniel said yes, and Grandpa got up and took one out of the brown paper bag, holding it in his hands for a moment, looking at it. " 'Twas a beautiful dream, for all that." He sighed. "The most beautiful of them all."

Kate and I tried all evening to cheer Grandpa up, while he tried to act as if he didn't need cheering. On the surface we all made out pretty well, but it was only on the surface.

It wasn't until after I had gone to bed and lay there thinking about Grandpa that I realized the failure of his corn meant the ruination of the one hope I'd had of bringing Maggie back to Roseville.

Chapter Fifteen

When Nathaniel didn't show up at school one Friday in the middle of December I didn't think anything of it. He was always saying he might go up to Chicago to visit his mother for the weekend. I supposed she'd finally said he could, and he'd talked his Aunt Julia into letting him skip a day of school so he could take the Friday-morning train, making the weekend a three-day one. Considering how long it had taken his mother to get around to letting him visit her—and, on the strength of that, how long it was likely to be before she agreed to it again—I didn't blame him. The fact that I didn't hear from him Saturday or Sunday convinced me I was right.

When he didn't show up at school Monday morning, I did think that was peculiar—so peculiar I began to be afraid he hadn't gone to Chicago for a weekend at all but—in spite of neither of us being able to put much stock in that any more—had finally gone back to Chicago for good.

I couldn't believe he'd go without telling me good-bye, but his mother had always struck me as being so erratic and so—well, not quite with things, it was easy enough to believe he hadn't had time, that the past Thursday evening she'd suddenly looked up from the paper she was reading and said, "What in the world has Nathaniel been doing down there in Roseville all this time when he should be home here with me?" And before she could forget what she'd finally wakened up to, she'd gone straight to the phone to call him up and say take the next train.

By the middle of the afternoon I was already mentally composing a letter to him saying not to feel bad he hadn't told me good-bye, I was just glad for his sake he was back home at last, and did he think his mother might let him come down for a visit between Christmas and New Year's, when the door to our room opened and the principal poked his head in.

He beckoned to our teacher, who went back to stand with him in the doorway, where he talked to her for a few minutes in a low tone of voice. She listened, nodding, her face gone solemn, while all of us sat twisted around at our desks staring at the two of them, wondering what was up.

When the principal left, the teacher walked back up to the front of the room and asked for our attention—as if she didn't already have it. She told us school was being dismissed now instead of Friday for the Christmas holiday, to gather together those books we would need, make sure we wrapped up warm and didn't leave our galoshes in the cloakroom, not to loiter on the playground but to go straight home, Merry Christmas and Happy New Year, please leave in an orderly fashion, class dismissed.

In the time it took me to find my galoshes, which I'd left there the week before, almost the entire school had emptied out, the thundering uproar in the halls dying away to a few scattered shouts. When I came out the front of the building, knots of high-school students were standing around everywhere buzzing with speculation, but it wasn't until I spied Kate standing on the corner a block away talking to George Garnett and a couple of girls and went running up to them that I found out what was going on.

Nathaniel had scarlet fever.

All they could tell me was what Mary Louise Fletcher had told Kate that morning. Nathaniel had awakened Friday morning with what seemed to be an ordinary cold and sore throat. On Saturday he started throwing up and having chills and fever. When the doctor came Saturday afternoon he said he thought it was the grippe, but he wasn't sure. This morning when Mary Louise went in to tell Nathaniel good-bye before setting off for school, he was all broken out with what looked like the measles.

Mary Louise, Kate added, had gone home for lunch and hadn't come back.

Neither Kate nor I had much to say to each other as we set off for home. When we went by the Fletchers' we stopped and stared at the red and white QUARANTINE tacked beside the front door. We walked the rest of the way in silence.

All through supper I kept trying to think up some excuse for calling the Fletchers, but I was too scared to call even if I'd been able to come up with anything.

Grandpa said we'd better both gargle our throats before we went to bed. When we couldn't find anything except salt to gargle them with, he put on his hat and coat and walked uptown to Ward's. Half an hour later he was home again with a bottle of ST 37. Sam McCutcheon had told him it was a new medicinal gargle and Grandpa was lucky to have come in that evening. He was nearly sold out of it.

The next morning at breakfast I was back to thinking up excuses and all set to ask Kate why she couldn't call Mary Louise when the phone rang. It was Mary Louise calling Kate.

"Nathaniel's going to be all right," Kate said when she finally got off the phone. "The doctor said it's not a severe case."

Considering the doctor had also said only three days before he thought Nathaniel had the grippe, I wasn't all that convinced, but as one day followed another, and Mary Louise kept reporting to Kate via the telephone that Nathaniel was going to be all right, I relaxed some.

The main reason for Mary Louise's faithful—and lengthy— telephone calls was she didn't have much else to do and nowhere at all to go. When Julia called Orn that Monday morning to tell him the doctor had said Nathaniel had scarlet fever, he told her to pack a suitcase for him, and he moved to his parents' house. Ellen, who was now away at college, joined her father there when she came home for Christmas. Mary Louise

296

wasn't so lucky. Since she was in the house when the sign was posted, she was stuck there, the ruling of the county health authorities being that once a house was put under quarantine, nobody in could go out, and nobody out—except the doctor—could go in.

Although Mary Louise told Kate the day after Christmas she was being driven nearly out of her wits, she had to admit she wasn't bothered nearly so much by the fact that she couldn't go out as Nathaniel was bothered by the fact that his mother was not allowed in.

Orn's reaction, according to Mary Louise, was that Nathaniel was behaving like a child, to which Grandpa retorted, when that bit of information was passed along to him, "Sure, and it is no wonder, when the boy is but a child. And a sick one, at that."

Julia, also according to Mary Louise, had explained the health ruling to Nathaniel, including the reason for it. Nathaniel understood that. What he didn't understand was why his mother couldn't be allowed to come in if she stayed in until the quarantine was lifted.

I couldn't understand it myself. I was sure she didn't work. Nathaniel would have told me if she did. Neither did she have a husband to cook and keep house for. If Nathaniel was sick and needed her, what could she possibly have to do in Chicago that couldn't wait a couple of weeks?

I didn't understand any better Julia's reply to Nathaniel, "Well, my dear, I know your mother would like to be here as much as you'd like her to, but I think it's best, really, if she doesn't come. What she wants you to do, what we all want you to do, is concentrate on getting well," followed by the usual parental admonition to eat his soup while it was hot and be sure to drink his milk, she'd come back later and read him a story, all of which served to do what anybody could see it was intended to do—change the subject.

It led me to wonder if Nathaniel's mother had been asked to come.

Apparently it led Nathaniel to wonder the same thing. Two days later there was a knock at the back door. When I went to answer it, George Garnett's younger brother Larry stood there holding out a folded sheet of paper. "Nathaniel threw this out his bedroom window to me this morning when I delivered some groceries to the Fletchers' back porch." He handed it to me. "It has your name printed on it, so I guess he wanted me to bring it to you, but I don't know why. It doesn't have anything else on it, inside or not."

I opened it. It was blank.

"Well," I said, "I guess he wanted to write me a note and didn't have the strength for it. But thanks, anyhow."

As soon as Larry was gone I went to the stove and lighted one of the burners, then held the paper stretched out above the flame. In a few moments brown lettering began to show.

I'd had a hunch it would. When Nathaniel and I were the A & N Club we used to write secret messages to each other that way all the time, using milk for invisible ink.

The A & N Club had never been formally disbanded. We'd just lost interest in it, that was all, deciding all that secrecy was silly when we didn't really have anything that amounted to anything to be secret about.

Nathaniel did now. When I read the message I knew why he'd resorted to using invisible ink. He didn't want Larry Garnett to see what he'd written or, if the plan didn't work and his Aunt Julia found the note, for her to see it either—his Aunt Julia because then the note wouldn't be delivered, Larry because he might make fun of him.

The message was: *Please ask my mother to come see me.*

I stood there staring at it, wondering how in the heck Nathaniel expected me to do that. Or what he expected me to do it with. In order for me to ask his mother anything I either had to call her up on the long-distance telephone or go see her in person. I shook my head, deciding Nathaniel's case of scarlet fever might not be a severe one, but he had to be sicker than everybody thought he was or he would have realized I didn't have that kind of money—or any prospect of getting it.

I wished, if he'd had to ask me a thing like that, he'd have asked it while Maggie was still at home for the Christmas weekend. She could have told me what I should do. She probably wouldn't have had me do anything. She'd have done it for me.

Done what?

I turned off the burner and went over to the kitchen table and sat down, still staring at Nathaniel's message, trying to think what Maggie would do if some friend of hers asked her what Nathaniel had asked of me.

I supposed she would do what the friend asked.

Whether or not Maggie would, by the same token, want me to do what Nathaniel asked, I didn't know. Maggie being a parent, she might side with Mrs. Fletcher.

She might even know why Mrs. Fletcher took the attitude she did.

I decided there wasn't any point in thinking about that. I had no possible way of finding out why Mrs. Fletcher's attitude was what it was short of asking her, and if she wasn't about to explain it to Nathaniel, she wasn't about to explain it to me either.

That brought me back to what Maggie would want me to do.

I supposed, Maggie not being there, I could ask Grandpa.

Grandpa was obviously on Nathaniel's side. He would probably think somebody ought to speak to Nathaniel's mother. But would he think the somebody ought to be me? I shook my head again. Since he was a parent, too, probably not.

But who else was there?

I stared at Nathaniel's message again.

The thing was, if I asked Grandpa, and he said no, I couldn't speak to Nathaniel's mother, that would be the end of it. Not just for me. For Nathaniel.

I thought a bit longer. If the situation was reversed, if Nathaniel was the only person I had to ask to do something for me, I'd expect him to do it somehow or other, wouldn't I? Otherwise, why would I ask him?

That brought me back to how I could do the thing anyhow when I didn't have any money to do it with. Even Maggie being home wouldn't have helped me there. Maggie had somehow managed Christmas again, but when I offered to give her back what I had left over this year from the dollar she'd given me to spend on Christmas presents, she took it.

I got up from the table and went upstairs to shake out my piggy bank. It was a useless trip. I knew before I went up there the piggy bank didn't have anything in it.

I went back downstairs and into the kitchen again. I supposed it would be cheaper to call Nathaniel's mother up on the long-distance telephone than to go see her—until the operator told me when I asked her what the person-to-person rates to Chicago were that the charge was one dollar and five cents for the first three minutes, thirty-five cents per minute for the next seven minutes, and twenty cents per minute after that.

I swallowed and hung up. Nathaniel's mother being the way she was, it would take a while to make her understand who she was talking to, let alone what about. Not to mention the fact that she might say, "Hang on a minute," every now and then while she went off into another room to tend to something. I'd be a nervous wreck watching all those minutes tick by, wondering how much it would end up costing.

The operator had told me it was a little cheaper to call station-to-station, but what if she wasn't there when I called? It would be bad enough if I called person-to-person, and she wasn't there. I'd have to pay a ten-cent report charge and try again. If I was going to have to explain to her who I was when I finally reached her, I couldn't very well leave a message asking her to call me back.

I put my coat on and set off for the depot on my bike. If I went to see her in person it wouldn't matter how long it took. The cost would be the same. And if she was out, I could wait until she came back home.

To my relief, the man at the ticket window wasn't anybody

I knew. "How much does it cost to go to Chicago?" I asked him.

That was when it hit me. I'd been so busy thinking it would be better to go see Nathaniel's mother in person than to try to talk to her on the telephone and wondering how I could get the money even for that, it hadn't occurred to me that going to see her meant I had to go to Chicago to do it.

The man peered out from under his green eyeshade. "Something the matter?"

I shook my head. There wasn't anything the matter he'd understand.

He looked me over. "You under twelve?"

I looked back at him. It had occurred to me to try to get by with half fare, but what if I got to Chicago and they found out I was lying and wouldn't let me ride back on it? Then I'd be stuck there. "No," I said.

"One way or round trip?"

I swallowed. "Round trip."

"Four dollars and sixty-four cents."

I stared at him, my mouth hanging open. Four dollars and sixty-four cents? Nathaniel had to have been completely out of his head when he wrote that message, and I'd be out of mine to take him seriously. As much as he probably did want his mother to come see him, he didn't really expect me to be the one to go to Chicago to ask her.

I heaved a sigh of relief, all set to turn away from the window, when the man said, "You planning to go up and come back the same day?"

I started to say I wasn't planning to go up at all, but I supposed I might as well hear what he had to say. I nodded.

"If you go on Saturday there's an excursion rate."

"How much is that?"

"Two dollars and six cents."

I frowned at him. Two dollars and six cents was still a lot of money, but it didn't sound as impossible as the other. I supposed Nathaniel had figured I could get it from Grandpa. Then when he was well he'd pay me back. After all, he couldn't have sent the money with the note without arousing suspicion. I sighed again, a different kind of sigh. "Okay. I'll go."

I didn't know I'd said it out loud until the man reached for a ticket and a stamp. I put my hand up. "I can't buy it yet. I have to get the money first."

He shrugged, and I left.

What Nathaniel hadn't realized was I couldn't very well ask Grandpa for the money without telling him where I was going with it.

I stood outside the depot for a bit, thinking. Then I got on my bike and rode over to old Mrs. Werner's house.

Mrs. Werner, in addition to being old, was a bit on the austere side. She was also, from the experience I'd had with her, which included running a few errands as well as picking currants and sweeping snow, strictly cash and carry. I wasn't too hopeful when I rang her front bell.

When she opened the door to me with a "Yes, child, what is it?" I lost what little hope I had. Still, I couldn't just stand there staring at her.

"I—there's something I have to talk to you about. Could I come in?"

She nodded. "Wipe your feet off first."

"Yes, I will."

"Hang your coat there on the hall tree."

I hung it.

She led the way into the parlor, told me to sit down, then sat down across from me, sitting so straight in her chair that I stiffened my own shoulders in an effort to look like her.

"Now," she said. "What is it you want to talk to me about?"

"Well, I—I have to go somewhere. On the train. There's something I have to do for someone, but I don't want—I mean, I'd rather people didn't have it to talk about."

She nodded and went on looking at me.

"Well, I was wondering if you had any jobs you wanted me

to do for you, and if I could make a deal with you—I mean, if I could agree ahead of time to do them." I frowned at her, feeling my face get hot. "You see, I don't have any money to buy the ticket, and I have to go Saturday, and I thought this way I might be able to get the money I need."

She looked at me a bit longer. "And how much money is that?"

"I'm afraid it's quite a lot. It's two dollars and six cents. But it might snow quite a lot this winter, mightn't it?"

So far that particular winter it had snowed only once.

I swallowed. "Or I could do other things. I'm—I'm pretty good at beating rugs."

Kate had told me the week before I was terrible at it.

"Yes," she said, "I'm sure you are. But you see, Mr. Werner and I are going to Florida next week to spend the winter."

"Oh." My shoulders slumped. "Well, then, I guess . . ."

I started to get up, but, putting a hand out to stop me, she got up instead and went over to a large walnut secretary and picked up her pocketbook. "I think if it's such an important trip—"

"No," I blurted out, wondering what in the world had come over me, "I couldn't just take it." My face went hotter than before. "I—it wouldn't be right."

"I see." She put the pocketbook down.

I had to take my eyes away from it.

She came back to her chair and sat down again. "May I ask —that is, if you feel you can tell me—where it is you have to go?"

I nodded, straightening up in my own chair. "Chicago."

"I see," she said again. She looked at me for a bit, frowning. "I wonder—have you ever been to Chicago?"

"No."

"Do you think, if I gave you the directions, you could find Marshall Field's?"

I stared at her. Was it possible she had an errand to be run in Chicago? "Yes. Yes, I'm sure I could."

"Then if you will wait a few minutes . . ."

"Yes. I'll wait."

She went back to the secretary, sat down in front of it, and, taking a pen from its holder, started writing, the pen scratching across the paper in the stillness of the room. When she finished, she came over to me with a sealed envelope in one hand and a sheet of paper in the other.

She handed me the paper. "These are the directions for getting to Marshall Field's from the train station." She handed me the envelope. "When you get there, go to the linen department and ask for the saleslady whose name I've written on the envelope. Give the envelope to her. It's an order and a check for some linens I need. She'll have them sent to me." She cocked her head at me. "Do you have it straight?"

"Yes," I said, repeating what she'd told me.

She went back for her pocketbook and gave me two dollars and twenty cents. "You'll need seven cents for the streetcar each way. It's too far for you to walk."

"Yes," I said again, though I hadn't the faintest idea of how far too far for me to walk was. I thanked her and headed for the hall to get my coat, unable to believe what had happened. I stopped and turned back. "Are you sure that's all—I mean, don't you want me to do anything else for the money?"

She shook her head. "No. That will be quite sufficient."

When I still hesitated, she looked at me again for a bit. "You see," she said gravely, "it saves me making the trip myself."

"Oh," I said. "I see." I supposed she felt the same way about Chicago I did.

I didn't know enough at the time about the New Deal to understand what Mrs. Werner had done, or, for that matter, enough about Mrs. Werner, who was such a staunch Republican that not even the dire needs of millions of unemployed could justify in her mind the make-work WPA, to appreciate the irony of it.

Riding home on my bike, I figured all I had left to worry

about now from the Roseville end of things was the weather. The only thing I could think of to explain being away from home for as long as it would take me to get to Chicago and back on Saturday was to tell Grandpa I was going on an all-day hike. If it rained or snowed I'd have to think of something else.

As it was, I nearly blew the whole thing anyhow. At supper Friday night I said to Grandpa, "How far is it from the train station in Chicago to Marshall Field's?"

"Which train station?"

I stared at him. "You mean there's more than one?"

He nodded. "Yes. There are several. It depends on what direction you're coming in from and what line you take."

"Oh," I said. "Well, coming from Roseville."

"That would be the LaSalle Street Station."

"Well, then, from that one."

"From LaSalle Street to Marshall Field's? Let me see now." He counted off on his fingers. "Three blocks east to State Street. Then five blocks north."

"What do you want to know that for?" Kate asked.

"Nothing," I answered, feeling my face grow hot again. I shrugged. "I just thought if somebody asked me, then I'd know."

Kate rolled her eyes.

According to Mrs. Werner's directions, I had to walk the three blocks to State Street to get the streetcar. Five blocks more didn't seem such a far walk to me, but then it wasn't really the distance that bothered me. "Grandpa," I said.

"Yes, love?"

"You remember the time when some other gangsters were trying to get Al Capone, and they drove through the streets in Cicero shooting off their machine guns into his hotel, only they had the first car in the procession shoot blank bullets so ordinary people would have time to get out of the way?"

"Yes," he said as I took a breath.

"Well, are they always that careful?"

Grandpa gave me a puzzled look.

"I mean, if a person was walking on a street right in downtown Chicago, and some gangsters decided to start shooting at each other, would they wait until the person got by?"

"Yes," he said. "I think they would."

I stared at him again. "You only think so?"

Kate frowned at me. "What are you looking so bug-eyed about? And why this sudden interest in Chicago? Or do you think somebody might ask you that, too?"

I could hardly bear to look at her. "I was just wondering, that's all. Can't a person just wonder about something?"

Kate shook her head. "You find the weirdest things to wonder about of anyone I ever knew."

Another thing I'd been wondering about all day Friday was whether Nathaniel might send me another message saying he'd changed his mind. I even went to the window once to see if Larry Garnett might be coming down the street. He wasn't.

Before I went to bed Friday night I had something else to wonder about—how to explain the Sunday clothes I'd be wearing Saturday morning for the hike I was supposed to be going on.

Not to Kate. She could be counted on to sleep until noon.

I ended up doing the only thing I could think of. I told Grandpa not to get up for me in the morning, I'd make my own breakfast—and hoped if he did anyhow, maybe he wouldn't notice what I had on.

He didn't get up, but when I came downstairs there was a lunch he'd packed for me on the kitchen table.

It was so gloomy out I thought sure it was going to rain, but it was only the gray that precedes the dawn. I'd been so worried I'd oversleep and miss the train that I woke up at six-thirty.

After I ate breakfast I felt in my coat pocket to make sure I had everything Mrs. Werner had given me. Then I took my lunch and left.

I hadn't bothered wondering if the train might not come. Sooner or later trains always came. This one came on time.

Nothing happened in the two hours or so it took for the train to get to Chicago. I hadn't expected anything would. I just sat in a seat by the window, and when I wasn't rereading Mrs. Werner's directions, I looked out the window at the flat landscape rolling by—barren fields with patches of snow here and there, an occasional town with its name on a sign at the end of the depot.

From the outskirts of Gary, Indiana, right on into Chicago there was so much to look at I could hardly take it all in, but it wasn't until I came out of the depot and looked up and down the streets at all the buildings—dozens of them taller than the courthouse in Roseville—that I sucked in my breath at the towering wonder of it all. And when, just a block away, an elevated train screeched against the rails as it turned a corner, grinding to a stop, I sucked in my breath again at the noise as well.

I stood there staring up at the train as it rumbled by practically over my head, ground to another stop, took off again, and went clanking on down the street to screech around another corner, looping back north, when suddenly a car swooped past the curb in front of me just as somebody poked something into my back. My heart leaped into my throat. But the car was only a yellow taxicab and the thing in my back some woman shopper's umbrella. I ducked back against the side of a building until my heart settled back in place.

I was trying to decide whether it would be better to go to Marshall Field's first in case Nathaniel's mother decided to take the train back with me, or whether it would be better to go see Nathaniel's mother first, so if she got to rambling on and on I could use Marshall Field's as an excuse to leave, when it hit me that I didn't even know where Nathaniel's mother lived.

I wondered how I could be such a jerk.

I started walking toward State Street, keeping as close to the shelter of the buildings as I could, trying to think of some way of finding out.

A sign on a tobacco store window, PUBLIC TELEPHONE, gave

me the way. If there was a telephone inside, there'd surely be a telephone directory.

There was. Nathaniel's mother lived on State Street herself, eight blocks north of Marshall Field's.

It occurred to me that maybe I ought to call her up first to say I was coming to see her, but when the proprietor of the store explained to me it would cost a nickel, I gave up the idea. Anyhow, nobody in Roseville ever called anybody up to say they were coming over. If they were going, they just went.

In the interest of economy, I decided to go see Nathaniel's mother first. I could walk the eight blocks back to Marshall Field's. If Nathaniel's mother didn't want to go there with me, she could meet me at the train station.

As I walked the rest of the way to State Street, I began to see why Grandpa could only say he thought the gangsters would wait until a person got by before they started shooting at each other. There was such a constant stream of people going and coming in all directions, if the gangsters waited for all of them to go by they'd have to give up the idea of shooting each other entirely.

On the other hand, with so many other people around for accidental targets, it seemed to me my chances of being hit weren't as high as I'd figured they'd be. I took what comfort I could in that.

Once on the street car and able to put the gangsters out of my mind for the time being, I started thinking about what I was going to say to Nathaniel's mother when I saw her.

I supposed she would think it was strange I'd come all the way up to Chicago to tell her Nathaniel wanted to see her when I could just as easily have called her up on the telephone.

Maybe I could tell her I'd had to come up to Marshall Field's and just thought I'd stop by as long as I was in the neighborhood.

Maybe she wouldn't ask.

I shifted in my seat and wondered if maybe nobody had told

her Nathaniel was sick. But if nobody had told her he was sick, how could she want him to concentrate on getting well?

The streetcar made a stop, and I looked over at the conductor, who had said he would let me know when to get off. He shook his head at me.

I wondered why Nathaniel's mother hadn't insisted on coming to see him whether the Fletchers had asked her to or not. And if the Fletchers actually hadn't asked her, why hadn't they?

Maybe she was more susceptible than other people to scarlet fever.

Maybe she was sick in bed with it herself.

I clapped my hand to my forehead with such force I knocked the hat of the woman sitting next to me askew. After apologizing to her, I sat there wondering how in the world it could have taken me all this time—and all this distance—to figure that out when it was such an obvious answer to the whole thing.

The conductor motioned to me. I was halfway down the aisle when the lady called out to me, "Little girl! Your package!"

It was my lunch.

The lunch tucked under my arm, I stood on the streetcar platform staring across at the apartment building Nathaniel's mother lived in, searching for the quarantine sign. By the time I reached the entrance I still hadn't spotted it.

Maybe it was then that I began to get my first glimmer as to why Nathaniel's mother hadn't come to see him—hadn't, in all probability, been asked to do so. The look the doorman gave me when I asked where Mrs. Peterson's apartment was may have done it.

All I know for certain is that as I walked up the stairway to the third floor I began to wish I hadn't come, and as I rang the bell at her apartment door, I found myself hoping against hope she wouldn't be home.

She was home.

I heard her coming to the door. I couldn't help hearing her.

309

She knocked two different things over on the way—one with a thud, the other with a crash.

When she opened the door I just stood there staring at her. She had on a pink wrapper, clutching it tight around her. Her hair was streaked, and it was mussed, lying flat on one side of her face, standing out every which way on the other. The circles under her eyes were darker than I'd ever seen them, giving her skin a yellowish cast.

But it was her eyes, which she had trouble focusing on me, that made me understand in less than a minute all of the things I'd been trying to understand about her in the last two years. Her eyes and her breath.

I knew she didn't remember who I was. I wasn't sure she'd have recognized Nathaniel at that moment if he'd been standing there.

When I thought of Nathaniel it was almost more than I could bear.

She swayed, caught the doorjamb, and leaned against it. "Well?" she said.

I struggled to get something out, to explain who I was and why I was there, but nothing came.

"Well?" she said again. "You just going to stand there and stare at me the rest of the day?" Her words blurred together.

I shook my head.

"Well, then?"

I had to say something. I couldn't have come all this way to not even open my mouth, whether anything I said got through to her or not. Taking a deep breath, I blurted out the only words that would come out. "Nathaniel needs you."

For a moment longer I continued to stare at her. Then I turned and ran—down the hall and down the stairs and out of the building and down the street until the breath was all run out of me.

I leaned against a lamp post to get my breath back. I didn't want to go to Marshall Field's. I wanted to go home.

But there wasn't any way to get home until the train left at a quarter to three in the afternoon, and it wasn't even noon yet. Besides, I had to go to Marshall Field's whether I wanted to or not.

The saleslady whose name was written on the envelope wasn't there. No, the man with the flower in his buttonhole said to me, she wasn't eating her lunch. She wasn't there at all that day.

An hour earlier it would have panicked me. Now it hardly seemed to matter. "Well," I said to him, "there must be somebody else then who can take an order. It's all written down." I gave him the envelope.

After reading what Mrs. Werner had written and glancing at the check, he would, he said, be happy to take the order himself.

I walked back to the station. Even the gangsters hardly mattered any more. Not that I wasn't still terrified of them, and not that I didn't jump whenever a car backfired or flinch whenever an unseen elbow jostled me. But I just couldn't believe that on top of everything else that had happened to me already, I was going to be hit by a machine-gun bullet, stray or otherwise. As Bernice Kaiser would have said to Marcella at Ward's Drugstore, "Now, really, that's too much."

Anyhow I didn't have anything else to do to kill time except eat my lunch, and the station seemed as good a place as any to eat it.

I tried window-shopping as I walked along, the way Maggie and Kate would have done, but I didn't really see any of the things I looked at. I kept seeing Nathaniel's mother leaning against the doorjamb in her pink wrapper trying to focus her eyes on me. Then I would see Nathaniel peering at me in that sidewise way of his, and I thought if I didn't stop seeing Nathaniel and his mother, there wouldn't be any point in eating my lunch.

When I passed the tobacco store I'd stopped in before, I went in and asked the proprietor if I could buy some paper and an envelope for seven cents. He rummaged around in his desk, saying I could have them for free. He looked up at me. "You have something to write on the paper with?"

I unbuttoned my coat and showed him the fountain pen on a ribbon Aunt Clarissa had given me for Christmas two years before. I always wore it when I dressed up.

While I was waiting for the train, and most of the way going home on it, I tried to think what I could write to Nathaniel, wondering if it was a sin to tell a lie when there wasn't any possible way I could see of telling the truth.

I wondered if Nathaniel suspected the truth. I think now he did, that his wanting his mother to come stay with him until the quarantine was lifted was as much in the hope of having his suspicion proved groundless as anything else. But even had I been sure then that he suspected it, I wasn't about to tell him he suspected right.

I began to despair of being able to write him anything at all. I couldn't even think of a lie that sounded any good. Or would do any good.

What I ended up saying was his mother couldn't come see him right then because she wasn't well—not sick in bed, just not well enough to make the trip, but she wished she could come. Meanwhile she wanted him to hurry up and get better, and she'd do the same for him.

That last was more of a hope than a lie, a hope so totally out of my power to do anything about that I figured on putting it into the hands of somebody who could, if anybody could, the next morning at church—God the Father, God the Son, and God the Holy Ghost, all three.

On my way home from the depot I dropped the letter into the Fletchers' mailbox, holding my breath from the time I turned into their front walk until I made it back out onto the sidewalk again.

I was hoping that when I got home I could slip in without Grandpa or Kate seeing me until I could change clothes, but my luck never had been much good in that department, and

I'd already used up what little I'd been granted. Kate was in the living room playing the piano.

She looked at me. "Those are pretty funny clothes to go hiking in."

I looked back at her. Then, as much to my surprise as hers, I said with what practically amounted to aplomb, "Well, I'm a pretty funny kid."

Leaving her sitting there staring at me, I went into the kitchen and called up Mary Louise to ask her to get the letter and give it to Nathaniel.

When Mary Louise reported to Kate on Monday morning that Nathaniel was still improving—had, in fact, been allowed to come downstairs for supper the night before—I decided he must have believed what I'd written him. Or else he had simply accepted his situation for what it was, the way he'd had to accept it for so long now.

Since nobody other than Nathaniel came down with scarlet fever, school reopened as soon as he was well again the second week in January.

He did, in fact, seem to believe the letter. He also said he was sorry it hadn't occurred to him I wouldn't have the money to go to Chicago, but he'd give it to me now.

I told him he didn't need to. When I told him why, he was impressed.

But then, so was I.

The first of March Nathaniel told me his mother was not only all right now, she was coming to Roseville to live. I couldn't believe it. I thought he was just dreaming in a new direction. But he wasn't. Two weeks later she arrived. She looked a bit drawn and shaky, but at least she was sober.

I didn't assume then, any more than I assume now, that my going to Chicago had anything to do with it. I doubt that she even remembered my being there. I'm sure it was Orn. From what he had said to Julia that day Nathaniel and I were trapped behind the davenport, he'd talked to Mildred before about her drinking. I think he kept on talking to her, in spite of his "for all the good it'll do," and with Julia's—and the guidance columnist's—urging, persuading her finally to go to a hospital to dry out, then persuading her to move to Roseville, where he and Julia could keep an eye on her.

I wondered some after seeing her if she would stay all right. But only some. The Sunday after she moved to Roseville, moving into a house the Fletchers owned around the corner from them, Uncle Donald and Aunt Clarissa drove down from Chicago to spend the day. As they were leaving, Aunt Clarissa asked Grandpa when the bank was going to foreclose.

I didn't know what she was talking about. Kate did. I could tell.

Grandpa, too. "The first of June," he said.

"Well," Aunt Clarissa said, "at least the children can finish out the school year."

As soon as I could get Kate aside I asked her foreclose what. "Our house."

"Our house?" I stared at her. "But where'll we live?"

Kate shrugged. "I suppose Maggie'll have us come live with her in Terre Haute."

The next weekend Maggie came home. I thought she'd be down in the dumps, the same as I was, but she wasn't. She came into the house all smiles, the yellow flecks dancing in her eyes.

We weren't going to Terre Haute. We were going back to Maggie's home—to Cincinnati.

Maggie told us she'd driven down there the weekend before to visit Great-Aunt Helen. While she was there she called on the man she used to work for before she married our father. He'd offered her a job, better than the one she had now. Best of all, Great-Aunt Helen wanted us to come live with her, to keep her, as she put it, from rattling around in her big house all alone.

Kate was beside herself.

I tried to act as if I was, too, but I wasn't. I didn't know why exactly. If there wasn't any hope of Maggie coming back to Roseville to live, then I didn't want to stay in Roseville either.

I wanted to be where she was. Ever since she'd left, I'd been wanting that almost as much as I'd wanted the other.

Well, now I was getting it. So why wasn't I happy about it? I didn't know. I just wasn't.

Even Maggie noticed it finally, saying, "What's the matter, Angel? You want us all to be together, don't you?"

"Oh, sure, Maggie," I said, and thought maybe that was it. I frowned at her. "Will Grandpa come, too?"

"Of course," she said.

Grandpa tried to tell her no. He said he'd find somewhere else to go. He'd only be a burden to her, now that she didn't need him any more.

We were in the kitchen at the time. Maggie was getting supper, and Kate was helping her. I was supposed to be setting the table. Grandpa was just there.

It was one of those times when, after something is said, it hangs in the air for the space of a breath, and you know that what comes after it can take you any number of different ways, depending on who says what.

Maggie said it.

She looked at Grandpa the way she looked at Kate and me sometimes—as if she wished she could give him something that he didn't have—and my stomach started hurting. But then she shook her head at him and said, "Who'll make our root beer?" Her eyes sparkled.

Kate laughed. "And fix pork liver for us?"

I laughed, too, and clapped my hands at him. "Remember the NRA, Grandpa—'We Do Our Part.' "

"Well," he said.

"Oh, Grandpa," I said, giving him a hug, "we love you!"

Maggie nodded. "Isn't that need enough?"

"Well," Grandpa said again. "Well, now." He beamed at us.

So it wasn't Grandpa. And I didn't know of anything else it could be.

I decided I really was a jerk.

Around the first of May Grandpa started collecting boxes

from Garnett's, and he and Kate and I began packing books and clothes and dishes and silver and kitchen utensils—everything except what we needed to live on.

The last two weeks of school had always crawled by before. This year they flew by so fast, before I had time to count them our home-room teacher was passing out report cards, saying, "Have a good summer. I'll see you in the fall."

While I was cleaning out my desk, Nathaniel came over and asked me if I wanted to go to Ward's one last time. Maybe if he hadn't put it that way, I would have gone, but I didn't want to do anything one last time. Anyhow I could see Bobby Jackson standing out in the hall with a baseball glove on, pounding his fist into it and frowning in at us. I said no, Maggie was coming home today, and we had to pack up what was left. The movers would be there in the morning.

Maggie was already home when I got there, helping Grandpa roll up the living-room rug and tie it. When I called out to them as I came in, my voice echoed back at me.

In spite of the furniture, and the boxes stacked up everywhere, the house looked as bare as it sounded. It looked a bit shabby as well. All around the walls were dark-rimmed rectangles where pictures had been hanging, showing how faded and dirty the wallpaper was everywhere else.

From the way Maggie watched me all through supper, I knew she figured I was probably going to throw up. I figured I was, too.

I did.

Kate said thank goodness I'd gotten it out of the way instead of doing it tomorrow in the car.

George Garnett came over after supper to see Kate one last time, looking as miserable as the first time he'd come dating her. She promised him she'd write, but he didn't look any happier when he left.

The phone rang a lot, before supper and after it—people calling Maggie to say they were sorry she was leaving, and they hoped she wouldn't forget all her friends in Roseville but would come back to visit whenever she could.

We listened to the radio awhile, then went to bed early. Maggie was tired from her long drive, and I felt kind of washed out, and there wasn't anything to do anyhow. Everything you could do anything with, like books or puzzles or cards, was all packed away.

The next morning I was standing by the turn in the stairway looking out the window there when Kate came down the top half of the stairs.

"Who are you looking for?" she asked. "The moving men?"

I shook my head. "I was just thinking. Did you know that in some places when a farm, for instance, is being foreclosed and auctioned off, all the other farmers around come and won't let anybody else in, and they buy it back for the farmer for almost nothing?"

Kate stared at me. "You expect that to happen to us?"

I shook my head again. "No. I was just thinking about it, that's all."

She frowned. "You don't really want to stay on here in Roseville, do you, the way things have been?"

"No," I said. "I guess not. It's just that—" I shrugged and turned to stare out the window again. There wasn't anything there to see.

"You'll like Cincinnati," Kate said. "You know how Maggie's always talked about what a great place it is."

I nodded, blinking, not looking at her.

"And you'll meet new friends. This time next year if I ask you if you'd rather be in Roseville, you'll say I must be loony."

I nodded again.

"And I'll say you were the one who was loony." Kate gave me a poke and went down the rest of the stairs.

I was still standing at the window when Maggie came down a few minutes later. "Who are you looking for?" she said.

I shook my head. I didn't know. Nobody, I supposed. Or any-

317

body. Warren White or Orn Fletcher or Barbara Kaiser. God, maybe. Maybe Loretta Gudeman coming to say I could have my seat at the movie back.

Somebody, I suppose, who might have come to pick up my Humpty Dumpty world and put it back together again. Even though I knew, as well as I knew I was standing there, it couldn't be done.

"Here comes Nathaniel anyhow," I said.

Nathaniel had ridden over on his bike to say goodbye.

"It's funny, isn't it," I said to him, "it's me leaving instead of you."

"Yeah," he said. "It is."

We were sitting on the back steps.

"I wish," I said, looking out at the stubble of our last year's corn crop, "It was because we were going to plant corn that you came over today."

He nodded. "It's about the time we always did."

I wished I hadn't thought about the corn.

I tried to think of something to change the conversation with, but I couldn't. It didn't matter. We weren't having any more conversation anyhow.

"Here." Nathaniel reached into his pocket and handed me his handkerchief.

"You want to walk a little?" he said.

So we walked a little. Around the house and up the block and back again. Then we stood in the driveway watching the movers carry furniture out on their backs.

When one of them brought my bike out, I touched Nathaniel on the arm. I did, after all, want to do something one last time. "Let's ride our bicycle route once more, shall we?"

"Sure." He looked at me. "The new route or the old one?"

"The old one."

I retrieved my bike from the mover, and after calling in to Maggie that I'd be back in half an hour, we set off.

In the old days we had always stopped at the courthouse when we rode by, calling up to Maggie's open window, waving back to her when she put her head out and waved to us.

We didn't intend to stop there this time, since there wasn't anything to stop there for, but as we were pedaling along the sidewalk toward the southwest corner of the courthouse lawn, the chain on Nathaniel's bike slipped out of the sprocket, so we had to stop until he could fix it.

I don't know yet what made me do it. Habit, maybe. While Nathaniel was working on his bike, I leaned mine against one of the hitching posts and walked past the flagpole, staring up at it.

I stopped dead still.

The flagpole wasn't leaning.

I couldn't believe it. I backed up a few feet and walked past it again.

It still didn't lean.

I tried walking past it from the other direction. It stood as straight as before.

I didn't know what to make of it. I didn't know whether it was because I'd grown taller or what. I only knew that whatever had done it, the flagpole didn't lean at me any more.

I stood there staring up at it, wanting to shout to Nathaniel that the flagpole wasn't leaning at me, but I didn't. I just went over to get my bike, and as soon as he had his chain back in place, we rode off together down Main Street.

At the corner where the Fletchers lived, we stopped. Nathaniel stuck out his hand, and I shook it. "Good-bye, Angel," he said. "Maybe I'll see you sometime."

I nodded. "I hope so. Good-bye, Nathaniel." As I rode off, I turned to wave at him.

When I rode into our yard Maggie was putting some boxes into the car. I stood my bike up against the side of the moving van and walked over to her. I wanted to tell her about the flagpole not leaning at me, but then I'd never told her it had. Besides, I still didn't quite know what to make of it.

Maggie did. Even without being told. Just from the look on my face, I guess.

She grinned at me. "If they can't lick Mr. Gilligan—"

I grinned back at her. "—they can't lick me!"

She shut the car door and we headed for the back steps.

"Maggie," I said.

"Yes?"

"There never was a Mr. Gilligan, was there?"

"No," she admitted. "But because he never was, he always is. If you know what I mean."

Had Mr. Gilligan a beginning? Mr. Gilligan had no beginning. He never was, and he always will be.

"Yes," I said at last, "I guess I do."

It was almost noon when the movers finished. Maggie had made sandwiches, and we ate them and finished up the milk, warm now from sitting out. Then we took a few last things to the car.

And then there wasn't anything to do but leave.

So we left, Maggie and Grandpa and Kate and I, on the highway going south, and I turned and looked out the back window until I couldn't see anything of Roseville any more.